Praise for THE WOMAN IN THE DARK

"One of the best psychological thrillers of 2019."

—*Bookriot*

"Suspenseful and macabre."

—*Bustle*

"I'm weirdly drawn to murder house stories—who isn't?—and this one takes the cake. The story tackles elements of mental health and domestic abuse in a provocative way, while adding just the right dose of horror."

—MarieClaire.com, "Must-Read Books for the Beach"

"Kept us utterly spooked and utterly hooked."

—*Heat*

"Savage carefully sustains the growing tension to the final twist. Psychological thriller fans will be rewarded."

—*Publishers Weekly*

"I *LOVED* THE WOMAN IN THE DARK by Vanessa Savage. Unputdownable thriller that I devoured in a couple of sittings. One to look forward to."

—Laura Marshall, author of *Friend Request*

"A vivid portrait of buried tensions."

—*Daily Mail*

"An intense tale of deceit, treachery, and loss."

—*The Sun*

"I read this brilliantly creepy thriller in one weekend because I couldn't put it down! So scary, pacy, and compelling with a very clever twist. One I'm still thinking about now."

—Claire Douglas, author of *Do Not Disturb*

"Creepy, atmospheric, and with a tangible sense of growing unease which powers a compelling story and keeps you turning the pages. Vanessa Savage is a name to watch and I can't wait to see what she writes next!"

—Amanda Jennings, author of *The Cliff House*

"A real page-turner...The book has twists and turns you don't see coming and lead to a shocking climactic reveal...[Savage] will be one to watch in the future."

—*Red Carpet Crash*

"When a psychological thriller begins with a family moving into a home known as 'the Murder House,' you know it's going to be good. THE WOMAN IN THE DARK will have you hooked from page one."

—*Hello Giggles*, "Best New Books of the Week"

THE WOMAN IN THE DARK

Vanessa Savage

GRAND CENTRAL
PUBLISHING

NEW YORK BOSTON

This book is a work of fiction. Names, characters, places, and incidents are the product of the author's imagination or are used fictitiously. Any resemblance to actual events, locales, or persons, living or dead, is coincidental.

Cover design by Blanca Aulet. Cover photographs by Getty Image: © Jitalia17/ E+; © Ray Massey/Photographer's Choice. Photo illustration and photography by Scott Nobles. Cover copyright © 2019 by Hachette Book Group, Inc.

Grand Central Publishing
Hachette Book Group
1290 Avenue of the Americas, New York, NY 10104
grandcentralpublishing.com
twitter.com/grandcentralpub

Originally published in 2019 by Sphere in the United Kingdom
Originally published in the U.S. in hardcover and ebook by Grand Central Publishing in March 2019

First U.S. trade edition: February 2020

Grand Central Publishing is a division of Hachette Book Group, Inc. The Grand Central Publishing name and logo is a trademark of Hachette Book Group, Inc.

The publisher is not responsible for websites (or their content) that are not owned by the publisher.

The Hachette Speakers Bureau provides a wide range of authors for speaking events. To find out more, go to www.hachettespeakersbureau.com or call (866) 376-6591.

Library of Congress Cataloging-in-Publication Data has been applied for.

ISBNs: 978-1-5387-1430-0 (trade pbk.), 978-1-5387-3009-6 (ebook)

Printed in the United States of America

LSC-C

10 9 8 7 6 5 4 3 2 1

Headline from the *Western Mail*, May 2017:

**Two More Bodies Found
in the Murder House**

It's been so long since you lived here, and everything and nothing in this town has changed. The graffiti is dirtier, darker, the rot more deep-seated, a smell that lingers, a pus-stained bandage, a red streak of infection meandering away from the rotting heart of it.

This house has always been the entry wound, sealing in the infection so it spreads under the surface, hidden, insidious, swelling and killing the healthy flesh around it. And you. You at the center: the dirty needle, the rusty knife, the cause, and the result.

In my dream, the one I told you about, the dream I have where the house is still just a house and not yet the Murder House, all the rooms on the landing have doors and all the doors are closed. They're always closed. But last night, the dream changed. This time, the corridor was longer and there was a new door at the end. And instead of running, as I always do, from the dragon in the man suit, half falling in that world-tipping way of dreams and thinking I'll never get to the end, this time I knew I would make it.

But I don't want to anymore. There's a door at the end that shouldn't be there. There's another door and this one is open.

Part 1—Before

January 2017

SARAH

CHAPTER 1

"Happy anniversary, Sarah."

When I open my eyes, Patrick is next to the bed holding a gift-wrapped box. He's already dressed and I glance at the clock—eight a.m. Oh, God—the kids, Patrick's breakfast. I should have been up an hour ago.

"Relax," he says, sitting down. He pushes my hair out of my face and bends to kiss my forehead, smiling into my eyes as he does so. "Mia and Joe have already left for school. You stay in bed." He holds out the box and I sit up, pulling the quilt to cover me.

I look at the gift. The paper is silver and shiny, its creases sharp and perfect on the edges, curling silver ribbon tied on the top in an elaborate bow. "But it's not..."

"Not a real anniversary, no. This one is more important." He lifts my hand and kisses it. He turns it over, kisses my palm, then up to my wrist.

My mind is scrabbling for the date, but then I remember and relax: January 21, the date we first met.

"Open it," he says, pushing the box into my hand. My fingers fumble over the ribbons and he laughs and helps me, tearing off the paper and lifting the lid of the box.

It's a CD. I lift it out, frowning, then see what it is and the frown fades. That old Verve album I loved so much. On the track listing, "Bitter Sweet Symphony" is right there at the top.

"Do you remember?"

Of course I do. I close my eyes and I'm back at that student party: a dark, smoke-filled room, carpet sticky with cheap booze, all of us drunk, a tangle of teenagers sprawled on the floor, passing bottles. Then "Bitter Sweet Symphony" comes on and this man, this ridiculously out-of-place man in a suit, comes over and asks me to dance. All that noise and all those people, no one else dancing, and he twirls me around like we're in some grand ballroom.

"I thought we could dance to it tonight," he says. "You can dust off your Doc Martens and I'll soak the carpet with cheap rum."

He kisses me again and this time he lingers. I can smell his aftershave, the spicy, heady scent he's always worn. I can taste coffee on his lips, feel the rough brush of his cheek against mine. I'm half-asleep and groggy and I can't remember how long it's been: weeks? Months, even? How long since we had sleepy morning sex, slow and languid, quiet because of the children? I reach up to pull him closer, but he moves away, letting in the cold.

"Stay," I whisper.

"I have to go to work. Tonight, though... we'll go to dinner tonight—somewhere special. Just the two of us," he says, back to Patrick all grown-up, buttoned behind a suit, not the Patrick who lay on that booze-soaked carpet, laughing as I danced around him. But it's all still there, isn't it? That Patrick, that Sarah? In the curve of his smile, his soft laugh, the way he looks at me as the quilt slips down. All still there, just muffled by the day-to-day.

"Stay," I say again, pulling him closer and sliding his jacket off his shoulders.

He laughs and begins nuzzling my neck. "You're terrible, Mrs. Walker..."

When he leaves the bedroom, I fall back onto the pillows, closing my eyes, a smile on my face. I could sleep, sneak another hour before facing the day. But Patrick's calling me from downstairs. I get up and reach for the threadbare dressing gown hanging on the back of the door. Patrick always teases me about this ratty old thing: he bought me a new, thick, luxurious one I never wear because my mother gave me this a million years ago when I left home. I've worn it ever since and I'll wear it until it falls apart because I have so little left to remind me of her.

Patrick is in the hall, holding up an envelope. "When did this come?"

I feel a flash of guilt. I remember the letter. It arrived the other day, handwritten, addressed to Patrick. I picked it up off the mat, but instead of giving it to him, I stuffed it into the drawer because it's handwritten, because the handwriting is feminine.

"Sorry," I say. "I must have put it in the drawer instead of on the top."

I watch him stare down at the letter. I'm ready to apologize again as I go down the stairs, but when I see Patrick's face, I stop. I recognize angry and he's not angry. I don't know what this is.

"What?" I ask, and when he looks at me, his eyes are burning and full, like he might cry, and there are spots of red on his cheeks.

He glances at the letter once more, then pushes it into his coat pocket. "It's nothing. Nothing important."

It is, though. I've never seen Patrick look like that before: fear chasing elation chasing…something. Or have I? I have, I think. Once.

Caroline's text comes through half an hour after Patrick leaves, and she's knocking at the door ten minutes later, two steaming paper cups in her hands and a stack of travel brochures under her arm. "Cappuccino delivery," she says.

"You look disgustingly awake," I say, opening the door wider and pushing my hand through my tangled hair. It's only nine thirty, but Caroline looks like she's been up for hours, fully made-up, hair sleek and shiny.

"It's a gorgeous day out there—cold, but gorgeous," she says as she follows me through to the kitchen. "We're going for a walk after I've fortified myself with sugar and caffeine."

I put down the coffee cup and flip through the brochures. "Thanks for these—I've never even considered the Cayman Islands," I say, pausing on a page of turquoise sea and white sand.

"Have you chosen where you're going yet?" Caroline asks, and I sigh.

"You don't have to keep doing this, you know."

"Doing what? Bringing you coffee?"

"All of it, turning up every morning, this false-bright Caroline. Up until a few months ago, I don't think you opened your eyes before midday. But now, you and Patrick, it's like a relay. He goes, you arrive."

Her smile fades. "Yeah, well, up until a few months ago, I never had to worry about you being alone in the house, did I?"

"You don't have to worry now."

"Don't I?" she says, going to the cupboard and helping herself to cookies. I shake my head when she offers me one and sit down with my coffee.

I make a mental note to get rid of the coffee cups before Patrick comes home. He doesn't know—can't know—about Caroline's end of the relay.

When my best friend moved into a bigger, better house around the corner from us, she announced it by turning up on our doorstep, a bottle of Prosecco in her hand, saying, "*Surprise!*" Patrick thinks she did it deliberately to wind him up, and although I denied it, I'm sure Caroline took an extra bit of pleasure in the move, knowing how much it would upset him. She's known him almost as long as I have and, given how much energy they devote to trying to stop me from falling apart again, to keeping me focused on the future, they should be the best of friends. Instead, they're constantly at each other's throats.

But I know their concern comes from a place of love, even their petty squabbles, and if their cotton-wool comfort makes me a little claustrophobic, I won't forget it got me through the bad times.

"Are you going to Helen's book club tonight?"

"I can't—Patrick's taking me out."

She raises her eyebrows and gets another cookie out of the jar. "What's the occasion?"

I smile. "It's silly. The anniversary of when we met. He always says that's our real anniversary because he knew he loved me right away."

Caroline shakes her head and laughs, but I don't. *Do you remember?* Patrick said, and his words brought it all back. I fell too, the moment we started dancing. Sometimes, now, I forget. Patrick's right to make it an occasion, to remind us of who we were.

"Is this Joe's?" Caroline asks, going over to a small framed pencil drawing I've propped up on the counter, ready to go on the wall. Joe, at seventeen, is far more talented than I was at his age. He's captured Mia in a few bold pencil strokes, sharp, clean edges and soft, smudgy curves. You have to stand back, sneak up on it, squint at it from the corner of your eye to recognize her, but once you see her, it couldn't be anyone else. It's like he did it deliberately, tucked his beloved little sister away, hidden on the paper, a constant game of hide-and-seek. He should have done it as a self-portrait.

"It's funny, isn't it," Caroline says, her acrylic nails tapping on the glass, "how it's Joe that's turned out to be the artist?"

"Funny?"

"You know what I mean."

I step closer to the drawing, trace the edges of Mia's face. "It's not about DNA. Mia is my natural daughter and we couldn't be less alike."

"Nature versus nurture?"

Joe picked up a paintbrush all by himself. I never put it into his hand. But I encourage his talent, of course I do. I don't need to have given birth to him to do that. I step to the side and the sketch of Mia seems to turn with me. I wonder how he would draw me. Or Patrick.

"Why haven't you told him yet? About..." She hesitates "...about him not being yours." Caroline's husband is a social worker, and ever since Joe reached adolescence, she keeps advising me on how best to deal with telling him and I keep shying away from it. "Why not just tell him, Sarah? It won't matter to him, not really. You're the only mum he's known. And Patrick is still his father. He'd understand."

My stomach lurches and I look around, as I always do, to check that Joe isn't lurking and hearing those forbidden words.

Caroline sighs. "I can't believe you've gotten away with it for so long."

Me neither. The knot of anxiety grows. What happens if at some point he asks for his birth certificate? Is that what I'm waiting for? For the issue to be forced?

I touch the glass of the framed drawing. Joe has always been my boy. Mia and I clash all the time, she's always been Patrick's little princess, but me and Joe... Caroline's saying the things that nag at me in the middle of the night. More so since my own mother died and I was reshaped into this new, broken Sarah with a raw wound that just won't heal. If I tell Joe the truth, I'll be taking two mothers from him, me and the long-dead Eve. My own loss broke me—what would it do to Joe?

"I know... I know we have to tell him, I should have before now, but it seemed like the wrong time when he started getting into so much trouble in secondary school," I say. "All those fights, the bullying...all those bloody teacher-parent meetings where they talked about him seeing some kind of child psychologist. God, Patrick was furious with them. Our sweet little boy was being bullied and they were trying to make out that it was Joe's problem... I couldn't throw this on him as well. So I kept up the lie until it became impossible to tell the truth. And it's not just Joe, is it? How do we explain it to Mia?"

"Oh, God, Sarah..."

My throat tightens at the familiar worry in her voice and I swallow to clear it. "Look, his birth mother is dead. She's not going to come knocking on the door. We will tell him. But not now. I mean, the accident... he's not ready."

"I could ask Sean to see if any of Eve's family are on record," Caroline says. "So when you do tell him, you have the information in case he wants to find them."

"No. Don't. Please don't. I'm sure if I ever need it, Patrick can give me any information about her."

"You've always said it's Patrick doing the stalling, but I've always wondered if it's you who's more unwilling. Afraid of losing your boy."

"Of course I'm afraid. Yes, we've both lied, but when it comes down to it, Patrick's still his father. I'm just the wicked bloody stepmother."

"Hardly wicked," she says, putting her hand over mine and smiling.

My own hand curls into a fist under hers and I frown. "But is Joe going to see that?"

"Is he still seeing the therapist?" she asks.

I shake my head. Patrick ended the sessions. He said they were a waste of time. I argued until Joe stepped up and told me he agreed with his dad. I've kept the therapist's number, though.

"Is he getting along any better with Patrick?"

I sigh. "Not really. Not since he crashed the car."

Caroline nods, then touches the drawing again. "He's good."

"He wants to go to art college."

She looks at me. "Does Patrick know?"

"Not yet."

"Remind me not to be here when *that* discussion takes place."

We go to the park for our walk, coats buttoned to our necks, sunglasses shielding our eyes, Caroline badgering me about where we're going on our grand family adventure. My answer is, I don't know. There's too much else going on, and I can't quite focus. I think that's why she keeps asking me, to give me something to hope for.

The park around us is full of dog-walkers and mums pushing strollers, eager to be out on the first bright day of the year, pale-faced after being shut up indoors through weeks of rain.

"Patrick got a letter," I say to Caroline, when we stop to rest by the lake. Our breath puffs out in white clouds, and I wrap my scarf tighter around my neck. I didn't realize the letter was still in my head until I spoke. But I can't shake that sight—the look on his face.

"And?"

"It frightened him," I say. "Whatever the letter was, it scared him. And there was something else..."

"It *scared* him?" She frowns and I can see she's thinking the same as I did. *Nothing* scares Patrick. That's why the disquiet's growing. Caroline leans back on the bench. "Did you see what it was?"

I shake my head. "The envelope was handwritten, that's all." I look at her. "I was wondering if he was ill. Or if he's had bad news."

"Was it from a woman?"

"I was stupid. It arrived days ago and I hid it. I don't know why. It's not like I'm worried he's cheating on me."

"Aren't you?"

"Don't be silly."

Patrick wouldn't. He just wouldn't.

Caroline stares at me. She has a strange expression on her face and I can see my own face reflected in her sunglasses, pale and worried. "Look, I'm sure it's nothing. But maybe you should see if you can find out what was in that letter. Can't hurt, can it?"

Patrick's edgy when he comes home. Joe and Mia are gone. Freed by the knowledge their parents will be out for the evening, they've scattered. I've already changed into his favorite skirt, the one he bought me for my last birthday. I came back from my walk to find he'd sent flowers that fragranced the whole house, so I've dressed up for him.

"You look beautiful," he says, leaning down to kiss me. "But where are the Doc Martens?"

I laugh and follow him into the kitchen. There's a tense energy hovering around him, an electric something I can't work out as he pours wine for me, water for him. "A toast," he says. "To James Tucker."

I clink my glass against his. "To James Tucker."

James Tucker—the boy who stood me up a million years ago.

If he'd turned up for our date, I'd never have gone to that party, never have met Patrick. He even mentioned him at our wedding, getting all the guests to stand and toast James Tucker, a boy he'd never met.

He takes off his jacket and goes through to the sitting room, pulling open the curtain and staring out at the street. It's not late. The Sawyer boys from across the road are still out on their bikes, bumping up and down the curb. It hasn't been so very long since Joe and Mia were that age, but I don't think Patrick's watching the boys with the same wistful pang I am.

"Are you okay?"

"Do you ever feel...claustrophobic?" he says quietly.

"What?"

"This house, this street, everything so dull and hemmed in. Not enough space, not enough air."

I don't know what to say. That odd energy is still there, humming in the air, and it makes me uneasy. It's me, not Patrick, who says things like that, who longs for adventure. It's never Patrick with restless feet and airless lungs.

"Are you sure you still want to go out?" I ask. "You sound... Are you ill?"

He turns from the window and smiles at me, dispelling my unease. "I'm fine—just tired," he says. "Of course we're still going out. We'll have dinner and find some seedy club that plays all those songs you used to listen to." He pulls me into his arms. "Give me twenty minutes to shower and change."

The last time I saw my mother, I could see she was thinner, paler. She was quiet, distracted, just like Patrick. *Are you okay? Are you ill?* I said to her, and she wouldn't look at me. *I'm fine. Just tired*, she said. I turned away and didn't ask again. I found the letters from the hospital only after she'd died. A stack of them, unopened, hidden away. Maybe she thought that if she hid the letters the cancer wouldn't be real.

Is that what I was doing, in keeping the letter from Patrick?

Hiding from whatever truth is inside that envelope? But that doesn't work, does it? The cancer spreads and grows, however much you hide from it.

I go back out to the hall and listen for the sound of the shower coming on. His coat's right there, hung up. I can see the corner of the envelope still poking out of the top pocket. It's open, edges torn. I go over and reach for it, pausing to check that the bathroom door is closed, the shower still running.

My heart is hammering as I slide the envelope out of his pocket, trying to pull the letter out without tearing it further.

"What are you doing?"

I spin around, fumbling behind me to stuff the letter back into his coat, but I can't find the pocket without looking, so I shove it down the waistband of my skirt, pull my top loose to cover it. Did he see? He's standing in shadow at the top of the stairs, still wet from the shower, a towel around his waist.

"Nothing—I was just—"

"Come upstairs."

I can feel the envelope pressing against my back. Why didn't I just bloody ask him? It's Caroline's fault, making me suspicious, hinting Patrick's up to something, when I know he wouldn't be. I cling to the banister as I climb the stairs. He pulls me close when I get to the top, burying his face in my hair. His hand is on my waist and he slides it around to rest on the small of my back. His fingers trace the shape of the envelope through the silk of my shirt.

"I'm sorry," I whisper. "I was worried. I..."

"Ssh." He reaches under my shirt, pulls out the envelope, his damp fingers brushing my skin so I shiver.

"I saw your face. I could see you were scared and I was worried..." I'm babbling, but I can't stop.

His frown fades and he laughs instead. "Scared? God, Sarah, I wasn't scared. I was thrilled. Excited."

No, that wasn't excitement.

"What is it?" I ask him again. This time he opens the envelope and hands me the folded letter inside.

"I sometimes drive past it," he says, rushing the words out as I read the letter. "If I'm out on client visits, I sometimes take a detour and drive past it."

At first, all I feel is relief. It's not bad news—it's not some love note from another woman. But then I focus on the letter and my heart starts pounding again. Patrick takes the estate agent's details that accompany the letter and stares at the photo of the house on the front.

Dear Mr. Walker, the letter reads. *You asked us to let you know if this property ever came up for sale*... My scalp prickles. How many times has he taken that detour? "When did you contact them?" I ask, holding up the letter.

"A few years ago."

A few years ago. I swallow bile, bitter in my throat. How many years? Two? Ten? Fifteen? Fifteen years ago is when the family living in that house was stabbed to death by a madman. That was when Patrick started having the nightmares that made him wake screaming in the night.

"You just called them up and...?"

"All of them. All the estate agents in the area. I asked them all to let me know if it ever came up for sale." He looks down at the photo again and I see that his hand is shaking. "I never thought it would."

He puts the letter into the envelope and looks at me again, a mix of fear and excitement back in his eyes. "It should still be mine. It should always have been mine."

I shiver and hug myself.

"I've arranged to see it on Wednesday. Will you come with me?"

God, all that wistful hope in his voice... I don't want to step inside that house, but Patrick doesn't see what I see when I look at the picture. He sees the beautiful Victorian house he grew up in, with its pitched roof and gabled ends—a fairy-tale house before it became the county House of Horrors. He sees happy memories of a childhood lived by the sea. He doesn't imagine blood on the walls or whispering ghosts. He doesn't see the Murder House, but I do.

CHAPTER 2

Mia's watching something on YouTube that, judging by the stream of swear words, is wildly inappropriate for the dinner table. Joe's head is bent over his phone, but I can see his smile as Mia shows him her screen and dissolves into laughter. I hum a tune as I finish mashing the potatoes and bring the serving dish to the table. I haven't seen them so relaxed in weeks.

"Phones away," Patrick says as he comes in, lingering to stroke my hair before taking off his cuff links and rolling up his shirtsleeves. Joe's phone immediately disappears into his pocket, but Mia grumbles as she slides hers onto the table, staring at the screen as a text comes through.

"Phones *away*," he says again, pushing it back toward her, watching as she gets up and puts it on the kitchen counter. I see her hesitate as it vibrates again.

"Sit down, Mia," Patrick says, carving the chicken, passing slices of breast to me, a leg each for Mia and Joe. "The world won't end if you're parted from your phone for half an hour."

He shakes his head as she sighs and stomps back to the table.

"It's all kicking off between Tamara and Charlie," she says to Joe as she sits down. Joe shrugs and doesn't look up from his plate, but that doesn't stop her from launching into some convoluted tale of betrayal and heartbreak.

"Mia, please, give it a rest. It's like listening to a soap opera," Patrick says.

"God, Dad—you don't know the half of it."

"Good. I hope it stays that way." He looks at me. "We weren't ever like that, were we, Sarah?"

I raise my eyebrows, remembering the soaring emotions of our first few dates, both of us giddy with it.

We all jump as Mia's phone buzzes, then starts ringing.

Patrick puts a hand on her arm as Mia moves toward it, so she mutters something under her breath and turns away. "I swear," she says, "I don't know how you guys functioned without phones when you were kids."

Patrick carries on eating, not rising to the bait. It's me who answers. "Mobile phones were invented twenty years ago, you know. We just weren't slaves to them like you are."

"But how did you talk to people?"

"Well, it was very strange, and you might not be able to comprehend this, but we used to stand in front of the other person and speak."

"Oh, ha-ha, very funny."

"It was good, actually," Patrick says, putting down his fork. "Wonderful. I lived in a really small town, but all of us knew each other growing up. Properly knew each other. It meant I could go down to the beach in the summer and guarantee I'd see some of my friends. Or we'd meet up at the fairground. But mostly down on the beach. We'd all bring firewood and food, stay there for hours as it got dark, warm by the fire."

"Speaking of the small town your father grew up in..." My voice trails off as Patrick looks at me and shakes his head. We didn't discuss what we'd tell the children about the house viewing tomorrow, but I understand enough from Patrick's white-knuckled grip on his water glass to keep quiet.

Joe and Mia disappear to their rooms the moment they finish eating, but Patrick and I linger.

"Coffee?" Patrick asks as he gets up and takes two mugs out of the cupboard. "Or would you prefer a glass of wine?"

I would, but if I say yes, he'll see how little is left in the bottle he opened for me yesterday. Patrick doesn't drink—he doesn't like anything that makes him feel out of control, and it's impossible to hide a sneaky extra glass of wine when you're the only one who drinks.

"No, thanks," I say. "Coffee sounds great."

He stops me as I get up to clear the table. "No, let me do it—you cooked."

"How come you don't want the children to know where we're going tomorrow? I was wondering about changing it to the weekend, so Joe and Mia could come with us—have a day at the seaside, like we used to."

He shrugs as he picks up my plate. "It's not a big secret, but I want you to see it first." He pauses. "It's not going to look the same as when I lived there, is it? It's been a long time since it was a happy family home and I wouldn't want the children to see it like that."

"I wish I'd known you in your happy-family beach-picnic days," I say to his back as he leans over the dishwasher.

He glances at me over his shoulder. "Do you?"

"I picture it, when you talk about it. My teenage years were all stifling boredom. Nowhere to go and nothing to do."

He closes the dishwasher and turns to face me. I can't read the expression on his face. "It wasn't always picnic weather," he says.

"No, but at least you had the freedom to go out with your friends. I was lucky if I was allowed out of the house in the day, let alone after dark."

"Your mother could have done with a kick in the ass."

I freeze. I can't stand any mention of my mother, not since she died.

Mum was pretty much housebound by her own fears by the end. But each time we'd visit, I'd go with fingers crossed, hoping she'd be better, stronger, that this time she'd say yes when I suggested lunch out or her coming to stay with us. And each time I'd be disappointed. We'd sit in the living room of the terraced council house that hadn't changed since I'd lived there, Joe and Mia fidgeting, Patrick glazed with boredom, and I'd feel my cheeks burning as the usual mix of frustration and shame filled me. I'd be torn between wanting to shake her and yell at her to bloody snap out of it and needing to cling to her, the child in me yearning for her to comfort and soothe me. And then we'd get up to go and I'd hate myself for the relief I felt at leaving. I'd want to tell Patrick to drive us home faster, but I'd also want him to go back so I could try again, one more time, to drag her kicking and screaming into the world. All too late now.

Patrick watches me as I rise stiffly and start clearing the rest of the table.

"I'm sorry," he says, and his voice is gentle. "I shouldn't have said that. I want you to let the guilt go, that's all. You couldn't have done anything for her even if you'd been there."

The plates and cutlery rattle as I carry them over to the counter.

"I think I will have that glass of wine after all." I sense him watching me as I get down a glass and fill it to the top with red wine, emptying the bottle. "Not all of us had an upbringing like yours," I say, after the first numbing sip. "Some of us need to drink to forget. Cheers." I clink my glass against his coffee cup, but he doesn't return my smile.

"They've said we can look around on our own this time—the house is empty."

"This time?"

He laughs. "You got me. I couldn't wait. I went to see it on Monday when I got the letter. It's been so long, I wanted to see it again. We'll go for lunch after, make a proper day of it."

"Fish and chips on the pier? An ice-cream cone?"

He grins. "Well, I was thinking of a nice warm restaurant, but if you want chips and ice cream on the pier in January..."

He's taken off his jacket and tie; his shirt has come untucked at the back and his sleeves are rolled up. We're driving along the coast road and none of this seems real.

I'm staring down at the details Patrick gave me. I want to be able to share his happiness, his excitement. *My childhood home, my dream house*, he said, but I can't forget the other photo of this house, the one that was on the front of the newspapers fifteen years ago. Someone spray-painted the front door and that's the photo everyone used: a house, police tape still fluttering around the front, broken window boarded up, *Welcome to the Murder House* spray-painted in red on the front door.

If Patrick's parents hadn't defaulted on the mortgage and lost it, it would never have become the Murder House. Patrick and I could have raised Mia and Joe there—picnics on the beach, trips to the fair, fish and chips on the promenade, every shelf and windowsill filling with shells and driftwood and sea glass rubbed smooth by the tide. All the things Patrick remembers so fondly from his childhood that are such a contrast to my own: streets and streets of terraced houses, tiny patches of green, cooking smells seeping through shared walls, net curtains and fitted carpets; shoes off in the house and cushions on their points, my mother with her clinging, strangling arms, keeping me in, holding me back behind the double-locked door. The agoraphobia that only she suffered from still managed to keep us both prisoner.

We pull up outside and I blink to rid my eyes of the newsprint version of the house. The red paint has long been covered up, the broken window replaced. I'm surprised at how welcoming it looks, the gate standing open, a hanging basket of winter pansies swinging next to the door, the windows scrubbed and gleaming.

"Has anyone else ever lived in it?"

"Since the family who..."

"Was killed here, yes."

"It's the first time it's come up for sale. Wait here, I'll go for the keys."

I get out of the car and cross the road to lean against the seawall. The first time Patrick took me to visit his parents, he brought me here afterward and you could see the contrast sat bitter in his throat. After the house was repossessed, his parents had retired to an ugly, rented two-bedroom bungalow five miles from here, with no views and no garden. Tiny, cramped rooms full of too-big furniture in dark wood. It was hot and airless, immaculately clean, the TV turned up full volume because his dad was hard of hearing. His mother would follow us around, polishing away every trace of our presence even while we were still there. Taking Joe to visit was always a nightmare—he seemed to throw up his milk or fill his diaper the moment we got there and the smell would linger foul in the air. I could never imagine them looking after a baby Patrick—they looked at six-month-old Joe as if he were a weird alien and spoke to him as if he were an adult.

His parents lost the house when Patrick was in his early twenties, not long before he met me. Every weekend, beginning when we were first dating and for years afterward, as the kids grew up, he'd drive us down the Heritage Coast, stopping in different seaside towns, picnics on different beaches, hunched against the wind, sand in our sandwiches. He'd stand outside seafront houses we could never afford in a million years and he'd get angry. All the relaxed happiness from the picnics would disappear and he'd be all hunched and tense and gritted, and I'd see in him a frustration echoed in me, but on a far more muted level—he wanted it all *right now*, wanted back what he'd lost. With me, it was a yearning for what I'd never had.

When we went to the bank to apply for our first mortgage and he realized a terraced suburban new-build was all we could afford, he shrank a bit, defeat dragging him down.

"*This* should be mine," he said, the first time he showed me the house he'd grown up in, before that poor family was killed there. Its big bay windows offered panoramic sea views and Patrick would describe the apple tree in the back garden he used to climb. Who was living there then? Was it them—a young couple like us, children little more than babies, no idea how short their future was?

I asked him, last night as we lay in bed, what he wanted from this house, why he was so desperate to see it again.

I just want it back, he said. *Not only the house but the town, the whole life I had there. The life I should have had.* There was something in his face, a fierceness and a vulnerability I'm not used to seeing.

So here we are. I'm not sure what we're doing, really, beyond indulging a fantasy. Is it nostalgia? Our finances are not much different than they were when we bought the house we're in now, so it's not like we're any closer to living in one of his seafront dream houses. I think Patrick just needs to look, to have this moment of hope. And it's the least I can do for him after all I've put him through, even if I don't share the dream.

I look toward the faded Welsh seaside town he loves so much, remembering the scruffy cafés, seaside shops selling buckets and spades, the dingy pub, and, in the distance, the fairground, ancient and rickety when I was nineteen. God knows the state of it now. I look back at the house and, hard as I try, I can't see what he does.

He finds me on the beach and jogs over, an envelope of keys in his hand. "We've got an hour," he says. Seagulls circle above us, adding their lonely cries to the crashing of the waves.

"I was born in this house," he says as he struggles to unlock the front door. "My mother waited too long to leave for the hospital."

Patrick was born in winter and I picture a dark night, a winter storm, the house battered by winds as his mother screamed inside.

"It should never have left the family," he continues as the key turns and he pushes the door open.

The hall is long and dark and cold, all the doors leading off it closed. A dim light from some unseen upstairs window illuminates the stairs, but all I notice are the hidden corners, dark spots perfect for lurking ghosts. I reach for the light switch but the electricity is off. I shiver as Patrick closes the door behind him, shutting us into the Murder House.

I reach for the first door on the right, but Patrick puts his hand over mine, stops me opening the door. "That's the cellar," he says. "I don't want the first room you see to be the cellar."

He pushes open the door to the kitchen instead and I follow him in. It's twice the size of ours at home. There's a small window with peeling paint overlooking a long back garden choked with weeds, mismatched pine units, dusty gaps for appliances. The light from the window is inadequate for this big, cold room. The floor is covered with dirty linoleum that's warped and curling at the edges. Even though there's no stove here, the room smells of old fat and moldy food.

Still, I turn slowly, forcing myself to ignore the smells and the dust, taking in the space. I try to imagine Patrick's happy life here. I picture everything I've always envied from the pages of *Good Homes* magazine and more. How wonderful it would be to have a kitchen where it's not a struggle to squeeze a family of four around the table. When I lift a corner of the linoleum, there are black-and-white ceramic tiles underneath. Some are chipped and cracked, but I can imagine the broken ones replaced, how once the floor must have stretched out, shiny and beautiful.

"This is not what it was like," he says, shoulders slumped. "I remember it as warm and bright and homey. I wish you could have seen it like it was." He rubs his eyes. "God, they kept it *so* beautifully," he says, and there's longing in his voice. "Nothing out of place, no mess anywhere."

I try not to hear, in this, a criticism of my own habit of shoving messes into cupboards or under furniture and calling the house tidy. "I'm sure it must have been messy sometimes," I say. "I imagine you filled it with Legos and your beloved *Star Wars* toys."

He laughs. "God, no! Heaven forbid I should leave a toy lying around. You knew my mother. It was spotless."

"It was a long time ago," I say, walking over to hug him. "It's still the same space as the house you loved; it just hasn't had the right kind of attention over the years." I stop myself from saying anything about the murders.

He drops a kiss on the top of my head and smiles. "You're right," he says. "Picture this: a range stove and a big wooden table over there. We'll get new tiles for the floor and the window replaced." He steps over to it and looks out. "The back garden's huge—I remember how far back it goes. We could get an extension built, have those folding doors that open right up."

He sounds serious. I look down at the estate agent's details in my hand. According to Patrick, it's been hugely undervalued—advertised cheap so buyers will look beyond its history. But the house is already way beyond our budget, even undervalued, even in this state with all its original features hidden by fiberboard and woodchip. Patrick's talking about new kitchens and extensions as if we've won the lottery, when on his salary we'd struggle even to pay the mortgage.

He carries on like this as he walks around the house, planning built-in storage in the living room bay window, a window seat for looking out at the sea. There's original parquet wood under the rotting carpet in the living room and it's fun to think about having that restored, the fireplace unboarded, a crackling fire lighting the polished wood. Oh, to have a home like that—the idea makes my heart flutter and soar. I join in the game, picturing new bathrooms, new carpets upstairs, having it decorated throughout. I get better at ignoring the rotting wooden window frames, the icy wind rattling through the gaps, the black spots of mold in the corners, the uneven walls and floors, the cracks and creaks.

Until we walk into the smallest of three bedrooms. "This was my room," he says. It overlooks the back garden and a tall tree blocks most of the light, leaving it darker and colder than the rest of the house. The smell of dampness is stronger in here too, a musty tang that clings to the back of my throat.

"I hope it was warmer then," I say, rubbing my arms to chase away the goose bumps as a gust of wind sets the branches of the tree tapping on the glass. Did the tree do that when Patrick was a boy? Middle of the night, curtains closed, something tap-tapping on the window…

"Not really. The heat never seemed to work." He walks over to the window and peers out. "But I could get out by climbing down the tree."

"Sneaking out to meet girls?"

He glances at me with a half-smile. "Maybe. You jealous?"

I stand next to him, trying to imagine a teenage Patrick sneaking out to meet a girlfriend for moonlit walks on the beach.

"Come and look at this room," he says, holding out his hand. I notice he closes the door of his old bedroom as we leave. All the other doors he's left wide open, but this one he closes tight.

We stand together in one of the bedrooms at the front of the house, looking out the window. The sun has come out and, reflected by the sky, the sea looks blue rather than its usual churning gray-green. It's like Patrick ordered this weather especially.

"Can you picture it, Sarah?" he says, reaching for my hand again. "Everything you've gone through in the last year—everything *we've* gone through—it would all be wiped away if we moved here. No reminders, a fresh start."

"A fresh start? *Here?* I know this was your home and I see that it could be so beautiful, but how can you get past what happened here? Can you forget that people...that that family was..." I swallow my words.

He studies my face for a few moments too long, and then his smile is back. "It was a tragedy, I know. A horrible, horrible tragedy. But it was such a long time ago. The house is just a house, Sarah. What—do you expect their killer to come back fifteen years later?" He laughs and looks around the room. "You think he's still hiding in a cupboard somewhere?"

My smile in response is halfhearted, reluctant. He's right, of course he is. But still...

"Just think: this would be our room. This would be the view we'd wake up to every day. It could be like your doll's house—remember?"

Of course I remember. My dad gave me a secondhand doll's house for my eighth birthday, a beautiful, old-fashioned wooden doll's house. But when I opened it, the walls had been scribbled on by its previous owner, and there was no furniture, no family of dolls to inhabit it.

Don't worry, my dad said. *We can make the inside as beautiful as the outside*. And we did. Dad painted all the walls in soft, warm colors. He varnished the floors to look like they were made of polished wood. I made little rugs and curtains from scraps of material Mum gave me. That Christmas, a little wooden family appeared under the tree: a wooden mum, dad, and two wooden children. And each time Dad came back from one of his sales trips, he'd bring a new piece of furniture.

I'd stopped playing with it by the time Dad left when I was twelve. But in those horrible years after, when we were scraping by on benefits and Mum was barely functioning, I'd sit in front of that doll's house and stare at all those perfect rooms and the perfect wooden family and wish that was my real life.

And here's Patrick telling me it's possible. We could paint those walls and floors, fill this house with beautiful furniture bought one piece at a time, chase away the bad memories, give ourselves, and this house, a new start. We could be the perfect wooden family.

I close my eyes and for a second, I can picture it. I hear the faint sound of a wind chime. I see myself waking up in a room like this, sun streaming in; I see myself on the window seat Patrick's going to build. Curled up, watching the sea, watching the seasons pass, a fire in the winter, candles burning on the mantelpiece, windows open in the summer, the smell of the sea and the cries of the seagulls drifting in. If we lived somewhere like this, the children would lose their suburban pallor, get some color in their cheeks. For a moment, I *do* see this as Patrick's house, the house he was born in, the house he's always loved.

When we lived in Patrick's old apartment, and Joe was a baby, he used to laugh at my obsession with magazines like *Good Homes* and *House Beautiful*. I'd spend hours drooling over pictures of Victorian houses just like this one, all polished wood and open fireplaces. Alcoves with built-in shelving and heritage colors on the walls. Patrick would tell me stories of his childhood and the yearning would become a physical ache. When did I stop buying those magazines? Was it when we moved into our current house, so bland and boxy?

"I've missed this," I say, opening my eyes.

"What?"

"You. Like this. All enthusiastic and passionate—it reminds me of when we first met."

"Before the drudgery of careers and mortgages and children, you mean?" he says, eyebrows raised.

"No, that's not it... It's me as well, not only you. I miss... that freedom we used to have together, the moments of saying, 'Screw it, let's do it anyway.'" I glance at him.

He looks away from me and back out at the sea. All that yearning is right there on his face and, like the other morning when he bent to kiss me, I wonder again how long it's been since that look made me drag him to the nearest bed.

"Screw it," he mutters, squeezing my hand.

"What?"

"You're right. Let's do it. Let's say screw it and do it anyway. What do you say, Sarah? Another adventure?"

I blink. Wait. That's not what I meant. The Murder House isn't the adventure I'm after. It wouldn't be a roller-coaster ride—this would be a ride on the ghost train. I shake my head. "We can't. We can't possibly afford it."

He's still looking at the view, but even from the side I can see the way his face changes. "There's your mother's money."

No. In that moment, that gap, all the adventures I've ever dreamed of hover there. My mother didn't have vast amounts of money to leave. She didn't own her own home, but she did save small amounts over decades and decades for God knows what because she never went anywhere, never did anything. When the money came through after she died, I looked at that fucking savings book and cried for hours. What was it all for? A hundred pounds a month, every month for nearly two decades. A little over twenty grand and she never touched any of it. It broke my heart, and I got so sad and so angry with myself for not knowing, for not being there enough to understand her longing, to the point of trying to tear up that damn savings book. Patrick had to wrestle it out of my hands as I cried and raged. What was it bloody for?

I'm not going to do the same. I'm not going to let my mother's money stagnate in a mediocre-interest savings account. I'm going to have an adventure. I like to think that's what Mum meant it for. I've spent months looking through the travel brochures that Caroline brings me, reading itineraries of safari tours, cruises to see the Northern Lights, deserted beaches, and hot, crowded cities. I want to do it all. Me, Patrick, Joe, and Mia. We're going to have the kind of adventures we'll always remember, together as a family.

The only thing holding me back, besides the push and pull of everyday life, is...how do you choose? All the places, the whole world, how do you choose when you've never been anywhere before? I want to sink my toes into white sand on a deserted beach, swim naked in the sea, jostle my way through all the sights and sounds and tastes of a foreign marketplace, sweating and claustrophobic, buzzing and alive. Six months on, the money is still sitting there, untouched. Maybe that's what my mother did. Dad left when I was twelve, walked out without a word and never came back. Is that when she started saving? Hoping she'd head off on some grand adventure, where she'd get to the middle of the deepest rain forest and there he'd be: my dad, her missing husband, waiting?

I don't know yet what our adventure is going to be, but it won't be this house. No matter what dreams you pour into it, this *is* still the Murder House. How would we ever get past that? How could any of us forget? Someone died in this room—not just died: they were murdered. A whole family. Butchered, ripped apart, blood on the walls. Every wall that's been repainted, I would know what's underneath, what they had to cover up.

"I can't live here," I say.

Patrick's blue eyes stop shining.

CHAPTER 3

"Mum?"

The bruise has darkened overnight, changing from a red mark to a faint blue, deepening to purple. It's like a painting I once did of the Northern Lights, the aurora borealis there under my skin. I watch it, waiting for it to flicker and flash and change color right in front of my eyes.

"*Mum?*"

Mia touches my shoulder and I jump. I blink away the light show.

She's dressed for school, a familiar scowl on her face. "Where's my PE uniform?"

"PE uniform?"

"For God's sake, Mum, you said you'd wash it for me. I'll get a stupid bloody detention if I don't take it." She whirls around to storm out but stops, staring at my arm. Did the bruise change color again?

"Where did you get that?" she asks, a different edge to her voice.

"I hit it on the door handle," I say. I'd gotten up last night and stumbled, bashed into the door in the dark. We'd argued, Patrick and I. He'd stopped at the garage on the way back from the house viewing and bought a copy of *Good Homes*. He flicked through the pages, pointing out all those perfect period homes, telling me all his plans and ideas, and then I called it the Murder House, baiting him, bitchy after three glasses of wine and still raw from his wanting to use my mother's money.

"Maybe you should lay off the bloody wine," Mia says, half in and half out of the room, and I hear disgust in her voice, a coldness that never used to be there.

"Mia, will you just *stop*—" My voice is sharp.

"Stop *what*?" There's a challenge in her voice. She's doing what I did to Patrick—baiting me. She wants me to call her out, so she can let rip with the simmering resentment that's been building in her ever since my mother died and I fell apart. At fifteen she's growing up so fast, and while I try to cling to the mother-daughter bond, she seems to want to hack it apart as bloodily as possible. She's hurting, I remind myself. Because of me. She attacks because she's scared. Me shouting back won't help.

"Nothing, forget it," I say, and her shoulders slump as she turns away.

"Mia?" I call as she moves off. I'm looking for my little girl underneath the stretched gawkiness of a too-fast growth spurt. "Want to go shopping on Saturday?"

"Saturday? I can't. It's Lara's birthday. Dad's promised to take me for lunch, and I'm going to the movies with the girls before the party."

"Okay. Never mind. It's been a while, that's all. Another time."

She hesitates in the doorway. I see the conflict in her face, the teetering between her spoiling for a fight and the temptation of my peace offering of a shopping trip. "But I could do with something new to wear for Lara's party." She grins. "Dad said he'd get me something, but he'd probably take me to Laura Ashley."

Her grin is for Patrick, not me, but I smile back. She's right—Patrick wants her still to be seven, wearing frilly party dresses. "He probably would."

She chews the ends of her hair and I wait.

"What about today?"

"Today?"

"After school? I could come straight home—we'd be in town by four."

"That would be lovely. We could go for coffee as well, maybe pick up takeout for later."

"Can we go to Starbucks? Dad won't—he hates it there."

"If we have to."

She smiles at me, the big beaming one that takes up her whole face and makes my chest ache with so much love I could burst. She bounds back into the room and leans in to kiss my cheek and give me a one-armed hug. "Thanks, Mum."

Joe passes after she leaves, as silent as Mia is loud. "All okay?" I ask. There's none of Mia's anger on his face, but none of the smile either, and what is there is somehow worse. I've asked *all okay* or some variation nearly every day for the last six months, because I see on his face the same thing I see when I look in the mirror: he's haunted by some pain that lives below the surface, a weeping wound that cuts and spreads. If it came out it would consume him.

He hovers in the doorway and I can feel all the other questions I'm desperate to ask hanging in the air. I want to wrap him in a hug and not let go until he's my smiling little boy again. *Let him come to you*, the therapist told us, but he hasn't and I'm afraid he never will. We used to be able to talk, before my mother died, before his accident. But he stopped and I got too scared to ask what was wrong, scared I'd expose the wound and make it fester.

I think I'm coming down with something: I'm achy and shivery, my eyes gritty with tiredness, my head pounding. I thought sea air was supposed to be good for you. But it's the dead air from inside that house that clings to my throat and lungs. Despite my exhaustion, I couldn't sleep last night. Every time I closed my eyes I saw that awful place and they snapped open.

The house is quiet when I drag myself out of bed and I think they've all gone, but when I get downstairs, Patrick is in the kitchen. All the drawers are pulled open, their contents messed up. I'm heading for the kettle when I see what Patrick's holding.

"What are you doing with my bank book?"

He doesn't flinch, but I see his hand tighten on it. "Nothing. I came across it at the back of the drawer so I was"—he holds it out—"returning it to you."

I take it and stuff it into my dressing gown pocket.

"Sarah?" he calls, as I turn to leave. "Have you thought any more about..."

I grip the door frame. I hate this. I saw, when we were in that house, that this is his dream. With my mother's money, I could make my husband's dream come true. But in doing that, I'd be destroying every dream of my own.

"What about all our plans?" I say. "We've never had so much spare money before. We could do something amazing—something we'll remember forever. All the things my mother never did—go to all those places I've always dreamed about. There's enough for holidays for the whole family and time away for you and me..." I stop talking because I see from his face he doesn't get it.

"Think of Joe and Mia," he says, a pleading note in his voice. "You've seen how withdrawn Joe has become. Since the accident, he's been teetering on the brink. And Mia—I don't like those friends of hers or how she acts around them. Even her teachers commented on it at parents' evening, remember? It's affecting her grades. We have a chance to give them a fresh start."

"We'll travel together, Patrick. We've never traveled abroad as a family—think of all the new experiences. That's a fresh start, too."

I watch stubbornness flash across his eyes, and I feel my own stubbornness rise to meet it. "I can't," I say. "I'm sorry. I'm so sorry, but I can't help you buy that house."

"That's it, then," he says. "Someone else will buy it. Someone else will get to live in my house and we'll be stuck here."

Guilt tastes bitter but I swallow it. "I'm sorry," I say again.

"It's fine. It's your money, isn't it? Your name in that savings book. Your choice what you do with it."

I bite my lip when Patrick leaves the house. He doesn't slam the door, but I hear a slam anyway in the slow click. I hear hurt and accusation and all the other things my guilt feeds me. I get out my travel brochures, but even their siren song doesn't ease the nagging ache.

My phone, when I switch it on, buzzes and a birthday reminder comes up on the screen. The grief, almost a physical pain, doubles me up, hands squeezing the edge of the counter, eyes closed. Mum's birthday—it's Mum's birthday. I forgot to delete the reminder.

Last year I didn't manage a visit, but the phone reminder made sure I called her, checked that the gift basket I ordered had arrived. Why didn't I visit? I can't even remember now, but I always seemed to have some ridiculous excuse not to make the two-hour trek north, to the house where nothing had changed since the day my father had walked out twenty-four years ago, where she'd waited in limbo for him to return ever since.

After Dad left, she clung so hard to me I couldn't breathe. It suffocated me, terrified me: our roles became reversed—I had to be responsible for her when I was still very much a child. But when I did get away, when I left for college and the freedom I'd been craving, I discovered I didn't know how to cope with being alone. I felt so lost. Caroline used to worry about me settling down to marriage and motherhood so young, but what I could never explain to her was how safe I felt with Patrick. He offered all the security of home but none of my mother's clinginess. His uncomplicated strength and confidence were everything I needed in the world.

My visits home grew fewer and fewer as the children grew older. I always had reasons. I always called her on Sunday, like a good daughter. Why didn't she go away, live her life, use all that money to do something fulfilling? I'll never know now. I ran out of excuses six months ago when a neighbor found her, two days dead, mold growing on a half-eaten microwave meal.

That day, I broke.

I went into such a dark place I couldn't find my way out. Everything from that time is cloudy...It took a week in the hospital, then months of medication and therapy to find my way back here. And the children—I saw how my breakdown frightened them. I became a stranger to them in those months and none of us have recovered.

At first they hovered around me like I was made of glass, flinching every time I said a cross word or looked sad, as if we were all playing a waiting game...waiting for me either to be all better or to fall over the edge again. Then they began to move away, let hardness, bitterness slip between us, as if they were afraid to see my pain. But I *did* get better. I *am* better. I feel it in my heart and in my gut. I feel strong and well, but things won't ever be the same in their eyes—the children's and Patrick's—because when they look at me, I'm permanently tainted by the shadow of the woman who had a breakdown. That's who I'll always be now.

But I'm trying to show them. Trying to eradicate the shadow. I promised Patrick. I promised *myself*. No more.

I strip the beds, fill the washing machine, and switch it on, making a third coffee as I wipe down the kitchen. There's a half-full bottle of wine on the side and I'm tempted to pour some. Eleven in the morning and I already want a glass of wine.

I drop the damp cloth into the sink and sit at the table. God, I'm tired. I close my eyes and Patrick's house hovers there, looming and dark. My mother hovers, alone and dying. Panic flutters. No. Stop. But the other way is Patrick's dream and my guilt at denying it: a house on the seafront, windows open, the sea breeze billowing the curtains. A life straight out of *Good Homes*, our very own postcard destination, Joe happy and smiling again. But even in that picture I'm at the shoreline with my back to the rest of them, looking out to sea, wishing I could sail away. *Go to your happy place, Mum*, Mia used to say, in those first bad weeks after my mother died, when she could see me drowning, but could Patrick's house ever be that place? I can see it—what he wants it to be, what it was—when he talks about it, and part of me yearns for that too. I know we'd never in a million years be able to afford something else that beautiful. But I'm scared. Scared that what happened in that house since will feed on the dark shadows I've spent half a year pushing away and that it'll bring them back.

I open my eyes and my vision is blurry with tears. My headache's getting worse and I go upstairs to look for painkillers, washing down two Tylenol with water. I sit on the edge of the bath, teeth gritted against the throbbing pain. I grab the bottle again and take out another couple of pills—I need more than two to push this headache away. As I put the bottle back in the bathroom cabinet, I see Patrick's sleeping tablets.

He started having nightmares years ago. He can't remember what happened in them, but he'd wake up screaming, scaring me and the kids. It got so he was reluctant to go to bed and the doctor gave him these sleeping tablets. He took them and, after a while, the nightmares stopped.

God, I could use an end to my nightmares, too. I know the painkillers will just dilute the headache—the only thing that will cure it is sleep. I swear I can hear the echo of the clock ticking a floor below me. It's hours until I'm due to meet Mia for our shopping trip. I could sleep, eat up the hours in one greedy gulp—numb myself for a while and drift away to a dreamland where my toes sink into white sand and the sea is turquoise and pristine. I'll set the alarm and when I wake up, I'll feel better.

I take the sleeping pills out of the cabinet. *Take two tablets before retiring*, it reads. I press one into my palm, then add another. The second sticks in my throat and I gulp down more water to get rid of the bitterness. My heart's beating faster as I go through to the bedroom.

I sit on the edge of the bed. The clock is ticking downstairs. It's getting louder, but I'm still awake. The pills are probably expired after all this time. Maybe I should take another . . . I go to take out one, but two land on my palm.

My fingers close over them. I shut my eyes and drift. I try to find that soft white sand, but instead there's a rocky beach under a stormy sky, a house with staring black windows and a door swinging in the breeze, broken police tape fluttering from it. Lights pulse and flicker and I'm sinking into a dream where an unfamiliar door opens and a shadow comes in. I think I've had this dream before. I try to pull out of sleep—this doesn't feel safe anymore—but I've sunk too far.

Who's there? my dream self says, and it comes out slurred. The shadow shushes me, flickering in and out of focus, and in my dream it's Mum coming in, brushing my hair back, soothing away my headache, offering me water.

So tired now, I'll just sleep. Sleep for a few hours...

"Sarah? Fuck, Sarah—what did you do?"

Someone pulls me up, drags me out of sleep. There are fingers in my mouth, stretching it wide, pushing in too far, down my throat until I gag. I can't breathe and I pull at the hand, try to get it off, but I can't. It's Patrick. He's pushing his fingers farther down my throat and everything comes up with a choking lurch, vomit spewing out, down his hands, down me, all over the bed. Oh, God, the mess, I'm sorry, but he's dragging me up, off the bed. My legs won't hold me, I can't walk, but he hoists me up, dragging me into the bathroom, pushing me into the bath, turning the shower on cold, so cold. I gasp as the cold bites at the numbness and I struggle, but his hand holds me under the shower.

Someone's screaming, I think it's Mia but I can't see her, and Patrick's yelling, *Call an ambulance, call a fucking ambulance*, and I'm wondering, Who for? What's happened? But then the water stops and I'm still so tired and I just want to sleep and I'm drifting again...

"I won't let you leave me—not like this. Don't you dare, Sarah—don't you fucking dare," Patrick says, and he slaps me hard across the face, and I slip back in the bath and my head smacks against the taps and I—

"Sarah? Sarah? Wake up, Sarah. Sarah? Wake up, Sarah—please... I'm sorry I had to be so rough but, God, Sarah—I thought you were *dying*."

"Mum? Can you hear me, Mum?"

Mia. Mia's voice. She's crying. I fight my way to the surface, struggle against the heaviness trying to push me down. I open my eyes and she's in a chair next to me and I'm in a bed but I don't know where—this isn't home.

I remember...I don't know. I don't know what I remember. Someone. Pills. Patrick, his fingers down my throat. I swallow and a sound comes out of me. Not a word, more of a whimper.

Mia leans forward. "Mum? God, Mum—why did you do it?"

Do what? But Mia's out of her chair, in the doorway calling for someone. A nurse in blue scrubs comes in. I must be in the hospital. Patrick's behind her and I close my eyes again, let myself sink. Not yet. Not ready for Patrick yet.

When I open my eyes again, Joe's there, the chair pulled up close to the bed so he's only inches away. His hair hangs over his face, a black curtain hiding his eyes. He's so thin, his arm resting on the bed nothing but skin and bone. I move my hand to nudge his and he lifts his head, gives me a familiar half-smile when he sees I'm awake.

"I knew you'd make it," he says, then leans in even closer so I can feel his warm breath on my cheek. "Did Dad do something?" he says. "He did, didn't he? Is that why you tried to kill yourself?"

What?

What?

This time I stay awake. There's no one sitting next to my bed and the corridor outside is dark, one set of footsteps echoing away into the distance. My hand hurts. There's a tube and a needle going into it and a drip stand next to my bed. My throat aches and feels swollen. I'm cold and shivery, like I've got the flu, but I don't think it's the flu that's brought me here.

Joe's words are fluttering around my mind and I can't get them to go away. Kill myself? No. I don't understand. It was Mum's birthday and I was tired and I had a headache and I took some painkillers and...the sleeping pills. I remember them. But I didn't take enough to make people think I was suicidal, did I? It was only two, wasn't it? I can't remember. Fuck. I can't remember how many I took.

* * *

Patrick's holding my hand, the one with the tube going in. His thumb is stroking the bump in the bandage covering the needle, and although he's stroking gently, it's making the needle move and my stomach turns in slow, lazy waves. I try to pull my hand away and he squeezes, just for a second, long enough for my whole hand to throb. He lets go then and leans back in the chair.

"I thought you were dead." He whispers it and I can see fear on his face. "I came in and saw you sprawled on the bed and I thought I was too late. I thought you were dead."

"No..." My voice is a croak, a raw, grating rasp.

Patrick waves his hand, like he's waving away my protest. My words have wings too. "I don't understand—I thought things were better. I thought *you* were better."

"I didn't..."

"What do you think this is going to do to Joe?" He leans forward and he knocks the drip stand, making it rattle. He steadies it, looking down at me. "Do you know how close you came to dying? Really? Do you know what damage you could have done to yourself taking that many pills? The only reason you're not dying now is because you hadn't swallowed all of them. They were still in your mouth and I got them out."

Two. I took two pills. I got more out of the packet, but I didn't take them, did I? And a few painkillers. Too many, I know. But not enough for this. I was tired, not suicidal.

"Please, Sarah," he says, and it's his voice that sounds raw now. "I can't lose you, I can't." More than fear. It's panic—he reeks of it.

CHAPTER 4

"I brought you more brochures and a coffee—I guessed you must be sick of hospital dishwater tea by now." Caroline sets a steaming paper cup next to me on the bedside table and sits down. The coffee smells like heaven.

"Thanks," I say, pulling myself upright. I shake my head as she holds out a glossy brochure offering exotic safari adventures. The word *adventure* puts a bitter taste in my mouth.

Her hair is black, hanging straight and heavy, suiting a scowl. It was copper red the other day. I abandoned the hair dye years ago, giving in to the mouse, but Caroline still colors hers half a dozen times a year. Less of the blue and pink these days, though.

"What the fuck happened?"

"I didn't do it," I say.

"What?"

"I didn't mean to take an overdose."

She leans back, staring at me for such a long time. There are tears in her eyes and I wish I were stronger, that I could speak without it bloody hurting so I could make her believe me.

I reach for the coffee and take a sip. They've taken the drip away, but I can see Caroline staring at the back of my hand. It's purple, a big dark bruise, like a flower with a red center where the cannula went in. The bruise on my arm has faded, yellowed—this new one is much more impressive.

"How's Joe doing?" she asks, and I tense.

"He's fine."

"Really? Because last time you had a meltdown, he drove a car into a wall."

I flinch. "It was an accident."

"He accidentally stole your car?"

"You know what I mean. It wasn't..."

"It wasn't like-mother-like-son?"

"Fucking hell, Caroline." My hand jerks and coffee spills on my wrist.

"Where are the children now?"

"With Patrick."

She rolls her eyes. "With Patrick? Oh, yeah, he'll help. Christ, I should have grabbed you the moment I saw you two together at that party and steered you in the opposite direction."

"It's not Patrick's fault." I think of the first time I saw him—he was so beautiful. "And besides, I don't think I would have let you."

"I should have hit you over the head. Knocked you out and dragged you away."

"No—I was *better* after I met Patrick, happier. You may not like it, but it's true." I shift in the bed and wince. "And I wouldn't have Joe and Mia."

"And you wouldn't be lying in a hospital bed recovering from a fucking overdose." She glances back at the door. "You should leave now. Take the children."

Fear blooms, darker than my bruises. "I don't *want* to leave. And what about Joe? I wouldn't get custody even if I did want to leave."

"No," she says, her voice flat. "I guess you wouldn't. Especially not after this."

"This is not Patrick's fault," I say again.

"I know. It's yours." Caroline sips her own coffee, the heavy bangles on her wrist jangling as she lifts the cup.

I remember Patrick's fingers down my throat, his desperation to keep me alive. God, that perfect couple we used to be, so in love—how did it end up like this? Have I become like my mother? Shrunken, hollowed out? I let Patrick fill in all the gaps. My fault, not his. If he left me, would I end up like Mum? I imagine myself sitting at the table for the rest of my life, waiting for him to come home. Caroline gazes at me with frustration and I remember the hopes I had and I want to cry because I don't recognize myself anymore.

She looks down at the travel brochure I refused. "Is there any point in me bringing you these? Patrick told me about the house."

They've talked? What did he say? Did he tell her I refused to give him my mother's money?

"He wants me to tell you to go for it, to move. But I'm here to say don't do it. Don't even think about it. Stick with the travel plans—have your bloody adventure. Haven't you waited long enough?"

"He thinks moving will be good for us, for the children," I say, biting my lip until I taste blood. "Maybe he's right."

"You'll be totally isolated out there. Alone. How can that be good for you?"

She makes it sound like the house is in the middle of nowhere, cut off from civilization. It's in a town, on a bus route, just an hour and a half's drive from Cardiff.

She leans in closer and I can see her eyes are red-rimmed. "That house—its history...How can you possibly live there? How can Patrick want to live there?"

"You don't understand what it means to him."

"No, I don't. But I'm scared for you. You did this to yourself here, surrounded by friends. What the fuck do you think is going to happen to you there?"

"Caroline, trust me, I wasn't trying to kill myself. Patrick overreacted."

"Overreacted?" She taps her nails on her cup, her voice rising.

She doesn't believe me. She thinks I wanted to die. She's my best friend, but I can feel the distance between us growing, stretching. Is everyone going to think that? Are they all going to think I'm either suicidal or desperately crying for help? I close my eyes, but this time I picture what Caroline must be imagining. Me, shaking more pills into my hand, not just two—dozens.

I shake my head. "I didn't do it."

"I don't know what to do anymore," she says. She stands up, slamming down her coffee cup on the cabinet. "I've tried. I've been trying for six months, but I can't keep doing this, propping you up, trying to stop you from falling back into depression again. I thought you were getting *better*." She stops and takes a deep breath. "Damn it, Sarah, how could you do it to Joe and Mia? How could you do it to me? And now you're going to rip your family away from their lives and move them into the *Murder House*?"

She wipes away tears and smeared mascara. "You think it makes it better that you're here by *accident*? You care so little about any of us? Your children had to see you sprawled on the bed, surrounded by fucking empty pill bottles, thinking you were *dead*."

Pill *bottles*? "I'm sorry. I—"

"Don't. Don't keep apologizing. Get some help. Some proper professional help. And maybe...God, maybe Patrick's right. Maybe you do need a fresh start somewhere. But not that house. Come to mine—bring the kids. Come to mine and..." Her voice trails off as she sees me shaking my head.

"Stop blaming Patrick," I say. "You've always wanted everything to be his fault, but this is all on me, a stupid mistake. I will get help, but I need you to stop trying to blame my marriage for everything."

She walks away and turns back at the door. "You say none of it's Patrick's fault. Well, maybe not this, but you've been disappearing since you met him. And your breakdown? I'm not sure it was anything to do with your mother dying. You're a ghost of the girl you were in college. I've tried so hard to keep you...I'm sorry if I've said things you don't want to hear, but it's the truth. I'll...I'll see you at home, okay?"

I turn my head away. "Maybe you should leave it awhile. I don't need the tension between you and Patrick at the moment."

"Don't shut me out."

"I'm tired. Can you go, please?" I close my eyes and swallow a lump in my throat as she shuts the door behind her.

The next day, Patrick holds my arm as we leave the hospital, hand cupped around my elbow, steadying me when I falter. An icy wind whips around the front of the building and I can't stop my teeth from chattering, despite the coat and scarf Patrick's wrapped me in. My legs are still shaking after my meeting with the doctor—not the ward doctor, who took away the drip and checked my throat and looked into my eyes with a little white light, but a psychiatric doctor who sat next to my bed and asked sharper questions that slipped under my skin like needles.

I was all dressed and ready to go, to walk away like none of this had ever happened. Then the doctor came in and wanted to know why I'd done it and if I wanted to do it again. He asked all these questions about Patrick and Mia and Joe and the house and my mother, and I started crying, not because I was bloody suicidal but out of frustration because no one would *listen*. And, of course, that had to be when Patrick walked in—to find me crying and freaking out.

So my meeting became their meeting. They stepped outside the room, but I could hear them talking. I stood on the other side of the door on shaking legs, listening to the doctor talk to Patrick about my suicidal state of mind, each sentence another needle under my skin.

She had a breakdown.

Her mother died and the guilt left her mentally wounded.

Months of medication and therapy.

We thought she was getting better.

We thought the worst was over.

Stupid. I was stupid taking those bloody pills. I should have stayed calm when the doctor came in, explained myself. Explained it was an accident, not a suicide attempt.

When Patrick came back into the room, the doctor didn't

come with him. He was carrying a white paper bag from the hospital pharmacy. "Come on, Sarah," he said. "Let's take you home."

Mia and Joe are waiting on the corner, huddled together for warmth, the same look on their faces as on Caroline's. They flank us as we walk to the car, both staying at least three feet away from me, their unexploded bomb of a mother.

We drive home in silence, parking on the driveway, the car headlights shining on the front door. It's getting late. All the other houses have lights on—families eating dinner, sitting in front of flickering televisions, workday finished, happy to be home. The houses look closer, squeezing in on us. The air feels heavy and thin at the same time and I can't seem to breathe enough in.

How many of those neighbors are watching now? They would have seen the ambulance, seen me taken away. I close my eyes. I can't face it. I can't face the scrutiny and I hate—*hate*—the thought of the avid gossip and questions my family is going to have to deal with because of me. I want to tell Patrick to drive us away.

"Go on in, you two," Patrick says to the children as he switches off the engine and the house falls back into shadow.

Joe and Mia scramble out of the car. Joe pauses and looks back, but Mia grabs his arm and tugs him away.

When we're alone in the car, Patrick opens the white pharmacy bag, pulls out a box of pills. "I thought...I thought you wouldn't want to take them in front of the children the first time." He glances up at the rest of the houses on the street. "It's okay—no one's watching."

I stare at the box. No, it's too soon. Barely six months since the last time I came home from the doctor's with a box just like this one, after Mum died and I forgot how to get up. Maybe if my mother had had pills after my dad left, everything would have turned out differently.

But this is not the same. *I'm* different, whatever everyone else thinks. I'm not broken like I was then. I'm better. I'm...I look closer at the label.

"*Diazepam?* Jesus—that's... Am I really that bad that I need diazepam?"

"The other medications clearly didn't work—this is a short-term measure. It's just for a few weeks, to get you on an even keel. Then we can go back to the doctor and see... Come on, Sarah. They'll help."

He sounds so anxious. I did that, didn't I? Put that fear into his voice.

He hands me a the white pill and I shiver as I put it into my mouth. That ghost of a dream is back as I swallow.

"I'm sorry," I say. "I never meant to... I *swear* I never meant to die. But I'm sorry."

He takes a deep breath and stares at the closed front door. "When I met Joe's mother..." He sees me wince. "When I met Eve, I thought I could save her. I should have seen she was beyond saving. She was self-destructing so fast it was inevitable she'd end up dead. We weren't together when she died and there was nothing I could have done, but the guilt was overwhelming. Like with your mother. I felt dreadful that I wasn't there." He grips my hand. "And then I met you and you were so different—together and happy, and so amazing with Joe. But the last six months, Sarah... I've been so scared. I can see you falling apart and it's like Eve all over again and I've been so bloody afraid. I couldn't stand it if Joe found out the truth and then saw it happen again with you. I couldn't... I couldn't bear it." His voice breaks and he buries his face in his hands.

I'm shaking, my eyes stinging with unshed tears.

"The house—I just want you to be happy. I want us all to be happy like we were."

There's fear in his voice and it makes something tighten inside me. "But..."

"If we moved, it could all go away. We could start again."

I get that, I do. This was only ever meant to be our starter home, the first rung on the ladder. We outgrew it long ago, tripping over one another in the too-small rooms. But the second rung on the ladder has always seemed so high, so out of reach.

"Maybe we could move—maybe we *should* move," I say. "But why there? We could look around, find somewhere closer to Cardiff, something..."

Patrick laughs and it's a bitter sound. "We can't afford anything else. This is a once-in-a-lifetime opportunity. If someone else bought the house and did all the things we talked about, they'd sell it for twice as much. This is it. The only chance—not just for me to get the house back but for us ever to own anything like it."

He's right. His childhood home isn't just the next rung on the ladder: it's a climb right to the top. God—sea views, detached, Victorian... When he'd taken me to see those beautiful seaside towns and I'd heard the longing in his voice, I'd feel it too: a yearning for a life I'd never had. I'd feel the exotic pull of it.

He comes around to my side and helps me out of the car.

"It could be such a happy place," Patrick says. I know he's not talking about our current home. "It was perfect once, before the murders. It could be perfect again."

Caroline's voice is going around and around in my head, and the fear and wariness on Mia's and Joe's faces, the way they tiptoe around me. Patrick's words have sent panic chasing through me. I need to protect my children. Patrick's right. To do that, we need a fresh start, somewhere I can get better, *be* better. Somewhere that will take away the fear in Patrick's voice. After we do the work, that house could be the dream home we always longed for. Because it was his perfect childhood home long before it became the Murder House, wasn't it? We'll be safe. It's not running away.

"Okay," I say to Patrick, bitterness from the pill still on my tongue. "You can have the money. Let's do it. Let's buy the house."

Part 2—The Murder House

Headline from *Wales Online*, May 2002:

Brutal Triple Murder Shocks Community

A man has appeared in court today charged with the murder of three members of one family.

Headline from the *South Wales Echo*, June 2002:

Welcome to the Murder House

I have this dream. In it, I'm in the house and it's dark and I know someone's in there with me, even though I can't see them. In the dream I start running, and the landing stretches out so it's a big long corridor and I'm running and the dragon in the man suit is chasing me and I never get to the end. There are all these rooms off the corridor and all the doors are closed and that's good because I don't want to look in any of them. I know something terrible waits inside for me, and if I stop and open those doors I'll never get away.

The sign went up today on the house. People crept out to watch, standing around in silence as the big red Sold was slapped over the For Sale sign everyone assumed would be there forever because who the fuck was going to buy that house, right? All the others cling to the shadows, pretending they're not really watching, just happen to be passing. Not me: I stand in the middle of the street, arms folded—I'm not scared of the Murder House.

"Who do you think bought it?"

I look at the man who slunk out of the shadows to ask. He lights a cigarette, holding out the packet to offer me one. Close up, he smells dusty and his breath is meaty and sour. "Probably someone who doesn't know," I say, and he stares at me like I'm nuts.

I remember when the house was something else, not the Murder House, just a house. These people, all these people watching, they see only the blood. You can tell by the way they avert their eyes, the way they cross the road, like something or someone will snatch them up if they get too close.

In my dream, the dream I have about the house that's just a house and not yet the Murder House, there are carpets in the hall, brown and cream swirls, and there's textured paper on the walls. It tips and tilts as the hall stretches out into an endless corridor and I run and run. It comes to life, flowing in and out under those closed doors. It comes to life and drags at my feet like an angry riptide.

I lied to the man with the rotting breath. I do know who's moving into the Murder House. New people are arriving—time to be neighborly.

CHAPTER 5

APRIL 2017

Someone's watching the house. There was a whole line of them when we pulled up earlier, the moving van behind us: a dozen silent watchers who just happened to be passing by, pretending to be doing something else but really just staring at Patrick as he put the key in the front door. No one said hello. No one came over to welcome us to the town. They just watched as our furniture was unloaded.

I grew more and more tense, self-conscious in front of the curtain-free windows. I'm not sure if Joe and Mia have noticed them yet—they seem shell-shocked by the move. It's all been so fast. We've been swept along by Patrick's enthusiasm, but I don't think the children really believed it was going to happen until the van turned up this morning. Mia looked on the verge of tears for most of the journey, and Joe visibly paled when we pulled up outside the house. And Patrick...I pointed out the watchers and he laughed. "We're famous," he said. "Ignore them; they're just vultures."

"They look like they're waiting."

He put down the box he was carrying and joined me at the window. "They probably are," he said.

"For what?"

He smiled. "For us to become tomorrow's news. For the bogeyman to jump out of the cupboard and a new family to be killed in the Murder House."

He winked at me, like it was a big joke, but goose bumps rose on my arms and they haven't gone down since.

The line of vultures thinned out over the course of the

afternoon as the sky got darker and the rain started. I thought everyone had left, but when I look outside it seems there might be one figure left. It's probably a trick of the light. Patrick's dragged the kids off to pick up takeout, on the pretext of showing them the town, and it's only me here, exposed every time I pass a window.

I wash down a pill with water, then try to distract myself while I wait for it to kick in by unpacking boxes, pausing to stroke the built-in shelves in the alcoves, humming as I fill them with books. Every filled shelf makes the house look more like a home and I don't notice it getting darker until I can no longer read the titles on the spines. As I reach for the light switch, a floorboard creaks in one of the empty upstairs rooms.

I stop humming.

No, Sarah, this is silly. It's just a house.

I glance out the living room window, but the watcher has gone. My heart's pounding. There was no watcher, I tell myself. It's seven o'clock at night in a bloody seaside town in south Wales: Who do I think is trying to get in? I put down my box of books and go back to the kitchen to make tea, putting on all the lights as I pass. I turn to the sink to fill the kettle, glance up, and scream. There's a face at the window.

I drop the kettle, water pouring out in a flood at my feet, then realize. Oh, stupid, stupid me—it's my bloody reflection. I've just given myself a heart attack over my own reflection.

As I'm mopping up the water, though, laughing shakily to myself, there's a sharp knock on the front door and I have to put both hands over my mouth to stop the shriek. Did Patrick lock it when he went out? I stand, frozen, in the kitchen, until I remember I'm visible to anyone in the darkness outside. I creep into the hall and silently slide the security chain into place, but the front door rattles again and I watch it open an inch, stopped by the chain. Without thinking, I race over and slam it shut, my hand shaking as I scrabble for the latch.

"Sarah? What's going on?"

It's Patrick's voice, muffled by the door but definitely his. Not a mysterious watcher, not a ghost. "Patrick?" I say.

"Are you okay?" he responds.

I'm flooded with such relief I can't speak. I release the chain and open the door, stepping back to let them in, my heart still galloping. Patrick comes toward me.

"What is it? What's wrong?"

Joe and Mia are still standing in the doorway, and I realize how it'll look if I show my panic. They've been out to pick up fish and chips and come back to find their mother freaking out over nothing.

"I'm sorry," I say. "I thought I heard someone outside and I overreacted, but I'm okay now. I promise." I'm trying to sound calm, but I can hear my voice shaking. I manage a smile. "Ignore me—go and get changed. You're all soaking wet…I had no idea it was raining so hard. I'll set the table."

Patrick follows me into the kitchen after the children have gone upstairs, stopping when he sees the pool of water on the floor, the kettle lying on its side, the soaked towel in the midst of it. "What is it? You looked scared when we came in."

I grab a roll of paper towels to finish wiping up the water. "I thought…There was someone outside—watching the house."

He touches my arm. "Did he try to get in?"

I shake my head. "I don't think so. He was across the road, but watching."

"Across the road? So he might not have been interested in the house at all?"

"I heard something outside, *right* outside. I heard a knock." My voice is rising and I can hear the edge of hysteria in it. Patrick's hand tightens on my arm and I wince.

"Sarah, calm down," he says. "Look at me and listen."

My breath is coming in gasps.

"It's fine. *Fine*. Calm down," he says. "I'll go and look."

I watch him through the window as he crosses the road and is swallowed by the darkness. I start counting. If he's not back in a few minutes, I'll go out there. As the seconds pass, my imagination supplies me with a dozen images of what's happening in the patch of darkness that swallowed him. He's fighting with the watcher; the watcher has thrown him into the sea; he's killed the watcher; the watcher has killed him, is dragging his body down the beach.

Why is he still not back?

One more minute. I'll give him one more minute, then I'll…I hold my breath as someone crosses the road toward me, releasing it as I recognize Patrick. I rush to open the front door, stepping out onto the path to meet him.

"What happened? Did you see him? Did you…"

His hair is soaked, clinging to his head, rain dripping onto his face. "There's no one there."

Then why was he gone so long? Twenty seconds to cross the road, twenty seconds back.

"Are you sure you didn't imagine it?" he says.

I shake my head.

He stares at me. "Have you taken your pills today?"

I nod. "Of course." There's a note of irritation in my voice I can't hide. It's become a ritual—Patrick putting the box of pills next to my morning coffee, the whole family on parade to watch me take them.

"Okay. I…Come on, I'll make you some tea."

My foot kicks something as I turn back to the house and I look down to see a shell on the doorstep, one of the big ones you hold up to your ear to listen to the sea. It's not the sort of shell you'd find on the local beaches, too shiny and big and exotic. I pick it up and hold it to my ear, but the real sound of the sea drowns out any magic from the shell. I had one of these once: my dad brought it back from some adventure before he stopped coming home. That's what he told me when I was a kid—that it was magic inside the shell: a miniature ocean hidden inside just for me to hear. All lies—Dad was a salesman, not an explorer. He probably bought the shell in some tacky seaside town like this one. I look toward the sea again, half expecting to see the ghost of a man I once called Dad, who got lost for good on one adventure too many.

Patrick ropes in Joe and Mia to help him clean up after we've eaten and I go back to the living room to tackle another box, distracted every time a car passes and the flash of headlights hits the curtainless window.

"What's up, Mum?"

I glance away from the window to Mia. She's chewing her hair and frowning. She's been so angry with me since the hospital, angry and anxious as she trails around after me. "It's nothing—me being silly, getting spooked in a new house, that's all."

"Where did you get that?"

She's looking at the shell and I hand it to her. She puts it to her ear right away.

"Can you hear it?" I ask.

Mia leans against me, nearly as tall as me, nearly grown-up but sometimes still my little girl. I stroke her hair and kiss the top of her head. It's been a long time since she came to me for a hug.

"I can't hear anything *but* the sea. I'll never be able to sleep," she says, her voice muffled as she buries her head in my shoulder.

"Come on," I say. "Listening to the sea has *got* to be better than listening to the neighbors' kids arguing through the walls. I know it's weird. But it's our first day. We'll soon have it looking like home."

"But it's *not* our home, Mum. I miss my friends. I even miss my old school. Why do we have to do this?"

"The school here has a great reputation—much better than your old one in Cardiff."

She laughs, but it's more like a sob. "Seriously, Mum? You move me and Joe to the middle of nowhere halfway through the year and you're trying to make out it's because it'll be good for our *education*?"

But they were both failing at the school Mia claimed she would miss: Joe hardly turning up for classes at all and Mia struggling with half her subjects. I don't need to say this to Mia. However I put it, it'll sound like the move is a punishment rather than something that could help them.

"Please give it a chance. We just need to make the house our own...and you know how important this is to your dad."

She stiffens and straightens, little girl gone, flinging my shell onto the sofa. It bounces onto the floor, clattering across to come to a halt at my feet.

"So we have to lie? Say we're all thrilled to be here? Heaven bloody forbid we should actually tell him what we *really* think." At the door she turns back to me. "I begged him not to do this to us and I thought he was listening, but because you took those pills, I had no chance, did I? He's done this, ruined all our lives, for *you*."

She slams her door upstairs and I hear Joe knock and go into her room. He'll be better than me at soothing her. After a few minutes, I hear Mia laugh.

I follow the welcome sound and peek into her room. As the elder, Joe should have had this one, as it's bigger, but as soon as she saw the size of the third, she pleaded until Joe gave in. Mia is sprawled on her bed, which sits like an island in a sea of boxes, laughing at something on Joe's phone, almost doubled up with it, red-faced. Joe's leaning over, trying to snatch it from her, and she jumps up, on the bed, bouncing and holding it out of his reach.

They freeze as I come into the room and I wish I'd stepped back instead, stored the moment in secret for later. Now I've broken it. I try anyway, putting on a smile, a light tone in my voice. "What's so funny?"

"Nothing," Mia says, chucking the phone to Joe and sinking down onto the bed. "Just something stupid on Facebook."

"Cat video," Joe says, which for some reason makes Mia laugh again, so hard she buries her face in the quilt.

"Sorry, Mum," Joe says with a sigh. "She's being a total idiot. What did you want?"

"Nothing," I say. "Just checking if you needed anything else to eat."

Joe shakes his head and Mia ignores me. I hover for a few more seconds, but Patrick's calling. I hear Mia's door click shut as I walk away.

I go down to the living room, shoulders drooping. I'm overwhelmed by how much there is to do. The walls are damp-spotted. The parquet floor, in the corner where I pulled up part of the old carpet, is in a worse state than I'd thought. Most of it will have to be replaced. At least the mountain of boxes covers the worst of the damage. I'm back at the living room window staring out when Patrick steps up behind me. I jump at his reflection, thinking the watcher has lurched into view, looming and dark, but it's just Patrick, wiping his hands on a towel he drops onto the coffee table.

"The dishes are done."

I smile at him. "Thank you—you're a star. We'll have to make a dishwasher top of the list of things to buy."

He raises an eyebrow. "It's getting to be a long list."

I bite my lip and look up at him. "Patrick? Who do you think it was, watching the house?"

"No one. Just another nosy idiot from the town." He leans down to kiss me. His lips are cold and his sweater scratchy when he puts his arms around me. I open my eyes when his icy hand slides under my top, and his are open too, but he's not looking at me: he's looking out the window.

I try to stay relaxed, but his hands are still stroking, lifting my top higher, and all I can think of are the children upstairs and the watcher outside. I put my hands over Patrick's as they slide toward my breasts. "Not here, not in front of the window."

"Too much of an adventure for you?"

His teasing stings and I turn my face away from him.

He's still clutching the edges of my top and I think he'll keep going, strip me bare. Then he stops, lets his face hide in my hair again, wrapping his arms around me, holding me too tight. "You have to give the house a chance, Sarah, not get hysterical over every imagined thing. We're going to be so happy here," he says. "You wait and see."

"I didn't imagine it."

"Does it matter if someone stopped to gawk at the house? You overreacting so much is upsetting the children. They worry about you. They want you to be happy here as much as I do."

The wind rattles the windows and somewhere a door bangs. I shiver as a cold breeze arrives from nowhere.

Patrick sighs. "It's not a haunted house, not a monster house, or a murder house, or whatever they damn well call it. It's just a family home, *our* family home. You can't blame the house... It was Ian who lost it, who went mad, not the house."

"Ian? You mean the murderer?"

He blinks and looks away. "Ian Hooper, yes."

"Why did you say his name like you know him?"

He hesitates. "Didn't I tell you? I did used to know him. He was a few years older, but I knew him."

I frown. "When you lived here? When you were still at school?"

He doesn't answer immediately. "Yes. That's right," he says, after that too-long pause. "I knew him when I was still at school."

I look at the shell in my hands. Will you know what it means? Will you remember? I wish I could get into the house. I wish I could find those hidden, secret places again. I'd put the shell there, fill it with my words, and leave it hidden, waiting to be discovered. Leaving it on your doorstep is cruder, a shout rather than a whisper, but then she finds it, not you, and it makes me laugh as I hide in the shadows.

CHAPTER 6

In May 2002 a man named Ian Hooper came to this house and stabbed John Evans three times in the front hall. Before that, he went upstairs to the room that's now Mia's and stabbed Marie Evans twelve times. Billy Evans, who was nine, came out onto the landing and tried to stop Ian Hooper from killing his mother, but he was stabbed once and pushed down the stairs. He later died in the hospital.

The younger boy, Tom, lived.

Hooper was charged with all three murders but only convicted of John Evans's: there wasn't enough evidence to get a majority verdict on the others.

Why did he do it? None of the first stories I find seem to answer that. But I'm looking for a connection to the Evans family, something to explain *why*. It can't have been senseless and random, can it? I'm not sure I'll ever be able to relax in this house if I'm thinking that it could have happened to anyone. It could have happened to us.

No. There has to be a connection. A motive. If Patrick knew Hooper when he was still at school, maybe John Evans did too.

I click through to another story, skipping the more gruesome details. I'm looking for more about Ian Hooper, whom Patrick apparently knew, but I can't find anything that makes sense. Hooper would have been so much older—too old to be Patrick's friend, too young to be his parents' friend. But it's a small town. Patrick might have known him to say hello to in the street.

I zoom in on a photo of the Evans family until it goes all pixelated. The knowledge that a grown-up Tom Evans sold us the house makes me feel as if I know him somehow. When we were signing papers, his name on the contracts brought a lump to my throat. That poor little boy. I know he's older than Joe now, twenty-one or twenty-two, but it's the little boy in the newspaper photos I pictured signing away the house, a seven-year-old I imagined banking my mother's money.

I close my eyes. Maybe I didn't get the adventures I wanted from the money my mother left, but I like to think Tom Evans will. That he took the money from the sale of the house and is now traveling the world, freed from the ghosts of his past.

It's different for us. The house will be different for us. Patrick has only happy memories, and for me, Joe, and Mia, it's a house with no memories at all. We can make it better. We can make it new again. My phone buzzes—I glance down and see another text from Caroline. She's given up calling. I'll call her back, but not until we're settled, not until she can hear in my voice a conviction that the move was the right thing to do.

I step away from the computer and open another box, unwrapping a vase to put on the mantelpiece. There's a knock on the door and I freeze, remembering the knock I thought I heard last night. I step back from the window, then jump as someone appears in front of me, her hands cupped, peering through the glass.

It's a woman in her sixties with a bunch of daffodils tucked under her arm. She steps back and waves when she sees me. I can't think what else to do, so I open the front door to greet her.

"Hello—hope I didn't scare you just now. I wasn't sure you'd heard me knocking."

I glance back toward the living room. "No. Sorry. I was listening to music."

"I'm Lyn Barrett from number twenty-eight. I was going to pop in yesterday, but my husband said I should give you longer to settle in."

It's not even noon. We've been here less than twenty-four hours. "Yes, I'm very busy, as I'm sure you can imagine. A million boxes still to unpack."

She gives a big bright smile. "Well, I'm sure you're ready for a break." She steps forward. I have to move aside to let her in or she'd be close enough to kiss.

"Oh, yes," she says as I lead her reluctantly through to the living room, the only room vaguely presentable for visitors. "You *have* got a lot to do." I see her gaze drift to the computer screen and go over to close the browser window before she can see what I've been looking at.

I offer her a seat, but she follows me into the kitchen when I go to fill the kettle, my face warming as she trips on a box.

"I've brought you these. They should brighten the room nicely." She's looking around as she says it, at the falling-apart units, the open pill box with the bold red lettering shouting what it contains, the scrunched-up packing paper littering every surface.

I put the daffodils in a mug on the windowsill.

"So, I'm guessing your husband—Patrick, isn't it? Patrick Walker. He's gone to work?"

I nod, thinking if I stick to saying as little as possible, she might leave quicker. I don't like the way she's nosing around—I can tell she's dying to open drawers and cupboards. I half expect her to ask for a tour of the house. She steps closer to the pills on the table, her head tilting to read the box. I want to snatch them out of view, but that would only make her more curious.

"And your children, I saw them heading into town earlier. I guess they'll be going to the local school?"

"That's right. They start next week. Look—it's so nice of you to stop by, but it's a really bad time and—"

"Oh, don't worry. I won't keep you. Just wanted to pop in to say welcome to the street."

I don't mean to be rude, but that's what I'm being. I should welcome a friendly face. I don't want her to go away gossiping about the uppity woman who's moved into the Murder House. "Perhaps next week you could come over for a proper chat," I suggest. "When I have things more organized."

She takes a sip of tea and pushes it away. I've made it too weak and milky. My own tastes of milky water. It's lukewarm—I must have forgotten to switch on the kettle.

"I really am sorry."

She reaches over to pat my hand. "It's fine. I'll be off now. Can I use your loo before I go?"

I direct her upstairs, because the downstairs loo is full of boxes, and pour away the disgusting tea. I'm moving the daffodils to the table, gathering up the packing paper to clear it away, when I hear a floorboard creak above my head. I frown. It's Joe's room above the kitchen, not the bathroom.

I go upstairs and find the bathroom empty, no sign she's even been in there. I turn as she walks out of Mia's room, her face reddening. She has her phone in her hand.

"Were you taking photos?" I say, my voice rising in disbelief, my stomach turning.

"Ah, no—my phone rang and the signal wasn't very good in the bathroom, so..."

All the bedroom doors are open.

"As I said, I'm very busy. Perhaps you should go now."

I walk behind her down the stairs, and she turns to me as she opens the front door. "I always felt sorry for him as a boy."

"Excuse me?"

"Your husband—Patrick. I was always so sorry for him. Such a handsome young man."

"Well, I'll be sure to let him know you stopped in." I'm tempted to give her a shove as she hovers on the step. "Tell me your name again."

She ignores me. "There was always something a bit strange about this house, even before the murders," she says. "And his parents...*awful* when the house was repossessed like that. So *embarrassing* for them. Mind you, they never really seemed happy here...We *were* surprised your husband chose to come back."

She's watching me, an expectant look on her face. I won't give her the satisfaction of answering, even though her words are like worms crawling under my skin. I grip the door and start to close it.

"Well," she says, clearly put out by my rudeness and oblivious to her own, "good luck to you. And your lovely children."

I'm shaking when I close the door behind her. Is that what it's going to be like? A parade of faux-friendly neighbors sneaking around my bloody house taking *photographs*? Whispering poison, insinuating... insinuating *what*?

I feel sick as I imagine her googling the name of my medication, making all sorts of assumptions about her mentally unstable new neighbor. I grab the box from the kitchen, rummage through a cupboard to find a plastic-lidded container, and press out all the pills from their foil, emptying them into the anonymous box, no incriminating label to give me away. But the bad taste in my mouth doesn't go. Her words, her avid curiosity... No. It used to be a happy house; I know that from Patrick. It can be a happy house again.

Patrick is in the hall hanging up his coat, his suit creased, eyes tired. I tried to persuade him to take some time off after the move, but he insisted on going to work.

"Are you hungry?" I ask, and he follows me into the kitchen. The breakfast dishes are still stacked up ready to wash and the box of tissue-wrapped crockery I started to unpack is open on the floor but no emptier than it had been hours ago. I went to lie down after taking my lunchtime pill and fell asleep, not waking until four.

"How did you get on today with the unpacking?" he asks as I rummage in another box for something for dinner.

"Not too bad," I say, rubbing my eyes. A pulsing headache has set in and I feel as if I could go up and sleep for another hour. "Another couple of days and we'll be pretty much done. I've got the bedrooms mostly unpacked."

"Good, good," he says, taking off his jacket and unbuttoning his shirt cuffs. He sounds distracted and doesn't seem to notice the mess as he stares out the back window at the tangled garden.

"Are you okay?" I ask.

He blinks and turns away from the window. "What? Yes, I'm fine. There was a... It was a difficult day at work."

Patrick is a structural engineer. I used to ask about his job with genuine interest. He'd show me plans and schematics, talk about the buildings he'd worked on, and I'd try to understand. But I didn't, really, any more than he understood some of the paintings I did. It never mattered. He'd laugh and put the plans away, help me wash the paint out of my hair, the conversation would move on and maybe, at some point, we'd stopped listening to the answers we got when we asked, *How was your day?*

He must see my worry, because he squeezes my hand and smiles. "It's fine—I'm a bit tired and hungry, that's all. I haven't gotten used to the commute yet. These are pretty," he says, looking at the daffodils.

"One of our neighbors dropped in."

His smile fades, replaced by wariness. "Oh, yes?"

"I caught her taking photographs of the bedrooms." My earlier outrage stirs again.

"What on earth for?"

"Well, I don't think it was the IKEA furniture she was interested in. She was on a bloody ghost tour of her own making."

"Jesus," he mutters.

"She seemed to remember you."

I wait for him to answer, but he turns away, flipping through the forwarded mail.

"I could see she was dying to know why we moved here and..." I see his back stiffen. He doesn't need to hear it today.

"It made me think—we should ask people around, not nosy neighbors but people you used to know, have a reunion of sorts. It'll be a way of laying down roots here again."

"No."

"What do you mean?"

"I mean, no. Any friends I had here are long gone. Anyone who remembers me now is not a friend. They just want to spread lies and gossip. I won't have them in my house." He glances down at me. "If this *neighbor* comes around again, tell her to piss off."

I stare after him as he marches from the room. What does he mean? Surely there must be *some* people left here that he knew as friends. Wasn't that part of the idyllic picture he painted for me—the friendliness of a small town?

I find pasta, a jar of ready-made sauce. I'm chopping onions and peppers, and Patrick's stuffing packing paper into the overflowing bin and stacking plates in a wall cupboard that looks ready to give way. The children are in the living room: I can hear the rise and fall of Mia's voice through the wall. She came down for dinner dressed all in black, eyeliner thick around her eyes. She's like a little girl playing dress-up, wearing clothes I don't recognize, looking both older and younger in too much makeup.

Patrick opens the bin lid to pull out the garbage bag, cursing as he drops it and everything spills on the floor. I spot the empty pill box too late—he's already reaching for it, snatching it out of my grasp.

"What's this?" There's panic in his voice as he holds the empty blister pack and stares at me.

Oh, no, no—he can't think…"Patrick, I haven't taken them. They're here," I say, holding up the plastic box I put the pills in. "I've put them in here."

He looks from the empty pack to the plastic container in my hand. "*Why*?"

"Because that damn nosy neighbor saw the box. I was embarrassed—humiliated at the thought of our neighbors thinking I'm…"

"Thinking you're what?"

"Crazy."

"*Jesus*, Sarah," he says, running a hand through his hair. "Taking medication doesn't make you crazy; it makes you *better*. This, though, doing this... God, for a minute I thought... What if Joe or Mia saw the empty packet? So soon after your damn overdose? You could have just put them in a drawer, kept them out of sight."

"I didn't think! It doesn't matter, does it?"

"It doesn't matter?" His voice rises in disbelief. He squeezes the empty pill box, scrunching it up. "You're hiding again, refusing to face you have a problem, wallowing in your guilt instead of trying to get better." He shakes his head. "God, it's good the children are starting their new school on Monday. They need some distance from you—it'll be good for them."

"Distance?"

"Your guilt is so obvious in the way you're clinging. It's making them claustrophobic."

Guilt: my sour, bitter friend. Guilt over my mother, over Joe, and now guilt over what I put them through with those stupid pills.

"It's just the same as before," Patrick says. "With your mother. It wasn't your fault she died, you did nothing wrong, but you couldn't get past it, could you? You couldn't just grieve and move on; you let it break you. You almost let it break our whole damn family. You nearly died, and I couldn't bear it, couldn't stand..." His voice is hoarse and I don't know if it's with fear, frustration, or both.

His words have winded me and I can't catch my breath. I hate that I've done this, that I came so close to breaking all of us. In those awful weeks and months after my mother's death, it was all so *much*. I couldn't see anything beyond all that grief and guilt. It overwhelmed me. But the pills... That's wrong. I didn't mean to die. I *didn't*.

"I'm trying," he says. "I'm trying so hard, but I can't do it on my own. Give the house a chance—give *us* a chance. Make it better, Sarah. Make this work, because if you don't..." He takes a shaky breath. "I don't know what else to do."

His fear leaks into me. What have I done to us?

The other day I was talking to someone about this town. "It's lovely there," they said. "I went there on vacation when I was a kid." That's the thing, though. Everyone went on vacation here when they were a kid. When you're on vacation, you don't see the rot. You don't see the rust or the nasty words graffitied on hidden walls. You don't see the pain, the sadness, the evil, the dull, gray, never-ending boredom that leads people to drink and smoke and fight and die. You don't see the locked doors and the bars on the windows. You don't hear the screams and pleas behind those closed doors. You see the fair and the fish and chips and the ice cream. You see sand and sea and picnics and candy. You see pretty houses with net curtains and sea views. You don't see a murder house. You don't see anything.

CHAPTER 7

"I was thinking, now that we're here, I could get a job."

Patrick glances up at me as he turns a page of his newspaper. "With all your qualifications?"

"Excuse me?" I say, flicking his newspaper.

He laughs and puts down the paper. "I'm sorry," he says. "You know I'm only teasing. But one step at a time, okay? When were you last out there looking for a job? First you're getting the whole neighborhood around, now you want to take over the world."

I pick up his discarded newspaper and go through it for the jobs page. "I'm not looking to take over anything. I'm thinking about a part-time job. It's supposed to be a fresh start for all of us. I need to do more. I have to do something."

"Aren't you happy? We have this house, this beautiful house, in this beautiful town..."

"Yes, and now I need a life. A house isn't enough. Maybe if I'd had more before, I'd..." My voice trails off.

"What?"

"Maybe I'd have been better able to cope after my mother died."

My words hover and Patrick goes pale. I sit next to him and squeeze his hand. "I am *determined* to make this work, I promise," I say. "You, Caroline, the children—you've all been running around, trying to help me, but I have to help myself too. I don't want to be reliant on medication to get me through the day."

There's a look of panic on his face that makes me laugh. "I'm not planning a midlife crisis. I'm talking about a part-time job, or taking some art classes, or...I don't know, just something."

He reaches over, tucks a strand of hair behind my ear, and

strokes my cheek. "I can't tell you how much it means to me that you've done this—moved here, committed to making our new life. Of course you should look for a job, take some classes, whatever. But let's get the rest of the house sorted first. Then I'm sure we can find you something to do."

But now that we've moved, I find I want more. My feet itch to get out and *do* something. Isn't that what he wanted for me?

"A few weeks. A couple of months, that's all. It's only been a few months since your... illness," he says. "We've only been here two days. Give yourself time to settle, adjust."

He gets up and takes his cup to the sink. "Tea?" he asks, filling the kettle. "Fuel for the unpacking..."

I glance back at the newspaper. I can still apply for jobs. Do the unpacking and decorating while I wait to hear back from them.

"Oh, wait," I say as he puts on his coat for work. "I found something yesterday." I run upstairs and come down with my hands held out. "Look," I say. "It's C-3PO and Luke Skywalker."

His hands close around the figures. I remember him telling me about the magical Christmas when he got them. All the *Star Wars* figures he'd asked for, more than a dozen boxed up. "Best Christmas ever," he'd said. I'd found them sitting on the windowsill upstairs, like they were waiting there to welcome Patrick home.

"They were in our bedroom—Mia or Joe must have found them somewhere. Didn't you say you had all the characters once? I did look, but I couldn't find any more."

"These aren't mine."

"Of course they are—you told me about them."

"Mine were thrown away a long time ago."

"You threw them away?"

He ignores me and keeps talking. "It doesn't matter, even if they were mine. They're toys. Crappy old bits of plastic, that's all." He goes through to the kitchen and drops them in the bin.

If they're not Patrick's, they must have been here when we moved in. Which means they could have belonged to one of the Evans children. I reach into the bin and pull them out, brushing off the dust. Patrick watches me do it but doesn't say anything. They weren't on the windowsill before today. I would have seen them.

My hands are trembling. I don't believe in ghosts, but it's the little dead boy I'm picturing, halfway through an unfinished game as a madman came through the door. I know that's silly. I know Joe or Mia must have found them in some forgotten corner and put them there, but...it seems wrong to throw them away. Whether they're Patrick's and he's forgotten he still had them, or whether they belonged to one of the Evans boys, they were once precious to somebody. I put them away in the back of a drawer. Safe but hidden.

A breeze ruffles the hair at the back of my neck. I know it's from the open window, but it feels like a breath. The breath of a ghost as I close the drawer.

As I wave Patrick off, I see Mia on the beach, a few feet from the shoreline, her head bowed and shoulders hunched, her arms wrapped around herself against the wind. Why does she never take her coat? I get it from the hall and follow her across the road.

"Put this on," I say as I draw level, then step back as a wave breaks a little too close to my foot. Mia doesn't seem to notice and lets the water wash over her shoes.

She glances up at me and takes the coat but doesn't put it on. Instead she hugs it to her, a cushion for her front, the rest still exposed to the wind and saltwater spray. "Thanks, Mum."

"What are you doing out here?"

She shrugs and looks down at the phone clutched in her hand. "I wanted to call Lara, but the signal in the house is shit."

It is. It's making it easier to avoid Caroline's calls when they go straight to voicemail. "Did you get through?"

"Voicemail," she mutters. "I wanted to get a lift into Cardiff with Dad. It's the last day of the Easter break—I thought we could have lunch and then I could meet up with Lara, but he said no."

She looks deflated. Trips to the city were something she and Patrick used to do a lot on school breaks.

"He's really busy at the moment. I'm sure he'd love to do that on the next break, though."

"Yeah, right. He never has time for me anymore. It's all the house and work and you."

I've noticed it too. His preoccupation with the house, with work, with me. When was the last time they had one of their father-daughter lunches? Hers is the first room we're going to decorate, Patrick insisted. But he's talking about it in a distracted way, not involving her. He's doing it like it's expected Mia's room will be done first, not like he wants to do it. The thread of unease I've felt since we first stepped through the door grips me a little tighter. Patrick has seemed only half-present—what's distracting him? Is it worrying about me? Is it the house?

"Your dad used to bring me here years ago," I say, nudging a shell out of its sand grave with my foot. Mia bends to pick it up. "Not to this exact beach, a bit farther down the coast. I loved it when we visited. He'd buy me an ice cream and we'd walk along the beach and then get fish and chips. You and Joe would be in a double buggy and we'd feed you chips and ice cream like you were baby birds, sitting there with your mouths open."

Mia smiles and reaches down to pick up another shell. "Do you remember that vacation in Cornwall? When we got lucky with the weather and were on the beach every day? We had that cottage five minutes from the sea, and by the end of the week, I swear more sand and shells were in the cottage than on the beach."

I can feel the tightness in my chest begin to loosen. "We could make it like that here. When the weather picks up. I promise, the first nice day, we'll bring a picnic down here and I'll treat us all to ice cream and we'll finish the day with a bag of chips."

"Will you buy us buckets and spades as well? Remember, mine has to be red and Joe's has to be yellow."

"Of course. There's a shop that sells them a few minutes down the road."

Another wave races in and soaks our feet. Mia laughs as I scream and almost fall.

Mia's laugh, the pocketful of shells, the sea spray hitting my face, the crashing of the waves and the call of the seagulls, the hint of blue showing through the clouds…I feel something building. It's the promise, not just a week by the sea, then back to suburbia, boxy houses, and patchwork lawns. We live here now, we live *this*, and I can almost see it—the dusting of sand in the hallway, shell collections on the shelves, sun shining on bowls of sea glass in the window. Screw the neighbors. If I can make Mia see it too, maybe this could work for all of us.

But then I look around and the house seems closed up and dark, unlived-in, and I can feel that ghost-breath on the back of my neck. Mia follows my gaze and I see her shoulders sag again.

"We'll still have to go back, though, won't we, Mum?" she says. "After the picnic and the ice cream. We'll still live in the Murder House."

I take her hand and squeeze it. "It's for us to make it something different. Something amazing. It doesn't have to stay the Murder House, not if we don't let it. I'll go back now, open all the windows…"

"Let the dead out?"

"Let the *history* out. There are no ghosts, just memories. Ian Hooper is locked away and we're free to make the house whatever we want. We'll let the sea air blow it all out and fill the house with new memories."

"Have you noticed…"

"Noticed what?"

"There are cold spots in the house. The heat's on, but sometimes I'll walk across a room and it's like the temperature drops by twenty degrees."

"It's an old house—a lot of drafts."

She rolls her eyes at me. "Drafts. Right."

I smile and nudge her, refusing to let that ray of hope fade. "Come on, Mia—you're too old to believe in ghosts. You're letting your imagination get the better of you. I understand, I've been doing it myself, but we have to try."

"I suppose it could be all right." She says it reluctantly, but she *says* it. It's a start. "It's nice to have a bit of peace at least—not have Caroline in and out all the time, like she lives with us."

I'm startled. I didn't know it bothered her—Caroline was always there to step in, especially in the last few months, there to be the parent when I was failing at it. "You used to call her Aunty Caroline."

Mia snorts. "Maybe *Aunty* Caroline isn't as good a friend as she pretends."

"What do you mean?"

"Nothing. Forget it." Mia glances at me. "It's nice to see you so..."

"What?"

She shrugs. "Positive? It's not Caroline who's managed to do that, is it? I guess there's got to be some hint of a silver lining to all this."

Joe's coming down the stairs as we go back to the house, zipping up his hoodie.

"Where are you off to?"

"The fair," he says, pulling a handful of change out of his pocket. "I'm going to make our fortune in the arcade. Want to come?"

"I have to get on with the unpacking. Why don't you two go together?" I get out my purse and give him a ten-pound note. "Go on—blow the lot."

He grins. "Come on, little sis," he says, tugging at Mia's hair.

I watch them from my bedroom as they walk down the street, laughing and pushing each other. Seeing Joe smile like that—I can imagine telling him the truth, imagine him understanding and being able to cope with it. That feeling, that *good* feeling, in the pit of my stomach grows. We'll be able to make it, I can tell. Patrick was right: it's a good place. I wonder, for a moment, if Marie Evans felt this way when she moved in, but I push the thought away.

I hear that wind chime again and open the window wide to see whose house is providing the music. As the sea breeze sweeps in and around the room, it feels like it's blowing away more than lingering memories of death and murder: it's blowing away some of the darkness and cobwebs that have taken residence in me. I was like the house, locked up and lost for too many years, slowly sliding into a pit I didn't see coming.

A stronger gust pulls the window wider and the vase of daffodils on the sill falls. The flowers get caught up and blown out into the street, landing at the feet of a woman walking past. "Sorry," I call.

She looks up, laughing. "Don't be—it's the first time anyone has ever scattered flowers at my feet." She bends down to gather them up. She holds them and I smile at how it must look, her offering a bunch of flowers to me in the window. "Do you want them back?" she asks.

"Keep them," I say.

She buries her nose in the daffodils, looking at the stack of boxes I've put outside the front door. "Thank you," she says. "Have you just moved in? It should be me bringing you flowers to say welcome to the town."

"I like to do things differently."

"You'll be very welcome if you greet all your new neighbors like this." She smiles again. "I'm Anna, by the way."

"Sarah."

"Well, it's nice to meet you, Sarah. Good luck with the unpacking, and I'm sure I'll see you around."

I watch her walk away, my flowers in her hands, and I think I hear her humming. She showed no sign of morbid curiosity and I get that feeling of hope again. I'd never stopped to consider what this move could offer me—a new town, new friends, maybe a new job. It could be an adventure. It could be just the adventure I need.

The wind from the sea blows in again and it feels, for a second, like it lifts me off my feet.

But then I see Lyn Barrett step out of her house and I'm brought down with a thump. What's she saying to make Anna glance back like that? Does she think I threw out her flowers deliberately? Is she telling her about the house, the murders? Is she telling her about Patrick, more of those needling innuendos? Or is she talking about the pill-popping rude woman who kicked her out? I lean out farther, as if their words might carry on the wind to me. What poisonous things is she saying?

They'll be next, the wind whispers. *You don't want to be friends with her. She'll be dead soon, like Marie Evans, dead, dead, dead, nothing left but blood on the walls.*

I slam the window shut.

No.

Stop.

I should be unpacking the rest of the boxes, but the sun's shining and I have to get out, away from my thoughts. I'm chasing that feeling of hope again. I've walked the length of the promenade into town. There's something particularly sad and lonely about a seaside town out of season. It's Easter but half the shops are closed, and the beach is deserted, apart from the odd dog-walker. I'm thinking I might head over to the fair, buy my children that bag of chips. I wander onto a side street, stopping when I pass a gallery. *This* is the kind of place I imagine myself working. I could go in and ask, couldn't I? Even a bit of volunteer work would put something on my résumé.

The window display is taken up with a large seascape. Acres of blue, and in the foreground, a back view of a bench on the coast path, two figures seated, looking out to sea, a small dog curled up at their feet. It's nice enough but unexceptional; cozy and chocolate-box. The paint is flat on the canvas, no sense of depth or awe in the landscape, despite the size of the painting.

"What do you think?"

I gasp and turn from the window to the woman who spoke. She grins at me, a big smile that's somehow familiar.

"Sorry, did I make you jump?" She's laughing and I blush at my too-extreme reaction. It's Anna, the woman I met earlier, the one who took my flowers home.

"They survived the fall—the flowers. They really brightened up my apartment and my day. Thank you."

We smile at each other.

"I pass this every day and I still haven't decided," she says.

"Decided what?"

"Friends or lovers?"

"What?"

"The people in the painting." She nods at the seascape. "I can't make up my mind if they're an old married couple out for a walk or two friends stopped for a chat. Or illicit lovers on a secret rendezvous."

I look at the painting again. One of the figures is leaning in toward the other as if for a kiss or to whisper in her ear.

"I think they're strangers," Anna says. "They've just met, right that minute, on the bench."

"They look closer than strangers."

"That's because there's a spark. Not romantic. That spark you get when you chat to a stranger and you think, we could be friends. Instant connection."

I had that with Caroline. We exchanged hellos on the first day of college and I knew instantly we'd be friends. I glance at Anna again. She's taller than me, my age or a bit older. Short dark hair, sharp cheekbones. She's wearing jeans, like me, but she has an edge: that thick black eyeliner, the cropped hair. Swap her Converse for DMs, add a few more piercings, and she could be one of the girls I wanted to be in art college.

She smiles again. "Shit painting, though."

I laugh in surprise. I don't want to admit it, but ever since I saw it, I've been thinking, I could do better.

"It's okay," I say instead, an answer as insipid as the painting.

There's a silence that should be awkward but isn't. "So, do you paint yourself, or are you just a critic?" I say. Maybe she's familiar because she *is* one of the girls from art college I wanted to be, if not from my college, then some other fine arts course.

"Not really," she answers. "I wanted to, once. I was good at it at school, but...I don't think I was ever good enough to do it for real. These days, I look at other people's paintings, save up to buy some for my walls, and that's enough for me. How about you?"

I open my mouth to answer, then close it again. What am I these days? Can I call myself a painter? "I used to," I say. "I used to paint. But, actually, I'm here trying to pluck up the courage to go in and ask for a job."

She makes a face. "Not many jobs around this time of year. Half the shops are seasonal—you might have better luck in the summer." She steps closer to the window. "This painting always makes me laugh," she says, and I look for the comedy in the seascape in the window.

She points to the title card propped up against the canvas. "He's called it *The Heritage Coast* but, come on, really? Bright blue? Calm water, not a cloud in the sky? Have you ever seen a view like that around here?"

I shake my head. "It should be gray," I say. "Gray and bleak and stormy."

She looks at me. "Not always. I know places where there are colors a million times more beautiful than this. Real colors too."

"Around here?"

She nods. "Seriously. Beautiful, beautiful places."

I think for a moment she's going to offer to show me and I stiffen, ready to make polite apologies and sidle away. But she sighs and picks up her shopping bag.

"Better get back to work," she says. "Nice to see you again. Maybe I'll call around—bring *you* some flowers to say welcome to the town."

She turns at the corner. "Listen, I work part-time in the café on Broad Street when I'm not critiquing the town's artists. Shit coffee but great service. Come in sometime—I'll tell you where the good beaches are."

I should go home, carry on scouring the jobs ads in the local paper, but less than an hour after seeing Anna outside the gallery, I find myself heading for the café on Broad Street, choosing a table in the window and picking up the laminated menu. Anna slides into the seat opposite. "I didn't think you'd take me up on it," she says. "I'll have to confess now—the service is as shit as the coffee."

"But aren't you the service?"

She laughs. "I'll get you a coffee in lieu of the flowers I owe you—but don't say you weren't warned."

After she leaves I get out my sketchbook. I haven't opened it since we got here. I've barely opened it since my mother died. Then the world seemed coated with a layer of gray and I haven't wanted to draw or paint anything. Perhaps that's where the distance between me and Joe has come from—we were always closest sketching together. I'm looking at a drawing I did of Joe and Mia, the two of them huddled together on the sofa, laughing, when a shadow appears on the page.

"God, that's good. Did you draw it?"

I glance up, resisting the urge to snatch the book away as she pulls it toward her to look closer.

"Are these your kids?"

I nod.

"They look so alike," she says with a smile.

I grimace and she notices. "Sorry, did I...?"

"It's not a very good drawing." I look closer at the sketch. I'm not doing the false-modesty thing—it's not the best drawing of them I've done, but it's one I keep coming back to. Anna's right—despite the difference in their ages, I've made them look like twins.

"Sarah," she says, "I've got something for you."

She goes over to the counter and comes back with a leaflet. "We're meant to be displaying them for the gallery, but I haven't gotten around to putting one in the window yet. It's not a job, but it is an opportunity."

The leaflet is advertising an open exhibition of local artists.

"They have them quite often," she says. "And they're always looking for new artists to showcase. As you can imagine, the talent's a bit limited in a town this size. You'd blow them away."

I shake my head. "I can't—I couldn't. I haven't painted anything properly for months."

She's flicking through my sketchbook again, pausing on a charcoal drawing of Patrick. I didn't fix it, so it's gone soft and blurry, but he's still there.

"It doesn't have to be paintings. Why not frame some of your drawings? Come on, please give me something decent to look at in the gallery window." She pushes the sketchbook toward me. "Speak to Ben Owens—he runs the place. Show him this book, see what he says."

She leans back. "Sorry. I'm freaking you out, aren't I? I do this all the time. I'll stop pestering you and leave you to your coffee. But come back in anytime. And if you change your mind about the gallery..." She scribbles her number on the leaflet, tucks it inside my sketchbook, and gets up. "It was nice to meet you again, Sarah."

She walks off, bangles jangling, and I think I've figured out why she seems familiar. She reminds me of Caroline, of the way we met, when she marched up to me, all two-tone hair, pierced nose, and confidence, on the first bewildering day at college.

I clutch the leaflet as I walk home, and my heart pounds as I imagine it. I haven't exhibited since college. I nearly had something lined up once, when Joe and Mia were in nursery part-time, but in the end, there wasn't room for me. Caroline exhibited there instead and I stopped trying.

"What's this?" Patrick says when he gets in from work, picking up the leaflet I left on the table.

"There's a gallery in town," I say. "It has exhibitions of local artists. I was thinking I could take some of my work down there and see if they'd be interested in me for the next one."

He doesn't respond, so I continue: "I think it would be good for me—good for *us*." I speak faster, words tumbling out in my rush of excitement. "If I did this, I could go out, start painting something new again. It would give me a purpose. And maybe I might sell a couple and that would help, wouldn't it? It would help pay for paint and wallpaper at least." I could help him make this place perfect.

Patrick is frowning down at the leaflet.

"What is it?" I say.

"Are you sure?"

"What do you mean?"

"Well...you did less than two years at art college." He takes my hand and gives it a squeeze. "I think you're an amazing painter, you know that. But everyone else will be a professional, with years of experience. Wouldn't it be better to start smaller? Something less...public?"

I can't help but look toward the hall, where Patrick's put one of my paintings on the wall. I did it after I agreed to move here, when I got out of the hospital. It was supposed to be this house as Patrick sees it, but it came out wrong, something a bit weird about the angles and colors. I tried to hide it, but Patrick found it and insisted on displaying it. He follows my gaze.

"I love your paintings, of course I do, because *you* painted them." He sighs and pulls me into his arms. "It's fine as a hobby, but an exhibition? Are you really ready for that?"

I pull away. "It was just an idea."

I'm halfway out of the room when he calls after me, "Hey, don't worry. If you really need to do this and no one wants your paintings, I'll come in and pretend to be a stranger and buy one. I won't let you be the only one with nothing sold."

He's right. I got carried away listening to Anna raving over my drawings. I'm being silly. I pick up my phone and make a call as I go upstairs.

"Anna? It's Sarah...Yes, Sarah with the flowers. Listen, I shan't go for that exhibition. I'm—I'm not a real painter; I don't want to make a fool of myself. But I was wondering...have you got time for a coffee?"

In my dream, the dream I have about the house that's just a house and not yet the Murder House, all the rooms on the corridor have doors and all the doors are closed. Whenever I have this dream, the doors are always closed. But. But... I think... one of the doors was open in my dream last night. I woke up and I think I shouted or yelled or something but it was okay: there was no one to hear.

Did you wake up last night? Did the sound of my screaming carry? Did the sea wind pick it up and carry it through the town, through your walls? Did you wake up to the echo of my voice with the hairs rising on the back of your neck?

CHAPTER 8

I make sure I'm up early for Joe and Mia's first day at school. Joe's putting drawings into his portfolio and Mia's pushing toast around a plate, but they both stop to watch as I take my pills out of the cupboard. The whole house hovers on pause until I swallow the pill and the play button is pressed again. I follow Joe and Mia out onto the path to wave them off. Their new school is only a short distance away and I wish they were still young enough to want me to walk them there. But my children are seventeen and fifteen—they'd rather die than have their mother with them. I get a muttered goodbye and I stand on the path, my arms wrapped around myself to ward off the sea breeze, watching them until they reach the end of the road.

I swallow, force a breath, and walk back toward the house, stopping when I see someone on the coast path, half-hidden in the morning mist. They're facing away from the sea, looking at me, and in the cold morning light, it's anger surging, not fear, as I stride over the road onto the path.

"Hey," I call to the figure, now walking away. "What is your problem?" But I'm shouting at nothing, shouting into the wind. Whoever it was has disappeared over the hill. I'm halfway up, out of breath and freezing in a thin T-shirt. I walk back down, passing number twenty-eight, where Lyn watches me from an upstairs window. Patrick's in the doorway of our house, putting on his jacket, and I brush past him on my way back inside.

"Everything okay?" he asks, and I nod, lifting my face for his kiss.

I don't want to tell him I was chasing a watcher he doesn't believe is real. "Thought I saw someone I knew," I say, wincing at how feeble it sounds when I don't really know anyone in the town yet.

He frowns and glances up at the now-empty path. "I'll try to get home early," he says.

"Don't be silly—I'm fine."

He hesitates, his hand on the door. "Don't forget to take your pills, okay?"

I jump when the door slams behind him and have to take a deep, shaky breath. I look out of the window—the coast path is still empty. I go back to the kitchen via the front door, making sure the security chain is on and the latch down. I hear the sound of wind chimes again, but this time it seems louder. It sounds like they're hanging right outside the house. I've looked in the neighbors' gardens and haven't found them. I liked it at first, the melodic clang. But sometimes the chimes sound *off*, a discordant note that unsettles me.

I put on the radio, turning it up loud to sing along as a classic Prince song comes on. I get a cloth and clean the kitchen window, opening it wide when I've finished. It does make the room brighter and eases some of the tightness in my chest.

When the surfaces are clean and every dish washed, I turn to the mountain of boxes. I swear it's grown since yesterday—yesterday the Andes, today the Himalayas. I wish I could snap my fingers, like Mary Poppins, and have it all unpacked in seconds. I want to see it as it could be: paintings on freshly decorated walls, polished wood, and fresh flowers everywhere. Beautiful antique furniture and the floors restored. My doll's house come to life. It's childish, but I'm impatient to get to the fun stuff.

My phone buzzes and another text from Caroline comes through. I still haven't taken any of her calls since the move—I don't want to hear her warnings and the constant edge of worry in her voice. I'm going to wait until everything's settled here and I'm back off the pills, then invite her around. Prove to her that this move was the right decision. *I know you said you were going to tell Joe soon, so I've asked Sean to check where Eve was in care.*

Like I said, they may not be able to give you any information but it could be a start if he wanted to track her family down.

I squeeze the phone. Damn her for still interfering. This is not the right time, not yet—and it's not her decision to make. Joe needs to be settled: he needs to be in a *good* place when we tell him. His smile needs to be more fixed. This is too soon after his car accident, too soon after the aborted therapy sessions, too soon after the move. When we tell him, he'll have questions about his mother, and how is he going to handle the knowledge that she was a drug addict who died from an overdose? Oh, the bitter irony of Eve's fate compared with my own recent experience. Was her overdose as accidental as mine? I reply to Caroline with a terse three words: *Leave it alone*. Me and the pills—I've made it harder than ever to tell Joe the truth.

The sun breaks out from the clouds and shines on the peaks of the cardboard mountain. I live by the sea and the sun has come out: I don't want to spend my time hiding inside, trapped by the fear of a watcher who might simply be someone out walking the cliff path, curious about the Murder House and the family who moved into it.

Make this work, Patrick's pleading voice whispers in my head. *Make it better*.

"Screw it," I mutter, putting away my phone and snatching up my keys. Isn't that supposed to be our new philosophy? Isn't that what brought us here? It's not running away; it's running *toward* something. It's not my tropical beach, but it is an adventure, or it could be if I make it one.

There's a DIY shop in town, small, dark, and cluttered with old wooden cupboards and shelves filled with nuts, bolts, and hinges. It smells of sawdust and damp, and everything is covered with a layer of dust. The small supply of paint and wallpaper is probably twice the price it would be in one of the big out-of-town places, but I don't want to wait. I want to see that look on Patrick's face again: excitement, exhilaration, the bright edge of promise.

I can help. This pot of chalky white Farrow & Ball paint, this roll of Osborne & Little wallpaper patterned with butterflies, this can bring happiness. I add more cans, more rolls of wallpaper to my pile, though it makes me twitch when I see the total. It's okay, I tell myself. My mother's money was there to make us happy, and this is how I'm going to use it: to heal our family and give us a home.

The back of my neck prickles as I stand at the counter and I spin around, expecting to see someone watching me, but the shop is empty.

"You'll be busy," the man serving me says, nodding at the bags around my feet as we wait for the card payment to go through.

I laugh. "That's the plan."

"Hey," he calls as I leave. "Aren't you from the—the house on Seaview Road?"

I hear the omission in his words. *Aren't you from the Murder House?* That's what he was really asking. My laughter dies. Is that who we are? The new Murder House family? I clutch my shopping bags tighter and walk faster, ignoring the question. No, that's not who we are going to be.

I stop and sit on a bench on the coast path, bags of paint and wallpaper at my feet.

"I thought it was you."

I smile as Joe sits down next to me. I don't like his new school uniform—too much black. He looks so pale in contrast, purple smudges under his eyes, too thin under the baggy layers. "You're out early," I say.

"I had a couple of free periods."

"Not playing hooky like me, then?"

"What from?"

I sigh. "I promised your dad I'd spend the day emptying boxes. But there are so many and the sun was shining, so..."

"You skived off."

"I know it's got to be done, but..."

"It's okay, Mum. You don't need to explain to me."

"How's your first day going?" I ask.

He shrugs and leans back against the bench, lifting his face to the weak sun and closing his eyes.

"Classes are okay, I guess," he says. "It's got a decent enough art room and I like the art teacher. She's going to help me put my portfolio together."

I spend so much time worrying about Joe—about him finding out, about losing him—that sometimes I forget to enjoy him in the moment. It's so nice to hear enthusiasm in his voice, to hear him planning a future. I could tell him now, here, neutral ground, just me and him. Confess it all and make him understand our reasons for the years of lies, help him understand how fully I love him, how much he is a part of our family now. Then the sun goes behind a cloud and the shadow it casts over his face makes him look younger and older and fragile, and I picture my words breaking him. I swallow the words.

"Do you miss it?" he asks.

"What? The old house?"

He nods.

I stare out at the sea as I think about it. Do I? I miss Caroline. I miss having a choice of shops and restaurants. But even after all those years there, did I really love the house? It was so small and new and featureless. Anonymous, very much a blank canvas. Our new house is all features. Full of potential. But full of other things too.

"I'm excited by the possibilities here," I say. "With the house and the town. I keep looking forward to the summer, when we can get out more and the house is finished. But I kept waking up last night—the wind outside, clanks and creaks from the house, the sea... I keep waking up with my heart racing, imagining..." My voice drifts off, but Joe nods anyway.

"Yeah. I know." He hunches forward, his head down, his face hidden under his dark hair. "So what's this?" he says, nodding at the shopping bags.

"I want to make the house ours," I say. "I want to make it beautiful. I want it to be a home."

When Joe heads back to school, I walk home. The phone rings as I unlock the door. I pick it up and there's a crackling on the line, a whistling noise that sounds like the wind. I wait, but no one speaks. It's probably a bad connection or a wrong number. I won't let it spook me, not today. The half-full bottle of wine in the kitchen calls me, but I put it away at the back of a cupboard.

I push the boxes stacked in the living room out into the hall and start on the painting, soft dove gray covering yellow-stained, damp-spotted magnolia. The room comes alive with every sweep of the roller and I laugh again, alone in the house. I'm painting away the house's history, painting out Ian Hooper and his awful crimes. I'm making it Patrick's again, alive, not dead. A happy house. A home. I can't wait for Mia and Joe to see what this place can be.

I hesitate as I get to the edge of the wall by the door. Halfway up, there are pen marks and initials scribbled on it. A DIY height chart: TE and BE. Tom and Billy Evans—Billy, who never outgrew the last pen mark, age nine, seven-year-old Tom, who hid under the bed from the monster and vanished after the trial. The roller drips paint on the floor as I waver. Must I be the one to erase them this one final time? I take a deep breath and put the roller to the wall, painting up and down, covering the scribbled pen marks, covering the ghosts of two little boys who once lived here.

"Screw it," I say, but any urge to laugh is gone and tears build. A lump forms in my throat. I paint the wall to the edges, then drop the roller in the tray and stand back to look. The height chart is gone. The wall is smooth and blank.

Mia gets in first from school and I greet her in the hallway, trailing after her as she dumps shoes, bag, and coat on the floor. I resist the urge to remind her to hang up the coat and the bag.

"Well, how was it?"

She shrugs, going through to the kitchen and opening the fridge. "It was okay. Felt like a bit of a freak show, turning up so late in the year."

"Were they nice to you?"

She laughs. "Mum—it's not kindergarten."

"But still..."

"Well, they didn't sit me in a circle and sing welcome songs, but most of them were friendly enough, I suppose. The teachers were the same as all teachers. There were a few idiots, nothing major."

"I'm glad," I say, opening a cupboard and getting down some cookies. "I really am."

"What have you been up to?" she asks, licking the chocolate off a cookie.

"Come," I say, leading her through to the living room, eager to see her reaction.

"Nice job, Mum, but you missed a bit," she says.

"What? Where?"

Mia points to the wall opposite the window, to the edge by the door. Butterflies have escaped from the wallpaper and taken up residence in my stomach. There are lines in the paintwork, scribbled marks halfway up the wall. I step closer and I can see it—TE and BE, fainter than before but still there.

"I'll cover it if you like," Mia says, leaning to pick up the roller.

"No," I say, grabbing her hand before she can touch the wall. "Leave it."

Mia leans in to look at the initials and draws in a hissing breath through her teeth. "Jesus—is that them?"

I nod. Her turn to shiver.

"Why don't you want it painted over? It's bloody creepy."

I don't think she needs to hear that I've already tried to cover it. None of the other marks on the wall are showing through. They must have used a permanent marker to immortalize the chart, I tell myself, though I know how unbelievable that sounds.

She touches Tom's initials, wobbly letters that suggest he wrote them himself. "It's so sad," she whispers.

We both jump as the front door slams and Patrick calls hello. Mia bounds out to meet him and I hear her talking, a bright string of stories about her first day when all I'd gotten was a shrug and one sentence. I look at my watch—it's only four thirty. What's he doing home? I go out into the hall to find him staring up at the cardboard Mount Everest. He looks at me then and I reach to smooth my hair, wishing I'd taken the time to change out of the faded T-shirt and sagging jeans I'd put on to paint. I haven't bothered with makeup and I never got around to a shower this morning.

Patrick, in contrast, looks the same as he did this morning, as perfect as he always does: no crease in his shirt, no sign of sweat or dirt or tiredness. He still smells of shower gel and his favorite spicy aftershave. I go in for a kiss and don't think I imagine his slight recoil.

"Get a room," Mia mutters as she pushes past to go upstairs.

"I'm sorry," I say, brushing down my T-shirt. "I lost track of time."

He looks at the pile of boxes again. "How have you done with the unpacking?"

"Ah...not that well today."

"No? How many boxes did you get done?"

I wince. "None."

"What?"

"Wait, though—there's a reason. I have a surprise."

His face stays wary as I grab his arm and tug him through to the living room. "Close your eyes," I say, dragging him in to face the painted walls. I've finished two and made a start on the wallpaper. I've done enough so he can see how beautiful it's going to be—just like my doll's house.

I made another decision too, while painting walls. I get my phone out of my pocket. I'll tell Patrick about Caroline's text tonight, as we sit in our beautiful new living room. We'll make a plan, work out what we're going to say to Joe and when. A fresh start for all of us in our new home.

"Okay, you can look now."

He opens his eyes and I grip his hand, squeezing as he stares at the walls, then at the half-dozen shopping bags spilling rolls of wallpaper and cans of paint.

"Surprise," I say, my smile growing as he spins to take it all in. "It looks just like those magazine pictures, doesn't it?"

My excitement fades as he doesn't say anything. He leans and picks up the receipt that's fallen out of one of the bags. "Did you really spend over three hundred pounds on paint and wallpaper? For one room?"

"I know it's a lot, but look at the colors. They're so beautiful and just like the ones in that magazine you showed me."

"Yes, but *three hundred pounds*?"

"I'm sorry. I wanted it to be a surprise."

He sighs and pushes a hand through his hair. "I'm sorry, too. It's great, but…" He looks down at the bags again. "Maybe we could take some of it back."

"I'm sorry," I say again. "But you said there'd be plenty of my mother's money left to do the house up."

He hesitates, looking away from me to the unpainted wall. "The bank asked for more of a deposit than I anticipated."

"So what does that mean? How much is left?"

He hesitates again. "None. I had to use it all."

I bite my lip hard, tasting blood. *All gone.*

"It's not a problem—we have to be careful, that's all," Patrick says. "If we want to do everything, we have to plan what order we do things in. I want to do the kitchen first, the flooring and the electrical. The big things, the important things. Decorating can wait."

"How will we pay for it if my money's all gone?" I don't mean the words to come out so bitter.

Patrick folds the receipt for the paint and wallpaper and puts it into his pocket. "I'm not saying we can't do anything. But I'll get some white paint. We'll start with that. A coat of white everywhere will freshen things up, provide a base." He touches my arm. "Thank you, though, for doing this. For trying."

I scrub clean the palette in my head, the Naples Yellow and

Rose Madder, the Burnt Sienna and Viridian. I thought the house could be my canvas. I got carried away.

"I'm sorry," he says. "It won't be forever—we just need to build the savings back up." He steps behind me and slides his hands around my waist. "Let's get your old decorating magazines out tonight, plan all the rooms. You can make mood boards, get samples, and as soon as things are straight..."

I push away my sense of deflation, smile, and turn in his arms. "See? I'm dangerous left here with nothing to do. I definitely need to get out and find a job."

He leans down to kiss me. "Come on—I'll make you some tea."

He pauses at the door. "Listen," he says. "Why don't we all go to the fair this weekend?" He laughs. "You told me you were pregnant with Mia when we were there, do you remember?"

Of course I do. He'd won a cuddly toy for Joe at one of the stalls and I told him he'd better try to win another.

"Wasn't it perfect?" he says. "God, I was so happy."

It was. One of those moments to put away and keep forever. I look down at Caroline's message on my phone. Does it matter if we wait a few more months to tell Joe? We can be that happy again—here, now. I need to make this work for all of us.

She's pretty and thin, the woman you moved into the Murder House, long pale hair, small pale face. Younger than you, smiling but brittle, circles under her eyes like she's been up all night. I wonder if she has dreams too.

I watch her moving around inside the house, reluctance in every step. I watch her step outside and take in great lungfuls of air, like she's been holding her breath the whole time she's been inside.

Someone stops and speaks to her. She smiles, and even across the road I recognize in her a desperation. I see a woman so full of fucking need and I realize how easy it would be to smash her to dust.

I could tell her some stories that would kill her smile. I could tell her what's hidden under the wallpaper. I could tell her about the holes in the walls and what made them and how they became places to hide... things.

She doesn't know. She only sees the fresh blood.

CHAPTER 9

"Sarah? Earth to Sarah?"

I look at Patrick. How long has he been talking? What was he talking about? "Sorry."

"Did you hear anything I just said? It's time to go." His gaze moves to the pills in front of me. "You're not skipping your medication, are you?"

"No," I say. "But I'm not sure they're working like they should. Shouldn't the side effects be gone by now? I don't feel better—if anything, I feel worse. Tired. My head aches all the time and I don't want to do anything."

"It'll be fine—the doctor warned us of the side effects, didn't he?"

"Yes, but he said to go back if they don't fade. I'm not supposed to take them for long, am I?"

"Give it more time. I've seen an improvement—you're less anxious, calmer. Joe and Mia have commented on it too."

Have they? I'm on different pills from the diazepam—supposedly milder, with fewer side effects, less addictive potential. But my mouth is dry and my hands are trembling. We've only been here a week and I've spent half my days sleeping. How is this better?

"Give it time," he says again.

Time. How much am I meant to give it?

The phone rings in the hall and Patrick goes to answer it. I hear his repeated hello and he comes back in shaking his head.

"Who was it?"

"No one at the other end—probably some international sales call. Come on," he says, pulling me to my feet. "Let's go and get ourselves a new kitchen."

* * *

"Are you sure you have time for this? Shouldn't you be at work?"

We're standing in the middle of a DIY-shop showroom, hoping to turn our sterile measurements and pictures into a dream kitchen. Patrick opens another cupboard, compares it to the brochure in his hand. "This is more important."

He looks tired, the circles under his eyes as dark as his jacket. A strand of his hair is sticking up at the back and it bothers me more than the creases in his shirt and the new lines on his face. "But..." He's frowning. I'm spoiling it for him. "Sorry, I remember you saying things are busy, that's all."

He blinks. "They've given me the day off."

They've given him time off now? I search his face, but he's looking at his brochure. He told me last week it was far too busy for him to have more than the moving day off. I'm glad, though. He needs some time to himself. He didn't sleep last night. I'd gone up early, out like a light before nine thirty. When I woke up, I'm not sure what time, he was moaning in his sleep, whispering something over and over again. Gibberish, incoherent, but it made my skin crawl. It was like when he used to have nightmares before, but this was different somehow, worse.

He woke, sitting up and gasping, but I pretended to be asleep. I don't know why I didn't sit up and comfort him.

"This is where it starts, Sarah," Patrick says, tilting his chin at the picture of a beautiful kitchen he's circled in the brochure. "This is where it becomes perfect. You'll see what the house can be. All new appliances, decent electrical and plumbing. We'll finance it on top of the mortgage, and then we'll get to the decorating when this is done, I promise."

I'm caught up too. We have walked through the room sets, like it was a giant doll's house just for us. We let the salesman seduce us with talk of hidden drawers, double ovens, and recessed lighting. We said yes to everything, though we don't know how we'll pay back the loan.

"We'll choose flooring and tiles then, and when it's all done, we'll look at a new bathroom," Patrick whispers. His lips touch my ear and I shiver. I started laughing earlier—we were practically drooling over a bloody tap that supplies instant boiling water. When did we turn into people whose highlight of the week was a trip to the bloody home repair store?

Now I trail after him as he approaches our hovering salesman. It's better this way, I tell myself. Better to be this woman than who I was before we moved here. Maybe the house, the new start, is helping after all. The salesman, fifteen years younger, sees a couple approaching middle age talking about family dinners and cupboard storage, one of hundreds of such couples he must see every week. He doesn't see a woman, three months out of the hospital after taking an overdose, who's living a lie. Better to be the woman the salesman sees, the woman Patrick imagines in this perfect kitchen of his, with its pale-painted units and built-in wine cooler.

The salesman clears his throat and I look up. His big sales smile is gone and there are red spots on his cheeks. "Um, sorry, Mr. and Mrs. Walker, but I'm afraid the application for finance has been declined. Do you have any other means of financing the kitchen?"

I'm half jogging to keep up with Patrick's stride. We get in the car, and Patrick slams his door so hard the car rocks. He sits there, his hands white-knuckled on the steering wheel, but he doesn't start the engine.

I thought, for one stupid moment back there, that he was going to launch himself at the salesman. The look on his face... But that isn't Patrick. Patrick doesn't lose control. He rarely gets angry, and when he does, it's a cool anger, not violent.

"It doesn't matter," I say. "We don't need a new kitchen, not yet. We can paint the cupboards we have. They'll look just as good as the ones in the showroom, and we can make do with the appliances we already have."

"I don't want to *fucking make do!*" He shouts the last words, banging the steering wheel, and I jump.

My heart is thumping as Patrick starts the engine, pulling out of the parking lot without another word. There's a tic going in his cheek and I'm frozen, his shouted words ringing in my ears, breath held in the charged tension. I'm still hot from the humiliation of having to walk out of the shop after being turned down. I have no idea why we didn't get the financing—we've had it before for cars and credit cards, and we don't have any debts, as far as I know. Other than the mortgage on the house, of course. Is that what's done it? Everything is in Patrick's name—I have no income and had no savings other than my mother's money. Patrick arranged it all and he told me that, with my mother's money, we'd be fine. We do have some other savings, Patrick's pension fund…My heart rate speeds up again. The bank would never have let him put *everything* into getting the mortgage, would it?

We're parked outside the house before Patrick speaks again. "When my father lost his job, he re-mortgaged the house. He let it fall apart, turned into…someone I didn't recognize. It used to be so *perfect*. My parents prided themselves on how perfect it was. Back then, when I still thought it would be mine one day, I told myself I would continue that. I'd make it even *more* perfect. How it used to be. Everything perfect and everything beautiful. But I'm no better than him, am I? I can't even get financing for a fifteen-grand kitchen."

"Patrick…" I reach to cover his hand with mine, but he snatches his away.

"Don't. Okay, Sarah? Just don't."

I call Caroline the next day, but it goes straight to voicemail. "Caroline, it's me. I'm sorry I haven't called you back. I needed to give this move time—to give me and Patrick time. And it's good, I know you won't believe me, but it is. This has been a good move. I'm better here. Patrick's…" No, his outburst was a brief loss of control. And completely understandable. "Patrick's happy, we're happy." I pause. I was going to say, "Come and visit," but maybe we need longer to settle first. "It's still a bit chaotic here, but call me back and we can arrange a visit in a few weeks, okay?"

I put down my phone and look around the room. Determined to do what I said and make this work, even without flashy new kitchens and bathrooms, I've embarked on a massive spring-cleaning. I've put cushions on the sofa in the living room, pictures on the walls. The old gas fire is not exactly the wood-burning stove of our dreams, but it gives off a cozy glow and warmth. I've lit scented candles and put flowers on the coffee table. It smells of cinnamon and polish. Not beautiful yet, but getting there.

But the room, which should be bright and sunny, stays in shadow because the windows seem to be clouding, growing opaque. I first noticed it over the weekend, but today it seems much worse. I stand in front of the big bay window and outside a ghost walks past, indistinct. I step closer to the glass until the ghost turns into an old man walking his dog.

I lean to touch it. Smooth. Whatever is clouding it is not on the inside. It's as if the house is growing a seal to hide us from the outside. My throat tightens as my imagination feeds me images of waking one day to find all the windows and doors gone, trapping us forever in the Murder House.

No. Stop. I press my hands to my stomach as though I could push back the growing anxiety.

I find a cloth, fill a bucket with hot water, and step outside. There's a dug border outside the window, freshly turned over by Patrick, ready to fill with bedding plants. Rich dark brown earth, full of wriggling worms. I know this because I've been watching the birds flutter down to get them, the few that haven't flown off for some winter sun.

I lean across the border to touch the window. The glass isn't smooth; it's grainy. I lean farther over and on impulse touch my tongue to it.

"It's salt," someone behind me says, and I stumble, my foot sinking deep into wet, wormy mud.

"Shit."

"No, definitely salt," he says, laughing, and I turn to glare.

I don't know him, but he's not looking at my mud-caked foot or the madwoman who licks windows: he's looking up at the house. "It's because you guys are so near the sea," he says. "Salt deposits. This road's the worst—you get the wind on the house all day. It's not too bad at the moment, but it'll get worse if you leave it. You need to clean them every week, really, especially in winter. They had someone here cleaning them a couple of weeks before you moved in—you should check with the estate agents, find out who they used."

It seems odd to have a stranger telling me when my windows were last cleaned. I try to picture this man where I saw the watcher. Is he the same height? I've never been able to get a clear glimpse of the person, except as a vague shape.

"You've probably noticed it on your bedroom window too." He points up at my room.

I take a step back toward the front door. Has he seen me looking out the window? "How do you know which is my bedroom?"

He blinks. Smiles. "I guessed. It would have the best view."

"What are you? A window cleaner touting for work?"

"I'm Ben Owens. From the gallery? Sorry to drop in on you, but your friend Anna said you had some paintings to show us."

"Oh, right. She didn't say...I don't have anything ready to show. I wasn't expecting..."

His smile fades. "I'm sorry, I assumed you knew I'd be calling by. Anna did give me your number, but I was passing, so..."

He was walking away from town, not toward it. Passing on the way to where? I look around, but there's no one else in sight. I take another step back toward the house. My phone buzzes and I look down to see a message from Anna: *Don't hate me but u r too good 2 hide away ur art! Thought u might never get the courage 2 go 2 the gallery, so Ben said he'd get in touch with u today—meant 2 text u last night 2 warn u, sry!!* ☺

I glance past Ben, half expecting to see Anna. How did she know to send the text now, just as he arrived? Ben's gaze drifts past the open front door to the painting Patrick has put on the wall in the hallway, my sharp-edged lie of Patrick's childhood home on canvas.

"Is that one of yours?" Ben asks, and I nod. "You've made it look..."

"I know."

"I used to know the family who lived in this house."

My face goes hot. "Do you mean..."

"No, no. Of course I knew the Evans family, but just as neighbors in town. I was away at college when all the...when it happened. I meant the people from before. They had a boy my age—his name was Patrick," he says.

"You know Patrick? He's my husband. I'm Sarah Walker."

His turn to retreat, a startled look on his face. "He's *back*?"

"The house came up for sale and he's always wanted to move back here. *We've* always wanted to, I mean."

"That's...God. Sorry, but Anna never said. I never thought..."

I force a smile. "I'll have to tell Patrick you came by—I'm sure he'll want to catch up with an old friend." I stop, remembering Patrick's words: *Anyone who remembers me now is not a friend.*

Ben shakes his head. "I wouldn't call us friends. We were at school together." He looks at the painting again. "Can I see the rest?" He steps closer, but despite his smile, I stay wary.

"I haven't done anything new for a while," I say. "But I have some canvases inside. Do you think people would buy them?" I want money back in my savings account. The failed visit to the kitchen showroom has sparked a panic that won't die down, chasing memories of that awful time, almost ten years ago now, when Patrick was between jobs and we were forced to pay all the bills on credit cards. Didn't we vow never to end up in that position again?

"If they're as good as that one? Definitely. Sorry if I've caught you off guard. Anna was raving about you and"—he shrugs—"it was an impulse. Sorry." He turns to walk away.

"Wait," I call.

I don't know this man: he's a stranger. He used to know Patrick, but Anna knows him. She wouldn't have sent him here if she didn't trust him, would she? I'm sure it's safe. But I'm still uneasy, so I don't invite him in.

"Can you wait here a moment?" I go back inside and through to the living room, where half a dozen canvases are stacked behind the door.

I let Ben look at them in the narrow confines of the hallway, standing between him and the open front door, behind him so I can't see his face, my arms folded, my nails digging into my palms. He glances over his shoulder at me and smiles a smile that uses his whole face: no frown lines for him, all laughter.

"These are wonderful," he says, and those three words wash away all of Patrick's warnings. "You have to show them."

"I'm not sure my paintings will fit in with what you exhibit." I wince. Oh, God—should I have said that? What if he loves that painting in the gallery window? He doesn't seem to take offense—he laughs.

"Don't worry. The artist in the window is popular with tourists, so I always have a couple of his on show. But your work is far closer to what I'd like to exhibit."

Our conversation washes away all my hesitation about Ben, too. He's a painter himself. He has kind eyes the color of the pebbles on the beach. He paints seascapes, but not like the offensive primary-colors one I saw in the window with Anna. He shows me some photos on his phone. Ben's paintings are quiet and lonely, mist rising on water, shadow and reflection.

He stands next to me as he tells me about the coves he visits to paint. His shoulder brushes mine. I think he's flirting with me, this man who has paint under his fingernails, whose creased shirt smells of linseed oil, cigarette smoke, and the sea. I should mind, but I don't.

He flirts with me as we stand in the hallway of the Murder House and he tells me I could have a solo exhibition if I produce some new paintings. What will Patrick think when I tell him?

I bite my lip. No need to say anything yet.

"Can I buy you dinner?" Ben says as he steps back outside and holds out his hand for me to shake. "To toast the gallery's newest artist?"

His palm is warm and dry and I swallow as his rougher skin brushes mine. It's a handshake, nothing more, a meeting between strangers, so why do I snatch my hand away so quickly? Why do I look around to make sure no one sees us?

"Me and Patrick, do you mean?"

He hesitates. "Sure. If you like."

But I can see he doesn't mean dinner for three. Why is he asking me to dinner, flirting with me in the hallway of my own house, when he knows I'm married? When he knows the man I'm married to?

"I don't think that would be a good idea," I say.

Ben, with what he's offering, is not the adventure I want.

"No painting today?" Patrick says when he gets in, looking at the stack of untouched paint pots.

"No, I…I got distracted." I turn my face away from him in case he sees guilt in my expression. Silly, I know. I have nothing to feel guilty about.

"Distracted? By what?"

"I wanted to go out. Explore the town some more."

There's a pause as Patrick hangs up his jacket and leans forward to check his reflection in the mirror, smoothing back his hair. "Didn't you do that last week? I don't think you really have time for going out, do you?"

"Come on, it's not my fault we didn't get the financing for the kitchen. Don't be grumpy with me."

"I don't want to talk about the damn kitchen. I'm just saying you need to finish unpacking and painting before you go skipping off again."

"Are you going to lock me in until I've finished?" I say it with a smile, but he doesn't smile back.

"It would be nice if you could do *something* while I'm working a sixty-hour week."

I take a step back, startled at the bitterness in his voice. I meet his gaze in the mirror and, behind me, I see a reflection of the cans of cheap white paint lined up in the hall.

I fold my arms and turn my back on the paint, walking away from him into the living room. My shoulders are rigid as I hear him come in.

"I'm sorry," he says, a heaviness in his voice. He sounds tired. "I don't want to fight. But I wish—"

"Look," I say, interrupting him, pointing at the window. "The glass is clouding over."

He leans over and frowns. "I'd forgotten this. Leave it. It's cheaper than curtains."

"What?" I let out a startled laugh at his reaction.

"That's what my mother used to say."

"Your *mother*? The woman who could spot a speck of dust at a million paces?"

Patrick shrugs. "Better cloudy windows than people looking in. You should be happy about that."

He doesn't believe anyone is watching the house. I can tell from the sarcastic tone in his voice. Humor the little idiot who jumps at every noise and sees people looking in at her.

"But..."

He sighs. "I'll ask around, find someone to clean the windows. But leave it for now, okay? I don't need this on top of everything else."

But it seems *wrong*. So out of character for Patrick and his obsession with perfection. More wrong to imagine his mother having the same casual reaction.

After Patrick leaves the room I step closer to the window. The sea is gray and choppy today, the sky a brooding dark cloud. The glass is lined with salt, except for the clear patch where I licked it. It looks like an *I*—like I'm asserting my claim: *I* live here, *I* exist. And it's a perfect spy-hole—I can look out, but no one can see me.

CHAPTER 10

I'm washing the breakfast dishes when Patrick comes in to say goodbye the next morning. He pulls me into a hug and rests his head against mine for a moment. "I'm sorry I was in such a bad mood yesterday. You were right—I was so disappointed about the kitchen and I took it out on you."

"It's okay," I say. "I understand. But it'll work out—we have our whole lives to get new kitchens. It doesn't have to be perfect right away."

"But I *want* it to be." He steps back. His tone is light, but I hear an edge of frustration. "Unpack the rest of those boxes, okay? Get them all done, and we'll buy some more paint to finish off the living room."

My hand squeezes the sponge. Water drips and splashes my foot. I remember the early days, when Patrick would tell me to leave the housework, to spend the day painting, enjoy the kids being at school and having time to myself.

I'm angry with myself more than him. He didn't put me in this situation: I let myself be put here. No qualifications, no employment record, I've turned myself into a Stepford Wife for him. Isn't that half the reason I'm reaching for the wine at six o'clock and yearning for the chemical calm the pills give me?

The front door slams and I grit my teeth as I turn away from the sink to make coffee. I'm walking through to the living room with my mug when I notice the cellar door is open. It definitely wasn't a few minutes ago. The first thing Patrick did when we moved in was make sure the door was locked.

"There's going to be dangerous things kept down there—chemicals, paint thinners, bleach. It's not safe for the children," he'd said while he turned the key in the rusty lock, as if Joe and Mia were toddlers.

But the door is open now, the key in the lock. My heart pounds and the hairs rise on the back of my neck. Patrick must have opened it before he left.

But he didn't. I saw him pick up his wallet and keys from the hall table and I followed him to the front door to say goodbye. The door wasn't open then. I don't even remember seeing the key in the lock. Didn't Patrick put it away in the drawer in the kitchen on a key ring with all the spare keys? I hesitate before closing the cellar door. Of course Patrick must have opened it. I try to turn the key, but it won't move, so I'm forced to leave it unlocked as I back away into the kitchen. I pull open the drawer and take out the bunch of keys as an icy trickle of fear seeps through my veins. The cellar key is still on the ring.

Calm. Be calm, Sarah. Patrick must have had another key cut, that's all.

But neither key looks new.

I'm still standing—hiding—in the kitchen when someone knocks on the door. I jump and then laugh because at first, for a stupid moment, I think it's someone in the cellar, knocking on that unlocked door.

I'll have to pass the cellar to get to the front door and my instinct is simply to hide, to wait till the knocker goes away. Then I think it may be Caroline, whom I've barely spoken to, in person or on the phone, since that day in the hospital. I've been avoiding her calls, putting off inviting her here, but right now all I want is for her to have ignored all that and come here uninvited.

But it's not Caroline; it's Anna. She's dressed in black: jeans, boots, leather jacket, a black scarf with white stars on it. The covered dish with a red gingham cloth draped over it looks incongruous, like a joke. Lift the cloth and something will jump out at me.

"Sorry, I know I'm a bit early," she says. "But I'm working later. I've brought pie—not homemade, sorry. Left over from the café."

I'd forgotten I asked her to come today. She's standing a wary six feet from the front door, looking like she might bolt at any second. Behind me, the cellar door clicks open again and swings gently back and forth in the breeze from the open front door.

I take the pie and put it on the hall table before stepping outside, pulling the door closed. "Thanks so much, but...change of plan," I say. "Can we go out somewhere?"

She hesitates, and I wonder if she's going to be like Lyn Barrett, if it's not me she wants to see but a guided tour of the Murder House. But she shrugs. "Sure," she says, turning away from the house. I feel lighter as I lock the door and follow her down the street.

She takes me to the fairground. "I come here all the time," she says. "I love it, bloody love it. It ignites my inner child—isn't it the best thing ever, to have a fairground on your doorstep? I don't even go on the rides, just come and people-watch. All the lights and the noise and the smells. You can't beat it."

I can smell sweet cotton candy, a meaty waft from the hot-dog stall, mingled scents of sweat and perfume from the people walking past. It's quiet this early, but the lights still flash on all the rides; tinny music clashes and merges as we walk around; a lone lost unicorn balloon floats into the distance. I know what she means: it smells like childhood—seaside trips with donkey rides, chasing the seagulls away from your chips.

"I forgot to tell you—and thank you. I met Ben yesterday, the guy from the gallery."

She looks blank for a moment, then smiles. "Ben, yeah. He's a nice guy and a *really* good painter. I don't know him that well, but we got chatting when I went in the gallery one day." She laughs. "He invited me to one of their exhibition opening nights last month and I thought he fancied me, so I got all dressed up, but he just talked about the paintings all bloody night and ignored my pathetic efforts at flirting."

I remember the feel of his hand in mine. Perhaps his invitation to dinner *was* innocent. Perhaps I misread the situation just as Anna did. "He was nice. I was a bit surprised to find him on my doorstep."

She raises her eyebrows. "That's probably my fault—sorry. When I mentioned your name and that you were new to town, he guessed right away which house. But I did tell him to call you first."

"Oh..."

"I suppose it was easy for him to figure out where you were. Small town and all. He really is nice, I promise."

"I guess." It unsettles me, though. I thought Anna had sent him—that was why I invited him in. And if she'd told him my name, why did he look so surprised when I said I was married to Patrick?

"So what did he say?"

"That I can have a solo exhibition."

She smiles wider. "Seriously? I was worried I was interfering too much, telling him about you. That's wonderful. Oh, wow... When?"

My own smile fades. Do I tell her I think he asked me out? And even if I was mistaken, how inappropriate Patrick would find it? That I haven't told Patrick about the possibility of me exhibiting because he might ask me not to because he used to know Ben? "I need more paintings. I haven't done anything new for so long...I have to find somewhere to work. What will I paint?"

"I told you I'd show you some beautiful places if you want. There's a beach—it's difficult to get to, but worth it. Bring your sketchbook, a camera. Bet you're inspired to paint after you see it. I hope you have your exhibition before the summer, anyway. I'm planning to spend it in Europe—find myself a job in Spain or Greece. I'll rent out my apartment here and go soak up the sun."

I close my eyes against the gray skies and cold wind and imagine it. Heat and sunshine and sleeping under the stars. "I wish I could come with you."

Anna laughs. "You? You're married, two kids, a million walls to paint. Have you forgotten?"

I open my eyes. Of course.

"You could, though," she says, after a pause. "Come with me. Run off, leave it all. We'll do a European Thelma and Louise."

"What? And end up driving our rented Peugeot into the docks at Calais after an epic police chase?"

"You screaming at the cops, 'I couldn't take any more decorating'?"

I laugh and it settles the unease in my stomach.

"Look—the carousel's just stopped. Let's go on," Anna says.

"What? No—we're too old." I laugh, and she turns to me, a huge smile on her face, her eyes shining.

She grabs my arm, tugging me along. "Come on," she says. "Pretend you're twelve again."

As we spin faster and faster I close my eyes and rest my forehead against the painted mane of my carousel horse. Everything whirls, like I've been drinking, and the music runs a bit too slow, a bit off-key.

"How long have you lived here?" I ask as we stagger off and walk toward the beach. Maybe Anna grew up here too.

She stops at a stall to hand over money for two coffees in polystyrene cups. "Not long. I moved here last year."

"In small-town terms, I guess that makes you as much of a stranger as me."

She nods. "It is a bit like that, isn't it? I used to be a nomad, traveling around. I was passing through, no intention of staying. I've always lived in cities, thought I needed that buzz. But this place…it's the peace, the space, the air, something about it. I drifted away again, but the town had gotten in my blood, you know? It drew me back."

"I hope it gets me like that. I *want* to love living here."

"Careful, though," she says with a grin. "Before long, you'll know everyone's name and they'll have *all* the intimate details of your life. Definite small-town hazard."

I pull a face, thinking of Lyn Barrett's needling questions about Patrick, her avid gaze on the pill box I'd left on display. This town already knows too much.

"Well, I'm very glad you moved to town, Sarah Walker."

"Me too." But am I? Am I really glad to have moved here?

"It's good to have a new friend," she says. "It seems like every week more people move away—it's becoming a bit of a ghost town."

A ghost town with a murder house. Which is where I sleep, where I brought my children to sleep. I think about the cellar door again and shiver as the wind picks up, whipping at my hair.

"How come you bought the house? Sorry if I'm being nosy, but you must have known its history," Anna says.

"Patrick loves it. He grew up there, so he's not a stranger to the town. He was long gone before the tragedy, before any of that happened, so for him it was a happy house. He thinks we can make it what it was."

Anna looks at me oddly.

"He's told me stories of what it used to be like," I say. "I can imagine it—I can almost see it. But then again, how am I supposed to forget what happened there? Can anyone really forget that?"

She looks down and brushes sand off her knee. "Wow. Imagine growing up here..."

I smile. "Patrick makes it sound like Paradise."

"Well, I think it's brilliant you've taken it over. It's always been such a depressing sight, empty and tainted by what happened."

"Patrick and I are determined to make it into something special, get rid of the taint. That poor family is gone and the man who did it is locked up for good, so..." Her smile is replaced by a frown. "What?"

She leans forward and lowers her voice. "You don't know? He's out!"

"Out? Who?"

"Ian Hooper—the murderer."

"What do you mean he's out? I thought he got a life sentence."

"Not sure, but I know he was released a few months ago. It was in the local paper."

I think of the person I saw watching the house and my stomach turns. Oh, God. He watched us move in. I pour the remains of my coffee onto the sand. "I have to go," I say.

I've got my phone out to call Patrick when I see his car in front of the house. It's not even lunchtime—what's he doing home?

"Patrick?" I call as I open the door.

He steps out of the kitchen. "I was wondering where you were. I had a meeting in the area, so I thought I'd pop home, see how the unpacking was going."

I can't tell him about Ben yet, but I can tell him about Anna. "I went out for some fresh air," I say. "With someone I've met—her name's Anna, she works in a café in town. She said..." I stop, take a breath. "Did you know Ian Hooper was out of prison?"

He looks away.

"Why didn't you tell me? Jesus, Patrick, didn't you think it was important?"

"It's *not* important," he says.

"How long has he been out?"

"A couple of months."

My nails dig into my palms. "Since before we moved in here? What if it's been him watching the house?"

"This is why I didn't tell you—I knew you'd freak out about it."

"And why wouldn't I? You know what he is—what he did. You moved our family here and... Oh, God—did you know before we moved in?"

"Of course not, but it doesn't matter, even if I *did* know."

"It doesn't *matter*? He murdered a family—he murdered a *child*."

"For God's sake, it was fifteen years ago. It wasn't a random attack. He had reasons, a motive—he knew them."

"You told me he knew *you*," I say. "All your talk about how scared you were for me after the pills, after what happened with

Eve, was that all lies? You lied to make me agree to move here before I knew Ian Hooper was out. You knew I'd never agree if I knew he was on the loose."

"He's been released, Sarah; he's not on the run. Yes, he committed a horrible crime, but it's not like he'll come back here. He'll be looking for a fresh start somewhere completely different, under the watchful eye of the probation service. Why would he ever want to come back? I would never have moved us here if I'd thought there was any danger."

He doesn't answer my question, though. "But he has come back, he's *here*. He's here, watching the damn house."

"No. You need to stop listening to bloody gossip. Those damn murders ruined my family once already. I'm not letting it happen again fifteen years later."

"What do you mean, ruined your family? You weren't even here when the murders happened."

"Enough, Sarah. It isn't him watching the house; it isn't *anyone*. He would never be stupid enough to come back. You need to let it go."

Let it go? How am I supposed to do that?

I wait until she leaves the house to play postman. It took me a while to source the perfect gift to leave next. After she found the shell, it struck me that your wife is the right person to leave my next gift for. I've seen her looking out the window, double-locking the door, little paranoias creeping in. It seems fitting that she's the one bringing me, piece by piece, into the house, the house that used to be just a house once upon a time. Like the darkest of fairy stories, I'll send in my truths and tales, let you find them with her fingerprints all over them—hers, not mine. Do you know? Have you already guessed I'm haunting your house? Not yet. I don't think you've scented me on the sea air that creeps in and wakes you at night.

It won't take you long, though, will it? To remember me. After all, haven't I always been there, in a dark corner of your mind?

CHAPTER 11

Over the next few days I find myself drawn back to old press stories about the murders. I'd stopped looking, determined to keep my promise to Patrick and make this a real fresh start, but now Ian Hooper is out of prison and I have to know. I have to know exactly what happened in this house.

Did Tom Evans know Ian Hooper had been released? Was that why he finally put the house up for sale?

"What are you doing?"

I go to close the browser window, but Mia gets to the mouse before I do and zooms in on the newspaper article I'm reading. "That's them, isn't it?" she says, her voice flat.

It's a picture of the murdered family, one of those smiling portraits you have done in a photographic studio. We have our own version on the wall in the hallway. This one of the Evans family was taken a few months before the murders. The little boys are grinning, gap-toothed, and Marie and John Evans look sweetly, almost painfully young.

In a smaller photo beneath it, Ian Hooper is blank-faced, good-looking. The old articles hinted at rumors about him and Marie Evans—the bad boy who seduced the married woman, then murdered her and her family.

"God, it gives you the creeps, doesn't it?" Mia says. "To think we're living in the same house where they were killed."

"Not all of them."

"No." Mia touches the face in the picture with the younger boy. He's like Joe was at that age. The look in her eyes makes me think Mia sees it too, but then her smile dies. "Lara and the others thought it was so cool when I told them where we were moving. She started a Murder House WhatsApp group and kept posting old pictures and stuff. God, even *I* did for a bit—like we were moving to some Gothic horror place from a film or something. But this isn't fun anymore. I'm sure I've felt those cold spots in the house, Mum. They're *real.*"

I look back at the screen, a chill creeping up my spine.

Mia's biting her nails again, so far down that her fingers are sore and red. I see the circles under her eyes that match the circles under mine. I've heard her moving around at night, long after she should have been asleep.

Mia has shown me the cold spots—six areas in the house that are cooler than the rest, places that make the hairs on my arms rise, where the air is damp. I don't know if it's real or my imagination, fueled by Mia's ghost stories. Mia's room is one, a place in the hall next to the stairs another, on the landing, in the bathroom, the kitchen, and Joe's room. The living room is fine, and so, according to Mia, is my room.

Three people died in the house, but there are six cold spots. It makes me imagine undiscovered bodies rotting in the garden. When I wake up at night with the wind from the sea rattling the window, I wonder if there are hidden bones under the floorboards. Some nights I swear I can hear scratching from under the floor. Like bones scraping at wood. Is that what keeps Mia awake too? I can't tell any of this to Patrick.

"Close it down, Mum—it's giving me the creeps."

I'm washing up when the phone rings. I go to answer it, wiping my hands dry.

"Hello?"

No answer.

"Hello?" I say again. I press the handset closer to my ear. Is Patrick right—is it someone in a call center in India, dead air as another call connects first, or do I hear breathing at the other end? I disconnect and turn away, spotting an envelope on the mat. I frown and glance at the clock—it's five, way too late for the postman. Leaning to pick it up, I see the envelope is blank but sealed. It makes me think of the letter that started all this, the one to Patrick from the estate agent. My hands are shaking as I tear open the envelope.

There are two pages from a newspaper folded up inside, and I sink onto the bottom step to read them. *Inside the Murder House*, the headline reads, with a small inset photo of our house. It's the bigger photographs that make my hands shake even more, the interior photos, barely recognizable as this house, even the state of it when Patrick and I first looked around.

They're grainy, black-and-white, but I can see what look like holes in the walls, as though someone has punched through them; floorboards are pulled up, carpets stained, curtains torn. I can't quite read it, but it looks like there is writing on the walls in the hallway.

What I can make out easily is the police tape across the open front door, but there's no way to say how much of this was done in the course of the police investigation or how much before the murders were discovered. All the newspaper articles I remember from back then, all the websites I've visited, talk about the Evans family as loving and happy, making the murders so much more tragic. It doesn't marry with the photographs on these pages, which are also a million miles from the pristine Paradise in which Patrick grew up. The newspaper's title has been ripped off, but the date is still visible, timed to just after the murders. Who put this through the door? Why? Was it one of Mia's new school friends, a cruel teenage joke?

I reach out a hand to touch the wall that, in the newspaper report, has a hole punched through. Is there a dip? A fist-sized curve in the wall that's since been filled in?

When Patrick comes in, he finds me still sitting on the stairs, newspaper article in one hand, the other feeling the wall. "Someone put this through the door," I say.

He takes the newsprint pages, his face expressionless as he looks at them.

"The state of the house in these photos... Was all this done after the Evans family moved in?" I can't correlate these photos, the way the house was when we looked around, with the beautiful family home Patrick used to describe.

"They were here for two years after my parents moved out," Patrick says, his face still blank, not really answering my question.

"I think he put this through the door," I say. "I think it was Hooper."

Patrick sighs and rubs a hand across his eyes. "This again? Sarah, it wasn't him. How can it have been when he—"

"When he *what*?"

He sits down next to me on the step. "Do you think I haven't seen the websites you've been looking at? All those clickbait stories, all rubbish. They've made you paranoid, thinking Ian Hooper's waiting around every corner."

"Come on, Patrick—you can't expect me not to be worried. He murdered three people."

"There's no need to worry. What you don't know is how the town reacted after the murders. Hooper's family was practically forced to leave."

"By local people? What did they do?"

Patrick smiles faintly. "Nothing really bad, apart from some idiot throwing a brick through their window. It was more things said, ranks closing, problems for the kids at school, Hooper's wife losing her job for no reason."

He folds the article and puts it back in the envelope. "My point is, what do you think would happen if Hooper came back? Do you think no one would notice? Do you think he could check into a B-and-B, shop at the mall, drink in the pub? Everyone who lives here, everyone who remembers, would shout and be dialing the police at any hint he was around."

I look at the torn envelope, held loosely in Patrick's fingers.

"It's not him," Patrick says in a softer voice.

"Then who? Someone was watching the house, we've had dropped telephone calls, and someone..." I was about to mention the shell, but I didn't tell Patrick at the time. "Someone put this through the door," I say instead.

"A local gossip, probably. Or a kid trying to scare us for a laugh."

"Patrick?" I say as he gets up. "How come you know so much about what happened afterward here?"

He stops in the kitchen doorway. "My parents were still around. Not in town, but close by. News spreads."

But he's never mentioned any of this to me before.

I trudge upstairs with a basket of clean laundry, knock on Mia's closed door, and push it open. The room's empty and I lay her pile of clothes on the end of her bed.

I'm almost out of the room when something at the corner of my eye catches my attention. There's a pile of papers on the edge of her dressing table. I assumed when I came in that it must be homework, or revision notes, but that photo on the top page—I've seen it before, downstairs on the computer. It's Ian Hooper. I go back into the room and pick up the pile of paper. There are printouts of stories about the murders, dozens of them, not just the ones I found earlier. Ian Hooper's face, the same photo, staring out of all of them.

"They give me nightmares."

Mia's voice makes me whirl around. She's staring at the pages in my hand.

"They give me nightmares, but I can't stop reading about it."

I know exactly what she means. I keep going back to that same website, that same newspaper story. It's their eyes, I think. Their faces. Ian Hooper's eyes seem to burn into me, and the Evans family looks so happy, unknowing and innocent, no idea what's to come. But I can't say any of this to Mia, can't let her see her own worries reflected in my eyes.

"I know," I say. "But it was a long time ago. You were a

baby when it happened. There's nothing to be scared about anymore."

"Every night I have horrible dreams about it," Mia says. "It happened *right here*, Mum. In my bedroom. This is where he killed her. Sometimes I'm watching as he comes in and murders them, but I can't move or say anything. Sometimes I'm one of their family, or it's us, our family, but we're living in the house back then and Ian Hooper comes in with a knife and it's us he's here to kill..."

I let the papers drop onto the bed, go over to her, and pull her into a hug. I stroke her back as if she were a much younger child.

"I'm so tired, Mum, but I dread going to bed every night because of the wind...and something keeps rattling my window, and I know if I go to sleep with that howling and rattling, I'll fall straight into those nightmares. I've spent more time in Joe's room than mine—I might as well move my bed in there."

"Okay, okay," I say, tracing slow circles across her back. "It'll be summer soon, lighter nights and fewer storms. We'll cut away the brambles by the windows and I'll ask your dad to see if he can do something about the rattling."

Mia pulls away, rubbing eyes that seem more dark-circled and bloodshot every time I look into them. "Then I'll just get to sleep quicker and have more time for bad dreams."

"Come and wake me if you have nightmares again. I'll make you hot chocolate, like I used to. I'll sit with you until you get back to sleep." I reach past her and pick up the pile of papers. "I'll take these away. Maybe if they weren't lying around your room, you'd stop having bad dreams."

She nods, then reaches into her dressing table drawer for a book she holds out to me. "You'd better take this as well."

I flinch at the title—*Murder Houses of the UK*. It's a thin book with a flimsy cover, no sign of a publisher's name. There's a black-and-white picture of a Victorian house on the front, not ours, but similar enough to make me look twice.

"Someone left it on my desk in school as a joke," Mia says.

"Not a very funny one," I say.

"Not really—especially as we're in there. Well, the house is. This place has its own chapter."

I almost drop the book, fumble, and manage to bend the cover before I have hold of it again.

"Page forty-three," Mia says. "There are photos and everything. Some of the things this bloke says...I mean it's obviously rubbish and all made up, but he talks about the history of the house." She stops to take a breath. "His theory, if you can call it that, is that there's something wrong with the murder houses themselves. That some evil exists in them to make awful things happen."

"That's—"

"Crap. I know. It's rubbish, but he mixes all the crap up with the truth and then I got to reading the newspaper stories."

I tighten my grip on the book. "I'll throw it away."

She nods. "Okay. Yes. Please do. Thanks, Mum."

I go straight out into the back garden with the intention of putting the book and all the pages Mia has printed into the bin. Glancing up, I see her watching me from Joe's room and I wave as I lift the lid and stuff the pages deep inside. I go to drop the book in too but pause. Mia has disappeared from the window. I don't know why, but instead of putting the book into the bin, I hurry back into the house and shove it to the back of one of the kitchen drawers.

In the living room, I try to reassure myself of our new start, that the past really can be erased. The decorating is only half-finished, but with the pretty wallpaper, the cushions, the flowers in the window, it's clearly not the house in the newspaper pictures anymore. It's not. It's what it should be—a home, a place we'll be happy. It's hard, though, to put the pictures and stories out of my mind, when in the corner of my eye, a faint height chart still shows through the paint, when I know that somewhere under the butterfly wallpaper, under the layers of old lining paper, the Evans family left their marks, their stories.

And, God, those pictures. How could the Evanses have been the happy family the press said they were if the house was in that state? I can't stop thinking of what Mia read in that book, and what I see in my mind is Marie Evans doing what I'm doing, pretending everything's normal—height charts, children playing with *Star Wars* figures upstairs—while someone punches holes in walls and the house rots around them.

My throat tightens as I stare at the wobbly letters on the height chart. I have to know when and why the house turned from happy family home into . . . into the Murder House.

I push open the estate agent's door. The girl behind the desk looks up with a bright smile. "Hi, can I help?"

"Um, I'm not sure. I'm Sarah Walker—we just moved into the . . . into the house on Seaview Road?"

Her smile dims.

"I had a few questions," I say, "for the previous owner. I was wondering if I could . . ."

Her smile has turned into a frown. "I can't give out client information." Her tone is abrupt and I wonder if she believes me or if she thinks I'm a journalist or a ghoul looking to harass the Murder House survivor.

"I know, and that's fine," I say. "Can you just give him my details? Ask him to get in touch with me?" I scribble my name and cell phone number on a piece of paper. "Tell him . . ." What can I say that would make him ever want to speak to me? I think of the *Star Wars* figures. "I found some things in the house that might have belonged to him. Him and his brother."

It's changed, the house that, once upon a time, was just a house, then the Murder House, and now... What is it now? Painted French furniture and Farrow & Ball colors, cans of white paint stacked in a hallway that was once dark and bare.

But look closely and there are black spots in the paintwork, the wallpaper's peeling at the edges. Look closely and she's biting her lip, her shoulders hunched and rigid with tension.

There's a photo on the wall behind her, two toddlers, could be twins, different coloring but matching smiles. How stupid—haven't you realized? Hasn't she realized?

It's not a house for kids.

CHAPTER 12

I watch Mia mooching around the kitchen, opening and closing the cookie jar without taking one, opening and closing the fridge. I took a couple of boxes upstairs this morning and her room smelled of cigarettes. In the old house, her walls were covered with photos of her and her friends, but this morning I found most of those photos torn up in her bin. She looks tired, thin under her baggy school sweater.

She goes to the table and picks up the two *Star Wars* figures I've put there. "Playing with toys now, Mum?"

"No—I found them upstairs. I thought they were your father's but...Did you find them somewhere when you were unpacking?"

"Not me."

When I asked, Joe said it wasn't him either. But they definitely weren't there when we looked around the house or on the day we moved in. I would have noticed, wouldn't I?

Mia pulls out of the fridge the remains of the pie Anna brought and puts it on the table. "Where did this come from?"

"What?" I pull my thoughts away from those little plastic toys. "Oh, a friend brought it around. It's a welcome-to-town offering."

"A friend?" She picks a bit of pastry off the edge.

"Her name's Anna. I met her in town—she works in the café. We've been meeting for coffee." I push the plate closer toward her. "Want some? It needs to be finished."

She pulls a face and shakes her head.

"How's school going?"

She gives me that look of hers, the blank one without any hint of a smile or even a scowl and somehow more hostile for it. "What do you think?" she mutters.

"Have you made any friends?" I grimace. I sound like I'm talking to a five-year-old.

She glares at me, and when she opens her mouth I'm expecting abuse. Then she stops and smiles, a new smile I haven't seen before. "Yeah, I've made a friend. He didn't turn up offering me pie, though."

I swallow a dozen questions. "I'm glad. I was worried."

She gives a snort of laughter and takes an apple out of the bowl. "Worried. Right."

"I am. Of course I am. All I want from this move is for you and Joe to be okay. To be happy. You look...tired."

She puts down the apple, one bite out of it. "I'm still having bad dreams."

I think of my own dreams last night, half-forgotten, splashes of blood on walls, bones under floorboards. I wonder if Joe has the same dreams, if he lies awake at night in his room, that tree tapping on his window. "The same dreams?"

She nods. "This house. Them. The Evans family. In the night, the sea sounds like whispering."

I shiver, see goose bumps rising on her arms as well as on my own.

She picks up the apple, rolling it between her hands. "I think I shouted out in one of the dreams last night. Dad must have heard me. He came in to check on me. He said we could maybe swap rooms. But the sea would be just as loud in your room, wouldn't it?" She laughs. "I wish me and Joe were little kids again. Then we could share a room."

Patrick didn't say anything to me this morning, about talking to Mia during the night—and he definitely didn't mention changing rooms.

"I guess, though, it's not really the sound of the sea, is it? It's not the sea making the cold spots or giving me nightmares."

"Of course we can change rooms. We can do it this weekend, if you like. And remember what I said—if you have more bad dreams, why don't you come and wake me up? We'll break open the hot chocolate and I'll sit with you."

She looks at me incredulously for a moment, then lets the apple drop with a thud. "Oh, please..."

"What?"

"Forget it," she says, leaving the room and running up the stairs.

I see the shell as I go to check on her. It's sitting on the hall table and looks like the one I found on the doorstep but smaller, more like the shells the children would collect on seaside trips when they were younger. I pick it up to look closer and a spindly leg and a red claw brush my hand. Hermit crab. I drop the shell with a clatter, letting out a small scream.

"Christ—what now?" Mia has come out of her room and stands, half in shadow, at the top of the stairs.

"Did you put this here?" I say, pointing to the crab. My heart is racing. The unexpectedness of those skittering legs scrabbling at my hand. Worse than a spider. Worse than that beetle I once found in my shoe that made me scream the house down.

Mia shrugs. "Not me."

It must have been Joe. I thought I saw him on the beach earlier, talking to some boy from his class, huddled together against the wind. I was so glad to see he had a friend. He must have brought home the shell, not realizing it had a resident.

A piece of the shell broke off when I dropped it and now I can see the crab's body, vulnerable, exposed. My bitter friend, guilt, makes a fresh appearance. I'm a home wrecker.

I'm setting the table for dinner when the door slams. I go to the window and see Mia marching down the street toward town. She's wearing a short black skirt I haven't seen before and high heels. I glance at the clock. It's getting dark but only eight o'clock, and she hasn't eaten.

"Where's she going?" Patrick asks.

"I don't know. She didn't say anything to me... You don't think she has a boyfriend she's not telling us about, do you?" I'm thinking of that smile, small and sly. A smile that said, *I've got a secret.*

Patrick steps away from the window. "No, I don't. Mia would tell me."

"During one of your middle-of-the-night chats?"

"What are you talking about?"

"Last night. Mia said you went in to her."

"And?" He stares at me. "She had a bad dream. It's a good thing *one* of us was awake, isn't it?" He shakes his head. "The food's going cold—go and get Joe."

I knock on his door, but he doesn't answer. The door isn't all the way closed, so I push it open and peer in. Joe is on his bed, staring up at the ceiling, his sketchbook open on the floor. He's drawn a boy standing on what looks like a cliff edge.

"Are you coming down for dinner?" I ask.

"Not hungry," he mutters.

I sigh and step into the room, walk over to sit on the edge of his bed, and let my eyes wander around the room. We really need to work on this room next, as soon as the living room is finished. In the corner near the bed, the edge of the wallpaper is peeling away—not just one layer, years' worth of it, right down to the plaster. I chew at the inside of my cheek and pull the edge. It lifts away easily, but so does the plaster, crumbling chunks of it clinging to the wallpaper.

"I made that mistake too," Joe says.

The wall underneath is damp, black-spotted. I can see the scribbled edge of a child's drawing. It makes me think of the DIY height chart on the living room wall and I smooth the paper back down, trying to make it stick.

"You should see what else is under there," Joe says.

I keep smoothing the paper. "Not now," I say.

"Not now?" He laughs, but the sound is not a happy one.

I get up to leave and I'm at the door when he calls me back.

"Mum? I saw Dad earlier."

I raise my eyebrows.

"He was in my room. I came upstairs and he was in here looking out the window and it was... weird."

"Weird?"

There's that hesitation again. I'm tempted to pick up the sketchbook—is the boy on the cliff edge him?

"I think he was crying," Joe says.

"Crying?"

Joe nods. "But I thought I had to be wrong. Because it's Dad."

I look at the sketchbook again. Maybe it's not Joe on the cliff edge. Maybe it's Patrick. But, no, like Joe said, Patrick doesn't cry.

"You don't believe me, do you?"

"It's not that, it's just... Your dad, why would he be crying?"

Joe shakes his head. "This whole *fresh start* thing? It's crap, Mum. Things are worse, not better. And all your talk about turning it into a home, it's never going to happen."

"Come on, Joe—it's only been two weeks."

Joe picks up the sketchbook, closes it, and puts it under his pillow. "Can you go, please?"

My throat is tight. There's a darkness rising in my son and it makes him a stranger, unreachable. I've seen it happen before. I know what happened to his birth mother and it terrifies me that Joe could end up the same.

My phone starts ringing in my pocket, but I ignore it.

"Joe..."

"Just fucking *go*."

My phone rings again as Joe closes the door. I put my hand on the wood as I hear a thud inside the room. The ringing stops but starts again almost immediately. I pull my phone out of my pocket. The number is unfamiliar, but I answer with a distracted hello.

"Mrs. Walker? It's Tom Evans."

Tom Evans is sitting at a table in the window. He's thin under a dark blue shirt, sleeves rolled up to reveal the edge of a black tattoo, and his dark hair is cropped short. I couldn't believe he'd actually called and agreed to meet me. I didn't suggest Anna's café as a meeting place. I don't need her questions—I have enough of my own concerns about why I'm doing this. I recognize Tom right away even though I've never met him. I recognize him not from the gap-toothed boy in the newspaper photographs but from the ghost of his father in his face. John Evans was only twenty-nine when he was murdered. Very young to have been married with children, tragically young to die. And Tom's brother... The thought of little Billy Evans squeezes my heart. He's here too, in the space next to Tom, the absence, the gap.

I can't imagine what it would do to Mia or Joe to go through what Tom Evans did. I don't know how much he saw or heard during the crime or how much he remembers, but like the taint that covers the house, it's a darkness you could never recover from.

He glances up as I approach his table and smiles, a hint of the old gap-toothed grin still there. "Mrs. Walker?" he says, standing and holding out a hand.

"Call me Sarah," I say. His hand is cold. He doesn't shake but holds my hand and squeezes, his thumb stroking my palm as he lets go. I automatically wipe my hand on my jeans, wanting to rub away that accidental caress, and he continues to smile. I want to shout, *This was a mistake*, and run. What the hell was I thinking? His eyes flicker as he stares at me and the look on his face is odd.

"Thanks for agreeing to meet me." I'm still standing, half facing the door. I swallow, glad it's a Saturday afternoon and the café is full. I think I *would* have run if we'd met somewhere more private. Glancing around, I see no one else is paying us any attention. The tension here is all in my imagination.

He shrugs and sits down again, pulling his coffee mug toward him, opening a sugar packet and pouring it in. "I wasn't sure whether to, but I don't live far away and you said you'd found something of mine."

I sit opposite him, take the *Star Wars* figures out of my bag, and slide them across the table. "I found these. I thought they might be yours."

He picks them up and squeezes them in his hand. "They were

probably Billy's," he says, his voice unsteady. "I didn't take anything from the house after. I didn't want anything. My grandparents cleared it and we moved away from the trial and the press. I don't know how these got missed."

I think of how I found them on the windowsill, set there as if little Billy Evans had left them mid-game.

"Thank you," he says, not looking up from the figures.

"I'm sorry if I've upset you."

He puts the toys into his pocket. "It's okay," he says. "I wanted to come anyway. I was curious."

"Curious?"

He glances up. "Curious about who'd bought the place. I thought it would never sell. Or if it did, I assumed a property developer would tear it down and build something new." He starts ripping a napkin into neat strips that he stacks next to his mug. "Then the estate agent told me they already had someone interested—someone *waiting* for me to sell it." He gives me that odd smile again. "And it turned out to be you. Like I said, I was curious. I almost called the house."

Maybe he did call and lost courage. I think of the dropped calls I'd thought might be Ian Hooper. Is it better or worse to think it was Tom Evans?

"Have you been back here since..."

"This town was the only place I knew until I was seven years old," he says, not answering my question. "I never wanted to live anywhere else."

"My children are struggling to see the benefits of living here," I say, forcing a smile.

"You have *children*?"

"Two—a boy and a girl. Teenagers."

His hand jerks, knocking over his mug. Coffee spills and soaks the torn-up napkin. "And you?" he says, clutching my hand and leaning close enough for me to smell his breath. "Do you see the... *benefits*, Mrs. Walker?"

I can't help but recoil, pulling my hand away and jerking back in my chair so it scrapes on the floor. "I...It's a beautiful town," I say. "And the house..."

"Why *did* you want to meet me?" he asks. "It wasn't to give me these toys, was it?"

I think of that newspaper cutting shoved through our door. I can't ask him about that, can I? Can't ask him if he believes the house is some evil thing that made Hooper murder his family. God, oh, God—what am I *doing*?

"Ian Hooper's out of prison," I blurt, wincing as I see him react to the name, shoulders hunching, face twisting. Jesus—could I fuck this up any more?

He stands, dropping a couple of pound coins on the table. "I'm sorry," he says. "This was a mistake. I shouldn't have come."

"Tom—wait," I say, putting my hand on his arm. "I'm sorry, I'm doing this all wrong. I didn't mean to upset you. I'm just...I found out he was released from prison, and we're in the house and it's all...it's all going wrong and I wanted—"

He pulls away from me. "Wanted what? The inside scoop on the infamous Ian Hooper? Reassurance that he won't come roaring back to slaughter *your* family?"

I'm unable to face the burning pain on his face. When I turn back, he's gone, the door swinging shut behind him. I sink into my chair, my legs shaking.

You come out of the house in your sharply creased suit, get into your shiny car, and drive off to your big office in the city. I can see your wife through the windows, drifting in and out of rooms, doing nothing. Your Stepford Wife is defective.

I was never supposed to end up here. I was never supposed to end up like this.

I was getting out. I was moving up. I was going to live the dream.

Then I woke up and I'm back here in this dying cesspool of a town, and I see you with your high-flying career and her with her dreams and smiles, and I say no.

No fucking way.

CHAPTER 13

When I get home, Patrick's in the back garden, poking at a fire he's lit in an old metal bin. It looks so beautifully domestic and normal I have to lean against the kitchen counter, my hands white-knuckled, gripping the edge, as I try to get my story straight as to where I've been. I can't tell him I was meeting Tom Evans: he'd never understand why. I'm not sure I understand myself. I wanted to know more, to understand how things went so horribly wrong for the family who lived here before us, but faced with Tom...He's not the little boy with the wobbly initials on the height chart anymore. He was right to walk out of the café. It was a mistake. I shouldn't have met him—what exactly was I looking for? Was he right? Was I just seeking reassurance that Ian Hooper wasn't watching the house? Did I want him to comfort me that Hooper's murderous spree was a one-off, a crime of passion, like Patrick said? Had I really gone seeking that reassurance from the man whose entire family had been murdered?

I make coffee and go out to join Patrick. My hands are shaking and hot coffee spills, stinging drops hitting my hands. It's nearly May, but the smell of the bonfire, the chill in the air, makes me think of autumn, crunchy leaves on the ground, the year winding down. Last summer and autumn I was in a fog of grief. Half a year passed and I barely noticed. I was so determined that this year would be different. *I* would be different. In some ways I am—my mother seems farther away here, my grief less sharp-edged. But is that the move or the pills? Meeting Tom has made me jittery. My throat is dry, my heart racing.

There's an apple tree at the bottom of the garden, the only thing thriving; the rest is an overgrown mess, weeds choking any sign of shrubs or flowers, the grass patchy, half-dead. But the apple tree already has blossoms on it.

"You making a start on clearing the jungle?" My voice is false-bright. I hold out a mug of coffee and he takes it.

"You're back. Where did you go?"

"Shopping. I found some of my old recipe books and I felt like making something different for dinner."

He's frowning. Is it as obvious to him as it is to me that my breezy tone is a lie?

"I'm thinking, making plans," he says, turning back to the garden. "We could have started this earlier, but a few weekends of hard work and we can clear this space. Stock up on plants, some new garden furniture, and it'll be beautiful by summer. Like it used to be."

He's ignoring my efforts at painting and DIY inside. He has found himself a new project. I think it'll take more than a few weekends to make this beautiful. So far, he's made a two-foot space in the weed jungle. A whole afternoon's work for a two-foot patch of yellowing grass and mud. He's sweaty and dirty, his hair all over the place.

"By the way, there's a message on the house phone for you." There's an edge to his voice, and I wonder what he knows. Too many secrets. We've never had secrets before. At least, I never thought we did. The wind picks up, whipping across the back of the house, blowing black smoke that stings my eyes.

He picks up another pile of garbage for the bonfire, and I'm turning to go back inside when, through the smoke, I see Joe's face, younger, smiling, sketched in fine pencil, eaten in from the curling edges by the fire. I reach to snatch it out, but Patrick grabs my hand.

"Don't be stupid. You'll get burned."

But the flames are licking at Joe's face, turning it to black ash, and only now do I recognize what Patrick has found for his first bonfire. It's my sketchbooks, the ones I showed Anna, my drawings of Joe and Mia growing up, Patrick sleeping, Mia dancing, Caroline laughing by the lake. I make another lunge for the pile, frantic, but he stops me with his body.

Chest to chest, I look up at him, speechless.

"The message was from that doctor you sent Joe to," he says calmly, as if we're chatting over a cup of coffee. "Apparently you called her about another appointment for him."

"I'm worried about him. He—"

"He is *fine*."

"He is not fine. God, Patrick, he's sinking again. I can see it."

"Why can't you ever just leave things alone?"

"So what is this?" I say through numb lips. "You burn my sketchbooks—a fucking lifetime of work—for calling a *doctor*?"

"You told me you'd finished unpacking but I found all this stuff," he says, poking at the ashes, not rising to the bait. "Boxes hidden behind doors. Stuff dumped in bags in the corner of the living room. You told me you'd finished and went running off *shopping*, so I assumed what was left had to be garbage."

Furious, I break away and run back into the house, pull open the living room door. I'd stored it all there—my sketchbooks, my brushes, my paints and pencils. Stored it all there while I waited to find a space to work in.

It's all gone. Damp spots are climbing up the wall, exposed now that all the bags are gone. Goddammit, Patrick. Where are my paintings? Where are the canvases?

"So, now we can make this place perfect," he says, so bloody cheerfully when he comes in and finds me staring into the empty corner. Doesn't he see the spreading spots of green and black rot? How is this ever going to be perfect?

"What did you do with the paintings—the canvases? You didn't..."

"They're in the cellar," he says, and my fury turns cold.

Patrick looks at my face and sighs. "I'm tired of *making do* while you're going behind my back, wasting money on therapy for Joe, going *shopping*, walking around all doom and gloom, upsetting everyone," he says. "Come on, Sarah, cheer up. This time, it's all going to be perfect."

"Cheer up? *Cheer fucking up?* Do you have any idea what those sketchbooks meant to me?" There's an aching lump in my throat and I want to punch him, scream in his face.

"They're just old drawings," he says. "God, it's not like I've set fire to a puppy or something. Get new books, if you want—it's not like you've used them recently, is it? When's the last time you did any drawing? Let it go, Sarah."

Let it go. Fuck. I grit my teeth and turn away. I know if I say anything else, it'll be something we can't move on from. I'll be setting fire to more than sketchbooks.

He goes out early on Sunday morning, saying nothing, slamming the door and making me jump as I sit at the kitchen table drinking coffee. I put beef in the oven to roast, peel potatoes, and refuse to think about the empty bags that held my sketchbooks.

"I'm sorry," Patrick says when he comes back in. He's wearing his coat and holding out a bag. There's a new sketchbook and a box of pencils inside. It's a beautiful book, hardbacked, thick, expensive paper—perfect, just like Patrick wants. But the pages are all blank and I feel no urge to draw anything.

I don't answer him. I can't speak to him with the anger still lodged in my chest, hurting and desperate to come out.

"I'm sorry," he says again. "I was wound up, angry that you called the doctor without talking to me, frustrated by the slow progress of everything. But I didn't know that stuff was important. I thought it was garbage. If I'd known, I would never have burned it." But he turns away from me as he says it. I slam the potato peeler onto the counter. *Of course you knew, Patrick.* The sketches were visible as they burned.

He walks past me and goes upstairs. I put the potatoes into the oven and go into the living room, my arms folded, wrapped around the aching anger inside me. There's someone across the road again, standing in exactly the same place as the watcher stood on the first night. The figure is looking out to sea, wearing a dark coat with the hood up, but I wait for the head to turn, to show me Ian Hooper's face. A breeze makes me shiver and, for a second, it feels like it's coming from inside the house, a cold breath on my neck.

I remember the first time I saw the house. It reminded me of something—took me a while to figure it out. It was that ghost house from the fairground we hung out at—remember that? Not inside: the house was nice then on the inside. But outside. Wasn't there always something about it? Something off? Don't tell me you didn't sense it as well.

Inside it all looked so nice. Then you showed me your room with its brand-new wallpaper and you showed me what was behind the wallpaper and you laughed like it was the funniest joke.

CHAPTER 14

From Murder Houses of the UK, *Page 44:*

When did Ian Hooper come into the picture? Rumors put him in the house almost from the beginning, his affair with Marie Evans long-standing and ongoing at the time of the murders. But Hooper himself insisted during the trial that the affair only began a couple of months before the murders. He claimed that he was drawn to Marie when he found her crying and bruised after being attacked by her husband.

This was denounced in court by the prosecution, backed up by John Evans's parents, who were adamant their son would never have hit his wife. But what never came to light in the trial, because charges were dropped, was that Marie Evans did once call the police to report her husband for domestic abuse. Marie's sister, Loretta Anderson, claims it was she who advised Marie to call them, but by the time an officer came to the house, Marie was claiming it was a mistake—she'd been angry over an argument, but John hadn't touched her.

Loretta, however, states that it wasn't the first time John hit his wife. But only after they moved into the house on Seaview Road. "It was the house, that's all Marie kept saying. The house changed him."

I put the book away, hiding it this time at the bottom of my bedside table drawer. Tom Evans's words and different bits from the book keep coming into my head as I shower and dress, each one setting off a stream of nagging worries. I can't get out of my mind the look on Patrick's face as he turned my sketchbooks to ashes.

He's always been so in control. I want to believe him burning my books was an accident because the alternative, for him to have done it deliberately...The anger I felt has faded to hurt, almost grief at the loss of all those years of drawings. It had to have been an accident or, at worst, a momentary flash of anger that I believe, I really do believe, he regrets. But that's what feeds my worries: Patrick doesn't have flashes of anger. Or he didn't before we moved here. It's one reason Caroline can't get along with him. She finds him cold, but she's never seen him like I have. But if she'd seen him burning my books, if she'd seen him banging the steering wheel and shouting after we left the kitchen showroom, would she still mock him for being so cool? And what would I say to her? *It's the house. The house is changing him.*

We were in the park once, talking about some film Patrick and I had been to see, a comedy, and Caroline said, *I've never seen him laugh. Not properly, not a doubled-over belly laugh.* I defended him—of course he laughs. He's not a bloody robot. But she went on, still digging. *I can't imagine him as a child either*, she said as we watched our children muck about in the falling leaves, shoes wet from the long grass. *I can't imagine him cutting loose and having fun.*

I know his parents were always remote, detached—the opposite of my mother. They were well into their forties when they had him and from the stories they told on our few visits before they died, and the way they were with infant Joe, they'd had no idea what to do with their surprise baby.

Patrick grew up in a beautiful house, in this idyllic location, and I believe, from the things he's said, that they loved him. But I could sense, too, in the pleasure he took from our family outings, Christmases and birthdays when the children were younger, what he might have missed out on with those older, awkward parents.

Everything Patrick has told me about his childhood relates to this house and the perfect life he lived in it. But if I think about it, they're more images than stories. As a boy, he couldn't have been so cool and in control, could he? Or as a teenager, that age of raging hormones and confusion, the roller-coaster age.

"Sarah?" Patrick calls as I walk downstairs. He's at the door, coat on, tapping something into his phone. "Don't forget about tonight."

"Tonight?" I echo, confused. But he's gone.

Once the house is empty, I pick up my phone to call Caroline, then put it down. If I call now, will I reveal too much? Will I confess that in the last few weeks I've sometimes looked at Patrick and not recognized him? That people keep telling me stories so at odds with what he's always told me. Or, worse, that as I watched him rage and bang on that steering wheel as we left the kitchen showroom there was something...familiar. Like déjà vu, like a didn't-I-dream-this-once moment.

"Mrs. Walker? Sarah?"

I'm walking, head down, into the wind and don't hear him at first. He puts a hand on my shoulder and I spin around, heart beating fast. "Tom?"

He smiles and steps back, buffeted by a gust of wind. I put out my own hand instinctively, to pull him away from the cliff edge. I was stupid to come walking up here on such a stormy day. I should have stayed in town, gone to Anna's café.

"I saw you and tried to catch up—you walk fast," he says, laughing.

"You were looking for me?"

"I wanted to apologize for freaking out the other day. It was being back here. It affected me more than I thought it would."

I shake my head. "It's me who should apologize. I had no right to contact you and bring up Ian Hooper and the..."

"The day my family died."

I nod.

"Can I walk you back into town?" he asks.

I don't really want to go home yet, but if I say no, will he follow me farther along the cliff path, farther away from town? Besides, clouds are gathering. I don't want to get caught in the rain. I've wasted another day, done nothing but doze between pills. Patrick will be home soon, wondering where I am.

"Sure."

It's easier walking down into the wind. Reassuring to see the town getting closer. It doesn't feel right, being up here alone with Tom—he's still a stranger even if it was me who made contact with him. He's walking too close, his arm brushing mine.

"I've not been sleeping," he says.

He's keeping up with me easily—was I really walking so fast before that he couldn't catch up to me before I got to the cliff-top?

"My doctor thinks it's to do with the sale of the house."

"Doctor?"

He smiles. "Head-doctor. I've been seeing him for years. I've been talking through everything with him. I think he's encouraged by the fact I finally sold it. I had to, when I found out Hooper was going to be released. Needed to." He slows almost to a stop as we reach the end of the coast path. "I almost didn't go through with it, though," he says. "When I found out who wanted to buy it, I didn't know whether to pull out or not. But I wasn't sure I'd ever get another buyer."

I chew the inside of my cheek, wincing as I bite too hard. "Why would you have pulled out?"

"I know Mr. Walker used to live there when he was a kid, and maybe the house was different then, but by the time... by the time of the murders, I wouldn't have wished that house on anyone. Especially not another family."

He leans in close to me and it unsettles me again, his way of invading personal space. "I was only a kid, so maybe I'm not remembering it right, but everything seemed to go wrong when we moved there. Dad changed, started fighting with Mum all the time. Billy got these awful nightmares, woke up every night screaming. We thought, me and Billy, that the house was haunted."

I think of the cold spots and take a deep breath. I thought any hauntings were the memories of the murders of Tom's family, that they were the first. Who else has died there? Who else is making those cold spots, and why weren't they apparent when Patrick lived there?

"I'm sorry," he says. "You probably don't want to hear all this, do you?"

Maybe I do. It makes me want to drag Tom in front of Patrick and say, *See? See what this house is?*

"I felt I should tell you, though. Warn you. Because you seem so nice. And since your husband and my dad were friends."

"What?"

"They were mates, weren't they? Mr. Walker and my dad? I recognized the name, of course, so I looked him up. I remember him, from when I was a kid."

"Your dad and Patrick?"

He cocks his head. "Yeah. What's wrong?"

I can feel my face grow pale and I'm light-headed. "No, that's not right. He never…"

"I don't have any family left. Seeing people I know in the house, it's almost like you're family. I just want you and your kids not to have any trouble there."

We've almost reached the house and I've broken into a cold sweat. He's lying. Delusional. Family? I've met him twice, for five minutes. And Patrick has never mentioned that he knew the Evanses.

The house is in darkness and there's no one out on the street. Neither option feels safe—going into the dark house or staying out here with this man, who is feeling more and more like a stranger. "I need to go in," I say as it starts to rain, fat drops that get heavier by the second. My heart is galloping again and I'm scared he's going to ask to come in.

"Of course," he says, stepping away from me. As I move toward the door he turns back and adds, "Stay safe, Sarah."

I double-lock when I get in and put on the security chain, rushing through the rooms to switch on all the lights. When I go into the living room, I can see Tom Evans walking away, hunched against the rain. He glances back, staring up at the house. I feel as if the cold spots themselves are snaking under my skin.

I jump when someone hammers on the front door, then hear Mia's voice calling. I hurry through to the hall to take off the security chain.

"Bloody hell, Mum! I've been standing outside for ages."

"Sorry—I didn't hear you from the kitchen."

"What's for tea?" she asks as she hangs up her schoolbag.

What time is it? Six thirty. Christ, Patrick will be home any minute.

"Sorry, Mia—I haven't...I forgot. I went out and...Where have you been?"

"For God's sake, Mum, you need to bloody wake up. I left a message to say I was going to the library. I'm *starving*."

"Library? Is it still open at this time?"

She glances at me, then away. "Well, I went to the beach after."

"Where's Joe?"

"He went to the beach too. He's still there."

I look out at the darkening sky. "Still?"

Mia's scowling at the empty fridge shelves.

"I'll cook now. I'll find something," I say.

"Forget it. I'll have a bloody sandwich." She turns back before she leaves the room. "Seriously, though, Mum, what are you going to say to Dad?" She's biting her lip, an anxious child again.

I haven't just forgotten to cook, I've forgotten to shop. Patrick said to do an internet shop if I didn't want to trek to the supermarket, but I never got around to it. The fridge and freezer are almost empty and I can't put a cheese sandwich in front of Patrick and call it dinner. I think of that story I used to read Mia, about the tiger who came to tea and ate everything in the house. I imagine saying that to Patrick and I laugh, an edge of hysteria to it. My hand is over my mouth and I'm laughing in front of the open empty fridge when I hear the front door open, Patrick's voice calling hello.

It'll be fine. We'll get takeout or something. "I'm sorry," I'll say. (*The tiger ate it all.*) "I forgot to do the shopping."

I go into the hall to greet him. He looks me up and down. I'm still in the jeans and sweater I put on this morning, the jeans paint-spattered. My hair's coming loose from its ponytail, so I tie it up again.

"You haven't forgotten, have you?" Patrick says.

"Forgotten?"

"David and Elly are coming for dinner. I told you about it days ago."

Did he? I don't remember. I mean, I know he's talked about having them here for dinner, but did he ever specify a day? We've only been here three weeks—why would he do it now, with the house still so unfinished?

Oh, God. I haven't shopped. I haven't even found the good plates and glasses. I'm trying to think if there's anything in the freezer, but Patrick's already opening the fridge, looking at its empty shelves.

"You forgot." It's not a question and his voice is heavy.

"I'm sorry," I whisper. I have no excuses. I glance at the calendar on the wall—there it is, today's date circled with "David and Elly" written underneath in red. But I'm sure—*sure*—it wasn't written there before. Didn't I look at the calendar yesterday, to check when Joe's parents' evening was?

"It's fine," he says, closing the fridge door. I can tell it's not. In the wave of his hand, the single crease that deepens on his forehead, I can see it's really not fine.

"We'll go out," he says. "I'll call them. Tell them there's a change of plan, make something up about a power cut or a broken oven."

My throat gets tight again with guilt. "We don't have to do that—I can find something quick in the freezer, or order takeout, or..."

"We'll go out." Two lines on his forehead now, so I know not to say anything else.

* * *

We march to the restaurant in silence. He gave me five minutes to change, so I'm aware I'm a mess. I put on a skirt and heels, but the skirt's creased and the shoes are already pinching. My hair is limp, and I'm not wearing makeup. Patrick has changed his shirt, but he's still in his work suit. David and Elly, already waiting outside the restaurant, are, in contrast, shiny and groomed. Elly looks like she's spent a week in the hairdresser's as she hands me a gift-wrapped housewarming present and kisses my cheek. David holds up a bottle of wine. "Sorry—I guess we should have left these in the car."

"It should be us buying *you* wine to celebrate," Patrick says, and I look at him.

"Celebrate?"

"David got a big promotion. Didn't I tell you?" Patrick's voice is light as he rests a hand on the small of my back and steers me into the restaurant.

David? David with his butter-blond hair and fake-tanned face, his BMW and kid-free life? David is thirty-two and was once Patrick's junior. Does this big promotion mean he's now Patrick's boss? I look from one to the other: Patrick seems smaller, shadowed by David's golden, glowing success. Clearly I haven't been listening enough when Patrick has talked about troubles at work.

Tonight was obviously important to Patrick, a chance to show off his dream house, a chance to keep some ascendancy. The guilt sits sour in my gut, and I stare at the menu the waiter puts in front of me, no longer hungry.

He's telling them all about the house now, about his plans for it and everything he's done so far. He makes it sound like I've done nothing. There's no mention of the damp or the state of most of the rooms. No mention of our disastrous trip to the kitchen showroom. No mention of his fifteen-year wait for it to come up for sale. No mention of the murder victim with whom Tom seemed to think Patrick had been friends.

"Excuse me a minute," I mutter, cutting across David's loud anecdote about some obnoxious client.

I wind my way across the restaurant floor toward the sign for the restroom at the back. It's crowded and hot, the air damp and filled with the aroma of frying fat, redolent with a stink of stale fish that's probably embedded in the foundations of the place. We've been seated in the middle of the room, at Patrick's request, surrounded by other couples and groups of tourists, fractious families keeping their kids up too late, all within elbow-jabbing distance.

It's not a good restaurant to show off to dinner guests. It's not a good substitute for a dinner party in a new house. Good wine in crystal glasses, soft music, and flowers in a house by the sea: that was what Patrick wanted, not scampi and fries and house white. I rest a pill on my tongue, lean over the washbasin to swill it down with water from the tap.

"I took the liberty of ordering for both of us, darling," Patrick says when I come back. "They had a special on the calamari."

The waiter goes past, carrying a small cake topped with a lit sparkler. Everyone at the next table starts singing "Happy Birthday" and they're loud enough to cover my gasp.

Once, when I was eighteen, on my one and only girls' holiday—eight teenage girls, one week in Crete—I ate calamari and was ill to the point I thought I was dying. Two days in a sweatbox of a room, crawling to the bathroom, unable to sip water without throwing it up, shaking, lips cracked, stomach racked with cramps, and, I swear, hallucinating by the end of it. I remember sobbing to my friends, *Just let me die, make it stop, kill me now.*

Now, the word, the sight, the smell, the very *thought* of calamari is enough to make me sick. Patrick knows this, I'm sure he does. I must have told him.

The calamari, when it comes, lies on a bed of brown-edged shredded lettuce drizzled with oil. I try to breathe through my mouth, but I can't close my eyes, not with them all watching me, so I'm forced to look at the glistening white rings. Sweat is trickling down my forehead under my hair. Beads build under my hair and I keep my breathing shallow as nausea curdles my stomach.

"Patrick, I..."

"Eat," Patrick says, his voice pitched low so no one else at the table can hear. There are red spots high on his cheekbones and I realize David and Elly are watching me with a weird look on their faces. Patrick watches as I raise a forkful of oil-drizzled salad to my mouth and he smiles.

It's that smile that makes me scoop up the smallest ring of calamari, put it straight into my mouth. Everyone relaxes and the conversation starts up again. I try to swallow without tasting, but then I breathe in through my nose and the smell combined with the rubbery texture in my mouth makes me gag. I drop the fork and put both hands over my mouth. It's Patrick's turn to hold his breath as he watches me. David and Elly have stopped eating and talking. They're all watching me, concerned.

I swallow, both the calamari and the surge of bitter bile that stings my throat. I pause to drain my water glass, then return my attention to the plate, concentrating on spearing tube after tube of maggot-white squid, in, swallow, in, swallow, no time to think, no time to taste, no time to breathe.

I keep going until every bit is gone, until my hand is shaking and my stomach is somersaulting. Then, I finally breathe and look at Patrick. He's smiling, his own plate still full, and I think maybe he's the tiger. Only three minutes have passed.

"Wow. You *did* enjoy that," he says, and I take this as permission to go and throw up, hoping I'll make it to the toilets before the ice in my guts melts and the gorge rises.

"I'm not actually that hungry," Patrick says as I scrape my chair back. "When you come back, you can have mine too, if you like."

I wake in the night, my stomach churning, and I know I'm going to be sick again. I run to the bathroom and this time Patrick follows me. He crouches next to me as I hunch over the toilet and he holds my hair away from my face.

"That dinner was so important to me," he says as my stomach tightens again and I retch, nothing coming up but bile. "I've been telling David about the house. All I wanted was to host them in *my* house, not some cheap, crappy restaurant. I wanted to show them I didn't *need* a damn promotion."

"Did you know John Evans?" I say, my voice hoarse.

For a second his hand tightens on my hair so he's pulling it, not holding it back. Then he lets go. "You're obsessing, Sarah. Stop it. Leave it alone."

He gets up, reaches for a towel, and hands it to me. I splash my face with water, my hands shaking, and take the towel. I see his reflection in the mirror and it's as if I'm looking at a stranger.

"I'm sorry about the calamari," he says as he turns to leave the room. "I'd forgotten. I forget things sometimes too."

CHAPTER 15

I sit at the table in the kitchen, massaging my temples. My head has been pounding all day as I got more and more tense, waiting for Patrick to arrive home. But he breezed in as if nothing had happened, and if it weren't for the sour taste in my throat from spending half the night throwing up, I'd have wondered if I'd imagined the whole thing.

Patrick's in the bath and I should be preparing dinner, but I can't seem to make myself move. There's a knock on the door and it makes me jump. I open it, expecting Anna, but it's Ben on the doorstep, holding up a pair of baby shoes.

"I'm sorry," he says. "I was passing and I saw these outside and thought you might have dropped them. It's about to rain and I didn't want them to be ruined."

I look at the shoes—I remember Mia having some very like these, cream satin with velvet trim and long silky ribbons. These shoes, though, are smudged with dirt, the edges of the ribbons frayed.

"They were on the doorstep," he says.

I glance back at the cabinet in the hall where I've put the shell I found, which was also on the doorstep. I wonder why Ben seems to be passing the house so often. We're not really on the way to anywhere.

"Not mine," I say, trying to keep my voice steady. "Someone must have left them as a joke or something."

"A joke?" he says, touching the silk ribbons.

"I'll throw them away," I say, but I don't take them from him. I don't want to bring them into the house—I don't even want to touch them.

"I'll do it," Ben says. "I'll put them in your wheelie-bin on my way back…Are you okay? You're very pale."

"It's nothing, really. I'm still feeling the effects of some bad seafood."

I didn't sleep last night. I couldn't stop horrible thought after horrible thought from building in my head. This morning, I welcomed the numbness that creeps in after I take my pill, wishing I could take two instead of one. But I don't want to tell Ben about the pills. Or about Patrick and the calamari.

I close the door a fraction, but Ben doesn't move. "Actually, I wasn't just passing," he says. My hand tightens on the door frame and I half expect him to push his way in. I glance back into the house—what if Patrick or Joe comes down to see me talking to Ben? I should never have opened the door.

"I've had an artist pull back his exhibition and wanted to discuss your going in his place next month. We'll promote it with posters and flyers—get some real interest."

I press my stomach to hold in the panic. "I can't. I told you, I don't have enough paintings. I haven't…How can I have a whole exhibition ready in a month?"

I could have framed my drawings, like Anna suggested, but they're all gone now and the loss is like a sore, weeping and raw.

He frowns. "Will you come into the gallery tomorrow or Friday? There's…I have something that might help you."

There's something wrong. Something different. I stand outside the house after Ben leaves and stare. The *I* on the window that I scrubbed away…there's another. Next to where mine was, smaller, fainter, but there: another line drawn through the salt already building up again. I look down at the border: tiny white stones are scattered through it that weren't there before. They're like the white pills I take every day, so much so I almost go back into the house to check that I haven't scattered them like seeds in the garden without even knowing I did it. But when I crouch down, I see that they're not pills or stones but dozens of broken pieces of shell. I put that poor hermit crab out here the other day and now the crab has gone, its broken home crushed into tiny pieces. And next to them, right under the new *I*, a footprint.

I hold my breath. This is too close. This isn't someone watching from the other side of the road. This is someone right outside the window. When did this happen? Earlier, when I was alone in the house? Last night? No—the baby shoes weren't there when Patrick and Joe came in, and it must be the same person.

My mind jumps from Ian Hooper to Tom to Ben, imagining all of them watching me through the window, wiping away the salt to spy. I shake my head. Nearly time to take another pill, time to be calm and numb again.

But what else have I missed in that drifting numbness? Would I have forgotten Patrick's dinner if it weren't for the pills? Would I have taken so long to unpack and decorate? Wasn't it both those things that drove Patrick to lose control? I take my pills and passively watch life happen around me. I'm never going to be able to paint enough for a whole exhibition like this. Instead, the pills will take root inside me, grow into something rotten while I sleep through it all and the *I* on the window will cloud over and disappear. I get the plastic box of pills from the house and take off the lid. I go out to the wheelie-bin in front of the house and lift the lid. My hand tightens on the box, unable to tip them in. Maybe I can hide them in my room somewhere, just in case...

I walk back up the path and stop by the border under the window again. The footprint looks less distinct, the line through the salt perhaps a streak from a raindrop. Am I imagining all this? Obsessing, like Patrick said? I look at the pills in my hand. If I took another now, the footprint and the *I* might disappear. But the baby shoes—I couldn't have imagined them, could I? Someone is doing this, messing with us, and I have to stop hiding from it. Using my hands, I dig holes in the wet earth. I kneel to do it, not caring as wetness seeps through my trousers. I bury the pills, scattering them among the pieces of broken shell, covering them with earth until the border is neat and there's no sign of white, no footprints.

I rummage through Mia's coat pockets in the hall, searching for the tins of mints she always has. They're bigger than the pills, but from a distance, in the opaque plastic box, you can't tell.

Patrick comes down as I'm putting the lid back on the box, rubbing his wet hair with a towel, warm from his bath as his arm brushes mine.

"Taking your pill? Good girl."

I nod, my heart pounding. My arm aches from holding it rigidly still—I daren't let Patrick see my hand tremble. There's still dirt under my fingernails. I couldn't get it out, but if he notices, I'll say I've been weeding.

I've always been so bad at lying. But if I tell him I want to stop taking the pills, he'll march me back to the doctor, who'll look at my records and won't let me stop. And after last night, after he burned my books, I'm scared of Patrick's reaction if I tell him. I'm learning to lie better, though. I'm learning as I take a mint out of the box and put it into my mouth.

I close the box again and turn away, my shoulders hunched and sweat dripping under my hair as I wait for him to grab me, to smell the mint on my breath and then see the lie.

He walks up behind me and puts his hands on my shoulders, leans down to kiss the top of my head. I turn and I'm in his arms, his hands stroking my back. He's nearly a foot taller than me and his arms are strong. I used to like this—how safe and secure I felt, locked in. Now I find it difficult to breathe and I have to try hard not to struggle. I move and his arms tighten.

"Patrick..." I try to bring my hands up to push him away and he shifts, but only an inch or so. My back is touching the high windowsill and I can't get away because he keeps his arms around me.

This house, this moment, feels like how his parents' house used to feel, when the claustrophobia would build and build until sweat broke out on my forehead and my breathing grew unsteady.

Patrick touches my chin, lifts my head, reaches down to kiss my cheek, moving to whisper in my ear. "What's wrong, Sarah?"

What's *wrong*? I can hear the frustrated edge to his voice. I get it again, the fear that everything is in my imagination. How can he be acting so normally? I *saw* the look on his face as he burned my books—I can feel his hand pulling my hair as I was sick last night. It's not just me. It's not. In my head, I see Tom telling me about Patrick and his father, I see Ben and the gallery, picture my paintings in the window, picture Patrick's reaction to it, and my pulse rate builds as Patrick stares at me. What if he can see inside my mind?

It's still dark when I wake. The streetlight outside shines yellow through a gap in the curtains, and when my eyes adjust, I see Patrick's not asleep next to me. His side of the bed is cold: he hasn't just gone to the bathroom. That's not what woke me. How long has he been gone? I came up earlier than him. It was only me and him downstairs and the silence got to be too much, but I'm sure I remember the bounce of the mattress as he got in next to me, a soft brush of a kiss on my rigid shoulder as I drifted off to sleep.

I wait for him to come back, but he doesn't. It's three o'clock in the morning: there can be no good reason for someone to be up at three o'clock on a weeknight. Is it the children? I listen in the dark, but the house is silent. I close my eyes, but my mind sends me pictures of Patrick burning more than my sketchbooks. It sends me pictures of Mia waking from one of her nightmares. I won't be able to sleep again without knowing why Patrick's up, so I reach for my dressing gown, pull thick socks onto my feet. I pause in the doorway, scared to leave the room. My heart is racing as I make myself step out onto the dark landing.

He's not upstairs. Joe and Mia are both fast asleep when I look in on them, which calms my thudding heart a bit. Didn't I have that nightmare once? That I woke in the middle of the night and Patrick was gone, and when I checked, the children were gone and I was alone?

I smell fresh paint as I go downstairs. The kitchen and living room are dark, but the cellar door is ajar and there's a light shining from down there. I don't want to go in. I don't want to find out what's happening. I've never been down there. I've never *wanted* to go down there. I want to go back upstairs, pull the quilt over my head, and go to sleep, pretend this is all part of that dream I once had. I wish I hadn't buried those pills.

But I'm here and I'm awake and there's a light on in the cellar and the smell of fresh paint is drifting up. It's surreal enough to be a dream. Slowly, numbly, I walk down the cellar stairs and see Patrick. He's wearing a faded T-shirt and old jogging pants and he's painting the wall, covering the water-stained beige walls with bright white.

"Patrick?"

He doesn't answer. He bends, dips the roller in the tray of paint, and straightens, rolling it up and down the wall, another two feet of white to cover the dirty, damp surface.

"Patrick—it's the middle of the night."

"Couldn't sleep," he says without turning.

The only light is a low-wattage bulb hanging in the middle of the room so the corners are all in shadow.

"You've got to get up for work in less than five hours. Come on, I'll make you a tea to take up."

He ignores me. He's missing bits as he paints in this stupid, inadequate light.

"Patrick, seriously, this is not the time to be doing bloody decorating."

"I *know* that," he says, throwing down the roller so paint spatters across the floor and my feet, polka-dotting my socks. "You think I really want to be doing this now? But I have to work all the damn hours to pay for this house while you sit around doing nothing, whining about having no storage for all your damn junk, having nowhere to paint your little pictures, expecting me to be pleased you've spent a fortune on paint before you've unpacked one fucking *box*."

His voice rises to a shout that echoes and I step away, glancing toward the open cellar door. He runs his hands through his hair and lets out a shaky sigh. "Sorry. I'm sorry. You're right. I'll come to bed in a minute. I'm sorry I shouted. I'm tired and the move stressed me out more than I thought, and work is so busy and... Never mind."

"Patrick, please talk to me."

He bends down to pick up the roller again. "There's been a problem at work. It was one of my buildings. Some safety issues."

"Is it serious?"

"They caught it in time. But *David* called me into his office today and *David* thinks I should take some time off."

"Will you?"

He shakes his head. "We can't afford for me to take time off now, can we? I wanted the dinner to smooth things over, but *that* didn't happen, did it? There's so much to do to the house. It'll be fine. It'll blow over. All this *nonsense* you keep coming up with about Ian Hooper and imaginary people watching the house is not helping. I try to sleep and I can't shut off. Work and Joe and you and Mia and the house. There's so much to do."

The butterflies in my stomach have multiplied. The hairline cracks in his control are widening. I take a breath and pick up a brush. "Want some help?"

He shakes his head. "Go to bed. I'll be up in a minute. I'll clean up here and then I'll come."

But when I wake again, it's past four o'clock and Patrick's still not back in bed.

CHAPTER 16

I've felt anxious and jittery all day. I don't know if it's not taking the pills, worrying about Patrick, or panicking about this exhibition Ben wants me to have. Patrick's hovering behind me as I chop vegetables for a stir-fry. He's distracted—he doesn't seem to have noticed my agitated state. I'm wondering if something more has happened at work today, but I daren't ask. The front door slams and he seems to snap out of his preoccupied state, turning with a smile as Mia walks into the room.

"Hey," she says, her eyes wary as she looks at us. Something's wrong, something that's making her hunch her shoulders and bite her nails.

"Hi, honey—nice evening?"

She shrugs, pushing her hair away from her face and already turning to leave. "We were just doing homework and watching TV. Is there anything to eat? I'm starving—Jane's mum did this stupid creamy pasta thing that was *disgusting*."

"I thought you said you were going to Betty's," Patrick says, and I see Mia flinch.

"She called me," I put in, before Mia can answer, "to say Betty had to go out and could she go to Jane's."

She frowns at me but nods and backs away before Patrick can ask anything else. Patrick's pretend smile drops as she leaves the room and he stares at me as I hurry after her.

"Thanks," she mutters as we pass each other on the landing. She stops with her hand on her bedroom door. "But you didn't have to lie for me. Dad wouldn't have minded."

Her defense of Patrick is nothing new, but the note of doubt in her voice is.

"Are you okay?"

"I'm fine. Why wouldn't I be?"

She opens her door and I see the walls are still bare, no photos of a gang of new friends. Maybe there is no gang. Maybe there's just one, the *he* she talked about, any photos of him hidden on her phone for her eyes only.

More worry. It's making my stomach ache. I want to ask her who she was with, what she was doing, but she's all hunched and defensive, and I know if I do, we'll have another fight.

"Are you still having bad dreams?" I ask instead.

Her knuckles whiten as she grips the edge of the door and I expect it to be slammed in my face. Instead she lets her hand fall and steps back, an unspoken invitation into her room. I sit on the edge of her bed and she hovers in front of me.

"Not as bad as before," she says. "Not since you made me get rid of those books and articles." She looks back at me, a faint smile on her face. "It's not surprising I had nightmares, is it? Did...did you read any of it?"

A line from the murder houses book comes into my head: *Neighbors report the children grew quieter and more withdrawn over the months leading up to the murders.* She doesn't need to know I keep the book in my bedside table, that it's become my bedtime reading. "I know enough about this house and the murders—true facts, not speculation."

I get up and reach out a hand to brush her hair. "Listen," I say, wanting to see a repeat of the smile, "we never had that shopping trip, did we? How about we go this weekend? I'll buy us lunch." I look at her blank walls again. "Maybe I can arrange for you to stay with Caroline for a few days. It'll be break soon."

She winces, like I've hurt her, then her face shuts down. We're back to the blank-faced hostility.

"I don't want to stay with Caroline," she mutters.

They used to be close. It made me jealous once, when all I got was slammed doors and attitude. "But it would give you a chance to catch up with your old friends."

"Jesus, Mum, can't you take a hint? Do I have to spell it out?" she says.

"What?"

"I thought that's why you did it—why you took the overdose."

My turn to wince.

She's gone even paler. "I thought you were punishing Dad," she says, her voice wobbly, "for cheating on you."

I can't take a breath. Her words have punched me in the stomach just as she intended. I'm remembering the letter, the handwritten letter that started all this. The one I saw and thought, *This is from a woman*, and my instinct was to hide it, bury it, forget it, pretend I hadn't seen it.

Did I know? Did I always suspect? Is that what's wrong with him—not the house, not money worries or work or me, but guilt over an *affair*? No. It can't be that. Mia's wrong. It can't...

"I saw him with her," she says. "They were only kissing, but it was obvious what they'd been doing." She shakes her head, as if she could shake away the memory. "So I shouldn't blame you, should I? Maybe I'd have tried killing myself too. If Dad can cheat on you with your friend like that..."

What?

Mia's staring at me. "Yeah, it was Caroline. He was kissing Caroline."

Caroline?

What?

I float in the bath, only my face above the water. It's so full that any movement on my part sends waves of water over the side to drip-drip onto the tiled floor.

We ate dinner, the four of us, Mia picking at her noodles, barely eating anything, me numb, frozen. Did I pick up my fork? Did I even pretend to eat? Patrick and Mia talked, Mia nervously prattling, shooting me worried glances. Joe was in a world of his own.

Mia has to be wrong. She must have seen something she misinterpreted. And Caroline hates Patrick: How can they have been close enough for Mia to think she saw them kissing? I can't breathe. Something's choking me. Caroline has been my best friend for nearly twenty years. She knew me when I met Patrick, when I was so in love with him, when I was floating in the clouds in love with him, first love, first lover, Caroline knew all of this. My best friend.

It can't be true. But a bitter voice in my head rewrites everything I've seen between them: the barbed words become flirtation, every moment they stopped talking as I entered a room becomes significant—not arguing, not talking about me, but making arrangements. Her concern at the hospital about my moving out here was nothing to do with me and all to do with Patrick. If I check his phone, will I see her number listed? Secret messages planning secret assignations?

Every thought is a stab, a hot needle direct to my bloodstream. I want to phone her, beg her to tell me it's a lie, a mistake, but what if she doesn't? What if she confirms it? What do I do then? I close my eyes, sink deeper into the water, but the voices won't go away.

"Who did it?"

Patrick's voice, raised and sharp, sends me lurching upright, water sloshing over the side of the bath. By the time I get out and run downstairs in my dressing gown, he's got Joe by the shoulder, shaking him.

"What's going on?"

They both look at me. I shiver not just from my wet hair but at the cold anger on Patrick's face, the fear on Joe's.

Patrick looks away from me, back at his son. "Did you do it?"

"Do what?" Joe mutters, and Patrick's dragging him off, through to the kitchen. I follow them in time to see Patrick unlocking the back door, pushing Joe out ahead of him.

"Look," he says, pointing up into the tree that grows outside Joe's window.

At first, I think it's a ribbon floating from the branches and I don't get Patrick's anger: it's close enough to Joe's window that he could probably reach out and hook it off. Then I step closer and see it's a pair of baby shoes, those soft satiny ones with ribbons that are just for show, for very new babies. It's the shoes Ben found, the ones he said he'd throw away.

I glance back at Patrick. He's breathing fast and the hand that's not holding Joe is white-knuckled at his side.

"Patrick, I don't think Joe put them there—why would he put baby shoes in a tree? It's probably kids messing about, a lucky shot from the alley."

Patrick isn't looking at me. He's looking at those shoes swinging in the breeze and it's there again. Fear. He's afraid of something and I don't know what. And I'm not only worried about him anymore—I'm scared too. Scared for all of us as to what that look might mean.

He lets Joe go, rubs his hands through his hair. "Sorry, I'm… sorry. Just kids, you're right." He glances up at the tree again and his face tightens. "Get rid of them," he growls, to both of us, as he walks away. I hear the front door slam and hold my breath, only letting it out when I hear the car start and drive off.

Joe straightens his shirt where Patrick twisted it when he grabbed him. "Still think this house is a good place for us, Mum? Still promise everything will get better?"

Anna's brought me to her secret beach. I stand on the steep path leading down, clutching a rock, as I'm hit with a disorienting wave of vertigo. I wasn't going to come—I walked away from the house, overwhelmed by everything: the fear on Patrick's face, my own fears about him and Caroline, about Tom's conviction of Patrick's friendship with John Evans. Everything that's happening in the house—the cold spots that I *swear* are growing, that height chart, which seems to be becoming more visible, the footprint, the marks on the window, those damn fucking baby shoes.

I press my hands tight against my temples, as if I could squeeze away the pounding headache. It's too much, thoughts like maggots eating away at my brain. Every muscle in my body is tense and I don't know if it's withdrawal from those damn pills or something more, but it's too much. I had to get out, but I was looking for the mundane, the normality of a café, or a numbing walk around a supermarket.

Then I saw Joe outside the fairground, and before I had the chance to go over, he was met by another boy in the same school uniform. They were mostly hidden in shadow at the back of the cotton candy stall and this boy leaned in to kiss Joe. Joe turned afterward and saw me. I lifted a hand to wave, but I didn't go over.

I wasn't sure what to do, so I ran away. Not literally running but almost. It's not that I'm surprised. We've never discussed it, but I think I've always known Joe is gay. I want to tell him it's okay, that I just want him to be happy. But if I'd gone over to them, what would I have said? Something stupid, probably: *Why aren't you in school?* or *I'm worried about you* or *Don't tell your father.* Something that would take away the smile on Joe's face and it's been so long since I've seen that smile. And I'm glad, so glad, to see him happy, but it ignites more worries: What if that boy breaks my son's heart when he's so fragile? What if Patrick finds out? Last year, six months ago even, would I have worried about that? But Patrick as he is now, would his reaction be rational?

So I waved and walked away, my feet carrying me in the other direction, to the coast path where Anna was waiting, sitting on a bench, looking out to sea, just like the painting in the gallery window.

"What do you think?" Anna calls as I climb carefully down onto the sand.

I straighten up. The beach is pebbly, like the one at home, but Anna was right: these pebbles have a million more colors—greens and blues and pinks. The water is slices of cobalt and jade and gray. That flat painting in the gallery chopped up and re-collaged into something real and interesting. I can see for miles along the coast and grass-topped crumbly cliffs stretch up behind me.

I glance at Anna. The walk down has put color into her cheeks and she looks younger as she jumps from rock to rock. I could bring Joe and Mia here. We could build a house made of pebbles and driftwood and hide from everything.

"I needed this," I say. "I haven't been sleeping. This is washing away all the sluggishness."

I want to tell her about Patrick maybe knowing John Evans, about Caroline and Patrick, but she doesn't know them. She won't be able to reassure me. She'll believe it, and the squirming fear in my belly will grow. If I told her about my husband's reactions to the baby shoes, the restaurant, the kitchen showroom, if I told her about my creeping fear that something's living in the house other than us, what would she say?

"Do you think this place might end up in one of your paintings?" she asks when we get to the water's edge. We look down, watching the water creep toward us, as far as our toes and back.

"Patrick doesn't want me to exhibit. He thinks it'll be an embarrassment." I feel the sting of humiliation again.

"But shouldn't it be about what *you* want?"

What I want is to grab Mia and Joe and move down here into the pebble-and-driftwood house of my imagination, away from everything. What I want is to be free of the clamoring panic in my head.

We stand in silence for a while, looking out to sea.

"I want to do it, I do. But I'm scared," I say.

"Of what?"

Of everything.

"I like your secret beach."

She smiles. "Then it shall be your secret beach, too. We'll share it, fifty-fifty."

Another secret to keep from Patrick.

She holds out a handful of tiny pebbles in a dozen pastel shades. Wet from the sea, the sun turns them into glittering jewels. "Paint this place," she says. "Have your exhibition. Do something for you."

I lick my dry lips and they taste of salt.

"I will," I say. "I'll do it."

* * *

I go by the gallery on my way back to talk to Ben, Anna's pebbles heavy in my pocket. I try to put the baby shoes out of my mind as I stand outside. Ben's talking to a customer but flashes me a smile as I come in. I leave them to their low-pitched chat and wander around the gallery. It's so beautiful, white walls and polished wood floors, huge windows, warm and bright.

"Sorry about that," Ben says, coming over to me after the customer leaves. I'm staring at a painting, lost in it. It's not big in terms of physical size. Its vastness is all within the picture, in the mist settling over the sand dunes, the way it eats the ground so the dunes appear to be floating.

"Is this one of yours?" I ask, and Ben nods.

"It's beautiful," I say. It is. Beautiful and powerful...but also full of emptiness and loneliness.

"It's not my favorite—too melancholy," he says. I nod. That sums up the mood of the painting perfectly. "It's one of a series I did after my divorce came through. The paintings I'm working on now are much happier." He says it with a smile, but I still see a drift of that melancholy on his face.

"You said you had something that could help me be ready to exhibit." Does he hear the agitation in my voice, the high-pitched edge of anxiety?

He looks at me for a moment, then turns and locks the gallery door. My stomach lurches—was I wrong about this? About him?

"Wait," I say as he walks toward the back of the gallery. "Did you—did you throw the baby shoes into our tree?"

"What?"

"The baby shoes. The ones you found outside our house."

He's frowning. "Throw them into a *tree*? Of course not. I put them in the wheelie-bin, like I said I would."

"They were dangling from a branch of the tree in our back garden."

He rubs a hand through his short hair. "I'm not...I promise you I took the shoes, put them in the bin, and that's it."

"Someone threw them there."

"What are you suggesting, Sarah? I'm guessing it was whatever joker put them outside your house in the first place."

He takes a step toward me and I take one back. His frown grows. "Look, I can promise you I'm not stalking you with baby shoes or planning anything terrible here, but if you're feeling uncomfortable, you can go and I'll get someone else to liaise with you over the exhibition."

I'm being stupid, made paranoid by whoever's been watching the house. I still don't know who threw the shoes, but it's clearly not Ben, and he's no threat to me. I came in here myself. It's a public place. I rub my fingers over my palms—they're tingling, itchy. My whole body is tingling and I can't stand still. "I'm sorry," I say. "You locked the door and..."

"I locked the door because we're going out of the gallery and these paintings are valuable. I wanted to show you something. That's all."

I hesitate and he sighs. "Please? It won't take a minute."

I follow him up a flight of stairs tucked away behind the door at the back of the gallery and we step into a large room. A rattling fridge and stained sink take up one corner; broken floorboards and damp, peeling walls frame the rest. But the light from two big windows floods the room.

"What do you think?" he asks.

"About what?"

"This as a studio space."

I spin in a circle, taking in the light and the space and the quiet. I could paint here. "Thank you, but I...we just don't have the money for me to rent a studio right now."

"Oh, I'm not charging for it, Sarah. I'm offering it to you to use as much as you need. I'll give you a key," Ben says. "It has a separate entrance as well as the one through the gallery. You can come and go as you please." He walks over to the window and looks out. "I used to live up here until I bought my cottage."

"Why?" I ask. He doesn't know me, not yet. Why give me

this when all I've done for him is throw paranoid accusations his way?

He shrugs. "I'm not using it, so why not?" He smiles as we walk out of the room. My room. "Besides," he says, "you look like you need this space. It's always been something of a sanctuary."

We go back down through the gallery in silence. I don't know if I'm comfortable with his... It's not pity. Sympathy? Concern? Whatever, I'm not used to such generosity from someone who's essentially a stranger.

"Sarah?" he says as I get to the gallery door. "If there's... if there's anything else I can do, or if you need help, let me know, okay?"

I nod and turn away, my eyes stinging. He sees too much. I'm giving too much away. He's offering more than friendship and, for a fleeting moment, I want to grab him and kiss him, make him lock the door again, rip his clothes off on the floor of the sanctuary he's tossed my way. I could take that home to Patrick, let him see the same betrayal in my eyes that I now see in his.

It plays over and over in my mind—us. Our time. Our years. Best friends, us against the world. That's what I thought. I spent a lot of time drifting, filling myself with whatever drugs and drink I could find so I didn't have to think about it. But the moment I'm sober, the projector clicks on, the film starts playing.

In a park, middle of the night, middle of the summer. "Doesn't it bother you that no one cares if you're out all night?" you said, looking to hurt. You lit a cigarette and passed it to me. A couple of our other mates had been there, but they drifted off home as it got closer to midnight. "Doesn't it bother you either?" I should have said, but I just shrugged. I don't think you ever saw how honest you were with me. How real. You would have been embarrassed by me earlier if you'd seen.

"God," you said, that night. "God, if I ever have kids, the perfect world I'm going to give them."

CHAPTER 17

I wait until the house is quiet, everyone busy doing their own thing, before I retrieve the stones from the secret beach out of my jacket pocket. I go upstairs and open my wardrobe. Right at the back there is an old wooden box my dad gave me. He made it himself and it's always been my treasure box.

I check that the bedroom door is closed and pull out the box, sink to the floor to open it. My head pounds harder as I lift the lid. Something's missing—it's much lighter than it should be. I move the bundle of postcards, scrawled messages from my dad sent from places I'd never heard of back then, the writing now faded. There should be a jewelry box underneath with all my mother's old necklaces and earrings. Nothing I'd wear, but all heavy and gold. Valuable enough to keep hidden, though that wasn't why it was in my treasure box. I take out everything—childhood diaries, the postcards, baby cardigans my mother knitted for Joe and Mia—but the jewelry isn't there.

I put the box back in the wardrobe and sit on the bed, my legs shaking. The bedroom door opens and Patrick comes in. "Everything okay?"

I nod. He must be able to hear my heart beating, it's so loud. "Fine," I say. I don't think I can stand up.

He turns to go and I reach out my hand to stop him. "Wait. Have you seen my mother's jewelry box?"

"Jewelry box?" He looks at the dressing table where my own jewelry box sits open, a tangle of silver necklaces and earrings. The combined worth of my jewelry is less than a hundred pounds, nothing worth hiding away there.

"Not that one. My mother's. The box with all her gold jewelry in—her gold chain and her engagement ring..."

"Why would I have seen it?"

"It's gone. It's missing."

He pauses. "Have you asked the children?"

I think of Mia's new shoes, all the unfamiliar clothes she's been wearing recently. I think of Joe hidden away upstairs on his own for hours on end. I think of how Patrick would respond if he thought they'd been stealing.

"It's probably just been misplaced in the move," I say, making myself smile.

"Okay..." he says, still frowning. He glances down at the sketchbook I dropped on the bed. "Are you drawing again? Can I see?"

I think of all the notes I've scribbled in there, the half-finished sketches, and I snatch it up before he can reach for it. "No—it's not finished. Not ready for anyone to see yet." But moving the sketchbook reveals the book about the murder houses I forgot to put away.

"What's this?" he says, picking it up.

"It's nothing," I say. "A book someone gave Mia. I thought..."

My voice trails off as he flicks through it, his face blank. If he grabbed my sketchbook as well, he'd see the notes I'd jotted as I read that stupid book, scribbled insane thoughts on the author's ridiculous theories. He'd see his name with a question mark next to it. He'd see Ben's name, Tom and John Evans, Ian Hooper, arrows joining them.

"Why are you reading this?"

"I was going to throw it out, but...I was curious."

"Curious? What on earth kind of curiosity do you believe is going to be quenched reading this crap?"

"What do you expect me to do?" I say, my rising voice surprising even me. "You never told me about Ian Hooper being out of prison. You never told me you were friends with John fucking Evans. It's supposed to be a fresh start, but how can it be? All these lies, all these damn secrets."

Caroline as well, another *secret*. My friend Caroline.

"Sarah, stop it. Just stop. I barely knew John Evans—that's irrelevant. All of it means nothing."

"What do you mean, nothing? Hooper's out—I can't just pretend it didn't happen, that it isn't still happening."

"But it's not happening to *us*. None of that and none of them matters. What matters is *us*. Our family. Here and now. And you just won't let it go; you won't let this work. You're the one ruining it, filling the children with rot, with your ridiculous obsessions."

He turns another page in the book and starts reading aloud. " 'Hooper has always insisted he is innocent. Did the police look elsewhere in their investigation? Did they question everyone who knew the family?' "

He looks across at me. "So what's your theory, Sarah? Do you think the whole town lined up to murder them? Or do you think I sneaked here with my mother, killed an entire family, then poured a bucket of blood over Ian Hooper and put a knife in his hand?"

"No, of course not. I—"

"You what? You fucking *what*?" He starts tearing pages out of the book, crumpling them and letting them drop. "These evil, vicious, whispering lies almost killed my parents. Did you know that?"

"How could I? You never said a word—wouldn't even *talk* about the murders."

After the murders, didn't we visit his parents less? Weren't there months and months when we didn't go there at all?

"The press found them. Hounded them for weeks, wanting background on their damn *Murder House*." He stops and takes a deep breath. I can see sweat shining on his forehead. "It upset them. My father had heart problems. And now I find you reading this vile garbage."

The pages of the book now litter the room, like giant confetti, and Patrick holds nothing in his hands but the cover. He closes it like it's still a book. "Please don't," he says. "Please don't read anything like this again."

He pauses on his way out of the room. "Clear this up, will you?"

I bend to start picking up the torn pages, words and phrases jumping out at me as I gather them up, whispering and settling in my brain.

Murder House.

Crying and bruised.

It was the house. The house changed him.

Neglect.

Bloodstains.

Horror.

Damage.

Was it the house?

Was it the house?

I hug the torn-up book to my chest and stare at the wardrobe, thinking of the empty space in my treasure box where my mother's jewelry should be. Patrick tried to persuade me to sell it after she died. We didn't argue exactly, but he didn't understand why I wanted to keep it when I never intended to wear any of it. I look at the mess of paper in my hands. I should throw it away now, give it to Patrick for burning. That's what he'll expect. Instead I put it under the mattress, tucking it away so it's hidden.

I follow Patrick downstairs, picking up Mia's coat from where it's fallen on the floor.

Joe comes down the stairs and tries to edge past us to the front door, but Patrick reaches out, pushing him back toward the stairs. "You're not going anywhere," he says to Joe. "No one is, not anymore. It's nearly dinnertime and dinnertime is family time."

"Since when?"

"Go back to your room and stay there until dinner."

"No. I'm going out," Joe says.

"Don't you *dare* take that tone with me."

Mia comes running downstairs. "What's going on?"

Joe goes to shove past his father, bumping me on the way, but Patrick hauls him back, pushes him against the wall, his hand clutching his T-shirt, pulling him away and slamming him back so Joe is gasping for breath, his arms flailing, scrabbling to push Patrick off.

"Patrick! Stop it—*stop it*." As soon as I touch him, Patrick lets go, breathing hard as Joe bends over coughing.

Mia's crying and I crouch next to Joe. "Are you okay?" I whisper, and he stares at me, tears in his eyes.

"No," he whispers back, his voice raw. He staggers up, pushes past all of us, and runs out the front door.

Patrick wipes his forehead with the back of his hand. "That boy is out of control," he says. "He almost knocked you over. Are you okay?"

I stare at him. "Me okay? Jesus Christ, Patrick, what the hell was that about?"

"I know," he mutters. "I went too far, but did you hear how he spoke to me?"

"He spoke to you like an angry teenager. A *boy*. Our *son*. You lost control." I'm saying it through clenched teeth, aware of Mia behind me. I'm shaking and I want to scream at him, push at him like he pushed at Joe.

Patrick's gaze flickers past me to Mia. He brushes his hair back. "Okay, I'll go out and look for him. I'll sort it out, I promise."

"No! I won't have you chasing off after him angry. Leave him alone. You need to calm down."

"Calm down? I'm perfectly calm. I'll find him, bring him home, and we'll talk—*calmly*."

I follow him to the door, disquiet building, my stomach somersaulting. I put my hand on his arm and he looks down at it. "Patrick..."

"What?" He lifts his head and smiles at me, calm Patrick again, hair smooth, jacket buttoned.

"Don't go. Stay here. Joe will come home when he calms down. Or I'll go and find him."

A gust of wind rattles the letter box and Patrick frowns. "It's raining out there and blowing a gale. It's not a good night to be out. Don't worry, I'll find him."

He's gone before I can say that Patrick finding him is exactly what I'm worried about.

Joe's door is open, his sketchbook lying on the bed. I sit down and pick it up, chewing my lip as I flick through the pages. I've never seen this one before and I can understand why Joe hasn't shown it to me: the first few are all sketches of me. Every page has two drawings, happy/sad, smiling/crying, asleep/awake; me divided, split in two, like he's trying to work out which is real. I wondered before how he would draw me and now I know: poised on the cusp, torn, pulled in two.

I expect the next pages to be Mia, but they're not. Instead, there are half a dozen pastel drawings of a boy with brown eyes, a stranger with a beautiful smile. It's not the boy I saw him with on the beach—this one is older. A man, really, not a boy. I look at the sketches Joe has done and I feel like I'm intruding. Is that where Joe's gone tonight?

Unsettled, I put the sketchbook away and go to my room, staring out the cloudy window, hoping to see Patrick's car returning, Joe safe in the passenger seat, Patrick still calm, storm all played out.

Instead, I see someone across the road, walking next to the seawall, almost lost in darkness. The figure stops and turns to face the house. I lift a hand to wave in case it's Joe but lower my arm as I realize it could be the watcher. Who is it—Ian Hooper or Tom Evans? Both of them tied to this house by a terrible crime. Whoever it is doesn't move and we stare at each other as the sky gets darker. It's like they're disappearing, eaten by the night. I wait until they've completely disappeared before I pull the curtains closed.

I look at the glowing numbers on the alarm clock. It's ten—Joe has been gone two hours and Patrick nearly as long. I try their phones, but they both go straight to voicemail.

Mia opens her door. "They're still not back?"

I shake my head, go back to my window to lift the curtain, and look again. Mia joins me. "Did you see someone watching the house earlier?" She speaks in a whisper, as if her voice could carry across the road.

I nod and she sighs. "Who do you think it is?" she asks.

"I don't know."

"I was wondering...I wondered if it was the boy," Mia says. "The one who survived. Not a boy anymore, of course, but I sometimes think...Could you ever really get free of this house? If you'd gone through such horror here? If you'd lost your entire family here?"

I think of Tom Evans—*Seeing people I know in the house, it's almost like you're family.* Could it be him out there? Still hiding under the bed from the monster, yearning for the family he lost? Or is it Ian Hooper, freed after nearly twenty years? I haven't told Joe and Mia he's out, and I'm starting to think I should have.

Mia shivers. "I'll never be able to see this house as anything other than the Murder House. Doesn't matter what Dad does to it, or how many stories he tells about how bloody wonderful it used to be, it'll only ever be the Murder House."

I let the curtain drop. "I'm not sure this house has ever been as wonderful as your dad remembers."

We pretend to watch TV, but I don't think either of us could have said what was on. I've tried Joe's and Patrick's phones again, but they're still not answering. Mia got out her homework, but she hasn't turned a page in ten minutes.

It's half past ten. The storm outside is getting worse and Joe has been out in it for two and a half hours.

We both jump when someone hammers on the front door. All of Mia's books and notes spill to the floor as she gets up and runs out, me behind her.

It's Anna, soaking wet and gasping for breath. "It's Joe," she says, and I can see she's shaking. "Oh, fuck, it's Joe. I called an ambulance, but I got there too late. I'm sorry..."

What? What is she talking about? She doesn't know Joe, she's never met him, only seen the old photos I keep on the wall and the sketches in my book.

She staggers as Mia pushes her out of the way and goes racing down the street.

"Mia!" I run out to call her back because Anna must be mistaken and that's when I see. I see someone lying sprawled under the streetlight halfway down the road, in a dark pool of— Oh, God, is that blood?

I got there too late, Anna said. "Joe…" I whisper. But as I try to run to Mia, to Joe, all the strength goes out of my legs and I fall to my knees. I want to slump like him, my boy, I want to lie on the cold pavement, but Anna's there, her hands digging into my arms as she drags me up again.

"Get up," she says, and there's anger in her voice as she digs her fingers in harder. I can hear sirens in the distance, getting closer. She shakes me and I stagger. "Get up and go to your son. Wake up, Sarah. For fuck's sake, *wake up*."

Part 3—Waking Up

Headline from the *South Wales Echo*,
a week after the murders:

Ian Hooper and Marie Evans Were Having Affair

A source close to the family has revealed that the affair had been going on for several months and that Marie was poised to leave Evans for Hooper. Is the alleged affair connected to the murders? Local writer **Wayne Matthews,** *who's working on a book about the Murder House, believes so.*

CHAPTER 18

I'd thought he was dead. I hunch, my arms crossed over my belly to hold in the pain. I can't breathe, I can't...I've been here before, after my mother died, and when Joe crashed the car.

I thought he was dead, but he's not. He's not. I repeat that to myself and stand up straight again. He is *not* dead. This isn't the same hospital I was in, but the smell is the same, same endless, windowless echoing corridors, same dry air, same creeping claustrophobia closing my throat. The wall is cold on my back as I lean against it. I've come out for air, but I can't find any, not here in these corridors. Mia's still in with him, holding his hand. She hasn't let go since we got here, while I hover useless on the edge.

I close my eyes and see the scars on Joe's arms. *Mrs. Walker?* the doctor said. I was waiting outside and I was on my own. *Mrs. Walker, we want to talk to you about these marks. Does he self-harm?* I press my hands against my closed eyes, trying to push away the images embedded there.

"Mum?" Mia tugs my sleeve. She's white-faced, makeup smeared under her eyes. Younger and older. "He's awake."

I pull her close in a hug and feel her trembling, still in shock. She gives me only a second before she pushes me away. I'd thought he was dead. When I came running out of the house and she was screaming and holding his head and there was all that blood. I looked for Ian Hooper in the darkness, Ian Hooper and his bloody knife. And, God, worse than that, worse than Ian Hooper, I looked for Patrick. I thought my son was dead and I fell, bloodying my knees and forgetting how to breathe.

Anna picked me up and handed me the contents of my pockets, which had scattered across the street. Part of me still feels like I'm there, boneless and numb, sprawled in the street, watching my son bleed on the road.

I help Mia to a chair and drape my jacket around her shoulders, but it's not the cold making her shake.

"Is it the house?" I say. "His arms—the cutting, the self-harming. Is it the house?"

She stares at me, like I'm mad. "You don't know a bloody thing, do you?"

"What?"

"He's been doing it for months."

What?

"Your precious *boy*—it's always been so bloody obvious who your favorite is, and Joe liked being someone's favorite for once. So he was never going to tell you he was struggling and fucking up, and would you have seen it even if he'd tried? Would you have listened?"

Of course I would have. Of course I...But I wasn't there when he crashed the car, was I? I was in that dark place, out of reach of everyone.

"It's your fault. All his scars are your fault!" she shouts, pale and shaking. "This? Now? All of it is your fault. You have no fucking idea what's happening to Joe, to me—and Joe's too scared you'll try to kill yourself again to tell you. But you're fine, aren't you? Tripping around with your new friends, feeling *better*. You're supposed to be the mother, the grown-up. You're supposed to protect *him*."

I reach out for her, but she shoves me away. "For God's sake, go and see Joe. Or are you going to run away again now that you know the truth?" She picks up her bag and rummages inside it, pulling out a crumpled box of Tylenol.

"Here," she says, throwing the box at me. "Just in case the urge overcomes you again—take the fucking lot and get it over with."

Joe is staring at the ceiling when I enter. They've cleaned away the blood, stitched his split scalp. I can't look at the shadowy bruise on his neck. He has two broken fingers where someone stamped on his hand and his face is bruised and swollen. He was lucky, they said—bruising, yes, the broken fingers, but nothing else broken, no internal injuries. *Lucky?* He's been beaten so badly he doesn't look like Joe. How could anyone describe this as *lucky*?

The scars on his arms are patterns of pink and white, new and old, faded and fresh. Mia's right: I've been hiding, I've been asleep. This is all my fault. I should have thrown away those pills sooner. I should never have started taking the damn things. The lump in my throat is so big it aches, but I take a deep breath and swallow it. I can't cry. I can't lose it in front of my boy. I have to be strong.

"Joe?" I say, leaning down. I run a hand over his hair, but he pulls away, then gasps in pain.

"Sorry." I go to move away.

"Don't." Joe whispers.

"Don't what?"

"Don't leave."

"I won't. I'll stay as long as you want."

"Please, Mum," he says. "You know what I mean. Please don't leave me. Promise me."

He stretches out his unbroken hand across the gap that's grown between us since my overdose and I hold it. "I will *never* leave you, Joe. *Never*."

I want to just sit with him now, holding his hand until he falls asleep, but there's something I have to ask him. Before anyone else comes in.

"Joe? I need to know who did this. You told me before you were worried about your dad, him shouting at you..." I lean in closer, but I can't say the next words. I can't ask him if Patrick did this. I can't believe Patrick would have done this to his own child.

"I don't remember what happened." He turns his face away, but I can see he's crying, salty tears weaving through the bruises. I'd thought he was dead. The ER doctor said he was lucky, but I'd thought he was dead.

"We have to get out," I whisper as Joe drifts back to sleep.

"Get out of what?"

I gasp and bump into the bed at Patrick's voice. He's right behind me, staring at me, not at his broken son in the bed.

"...of the room," I say. "To let Joe sleep."

He's still staring. "What happened?"

He looks...crumpled. His hair is wet and his shirt is creased. It could be because he got the message and rushed right here. It could be because he's been frantically searching the town for his son. But I'm thinking of him pushing Joe up against the wall, a look I've never seen before on his face. I'm thinking of his hands slamming on the steering wheel after we got turned down for the kitchen, of him ripping that book apart. I'm thinking of the dozen cracks in his control that have grown since we moved here.

I'm imagining Patrick seeing Joe on the beach with a boy and what his reaction would be. I look at his hands and I'm looking for blood on his knuckles, on his shirt. Joe's blood.

But his hands are clean.

Out in the corridor, Mia is asleep, stretched across three chairs with my jacket over her. Patrick reaches down and strokes her cheek, his hand brushing hair off her face.

I hold my hands behind my back because my instinct is to drag him away from her. He moves away from Mia and comes over to me, standing too close. The wall is behind me and I can't step away.

"What happened?" he asks again.

"I don't know. Joe told the police he doesn't remember. He didn't see who attacked him." I'm pressed against the wall and he's facing me, his arm next to me on the wall, leaning in to kiss my forehead.

"I rushed here as soon as I got your message. I'm sorry I missed your call before."

I turn my face away and duck from his kiss. "I thought it was Ian Hooper."

"This again? Sarah, why the hell would Ian Hooper attack Joe?"

He's right. But if not Ian Hooper…

"Was it you?" I whisper.

He steps back and his face shuts down. I shouldn't have said it. "You think I'd do this to my own son?" His voice rises as he looks down at his hands and I wonder if he sees the same thing I do: his anger as he turned toward Joe.

"He's been self-harming," I say. "His arms are scarred and Mia says he's been doing it for months."

"I know. I saw the doctor. I think—"

"Mia says it's my fault, because of what I did—the pills and—"

"Don't, Sarah. Don't blame yourself. Don't start that again. He's acting up, punishing you, looking for attention."

"He's not a toddler throwing a tantrum, he's *cutting* himself. We have to address this, Patrick."

Patrick shakes his head. "You're making too much of it. He needs to be grounded, not indulged."

"I'm going to make that appointment with the therapist."

"*No.*"

I reach for Patrick's arm to stop him from marching away. "*Yes.* We're not going to pretend this isn't happening. We're not going to pretend everything's fine while Joe is locked in his room, slicing his arms open."

I'm speaking too loudly, but Patrick turns to face me.

"He's going to get the help he needs," I say. "And I don't think this move has been good for either of them. I don't think it's been good for *us*."

"Didn't take you long to find another reason to leave, did it?"

"I'm not using our son as a fucking *excuse*."

There's a silence that lasts too long.

"But you're saying we should move? Give up after a month and sell the house I've waited half my life to get back?"

I make myself stand straight and look him in the eye. "Yes."

"No," he says. "*No.* Those scars on his arms are old. Moving here was the right thing to do, you'll see. The murders are nothing but bad history. Ian Hooper is *not* hanging around watching the house. Whatever is troubling Joe got left behind when we moved. I wish you'd do the same and let it go. If you insist, he can see the damn therapist, but honestly? Whatever is worrying him, it's not the house. And we are *not* moving. Ever."

But not all the scars are old.

"Hey, Sarah."

I recognize her voice right away but don't believe she's really here. I've picked up my phone so many times to call her and put it down again in the last two days, since Mia told me about the affair. I turn and my mind paints guilt and deceit on her face.

"How did you know?"

"Patrick called me," Caroline says.

The taste of vomit rises in my throat, sour and bitter.

"How is Joe?" she says.

I take a deep breath. "Physically, he'll be fine—a lot of bruising, a few breaks."

"But?"

I flinch. That awful, rusty knife of a *but.* "He's been self-harming. For months, maybe longer, the doctor thinks."

Caroline looks shaken as she steps away from me. "God. Fuck. Fuck, Sarah, I'm sorry."

"I didn't know—I didn't have a clue." I blurt it out like I expect Caroline to accuse me of letting it happen. But is it any better not to have known? Not to have noticed my son bleeding? I'm crying again. I'm trying to be so damn strong, but I can't stop the tears.

Mia is still sleeping across the chairs, so I turn away in case she wakes up and sees me crying. "What exactly do you want, Caroline?"

Her turn to have tears in her eyes. "I couldn't stand seeing you like that anymore," she says. "You were dying way before you took those damn pills. Fading away right in front of my eyes. I couldn't stand it anymore when you wouldn't listen to me. I'm so sorry I got angry with you at the hospital, but it's because I love you. Surely you know that."

"I'm not fading anymore."

She looks at me, my fighting stance, my windswept hair, whatever expression is showing on my face. "No. No, you're not. I guess Patrick was right about the house, about the move being a good thing."

I gasp. No, no, that's not what she's meant to see. "It's not the house." I say it louder than I intended and Mia stirs on her chairs. I hold my breath, but she doesn't wake.

"Listen," Caroline says. "I know...I know we have our issues, stuff to sort out, but why doesn't Mia come home with me?"

"What, now?"

"Yes. You need time with Joe. Let her come and stay with me for the weekend so you can concentrate on Joe's recovery."

"She won't want to," I say. "You know why."

She looks wary. "Sarah, I don't know what you mean. Did something happen with Mia? I could stay tonight, take Mia home for you?"

Caroline, Patrick, and Mia in the house, playing happy family. I grit my teeth. "I know," I say.

"Know what?"

"About you and Patrick. Mia saw you."

Her face drains of color. So it's true.

"No, Sarah. Listen—"

"*No*. I don't need this now. I don't want to hear your excuses and lies. You were supposed to be my friend. My best friend."

"It's not what you think."

"Oh, please." I pause as Mia stirs again. "I can't talk to you about this now while my son is lying in a hospital bed. You and Patrick—it's insignificant, unimportant. Now, please go. Leave us alone."

"Sarah?" Caroline calls as I turn away. "There's something you need to know. About..." She looks at Mia.

"Whatever it is, this is not the moment, Caroline."

But she continues: "I'm sorry, but I asked Sean to look up Eve and where she was in care."

"Don't say it," I hiss.

I can see fear in her face. My own fear rises as I glance back at Joe's closed door. On top of everything else, she's bringing up Eve? Now? How long until the secret comes out? How long until Joe finds out? He's going to be eighteen in seven months. I think of the scars on his arms and picture him finding out and cutting and cutting and cutting...My shoulders stiffen. "I told you to leave it alone."

She's chewing the inside of her cheek, her face twisted. "Sean found something else, though—"

No. I can't bear to hear anything more or to see her standing here any longer. "Get out!" I hear it come out of me as almost a scream. "Leave! And don't you dare—don't you bloody *dare*—mention a word to anyone about any of this."

CHAPTER 19

I'm putting on my shoes when Mia appears in the doorway.

"Don't come," she says.

I let go of my laces and look up at her. Patrick is waiting downstairs for us all to go and collect Joe from the hospital.

"You'll stress him out." When she sees my face, her tone softens. "Even without meaning to."

I shake my head. "I won't. I won't do anything to upset him—that's the last thing I want."

She folds her arms and frowns. "Bloody hell, Mum, even *I* can see it. You're so wound up. I know it's...Look, I'm sorry I said it was your fault at the hospital. Him cutting. It's more than you, more than your overdose. But if you go in there this stressy, he's going to worry again. He needs to be able to focus on himself, not you."

"I need to be there. Caroline said—"

"Caroline?"

"She was at the hospital. Your dad called her."

Mia frowns. "Fuck's sake," she mutters, nibbling the edge of a nail. "Did you...does Dad know I saw them together?"

I shake my head. "I haven't been able to—"

"Don't. I shouldn't have said anything. I wish I hadn't."

"Of course you should have told me."

There's panic on her face. "But if you tell him now, with Joe, with everything going so wrong—"

We both jump as Patrick calls up the stairs. "Sarah, Mia, we need to go."

Mia backs out onto the landing. "Please, Mum," she says. "Stay here and work on being less...less *everything*."

I follow her downstairs. Patrick's in the hall, car keys in hand.

"I'll stay here," I say. "Get dinner ready. The chicken will be cooked by the time you get back if I stay at home."

So Mia goes with Patrick to collect Joe from the hospital and I wait here. Is Mia right? Or is Joe going to see my absence as another rejection? I can't get it right. I'm either getting too close or stepping back too far. Everything that's been going on with them I've missed, and my punishment for that is evident in the scars patterning Joe's arms.

I pick up my phone to call Anna, but it goes straight to voicemail. The chicken's cooked and cooling on the table, the vegetables drying out in dishes in the oven. I should have gone with them. I look at the time—they'll be at least another hour. The house is too quiet. I walk through, switching on lights, avoiding looking at the cellar door, the marks of the height chart on the living room wall.

I shiver as I pass through the hall and the temperature seems to drop. God, I want a pill. I need something to quell the building panic in my stomach. It's rising and I can't stop the panicked voice in my head that's screaming at me to get out, get out, run away. I pull a bottle of wine out of the cupboard and pour a glass, spilling it down myself in my haste to drink it.

It's getting dark outside. They're late. Should I have let Patrick go to get him? No, stop. I won't go there. It wouldn't have been Patrick—it *couldn't*. I'm being paranoid, letting my fears get to me. This is why Mia asked me to stay at home. She's right: I wouldn't have helped Joe turning up like this. I switch on the television, pace the room flicking through the channels, unable to stay still.

Oh, God, there's the car. I go out into the hall. Joe comes in first and I gasp, my hand flying to my stomach as the knot of panic grows. He looks worse out of the hospital, pale and fragile and broken. He ignores the hand I reach out to him, holds on to Mia instead as she hovers next to him. He shrinks away from Patrick coming in behind him.

"I've got dinner ready—your favorite roast chicken," I say, wanting to hug him but unable to move.

"I'm not hungry," he mutters, still looking at the floor. "I just want to go to bed."

"The hospital gave us some medication to bring home," Patrick says, and the rustle of the hospital pharmacy bag acts like the chink of a bottle to a recovering alcoholic—my mouth goes dry and I want, so desperately want, to feed the panic with a little white pill. Joe limps upstairs with Mia trailing after him, and I'm left to follow Patrick into the kitchen, where we eat cold, dry chicken, then head silently to bed.

"Joe?" I knock on his door, hovering outside with a mug of tea for him. It's Tuesday morning and Patrick and Mia have left for work and school, Mia clearly relieved to be getting out of the house after a bank holiday weekend spent tiptoeing around, all of us hiding in separate rooms. Joe has barely spoken, barely eaten. But this is the first time in an awful lot of years it's just been me and him in the house for a whole day and maybe he'll talk to me.

He doesn't answer, so I knock again, louder. I remember the days when the children were little and there were no closed doors. When Joe would spend hours at the table with me, coloring and painting and sticking and gluing, talking nonstop, filling me in on every little detail of his day at school.

That's not the Joe who opens the door, though. This is hidden Joe, the boy who one day started shutting me out, who's been cutting his arms and living a life I know nothing about. I hate to think of him locked in there by himself, in that terrible old room of Patrick's with the peeling walls.

He opens the door a crack and I summon all my cheer, hold up the mug I'm carrying. "Tea?"

I think he's going to slam the door in my face.

"The police called earlier, to see if you've remembered anything else."

"I told them: I was mugged. They came up behind me—I didn't see anything."

"But they didn't..." They didn't take anything. Joe still had his phone and his wallet on him.

He looks down at his feet. "They must have been scared off before they robbed me."

Scared off by what?

"They want you to come into the station to give your statement. I told them you're not well enough yet. And I called the school," I say. "I've told them you won't be back until next week. I thought we could have a quiet few days and do something together."

He stares at me and I have to look away. I sometimes think, when Joe looks at me, that he'll see it all. And if he did, he'd hate me and I couldn't stand that. I'd do anything to stop it. So I step back and he laughs.

"Together?" he says. "What—will we go to the park so you can push me on the swings?"

"I thought we could paint..." My voice trails off as I look at his swollen, bruised hand. God, could I get this more wrong? It'll be weeks before he's able to pick up a brush.

"And you can forget about school," he says. "I'm not going back to school. I'm never going back to school."

I take a breath and hold it to stop more stupid words from coming out. *What about college? What about your exams?* "Can I come in?" I say instead.

He opens his door wider and I follow him inside, perching on the end of his bed.

"I'm sorry," he mutters.

"For what?"

He gestures down at his arms, hidden under the sleeves of his hoodie. "This."

"You don't need to be sorry. But I do. I should have seen, should have known."

"It doesn't have anything to do with you. I heard Mia shouting at you at the hospital, saying it was your fault. It's not."

"But would you have talked to me—if I hadn't fallen apart after your grandmother died? If I hadn't taken those pills?"

He leans back on his bed. "I don't know."

I reach for his uninjured hand and squeeze it. "But now, Joe, will you talk to me now? You used to. Couldn't we get that back?"

He looks at me, his eyes full. "You stopped being there. You stopped hearing me. Dad found out. He caught me with a boy the day Nan died. The things he said... It's why I took his fucking car. All that was going on and you knew nothing about it."

"Oh, God, Joe, I'm sorry."

"You never have room for anything but yourself and Dad, and it's gotten so much worse since we moved here."

I can tell myself over and over that this move was down to Patrick, this house is Patrick's dream... but I gave him that money. I took those pills—or, at least, everyone says I did. Us being here is down to me too. And now we're stuck because Patrick will never agree to leave and no one else would ever buy this house anyway. They'd walk through the door and feel the cold spots, sense what was behind the butterfly wallpaper. They'd see the history burned into the walls and they'd run like we should have. We're stuck in the Murder House, and I can see Mia drifting away and Joe self-destructing and Patrick losing control, and I know it's down to me and I'm overwhelmed by it. I can't see past it all to find a way out.

"You tell me to talk to you," Joe says, "but will you listen? Will you *see*?" He leans toward me. "You want to know what happened? I lied when I said I didn't remember. I was so angry with Dad I went out and... I picked someone up. He bought booze and we went to the beach to... I was so mad I was ready to have sex with some stranger right there on the beach. But I changed my mind."

"And he beat you up? God, Joe, you have to tell the police, you have to—"

"No, you don't *get* it. I started it. I had a go at him—I started the fight. I pushed him, provoked him. I said the things to him that Dad said to me. I'd gotten drunk and I was angry and hurting and wanting to hurt but, Jesus, what did I think was going to happen? Look at me—did I think I was going to win? Did I think he wouldn't fight back?"

He shakes his head. "If the police find him, he'll tell them I started it. I'll be the one arrested. He got angry and fought back, started hitting me and kicking me, and I thought I was going to die. I thought he was going to kill me. He was off his head on something and he wouldn't *stop*... but someone else was there."

I pull him toward me, not letting go when he resists. I pull him into my arms and hold him, not tight, careful of his injuries, but I don't let go. I hold him until he relaxes and lets his head drop onto my shoulder.

"Someone was watching us," he says, and my shoulder stiffens under him. "It was dark and... But I'm sure I saw someone. He watched this boy kicking me. He watched him stamp on me and scream at me and he watched me crawl back up onto the street and he did *nothing*."

"How's he been?" Patrick asks when he comes in, glancing up the stairs toward Joe's closed door.

"Fine," I say. I can't bear to look at him.

"Good," Patrick says, taking off his jacket and hooking it over the banister.

I follow him through to the kitchen, my hands clenched into fists. "Patrick? That's not true. He's not fine at all."

He sighs. "What's the problem? This will blow over. He's a teenager, that's all. He probably got dumped by a—a girlfriend."

You know, I want to scream. *You've known for months he's gay. You knew why he crashed your car and you've never said a word to me*.

"I think it's more serious than a teenage tantrum," I say, my voice rising in disbelief.

Patrick moves to the sink to fill the kettle. "Half of his problems are down to worrying about you. If you're fussing and stressing all the time, how is that supposed to help him?"

"But—"

"It makes him *weak*. Everyone has problems and everyone else deals with them without carving themselves up. This is down to where he came from and who he was before he was ours. We need to help him by being strong. Joe will be fine. Let your damn *therapist* do her job. Give him some space."

I step back from his rising voice. Careful. I have to be careful. He turns to face me and I can't help but recoil.

"For Christ's sake, Sarah, what is this?"

"Joe said someone else was there. When he got attacked. A witness. A *watcher*."

What's that look on his face? Is it fear? It's gone now, replaced by tight-lipped anger, a tic going in his cheek. I take another step back.

"*Enough*," Patrick says. "I can't deal with all this imagined nonsense right now."

Imagined? Are the scars on Joe's arms *imagined*? His fractured bones? The fact that he's refusing to go back to school?

I want to ask him about Caroline. I want to confront him. I want to ask him where he was while our son was being beaten up. But I can't.

It feels like there's ice trickling in my veins. This is my husband, the man I've loved for seventeen years, and I can't ask him because I'm scared of his reaction. I'm scared of what he might do.

There's a new lock on the cellar. Last time she opened the door, I saw it, shining silver, incongruous in the dull hallway. When I was here before, when it was just a house, there was no lock on it. You took it off. You laughed and told me you snuck down in the middle of the night and unscrewed the whole lock. You buried it deep in the back garden. You laughed as you told me about your dad's ranting confusion, how, because he woke up and saw his tools lying around, he thought he'd done it himself. You managed to convince him he was sleepwalking. Doing fucking DIY in his sleep.

"Why did you bother?" I asked. "It was just a rusty lock, wasn't it?"

You had that frown on, the bone-deep one. "Not just a lock," you said. "It's a lock that shouldn't be there, should never have been on that door."

CHAPTER 20

I'm trying to work Anna out as she paces on the sand, dressed all in black, her hair cropped even shorter than before. Joe was sleeping, so I brought her down onto the beach, where we're still in view of the house. It's been a week since the attack and this is the first time I've felt able to leave him.

"Are you okay?" she says, and she's looking at my hands, at the nails I've bitten so much the tips of my fingers are bleeding. I pull down my sleeves to hide them.

"Just worried about Joe," I say. "And Mia. And other things." I don't want to tell her about the cellar, or Caroline, or about Patrick's trouble at work. I don't think he'd like me telling other people about that. Anna stops pacing and reaches over to squeeze my hand.

"I'm so sorry about Joe. I know I said it before, but I wanted to say it again. It was awful. I saw him staggering onto the path, and I thought he was just some drunk kid, then he stopped under the streetlight and I saw the blood and I recognized him from your sketches. I'm still shaky remembering him there—God knows how you must be feeling."

"I wish we'd never moved here," I say, under my breath, not wanting to confess too loudly in case the sea breeze picks up my words and carries them to Patrick. "I've tried. I've tried really hard to make the house beautiful, but everything keeps going wrong. All Patrick wants is the perfect house he remembers—it's no wonder he's on edge."

"Perfect?"

I turn to face her. "Like it was when Patrick lived here before."

She sits down on a rock, starts scraping at the bark on a piece of driftwood. The noise of her nail on the wood sets my teeth on edge.

"I can't imagine it ever being perfect," she says, flicking a sliver of wood off the edge of her nail. "Not with the state of it before you moved in."

"He's told me what it was like." If I close my eyes, I can almost see the house as it was. Patrick has told me about it so many times: the soft, muted colors bathed in flickering firelight, the smells, fresh flowers and furniture polish.

"Still, anyone would be edgy, wouldn't they?" she says. "With so much to do to make the house *perfect*."

How much do I want to say here? Will voicing my hidden fears make them bigger? But she's smiling at me so warmly, and she brought flowers with her today, a huge bunch of sweetpeas, whose heady scent is now filling the house. "A couple of times, he's gotten a little... upset."

"Upset?" She raises her eyebrows.

"It's nothing, really. Like I said, he's been on edge."

"Do the police have any idea what happened to Joe?" she asks as I perch on a rock next to her.

"He thought it was a mugging, a random attack." Anna doesn't need to know.

"Do you think he really doesn't remember? Or is it that he doesn't *want* to remember?"

Unease is making the hairs on my arms rise. "Why do you care so much?"

She shrugs. "I can see the worry on your face every time you talk about Joe."

"Joe thought he saw someone—someone watching him get attacked—and I worried, for a while, if Patrick might have been there."

"Patrick?"

I nod.

"Because he was upset?" she says. "By upset, do you mean angry? Angry enough to go chasing after Joe? For what?"

"Not like that...I'm wrong. I'm being silly. Joe was half-conscious. He doesn't properly remember anything. And, besides, you were there, weren't you? Joe probably saw you and—"

"I didn't see the attack, Sarah. I saw Joe collapse, but I didn't see anything else."

I shouldn't have said anything. What I'm insinuating is...It's monstrous. No wonder Anna's looking at me like I'm bloody mad. Do I really believe Patrick would have been there and done nothing? Before the move, I would have said it was impossible. Patrick doesn't lose his temper. Patrick doesn't lose control. But, here, I can't help wondering what he'd have done if he had followed Joe that night and found him with a boy again.

No. God, better it be Ian Hooper watching. Anyone but Patrick.

Anna stares at me and her foot digs into the sand. "Don't take this the wrong way, Sarah, but I used to have this boyfriend," she says. "He'd get...*upset* and he'd hit me. It got to the stage where I knew—I *knew*—if I didn't leave, he'd end up killing me. I see you, and you have the same look in your eyes that greeted me in the mirror every day. Have you gotten to that stage?"

"No, he's never..."

"I used to pretend it wasn't happening too. Pretend every time was a one-off, pretend every time was the last time because every time he promised he'd never do it again. I let him hit me for too long, but if I'd had kids, I'd never have let him hurt them."

It's like a slap in the face and I gasp, sucking in the sand her foot sent spinning. "I haven't let him—"

"Why don't you leave?"

"What?"

"Why don't you take your kids and leave? Stay with a friend, go to a shelter—whatever."

"I can't. I don't need to. God, Anna, he's never *hit* us. He never would. *Never*. He's stressed, that's all, with the house and Joe and...other things. He needs help, not all of us abandoning him."

"So what are you going to do?"

"What do you mean?"

"You're going to sit here in the Murder House, waiting for him to put your kids in the hospital again?"

"No—of course not. He didn't *do* anything. He swore—"

"But you thought he could have. Might have."

I shake my head in denial but don't say anything else in protest because I have been wondering that, haven't I? I lie awake at night wondering about it, wondering about his growing fear and paranoia, wondering about the cellar. I imagine him lurking in the shadows, watching Joe kiss a boy and I wonder…God, I think the *worst* things.

"I can see the fear in your face. You have to find a way to do something about it before something really *does* happen. Because, Sarah? I know this—I've been there. Something worse always happens."

Anna pulls up her sleeves and turns her arms over to show me two silvery white scars running up her wrists and forearms. "It all got to be too much one day and I decided I'd rather be dead than keep living like that. God, he'd reduced me so much that killing myself seemed an easier option than leaving him." She looks up at me. "Don't ever let a man reduce you to that, Sarah."

My throat closes at the sight of those thin white scars. "It's not like that for me," I say. "I think it's the move. This house, that's all."

She leans forward and I recoil from her scarred arms, as if they might be catching. "You really believe it's all because of the house?"

"I want to move, but Patrick won't even consider it."

"Then maybe it's time you considered moving *without* Patrick. After your exhibition, take any money you make and go."

I know she means well, but Joe's not mine. If I leave, my mind whispers, Patrick will tell Joe the truth and I'll lose my boy.

A gust of wind tugs at her scarf and she ties it tighter. It's the black scarf with the white stars. I remember her picking me up the night Joe got attacked. She was wearing it and it had come untied. It floated in my face as she pulled me up.

"What were you doing?"

She frowns at me. "What?"

"The night Joe got attacked. You were there; you called the ambulance. What were you doing outside our house?"

She leans back and pulls down her sleeves. "Don't make me the villain of this, Sarah."

I check on Joe when I get back to the house. He's still sleeping, hunched on his side. I wonder if he's managing to sleep at night or if, like Mia, bad dreams make it impossible. I tiptoe downstairs to the hall. Patrick has left the key in the cellar door. I haven't painted all week because I've been staying at home with Joe. The exhibition is looming closer. The canvases Patrick put down in the cellar: I saw them stacked in the corner the night I caught him painting the walls. I need to get them to the studio. I rummage in the hall table drawer for a flashlight.

It's only mid-afternoon, but I still look out of the window for Patrick's car before I open the cellar door. It's not that it's out of bounds for any reason, but I've been careful not to mention my canvases since the day he burned my sketchbooks, and without confessing about the exhibition, how would I explain what I was doing in a cellar I've so far done all I can to avoid visiting?

I feel sick when I go down the stairs—three of the four walls are now painted, the floor's been swept and most of the rubbish stacked against the unpainted wall. When had he done the rest? How many nights has he been sneaking down here, painting walls? And why? Why the cellar when there's a whole house that needs painting?

Under the fresh paint, though, there's still the smell of damp, a fusty, unmistakable mix of mildew and ammonia. When I get closer to the first wall he painted and shine the flashlight on it, my breath comes out in a whoosh. It's worse, so much worse. Before Patrick painted, the walls had brown water stains, like tide marks, and a few darker spots in the corners. Now, against the white, great black-and-green flowers of mold bloom, as if the paint has made everything worse, not better. The walls are cold and it feels as if there's only a thin layer of paint between my hand and running water.

I step away from the wall and try to imagine bringing him down here later, pointing out how he wasted his time, how he gave up a whole night's sleep for nothing. As I turn away to find the canvases, the flashlight's thin beam hits the base of the wall he's yet to paint. I step closer. What did I see?

There's an old wooden table stacked with boxes pushed against the wall. Above the table, it is beige and damp-spotted, like the others were. But the flashlight beam caught something else in its low sweep.

I crouch and duck under the table. The cellar seems to get colder as the light shines on the wall. It's writing—the same words written over and over again in the same childish hand.

I've been bad. I've been very bad. I've been bad. I've been very bad.

I think of the kids who lived in this house before as I shine the light along the wall. The back of my neck prickles, hairs rising. It's written all the way along, fifteen feet of wall. *I've been bad. I've been very bad.*

Did Patrick see this? Is this why he stopped painting? As I straighten up and brush dust off my jeans, all I can think about is the height chart, the cold spots, toys that appear from nowhere. As I run up the stairs and lock the cellar door, I'm followed by a ghost's voice whispering those words. A little boy's voice. *I've been bad. I've been very bad.*

CHAPTER 21

I trip over Mia's schoolbag as I step into the hall. I didn't hear her come in—did she see me in the cellar? I run upstairs, cold from finding the writing on the wall. The bathroom door is closed, but Mia's is ajar and I can see clothes scattered across her floor. Did she realize I was down in the cellar and come up here to hide? No—it can't be her writing on the cellar wall. Why would she? But the jittery fear won't go as I gather up the clothes, frowning at how much there is I don't recognize.

There's money on her dressing-table too—coins in small piles and some crumpled notes. More than fifty pounds in fives and tens. I think of my mother's jewelry box. She wouldn't. But if not Mia, then who? Patrick?

"What are you doing?"

I spin around. Mia is all scowls, folded arms, and hunched shoulders. But underneath the truculent teenager pose, she's pale and tired. Her nails are as bitten-down as mine and her eyes are red-rimmed.

"I was picking up your laundry and I saw..." I nod at the money and she pushes past me, picking up the notes and stuffing them into her pocket.

"Where did you get it?" I say.

"What's it got to do with you?"

"I want to know how my fifteen-year-old daughter has this much money lying around when I know damn well it didn't come from me."

She laughs. "Oh, right—I get it. You think I stole it? You think I've been going through your purse?"

"I didn't say that. I'm asking where it came from because there's clearly something going on and after Joe..."

Her head jerks at my mention of Joe's name and mutters something I don't hear.

"What?"

"Dad gave it to me."

Patrick hasn't said anything. I told him about my mother's jewelry. I told him my concerns about Mia and her new clothes, and he hasn't said a word about giving her money.

"Why?"

"Because he cares, that's why. Because he gives a shit about me."

But why hasn't he mentioned it? That's what I'm really asking. Why hasn't he mentioned it when we're so skint he frowns if I come back from the supermarket with too many bags?

Mia won't meet my eyes as she sweeps up the piles of coins. I reach out and put a hand over hers, but she pulls away.

"Can you get out of my room, please?" she mutters.

Joe comes in as I turn toward the door. "What's going on?"

He still looks so bruised and fragile. I want to ask them both if they've been down in the cellar, but then I'd have to tell them about the writing and I can't. I can't add my fears to theirs.

We freeze as the front door opens and we hear Patrick calling up.

"Mum was just leaving—weren't you, Mum?" Mia says.

She barely waits for me to step onto the landing before she slams the door.

Patrick's standing in front of the locked cellar door, a plastic-wrapped roller and tray in one hand, a can of white paint in the other. From the top of the stairs, I can see the edge of light around the door frame. Shit. I left the cellar light on, left the flashlight sitting on the hall table.

"Have you been in the cellar?"

"I thought I could continue with the painting," I say, avoiding his stare as I come down the stairs.

My heart's thumping as he puts down the paint and unlocks

the door. Why did I lie? He's going to see I haven't done anything. He's going to see my footprints in the dust by the unpainted wall.

I think of this morning, when he was struggling with that bloody window in the kitchen and the handle came off in his hand. His *rage*... Disproportionate, it shocked Mia, who cringed away when he flung the damn thing toward the bin. It went nowhere near her, of course, but... That was just a window handle.

"Wait," I say, following him in. "I found something."

I go down the stairs ahead of him, switch on the flashlight, and shine it onto the wall he'd left unpainted. The damp, clinging and cold, creeps into my veins when the light shines on the scribbled words.

Patrick doesn't react. He stands motionless at the top of the stairs, staring at the words highlighted in the flashlight's beam.

"You must have seen it when you were down here painting. I wondered if it could have been Joe or Mia, but it's not their handwriting. So I thought it must have been..."

He comes down the stairs and stands next to me, his arm brushing mine. "It was just some kid playing about," he says softly, and all the hairs rise on the back of my neck.

I realize, as he says this, that before Tom and Billy Evans, the last child to live here was Patrick.

"A kid?"

"I'd forgotten," he says, and he reaches to touch the wall.

Forgotten? I look at the wall, the scrawled child's writing stretched all the way across. *I've been bad. I've been very bad.* How could he have forgotten?

The air seems to have gotten thicker. It's harder to breathe. "You wrote it?"

He glances over at me. "Of course I didn't," he says, a smile on his face. "You know what my childhood was like—do you really think I'd be down in the cellar scribbling on walls?"

But his smile isn't real. It's big and wide and entirely false.

"Sarah?" he says as we walk back up the stairs. "Don't—don't worry about painting down here, okay? We have enough to do in the rest of the house." He locks the door and looks down at the key in his hand. "I'll go and put this away somewhere safe."

I wake up in the middle of the night, my throat dry, my head pounding, caught in the aftermath of a dream I can't quite remember. I reach for the glass on my bedside table and gasp, knocking the water over when I see a shadow at the window. Then the shadow turns and I see it's Patrick, naked and only half-covered by the curtain, staring out into the night. He puts a finger to his lips, then beckons me to him, frowning when I hesitate. I step over the puddle of water as I join him.

"What is it?" I say, and he points at something across the street. I move closer to the window and squint into the darkness. A shadow detaches itself from the black, forms into a figure, and retreats. I blink but can't see anything else. The shadows shift and move as the clouds play peek-a-boo with the moon.

"Is it a person?"

Patrick nods. "Every so often the clouds clear and I can see him. He's been there for hours."

"Hours? How do you know?"

"I got up before midnight...I thought I heard something. He was there then."

I glance at the clock—it's ten past three. Has Patrick been standing here the whole time? I reach out to touch his arm. It's like ice.

"Come back to bed," I whisper, but he shakes his head. The shadows move again, but it no longer looks like a person. The street is empty. No one is out at three in the morning in the wind and rain.

"Patrick, are you sure someone's there?"

He steps fully in front of the window, not even trying to cover himself with the curtain. "Someone's watching the house. You were right the first night. Someone's watching us."

CHAPTER 22

I take a plate of toast up to Joe on Monday morning, after Patrick and Mia have left, to find him struggling to put his shoes on with his injured hand.

"Let me help," I say, putting the plate on the desk. I crouch and loosen his laces so he can slide his feet in, then tie them in a double bow.

"Are you going out? I could come with you." I put my hand on his, careful of his still-bruised fingers, but he pulls away.

"*Don't*," he says. "I don't want—I don't need my mother doing everything for me, following me around. Isn't it bad enough I can't do my own fucking shoes up?"

I step back from the frustrated anger in his voice. "I'm sorry. I only want to help."

"I know you do, but I don't need it. It's been ten days...I have to get out of this house. I feel like I can't breathe in here."

"But you shouldn't be on your own."

"I won't be. I'm meeting a friend. He's coming up from Cardiff."

"He?"

"Stop it, Mum. I can't stand the constant worry in your voice. I'm not going to get into trouble again, okay?"

I follow him to the door, trying to resist the urge to cling to him, beg him to stay home and safe. God, he's right. He's going to be eighteen in less than seven months and I'm acting like he's five, cutting up his toast and tying his shoes. But it's so hard watching him walk away when the fading bruises from the attack are still on his face.

He's right to get out of the house too. The silence when they've all gone is so *full*...I'm alone but I hear footsteps above me, the creak of floorboards. I know it's an old house settling, but here alone, it's a restless ghost pacing upstairs; it's Marie Evans, covered with blood; it's Billy Evans, playing with his *Star Wars* figures. It's a child scribbling on the walls of a dark cellar. I hear the quiet click of a door and freeze, my heart pounding. Just the wind, the crap windows letting in a sea breeze, like a breath that opens and closes doors. Not a ghost. Just the wind. But it doesn't stop me from staring at the kitchen door, waiting for one of the ghosts to appear.

There's a knock at the front door and I jump, my hand jerking and spilling tea on the table. I expect to see Mia on the doorstep, moaning about forgotten books and keys, but I gasp when I open the door because it *is* a ghost.

I realize my mistake in seconds—it's a grown-up Tom Evans, not the ghost of a little boy conjured by my own haunted thoughts, but it doesn't stop my heart from pounding, and it's too late to hide my gasp and lurch backward. He flinches and steps away.

"I'm sorry," he mutters. "I waited until your family left."

"What are you doing here?" I want to slam the door in his face and run away, my mind still full of ghosts and murder, but what if the neighbors see him standing there, see me slamming the door on him? Will they recognize him as I did? Some will have known the Evans family in real life, not just from newspaper stories. I almost told Patrick after I saw Tom up on the cliff path, almost confessed what I've invited into our lives, but there was never a good moment. And then Joe got attacked and I caught Patrick painting the cellar, found the writing and— I just can't. I can't add to whatever it is that's leaching away the Patrick I know.

"I wanted to see the house again," Tom says, and as he speaks, I think he might cry.

I don't see a ghost anymore. I see a broken little boy who never grew up. I can picture that broken boy writing on a cellar wall and, God, do I want it to be him, not Patrick? Do I want to imagine any lost boy scribbling such horrible words? I open the door wider. "Come in."

He takes a deep breath and steps into the hall, tensing as I close the door behind him. The outside world disappears and it's the two of us alone in the Murder House. I wonder if his heart is beating as hard as mine. He moves closer to me, too close, but I'm right by the wall and I can't back away.

"I haven't been back in here since..." He blinks. "I couldn't. I knew my grandparents arranged for it to be cleared and decorated, but I couldn't. I thought it would be so different with a family in it again. I thought I could see it and it might finally take away the images in my head."

His shoulder brushes against my hair as he turns away.

"When it was empty I used to come here and stand outside," he says, touching the dip in the wall by the stairs. "I always had the key in my pocket, but I could never use it, never bear to come in."

I go cold. How often has he been back since we moved in, standing outside? We decided not to spend the money to get the locks changed. Does he still have a key to the house where my family and I sleep?

"It was so old-fashioned when we moved in," he says, peering into the living room, "but Dad had all these plans to make it modern. All he seemed to do was wreck it. The colors he chose were ugly and he was terrible at painting and DIY. It drove him mad that everything he did made it worse, not better."

His gaze drifts to the still-visible height chart by the door. I wait for him to say something. He reaches out to trace his wobbly initials and I can see his hand is shaking, but he doesn't speak. He clenches it into a fist when he pulls it away from the wall.

He wanders into the kitchen and I follow. "Old Mr. Walker actually came around once, after Dad ripped out the dark wood stuff in the kitchen. Me and Billy thought he was going to have a fit and die right there on the path, he was so mad at Dad. He was shouting and ranting and tried to push his way in. I thought Dad was going to punch him."

Patrick's father? I can't imagine Patrick's father shouting at anyone. He seemed such a quiet, small man the few times I met him.

"Can I...can I see upstairs?" he asks.

I don't want him upstairs. I don't want him walking through my bedroom. I'm already wishing I hadn't let him in.

But he doesn't wait for a response—he's already heading for the stairs.

I jump when I hear a car door slam, imagining Patrick coming through the door, finding Tom Evans in his house with his wife. But Patrick will be safely at work now.

I follow Tom upstairs and find him standing in the doorway of Joe's room.

"This is where I was. I'd taken Billy's *Star Wars* toys again. He never liked me borrowing them. I'd take them without asking and play under my bed so he wouldn't catch me. I did that so many times when I had bad dreams and couldn't sleep. Played under my bed, soothed out of the bad dreams by Mum's wind chimes in the tree outside."

I shiver. "Wind chimes?"

"Yeah, she had loads of them. I don't know what happened to them after..." He looks lost again and those scribbled words are back in my head. *I've been bad, I've been very bad...*

"Tom, did you or your brother ever write on the cellar wall?"

"Write? What do you mean?"

"I found writing on the wall and I wondered. I thought it had to be you or Billy. No one's been here since."

There's a short silence. "No. We were never allowed in the cellar. Dad always kept it locked."

He moves out of the room and I pause there, pressing a hand to my stomach. It hurts, a nagging nauseous ache. I rub my eyes. God, I'm so tired. So tired of thinking and worrying.

When I leave the room, Tom's not on the landing and the nausea rises higher when I find him in my room. He's picked up my sketchbook and is flicking through the pages. "This isn't your husband," he says, gazing at a scribbled sketch I've done of Ben.

I snatch the book away. "Okay, I think that's enough now."

"It's starting again, isn't it?"

"What are you talking about?"

He steps closer and I back away until I'm pressed up against the wall.

"I'm sorry," he says. He bows his head and he's standing so close it almost rests on my rigid shoulder. "I sold the house to Patrick because he *knows*... I was angry and I wanted the house to make him admit what he knows. I didn't think about you and your children."

"What are you talking about?"

"You shouldn't stay here," he says. "It keeps happening. The same thing's going to happen. This house... Bad things happen to people who live in this house."

"You need to leave." My voice is steady, but my hands are shaking.

Oh, God, what have I done? I should never have gotten in touch with him, never have invited him into the house. What does he mean, Patrick knows? Knows what? I need to ask Patrick, but that means telling him about Tom.

I step back from the easel to look at the finished painting. I've painted Anna's secret beach, all those muted, beautiful colors, building them up in layers so it appears almost abstract. Step to the side and a whole new level of color appears, highlighted by the dying light coming through the window. Wiping my brush on a rag, I walk over to look out. The sky has clouded—it's going to rain. I check the time. Patrick will be home soon and I still need to shop. I clear away reluctantly. The longer I spend here, the harder it becomes to go back to the house. When I'm here, painting, I'm able to push everything else to the back of my mind, but the moment I leave, it comes back: Tom Evans, the house, worry about Joe, about Mia, about Patrick.

Ben was right: this is a sanctuary. But now it's time to go back to my real life. I make sure all the paint is scrubbed from my hands, lock the studio, and head for the supermarket.

I'm halfway back from the shop when I see it. Outside a jeweler's, I'm checking my list to see if I've forgotten anything.

I'd never normally bother looking in the window—it's all twenty-grand engagement rings and heavy gold jewel-encrusted stuff—but something is nagging, something I've seen in the corner of my eye. I step back and there it is: my mother's engagement ring, nestled in the middle of the section marked "vintage," pride of place on a blue velvet cushion, price tag tied to it.

I move closer and gasp. When I breathe out it fogs the window. As I wipe my hand across the glass, I want to be wrong. I want to see an emerald, not a diamond. I want to be mistaken. But I'm not. It's my mother's ring, tied to a price we could never afford to pay. I put down the shopping bag. This dinner was supposed to be a peace offering, Patrick's favorite meal, before I confess that I've invited Tom Evans into our lives and now I can't get rid of him.

I waver there for what seems like forever, then I turn right instead of left to go home. I walk down onto the beach and all the way to the water's edge. I kick off my shoes, scrunching sand between my toes, liking the salty smell of the sea, the sound of the waves washing over the pebbles at the shoreline.

I have to make a decision. I have to stop hoping everything's going to turn out all right on its own and make a decision.

It's beginning to rain and the few people who were on the beach are leaving. I look down at my empty hands. I left my shopping outside the jeweler's. It gets darker, darker than it should be at this hour, as the clouds get heavier and the wind picks up.

My scarf flutters and is snatched away by a gust of wind powerful enough to make me stagger. I spin to reach for it, but someone gets there first. It's Ben, a big smile on his face.

"I thought it was you," he says. "I live in the cottage up there, and I saw you walking down the beach." He's pointing up to a house on the hill. One of a row of cottages I sometimes daydream about living in.

Ben has phoned twice since I went to the gallery, leaving messages about my exhibition. I haven't returned his calls.

"The rain's getting heavier," Ben says. "The café's still open. Do you want to get coffee?"

I shouldn't. I really shouldn't. I should go collect that shopping and head home and cook like a good wife. But I think of Patrick and the house waiting for me, Tom waiting outside with a key in his pocket. I think of the ring in the window of the jewelry shop. I think of the decision I have to make.

"Why not?" I say.

"I thought you were avoiding me. I've seen you coming and going to the studio, but you never drop in to say hello."

He says this as he brings weak tea in stained white mugs over from the counter. The plastic tablecloth is sticky when I peel my arm off it to make room for the mugs. The rain is pelting the windows, the wind rattling the door. Every so often, someone else is blown in, windswept and dripping, seeking shelter. The windows are steaming up.

"It's not personal. There are…things going on at home. It's complicated. But I am painting. Anna convinced me to go all out for this solo exhibition."

"I'm glad," he says. "I'm glad I came over as well. I saw you on the beach and I assumed it was your husband with you so I nearly didn't."

I frown, lifting my tea. "I wasn't with anyone."

Ben shrugs, confused. "He was a few steps behind you, but since he'd walked with you all the way from town down onto the sand I assumed…"

I put down my mug without taking a drink. Tom. It was Tom fucking Evans following me. In the wind, I wouldn't have heard anyone walking behind me and I was so preoccupied, thinking about my mother's ring. Was he waiting outside the studio the whole time I was there? Is he outside watching now?

Ben puts out a paint-spattered hand and touches mine. "Sorry—I must have been mistaken. But either way I'm glad I came over."

Someone walks past the café window just as our hands touch and I imagine how this would seem if it were Patrick. I move, but part of me is tempted to leave my hand there for all to see.

A girl comes over to take our cups, pausing to turn the Open sign to Closed. The wind rattles the door again.

"It doesn't look like it's stopping anytime soon and they want to close up here. Why don't you wait it out in my cottage?" Ben says, pulling his jacket back on.

I shouldn't. I should be back at home, cooking, figuring out how to explain about Tom Evans. I should be home before Patrick or I'll have to come up with a whole new lie to explain where I've been.

"Why not?" I say again.

"Do you need to phone home, let them know where you are?" he asks as we stand at the front door of his cottage, waiting for him to unlock it.

I don't answer and he pushes open the door, walking in ahead of me. It opens directly into the sitting room, dimly lit by a wood-burning stove in the corner.

"I know it's ridiculous lighting it in May, but there's something about a stormy night..."

He gets a wine bottle and two glasses from a drink-ringed dark wood cabinet. I see paint under his fingernails as he hands me a glass filled with red wine. Cobalt Blue, Cadmium Red. It's a sight so familiar and so strange. It fills me with nostalgia for a time when everyone I knew had paint under their nails, smelled of turpentine and linseed oil, sweet rolling tobacco and cheap booze. Giddy days when I'd lurch from excitement to fear at how overwhelming and different my life had become, when a part of me longed to run home to the stifling safety of my mother.

Ben's telling me about his new series of paintings as we dry out in front of the fire—lost to me, his eyes turned inward to whatever he's creating in his studio. I imagine kissing him, pushing myself against his rain-soaked T-shirt, imagine the solid feel of his chest and belly.

What is this—a fantasy? Revenge for the hurt of what Patrick did with Caroline? A betrayal that festers inside me because I'm too scared to confront him? Is that why I'm sitting here with Ben, sipping wine, close enough to kiss, trying to stop myself from stroking the shorn ends of his hair?

I'm the same as Mia, yearning for someone to come riding in on a white horse to rescue us. I'd thought, with the painting, with the exhibition, that I was doing it this time. That I was the one doing the rescuing. So why am I here?

My gaze lands on a bowl of shells on his coffee table.

Ben shifts closer and I jump up, put my wine on the table. "I'd better go," I say. "I think the worst of the storm's passed."

The door to his studio is ajar and I go toward it as I put my coat on, intrigued by a glimpse of the canvas I see propped up on the easel in there. It looks dark: a large, swirling painting, so unlike his usual calm seascapes and still lifes.

"Can I see?" I ask, and he hesitates. But then he nods and pushes the door open.

It's a painting of two boys, children, but I recognize the half-shadowed face of the one on the left. It's Patrick.

I step away, almost stumbling, recoiling not only from the painting but from the artist. I'm alone with a stranger in his house and no one knows I'm here.

"I told you I used to know him," Ben says, halting my stumbling escape. I'm halfway to the door and I stop, turning to stare at him, at the painting still revealed through the open door.

"Is the other boy you?" I ask, and he nods. "You said you weren't friends, that you were just at school together."

"We were friends once, for a while. I met you and it got me thinking about him," he says. "It got me remembering everything because I could see there was something wrong."

"What?"

"I saw it that first day when you showed me your paintings. I saw it again when you came to the gallery. It's why I offered you the studio." He pauses. "I don't...I haven't seen Patrick for a long time, not since we grew apart as kids."

"You could have reintroduced yourself to him. You should have told me you were friends."

He frowns. "We didn't end up on the best of terms. It wasn't a friendship I wanted to revisit."

"But befriending his wife behind his back is okay?"

He shrugs. "I never asked you to keep me a secret. The fact you have proves I was right. Something's wrong."

He takes a step toward me, reaches out an arm, letting it fall before his hand touches me. Did he see me flinch?

"The studio was an apartment once," he says. "Basic, but livable. It could be again; I don't mind."

Here he is again, this stranger, offering me an escape. Offering me sanctuary.

"Well, I don't need anywhere to live. I have a house."

"I never thought he'd come back," Ben says. "When I came past the house and saw you, I worried for you even before I knew you."

He comes closer and touches my hair. I shut my eyes and imagine letting him kiss me, imagine going home to Patrick with the smell of my artist on me. Would that be enough to take away the sting of my mother's stolen jewelry, the aching hurt that my husband might have taken it, or of Caroline kissing Patrick? But this painting... *Is it you?* I want to ask. *Is it you, with your bowl of shells and paintings of Patrick, watching the house, leaving things on the doorstep? You, not Ian Hooper or Tom Evans? You, so suddenly friendly and always there.*

"I have to go," I say again, pulling away from him. I let the wind push me faster and faster as I leave, until I'm almost running.

I shouldn't have stayed out so late. And I should have gone back via the jewelry shop to see if my shopping bag was still there—come in brandishing groceries and tales of long checkout lines as an alibi. But I didn't think, I just went. Now I have to think. I hear footsteps echoing my own as I walk toward the house, the same reluctant, slow steps, getting slower as I approach the house.

When I look around, though, no one's there. A box sits on the doorstep. When I bend down to pick it up, I see an envelope taped to the top with *Sarah* written on it in scrawling, unfamiliar handwriting. I look around again, but the night has got darker, clouds covering the moon and stars, so even if someone is out there, I can't see them. I swallow and push the front door open.

I feel a hand tugging at my coat and I jump.

"Where were you?" Patrick's pulling off my coat.

"With a friend, someone I met in town," I say, and something, an expression I can't read, flashes across his face. His hands come down to rest on my shoulders, and in our reflection in the mirror they seem to be resting around my neck. But they're not squeezing, they're stroking, and somehow that's worse as I lie to his reflected eyes. Can he smell the oil paint? Did I scrub away the evidence hard enough?

"Is it the woman you mentioned? Anna, wasn't it?"

I hesitate, and for a second the hands do squeeze. "Yes, that's right. We had coffee in town."

The hands are stroking again, up to my neck, down my arms. I close my eyes.

"You wouldn't lie to me, would you, Sarah?" he whispers.

"Of course not."

"What's this?" he says, picking up the box.

"I don't know—it was outside." I reach for it, but he pulls it away from me, tugging off the envelope and crumpling it up.

"Don't," he says. "I think it's from an ex-coworker. Someone I got fired."

"But—"

"Forget about it."

But the envelope had my name on it, not his. He turns to leave and I grab his arm. "Patrick, wait." He glances back at me.

I want to confront him about the jewelry, demand an explanation. But now is not the time. I need to tell him about Tom Evans and I have no idea how he's going to react.

"I've done something stupid." The words come out in a rush. I want Patrick to reassure me, to make things right, like he always did.

He doesn't give me the indulgent smile he used to when I'd confess some silly cock-up. He looks at me warily. "What?"

"When I found out Ian Hooper was out of prison, I—I contacted Tom Evans." My heart is fluttering as I wait for his reaction. "I only wanted some answers," I say into the silence. "I panicked. But..."

"But what?"

"I think...he came to the house. And there's something strange about him. He was...He scared me."

Patrick stares at me. "What exactly did you expect, Sarah? You thought you could have a nice little chat about the man who murdered his entire family and that would be it? He'd make the bad man go away and everyone would live happily ever after?"

"No, of course not—I wanted to understand..." I take a breath. "Why did he sell now? Just as Ian Hooper gets out?"

"He sold because he needs the money. Why else? Even if he did sell because Hooper was released, does that matter? He's a disturbed, traumatized little boy and it was incredibly stupid of you to go to him."

"He's not a boy anymore."

"He'll always be a boy. Permanently damaged by what happened. What are you looking for, Sarah? Another boy to save because you failed Joe?"

I flinch as if he'd slapped me. "Don't you *dare*. That's not what this is. He said something else—something about you. About how you were friends with his father and that you know something."

"Know what? He was a kid when it happened. What exactly is it he thinks I know?"

"You tell me," I say, and hold my breath.

Patrick shakes his head. "Can you hear yourself? Can you hear how paranoid you sound? Fucking *hell*," he says. "I do not *need* this at the moment." He stops and sighs. "Okay. Do you have his number? Give it to me. I'll have a word, make him back off. I'll sort it out."

He's doing what I wanted, telling me that he'll sort out my mess, but I don't feel reassured. He hasn't answered my questions. I feel unsettled, fluttering nerves worse than when Tom was at the front door. As Patrick exhales in an angry sigh, I freeze. I can smell alcohol on his breath, a familiar sour-sweet smell but unfamiliar and wrong because Patrick doesn't drink. I've never smelled it on him.

"You're determined to ruin this, aren't you? Determined to destroy every effort I make?" he says as he copies Tom's number into his own phone. "I've done all this for you, Sarah—moved us here, fresh start, a new life. I've done it all for you and you're *ruining* it."

He's done it for me? Moved us to the Murder House? How could I ever have thought for a second this could be the solution to our problems? It's as realistic an idea as twelve-year-old me wishing a doll's house could become real.

"What are you going to do?" I step closer to him and there it is again. Not just a hint, it's a waft, strong and heady. Spirits, whiskey or brandy.

He frowns. "What do you think I'm going to do? I'm going to talk to him—make him see that stalking my wife is not acceptable behavior."

I feel a ridiculous urge to warn Tom, which is stupid. Tom's the one I'm worried about, not Patrick. But...

"Patrick?" I call as he walks away. "Have you..." My voice dies.

"What?"

I swallow past the dryness in my throat. "Have you been drinking?"

I feel sick as I watch his face twist. I shouldn't have asked. I was mistaken. It wasn't alcohol on his breath, it was—

"Yes," he says, then walks away, shutting the living room door behind him.

CHAPTER 23

I'm drifting off to sleep when I hear the front door slam. The floating, almost asleep part of my mind tells me to ignore it, to keep drifting, to dream.

But it's late. I open my eyes and sit up. It's way past eleven, nearly midnight. Who's going out at this time? It's a school night, a work night. I'm reaching for my dressing gown when I hear the first raised voice. Mia's, answered by Patrick, not as loud but getting louder.

I rush out onto the landing, tying my belt. Joe is out of his room too and I see he's fully dressed. He disappears into his room every night after dinner, shuts the door tight behind him, only Mia welcome to knock and go in.

"Wait up here," I say to him, putting out a warning hand.

Mia and Patrick are in the hall. Mia has her jacket on, a full face of makeup that looks smeared and blurry. It's end-of-night makeup, not sneaking-out makeup, and for a second I'm relieved. Then I realize it means she sneaked out earlier.

I look back at Joe and he shrugs. I think of all the nights she goes into his room, and his window, with the tree outside, that Patrick used to sneak out from. Not evenings spent together then, brother and sister, making me feel better, imagining them looking out for each other. Instead, Joe's been on his own and Mia's been out until God knows what time. Is that why Joe is still up now? Waiting to let her back in?

Patrick has hold of Mia's arm and I can see as I go halfway down the stairs that he's holding too tightly: she's wincing and his knuckles are white.

"Patrick."

He whirls to face me. "Did you know she was out?"

"No, of course not. She was in her room earlier. Mia, where have you been?"

"I was locking up and I saw her walking past the house to go up around the back. Almost midnight, when we thought she was in bed asleep, she's out walking the streets looking like *this*." He shakes her and she stumbles.

She smells of alcohol and cigarette smoke, her jeans are sandy, the hems wet and dark. Her feet are bare and she's carrying those high-heeled shoes in her free hand.

"Bloody hell, I was just meeting some friends at the beach," she says, pulling her arm away from Patrick. "Like *you* used to do—you told us so." She drops the shoes and rubs her arm where Patrick held her.

"I never went out at this time, in this state. You're drunk," Patrick says, in the soft voice that makes me want to run back upstairs and pull a pillow over my head. "You stink of smoke and you're drunk and you're staggering around in the middle of the night." He leans over and wipes his hand across her face, smearing the eyeliner and red lipstick. "All this crap on your face, you look like a cheap prostitute."

I gasp. It's intrusive, intimate, the way his hand presses over her mouth and eyes. I was right about a younger Mia being hidden under the mask of makeup, but this isn't how I wanted her back, a frightened, cowering child. Where's the smile? Where's the singing, smiling girl?

This—his hand distorting her features, dragging at her skin—is a violation, and I'm running down the rest of the stairs, shouting, half-incoherent, *Don't, don't you dare!* and now they're all looking at me, breathing heavily as I wrench his arm away from her face.

"Don't." A whisper this time.

I turn to Mia and reach for her, but she pushes me away hard enough to make me stagger. "Get *off* me," she says, and pushes me again. "Don't pretend you care what the fuck I get up to all of a sudden."

Her face is twisted in anger, but there are tears in her eyes as she looks at her father. "I could have walked out of the house naked for all the notice any of you take of me. It's all *her*—her and this bloody *house*."

"How did you get out?" Patrick says. "When did you go out?"

Her eyes flicker toward Joe, hiding in the shadows at the top of the stairs, and Patrick turns to stare at him. "I should have known it would be your fault."

"Dad, come on—Joe didn't know where I was," Mia says.

"Stop lying for him, Mia. Why are you still up and dressed?" he says to Joe. "Have you been out as well? What—you climbed the tree back in and left your sister to get into trouble?"

Joe's shaking his head. "I haven't been anywhere."

"Liar. You'd think you'd have learned your lesson."

"I fucking *haven't been anywhere*." Joe's come halfway down the stairs and Patrick steps toward him.

"Patrick," I say, stepping in front of him, making him look at me. "Patrick, calm down. Let's all sit and talk about this *calmly*. I'll make some tea and—"

"I don't want any fucking tea," he says.

"Watch out, Dad," Mia says behind me. "Don't want to bloody upset *her*—she might try to kill herself again."

Patrick spins back around, pushing me out of the way. "Shut up," he says, his voice rising. "Shut your dirty mouth."

Mia gasps. "For fuck's sake, it's true. It's not me who's the problem; it's her. That's all you bloody care about anymore." Her words end on a scream as Patrick lunges toward her.

Joe and I both lurch forward. Joe grabs Patrick's arm with his good hand and I reach for Mia, wrapping her in my arms, cuddling her, cradling her. She fights for a moment, then relaxes, holding me as hard as I hold her, her breath hot in my ear. I hold on to my daughter and we cringe against the wall.

"Patrick, stop. Stop it. Stop now," I say, and Mia's crying, weeping, and I think that gets in. I think that's what stops him.

He's shaking and Joe has to hold on less tight. "Okay," I mutter.

"Okay, we're all okay now." I don't know what the hell I'm saying. I'm shaking as much as he is and Mia's still crying, and when I look, Joe has sunk down onto the bottom stair and is holding his head in his hands.

Joe follows me into Mia's room. This was one of the first we finished decorating. Patrick did most of it, painting the walls apple-white and putting a new pink-and-pale-green rug over the bare floorboards. Looking at Mia hunched on the bed in her skinny jeans, black eyeliner, and red lipstick, I think how wrong it is because it's a little girl's room and that's not who Mia is anymore. But then she reaches for the battered old stuffed bunny she still keeps at the bottom of the bed.

I get a cleansing wipe out of the packet on her dressing table and sit next to her, carefully wiping away the smudged eyeliner and mascara, the smears of red around her mouth.

"Sorry, Mum." She sniffs, burying her head in my shoulder. All the fight has gone out of her and she sags against me.

I sigh and stroke her hair, dropping a soft kiss on the top of her head. "It's okay, baby. I'm sorry your dad lost his temper—I'll speak to him. We'll sort this out."

Mia lifts her head to look at me. "It was my fault."

"No, it wasn't," Joe says, coming over to sit on the other side of her. "He lost his temper and nearly hit you. How can that be your fault?"

"He didn't, though," Mia says, her voice rising. "He wouldn't have. He just *wouldn't*."

Joe looks at me over Mia's bowed head and I think of his whispered question when I was in the hospital after the overdose. *Did Dad do something?* I want to reassure him, to echo Mia's words, tell him Patrick would never, has never...but Mia's sitting between us, shaking, her arm red where Patrick's fingers dug in.

And this house. In this house, his tight control seems to be slipping. When I close my eyes now, I see Patrick painting the cellar at three a.m., I see him burning my sketchbooks, then that plate of fucking calamari. I smell alcohol on his breath.

I find Patrick in our room, standing by the window. He hasn't put the light on, but the streetlamp outside casts enough of a glow that I can see him. I don't know what he's looking at: on cloudy nights like this, the sea is just a black hole, like the world ends across the road from the house. I think I see someone outside under the light when I join him at the window, but before I can lean closer to see if it's the same watcher as before, the figure fades into the shadows.

"They've told me I might be suspended from work," he says, not looking away from the window. "That's why I was drinking."

"What?"

"The mistake. They're calling it negligence, *David's* calling it negligence. Fucking *David*."

"Oh, God, Patrick, I'm..." Sorry? Am I? Does that excuse what he did? Stress. Worry. Out-of-character drinking. A slip. A lapse. But it's Mia. *Mia*.

"How is she?" he asks.

"Tired. Upset. Patrick—"

"Don't. Don't say anything. I know what I did." He looks down at his hands as if they don't belong to him. "I lost it, I totally lost it, and I don't know why."

I don't know what to say to him. I can't tell him it's okay and it'll be fine and that we'll all forget about it and sweep it under the carpet because I keep seeing him going toward her with his hands curling into fists. I keep imagining what might have happened if I hadn't been there, and hearing the rage in his voice (*shut your dirty mouth*) and thinking, That's *Mia* he's saying it to, Mia, his little princess, Mia, our baby girl. *Bad things happen*, Tom said. Oh, God, oh, God.

I don't recognize him, this raging Patrick. He's not the man I married, the laughing man who once danced me around the room and promised me the world.

He looks at me, his eyes bloodshot, his hair a mess. "I'll never do it again, lose my temper like that. You know that, don't you? I'll *never* do it again."

My heart pounds and I feel faint as I think of Anna telling me about her own abusive boyfriend. It's an echo. His words are an echo. I feel as if I'm standing on the edge of a cliff and the only way is down.

CHAPTER 24

"Mia? Can we talk?"

She's sitting cross-legged on her bed, reading a book, school uniform on with the tie loose around her neck. She doesn't answer, but I step into the room anyway, pulling the door shut behind me. The sun is shining and she's opened her window. I can hear the seagulls and a dog barking in the distance. I walk over and look out: no families on the beach yet, it's too early, but lots of people walking their dogs.

A day like today makes me almost able to picture it, the life Patrick said we could have here. It's hard to equate this with last night, Patrick's white-knuckled anger, the fear and panic, but when I look at Mia, I can see the shadow of it in her face, the way she's hunched over, defeated.

She puts down her book and I see she's rereading *Little Women*, taking comfort in her childhood favorite. Bunny's on the floor, but I bet he was on the bed with her last night. I feel a sudden longing to do the same, to go to Vanity Fair with Meg, travel to Europe with Amy, fall in love with Laurie, anything but face what our life has become.

"Dad's already been in," she says. "He came in last night to say sorry."

Last night? We went to bed at the same time, so he must have waited until I'd fallen asleep before coming in to see Mia.

Mia looks at me. "What's going on with him, Mum? First he goes after at Joe, then me. It's not... it's not like him. He's not the same."

I take her hand. "Don't worry. This will get sorted. He's under a lot of pressure at work and with the stress of the move..." I'm making excuses to my own daughter now. "Maybe you and Joe should have some time away."

She pulls her hand out of mine. "No—don't send me away. I shouldn't have sneaked out. God, it's not like he hit me or anything, is it?"

"Mia, I just think—"

"I don't want to talk about it, okay? Dad said sorry and we're fine now, so we don't need to talk about it anymore."

She's got that frown, the one that's all him. She's had it since she was a toddler, when it would herald the start of an epic tantrum. I don't want to fight today: she may say she's fine, but I see fragile, not just in the hunched shoulders and pale cheeks but in the book, the stuffed toy, the comfort blankets of childhood she's tucked in around her.

"Okay," I say, putting my hand over hers. "No more talk of last night. Not now. Unless..."

"What?" Wary eyes to go with the frown.

"Unless you want to talk about who you were out with." I make it light, a mum-and-daughter gossip, not an interrogation.

She opens her mouth and closes it again. She doesn't pull her hand away, but she's tensed it, scrunching up the quilt in her fist.

"I remember, when I was your age, sneaking out to meet a boyfriend," I say. "His name was Daniel and he was beautiful. He was the year above me, already learning to drive."

Mia pulls her hand away. "It's not a stupid playground romance."

"I know—that wasn't what I meant. I only wanted you to know I understand."

She shakes her head. "No, you don't. This is different."

"How?"

"He's not just some *boy* from school. He's older."

My turn to frown. "How old?"

"God, I don't know. I haven't asked for his bloody date of birth. Seven, eight years older?"

"That's too old." I was assuming he was from her school. I was thinking...What was I thinking? That he could come around for tea in his school uniform and we'd play happy family and this would all go away?

"Doesn't matter anyway. I got it wrong," she says. "He was so different—older and working and wearing a suit. He asked me to dance and I thought..."

I freeze, forgetting to breathe. I'm not seeing Mia dancing with a man in a suit, I'm seeing a younger me and Patrick.

"I thought he would love me," Mia says. "I thought he would love me if I said yes. I wanted him to be my boyfriend. I wanted him to be our fucking *hero*—to save us. He kept asking and I thought he'd dump me if I didn't," she says, tears soaking my sweater as she buries her face in my shoulder. "So I had sex with him and he just walked away after. He didn't even wait while I got dressed again."

"Oh, Mia," I say. "I'm so sorry." I am. I'm so, so sorry for her, but is it better or worse that he was such a bastard? That he walked away, that he wasn't another Patrick, sweeping her off her feet into a future life like mine? "I'm sorry we've been so distracted that we've missed all this. Your father, and the house..."

Mia pulls away, losing strands of hair that tangle in my fingers. "It's not Dad's fault—it's *yours*. All your bloody fault. None of this would have happened if we hadn't moved to this shithole."

I wince at the loathing and disgust in her voice.

"I tried, Joe tried, we all bloody tried to talk to you, but you're always asleep. Even when your eyes are open, you're not really awake. And Dad...Dad's got no time for anybody else anymore."

I shift along the bed—the moment for mother-daughter closeness is over: I can tell by the hunch of her shoulders, the way she wraps her arms around her body. I thought I'd be better now that I've stopped taking the pills, but how much has changed? I've been here to listen, I *have*, but somewhere along the line, I think my children have gotten too used to me being half-present. They've lost faith in my ability to be there for them.

Her head flies up as we hear the creak of footsteps on the stairs. "Don't tell Dad," she says, her face full of panic. "Please don't tell him, Mum—he'd go *mental*."

I jump up as the door opens, standing in front of Mia as she wipes her eyes and smooths her hair.

"What's going on?" Patrick asks, looking past me at Mia.

I glance back as well. Mia's shaking, looking at me.

"Nothing," I say. "It's me. It's my fault. I was nagging Mia to tidy her room and we had a fight. That's all. It's nothing."

"You're pale," Patrick says to Mia, ignoring me.

"I have a headache," she mutters.

"Come on," I say, touching Patrick's arm. "Let's leave her to get ready for school."

"Sarah?" Patrick says, at the top of the stairs. He looks at me for a moment, then shakes his head. "It's fine. It's nothing."

I can't find any Tylenol in the cupboard above the bathroom sink, but I don't think Mia really has a headache anyway. I have my own ache, a lump in my throat as I mourn with her—not in a wanting-my-daughter-to-remain-a-little-girl-forever way, but in wishing her first time was about love, not drunken sex because she wanted to be liked. But my first time had been about love, hadn't it? I swallow the lump in my throat and think again: Is it better or worse this way?

My hand brushes against a bottle shoved right at the back of the cupboard and I pull it out, sinking to the floor as I look at it. It's the sleeping pills from the old house. When I took the pills, the bottle was at least three-quarters full. There are now only four left.

I lean back against the tub, staring at the bottle. I can taste the pills on my tongue. And I remember my dream, the hand pushing pills into my mouth...And after the hospital, I've been so tired. All the time. I've had days since we got here I barely remember. I drifted along, oblivious to so many things, and I thought it was the pills I buried.

But what if it wasn't? Since I buried them, have I really felt that much better? *You're always asleep*, Mia said. *Even when your eyes are open, you're not really awake.*

I return the bottle to the cupboard, pushing it right to the back.

Getting up, I stamp away pins and needles and go across to Mia's room. She's sitting at her dressing table, reapplying makeup, her hair smooth again, all traces of tears gone.

"Thanks," she says, meeting my eyes in the mirror. "For not telling Dad."

I open my mouth to answer, but she shakes her head. "Don't, Mum, please. Forget what I said, forget it all. I don't want some awkward mum-and-daughter chat about the bloody birds and bees. It's a bit late for that." She smudges more eyeliner under her eyes. "Go back to normal zombie-Mum mode and we'll all just pretend this didn't happen. That it's just a bad bloody dream."

"She's gone to school?"

I spin around at the sound of Joe's voice. He's standing in his doorway, the room behind him dark, curtains drawn over the sun.

"I think some normality is a good idea."

"A good idea to get out of the house—get away from Dad, you mean. You can't seriously think they'll both come home and it'll be like nothing happened?"

Is that what I'm hoping? No. We've gone past that.

"All Mia ever wants is to be adored. That's what the boyfriend's about."

"I love her—I love both of you. She knows that," I say.

"Sorry, Mum, but Mia's never chasing you for approval. It's not *your* neglect sending her off the rails." Joe sighs and retreats a step back into his room. "It's not just Mia who's changed since we moved here."

"Joe, please tell me what's going on with her."

He gives me that half-smile. "Mia thinks there are ghosts here," he says.

I don't believe in ghosts, but here . . . I think of the shadow stains on the walls, the creaking floorboards, the writing scribbled on the cellar walls. "She's looking for someone to save her from the ghosts?"

His smile fades. "I don't think it's the ghosts that are scaring her."

"What can I do, Joe? For Mia—for you?"

"You could take us away."

"Move again? The house will never sell. And I've tried talking to your dad, but he won't—"

"I didn't mean all of us. I meant you, me, and Mia." He says it so quietly, but his words land like a shout. I remember Patrick's clenched fists, the look on his face, and I think that's what Joe's seeing too.

He goes into his room and comes back with a sketchbook. "I have sketchbooks for all of you," he says. "This one is Dad's. Look," he says, opening it to the first page.

It's Patrick, outside the old house, dressed for work. He's all lines and angles, from the razor-sharp crease in his pinstriped leg to the angle of his jaw. Hair combed back, hand on his briefcase, face unsmiling, he's remote but calm.

Joe flicks through the pages, faster and faster so it's like one of those flip books, pencil-drawn Patrick coming to life, about to jump out of the book. But I don't want this Patrick to come alive, because the way Joe's drawn him... As the pages flick past, as time passes, Patrick's angles blur, his shoulders hunch, his hair rumples, and his face changes from calm to smudged and snarling. Still all angles, but thick drawn, sharp enough to cut. The Patrick in the last drawing is a storm unleashed. It's Patrick last night, a maelstrom of swirling rage, broken apart so you can only just see a figure in the lines and swirls, lines drawn so heavily the pencil has actually broken through the paper, as if he really is trying to break out.

Talk to me, I used to say to Joe, handing him a pencil and paper. *Talk to me*. I step back, away from the book, my hands shaking. This isn't talking; this is a roar.

"Do you see?" Joe says, holding the book toward me. "Do you see now?"

I take another step back. This house...He told me it was his dream house, his childhood Paradise. This is where everything was going to be right and perfect. This is where everything has gone so wrong. The decision isn't really a decision anymore. We have to leave.

Joe goes back into his room and pulls the curtains open. It seems brighter, and when I go to the window I see the tree is gone.

"He did it last night," Joe says. "I woke up—I don't know what time it was, but I heard a noise. He was out there in his fucking pajamas sawing the tree down."

There are branches all over the scrubby grass and littered among the weeds. Up close, I see the tree isn't completely gone, just the branches that reached up to Joe's window. It looks lopsided now, lightning-blasted. I glance down at Joe's sketchbook, open at the page where Patrick is the storm.

Last night, after everything that happened, I slept. I didn't hear him get up to go to Mia; I didn't even hear him sawing a bloody tree down in the garden. Patrick brought me a cup of tea, made so strong it was bitter, and sat with me while I drank it, apologizing over and over again. That was what I'd gone to sleep on, a lullaby of *I'm sorry, I'm sorry, I'll never do it again*...

"You have to get us out of here, Mum," Joe says again as I go back toward my room. I pick up my mug from last night and stare down into it. All those cups of tea he's been making me...It's not my future in tea leaves I'm looking for, though; it's white residue from crushed sleeping pills.

CHAPTER 25

When Patrick comes home, I can see the evidence of his nighttime activities. His eyes are bloodshot, black shadows underneath. His hair is rumpled and he's wearing yesterday's suit and shirt. His hands are scratched and bruised, black under the nails. I can't stop thinking about Joe's drawings.

"Have you been at work? Have they said anything more about..."

He dumps a shopping bag on the table and pushes his hands through his hair. "I've been shopping. I had some things I needed to get. I'm officially suspended from work. David called this morning."

He shakes his head at the look on my face.

"Don't worry, Sarah. The suspension is with full pay. We'll only be in trouble if they decide to fire me."

But aren't we already in trouble? It isn't the thought of Patrick losing his job that's making me panic; it's the thought of what it'll do to him if he loses the house. And if I leave, he loses us as well. His family and his house.

My phone buzzes in my pocket. I ignore it, checking that Patrick hasn't heard. It's going to be Tom Evans again. He's called five times today and I've declined all the calls, trying to stem the rising panic at what I've let—what I've *invited*—into our lives. I know it's childish to avoid the calls. I have to face it, stop hiding. I shake my head. I always do this—eyes tight shut, hands over my ears, hoping it will all go away if I just pretend it isn't happening. I can't do that anymore.

I hunch over the stove, stirring a pot of pasta. "Are you hungry?" I ask. "I can do dinner early."

I sense him standing behind me and have to force myself not to tense. I can't help but jump when he puts his hands on my shoulders and the wooden spoon drops into the pot, splashing me with drops of boiling water.

"No rush," he says. "I have things to do first." He steps away and starts rummaging through a drawer. "Have you seen the spirit level? And my drill?"

I pick up the spoon again, wipe my stinging hand on my jeans. "I think they're in your toolbox."

"And where's that?"

"Didn't you put it down in the cellar?"

He stops rummaging and goes still. He closes the drawer softly and glances at me. "I'm not hungry," he says, picking up the bag, which clinks as if there are bottles in it. "I have things to do. Don't wait for me."

Mia refuses to come down, so Joe and I sit in silence at the table, not eating our pasta. I don't know what Patrick's doing, but I can hear the drill going. I grit my teeth as the noise bites into my skull and settles as a throbbing headache. I've been sluggish all day, my eyes gritty. I feel hungover, even though I didn't drink last night.

I was going to joke about it, say it lightly when Patrick got home. I even rehearsed it, practiced my smile in the mirror, *Hey, what did you put in my tea last night? I slept like a log*... But the Patrick I smiled at in the mirror was calm, buttoned-up Patrick, not the Patrick caught in the storm who came home looking for a toolkit in the cellar. If I said it to that Patrick, it would be an accusation, not a half-joke, a casual comment.

Joe gets up and puts his plate in the sink, most of the pasta scraped into the bin. He stops on his way back to the table, staring at something in the hall.

"Have you seen this?" he says.

I get up to join him and go cold. Patrick has fitted a new lock to the cellar door, a big silver one with a padlock. We jump as something crashes to the floor upstairs and the light starts swinging.

"He's in my room," Joe mutters, heading for the stairs.

I follow him. I want to find Patrick fixing the wardrobe door that keeps sticking or, even better, putting together some new furniture so Joe's room looks like less of an afterthought next to Mia's, whose room he put aside a whole weekend to decorate straight after we moved in. But he's not doing any of those things. He's fitting another lock, this one to the window, a big, ugly lock-and-bolt thing that's hugely obtrusive.

"Jesus, Dad, you've already cut the fucking tree down," Joe says, and Patrick scowls at him. He's still holding the drill and I put a hand on Joe's arm. The shadows of his beating have only just faded. He shakes it off and takes another step toward Patrick. "Will it be a lock on my door next?"

I think of the shiny new padlock Patrick's put on the cellar door. What else has he got in that bag?

"I have to stop the sneaking out," Patrick says, and Joe laughs.

"It wasn't me sneaking out, though, was it, Dad? In case you hadn't noticed, I'm the one who's actually fucking here."

Back on the landing, Joe turns to me. "How long do you think it's going to be before he really does put locks on our doors?" The drill starts up in his room again and we back away.

"I've got a job," Joe says. "It's only in a coffee shop, and only part-time, but I'm earning money and I'm saving. I'm going to get out of here, Mum. I wish you would, too."

"Joe..."

"He won't be able to lock me away then. I'll be gone and I won't ever come back."

Something wakes me. I open my eyes and Patrick is sitting up in bed, his head in his hands. I hadn't noticed how thin he's getting, collar bones jutting behind his hunched shoulders, his scars standing out even in the dark.

The first time I saw him naked, I remarked on his scars. He had too many scars for a twenty-two-year-old middle-class man with an office job. *Where did you get them?* I asked. He told me stories for all of them—a fall from a tree, off a bike, a minor car accident, all perfectly feasible explanations for the scars patterning his body.

But now I wonder how many of those stories were true.

"What's wrong?" I whisper.

"Bad dream," he says, lifting his hands from his face but not moving from that hunched-over position.

I reach up to touch his shoulder and find it damp with sweat. He jumps as if I've slapped him.

"Do you want me to get you a drink or something?" The bed creaks as I sit up, tugging the quilt with me. Patrick is sweating, but I'm cold. I always seem to be cold in this house.

Patrick shakes his head. "No, I'll just... sit for a while."

Is he scared to go back to sleep in case he falls straight back into his nightmare?

"Was it like the dreams you had before?"

He wipes sweat off his face. "It was different this time. I was a boy again. The house was like it was back then, but the landing was longer and there were too many rooms. I was running and there was screaming... That was always when I woke up before. But this time, I found myself in the cellar and I knew whatever caused the screaming was in there with me."

I can hear our mingled breath, his fast and harsh. When he'd had these dreams before, I'd never thought they meant anything. But now we're here, in the house with the same landing, which *does* seem to get longer in the middle of the night. His dreams never took him into the cellar before—is it because I found the writing, or is it something more? "Is it... Do you think it is just a dream?"

"As opposed to what? You think it's real? What—a memory?"

I pull the quilt higher. "Is it?"

He looks down at his hands and I see they're shaking. I hold my breath as I wait for him to answer. "Don't be stupid," he says. "Of course it's a dream."

But I'm thinking of the cellar. I'm thinking of the writing on the walls. I'm remembering when he woke up from those nightmares before, the half-screamed words I thought meant nothing, that were just fragments left over from a nightmare. *I'm sorry, I've been bad. I'm sorry, I'm sorry. I've been bad.*

"Sarah?" he says. "You won't... you won't ever leave me, will you?" The pleading note in his voice, the *fear*, sets my stomach churning. "I see you drifting away and I can't...I don't think I could stand it if you weren't here."

I see the ghost of my mother in his face, a naked vulnerability verging on desperation.

The light on the landing flickers and goes out. I glance at the digital clock and that's gone off too.

"Power cut," Patrick says, but when I get up to check, the streetlight outside is still on. I hear a moan from one of the children's rooms.

"I'll go," I say as I see Patrick getting up.

"I can't sleep anyway, I'll check on them."

"Patrick." I reach for his arm. "Don't..."

He stares back at me, his face barely visible in the darkness. "Don't what?"

My heart's pounding, but I don't know how to say the rest of the sentence without making him...upset again. He shakes my hand off his arm.

I get back into bed and lie down, staring up at the ceiling. I can hear a tapping on the window. I know it's not tapping. I know it's the wind rattling the frame. Or the branches of the tree at the front hitting the glass. But it sounds like knocking, someone outside saying, *Let me in.*

I don't think I could stand it if you weren't here, Patrick said. What would he do to make me stay?

Patrick still isn't back. Maybe one of the children is ill. I think of Joe and his arms and I get up, tiptoe to the door. When I look out, Patrick is on the landing, facing away from me. He's leaning his head on Mia's closed door. He's holding the handle, but he doesn't open the door, just leans his head against it. His other hand is clenched in a fist at his side and his eyes are closed. I don't move, I stay where I am, heart pounding even harder, hidden behind our door, watching Patrick and waiting. Waiting for what? I stand and wait and watch, and behind me, the tapping on the window gets louder and the wind outside seems to whisper, *I'm sorry. I've been bad. I'm sorry.*

CHAPTER 26

I pick up my phone and hesitate. I waver, then make myself answer. "Hello?"

"Sarah? It's Tom."

Stupid. This is my own stupid fault for leaving my details with the estate agent, for trying to contact him in the first place.

"I had a message on my phone from Mr. Walker."

"I'm sorry, I—"

"He basically accused me of stalking you. Told me to stay away from you. What did you tell him?"

"You came to the house, Tom—you followed me onto the cliff path. That's not normal behavior."

"All I ever did was warn you. All I wanted was to help you." He pauses, and I can hear him breathing, harsh and fast. "Do you know—I called your husband once, when I knew he was buying the house. I called because he knows Hooper should still be in prison for what he did to my family. He *knows*. But he wouldn't take my calls. He never called me back. And so I left it. But then you contacted me and I knew it was a sign. And now you're doing the same, ignoring my calls."

"I'm sorry. I—"

"Is it because of the other man? The one in your sketchbook? Do you think he's going to rescue you, take you away from it all?" He stops and I hear his breath catch. "That's what my mother said to us about Hooper."

I feel a growing sense of panic, of things escalating. "Look, I'm sorry I got in touch. It was a mistake. Patrick can't help you. Ian Hooper is out, but there's nothing Patrick can do to change that. And you don't know me, we're not family—we're strangers."

There's silence. I'm ready to end the call when he speaks again. "We were never strangers. You're as caught up in this as I am, because of the man you married."

"What do you mean? What—" But I'm talking to dead air. He's hung up, and when I try to call back, it goes to voicemail.

I take my sketchbook out onto the coast path and sit on the bench that I believe was the star of the painting in the gallery window on the day I met Anna. I've got an idea for another painting using all the colors from Anna's secret beach, but working in the studio was stifling me, giving everything I paint an edge I don't intend to be there. Instead of it being a sanctuary, I'm too aware of Ben working downstairs, Ben, who I'd thought might turn into a friend but instead has become more of a stranger, because of his secret friendship with Patrick and his bowls of shells. I tried painting in the kitchen of the Murder House, but the draft from the broken window catch is like a cold breath on my neck, and the way the wind blows sometimes sounds like moaning.

"I wondered where you were."

My pencil slips on the page as Patrick sits down next to me. He's still suspended from work, but he got up at six as usual this morning and put on his suit. I came downstairs and he was sitting at the kitchen table, staring into space.

He puts a flask on the bench between us. "I brought you some tea." He pours some into a cup and offers it to me, but I shake my head. He shrugs and takes a sip, smiling. "What are you drawing?"

"Just some scribbled ideas. For a seascape, but something quite abstract."

"Not a portrait, then?"

There's something odd in his voice, an off-note that makes my shoulders stiffen and my heart beat faster.

He reaches into his pocket and pulls out a folded piece of paper. "I found this in the hall—it must have fallen out of your sketchbook."

He unfolds the paper and lays it on the bench between us. "Who are you drawing?"

Oh, God. I think of that painting of the couple on the bench and wonder if Anna's ever come up with *this* scenario for what's going on between the two figures. "It's just a drawing from my imagination."

It's not even a good drawing, not like Joe's sketches. It's a scribbled portrait done in an idle moment: an artist at work on a canvas in a cottage by the sea, shown from behind so you can see the view he's painting. It doesn't look much like Ben, not really. Any of the other pages in my sketchbook have better drawings, but they're of the beach, of Mia and Joe. Nothing in any of those to make Patrick wonder. Which is why I'd torn out the page. I thought I'd put it in the bin. I think again of Patrick sitting staring at nothing. Maybe I did. Maybe that's where he found it. Or...I think of Tom Evans looking at the sketch, Tom Evans, who might still have a key to the house, who's angry because I told Patrick about him.

Joe's sketchbooks reveal the truth, more than a photo ever could. Does mine do the same? Tom read something in this sketch that I never intended to put there. Clearly, so has Patrick. I notice his hand is shaking.

"I thought...at first I thought you were drawing the house. Us. I thought it was me in the sketch, looking at your paintings. Then I looked closer. Who is he?" he asks again.

"Really—he's nobody. An idea, a dream, I don't know."

"A *dream*? Is this what you want?" he says.

Everything I find out about the boy Patrick used to be, the more of a stranger my husband becomes. The house, the Murder House, is rotting, oozing poison and falling apart. Joe is at home, a boy made of scars. Mia is out, still searching for someone to save her. And at the back of the wardrobe, there's a gaping hole in the box of treasures that holds all that's left of my parents. "Yes," I snap. "This is my fantasy—everything I don't have."

Patrick's turn to go pale, to look scared. The fear in him is bleeding out, eating at his control. I didn't start it: that was someone else, something else. It was this house, whatever he's trying to undo and paint over by bringing us here.

He crumples up the sketch and I think he's going to hit me. I duck down, but nothing happens. When I look up, he's opened out the paper again and he lets it go. The wind picks it up and carries it away, over the edge of the cliff.

"You're killing me, Sarah," he says softly. "You're breaking my fucking heart."

I see Anna coming up the path and, for a moment, I'm tempted to hide. I've been avoiding her—at first because I was angry over her words last time we met, then, after Patrick nearly hit Mia, because I didn't want to have to confront my growing fear that she was right.

I take a deep breath and pull the front door open when she knocks.

"I'm sorry," she says, holding out a pot of daisies gift-wrapped in tissue paper and a bow. "I was ridiculous the last time we met. I'm oversensitive because of my history with my ex, but I had no right to question your relationship with Patrick. You told me he'd never touch any of you and I should have accepted that immediately."

The way she's holding out the pot of flowers, I can see the scars running up her arms. I reach to take the daisies. "It's fine, don't worry about it."

"Are you sure? I'd hate to think I've upset you in any way... You haven't taken my last couple of calls, so I thought I must have said something." She glances at me and away again.

I take the flowers and put them on the hall table.

"Are you okay? You look terrible." She reaches past me, picks up a fallen petal. "Do you think that was a loves-me or a loves-me-not?"

I want to smile and tell her again it's all fine, but Mia jumps every time Patrick enters a room and Joe is still healing after the attack. The attack he's too scared to tell anyone but me about. The attack someone watched and let happen.

Instead of replying, I rub my palm across my burning eyes. I didn't sleep again last night. Every time I closed my eyes, all those faces were there—Ian Hooper, John and Marie Evans, the little gap-toothed boys. God, Tom Evans, that sweet boy from the photos who looked like Joe once did, the man he's turned into... Is that what's going to happen to my children? Next to me, Patrick was sleeping heavily and I watched him in the dark, thinking about his obsession with this house, all those times he came here when he'd said he was working... Did he visit way back when the Evans family lived there? Did he just park and sit outside? Or did he sometimes knock on the door?

Tom is so insistent John and Patrick were friends. What is it he thinks Patrick knows that could have kept Hooper in prison? All those detours Patrick said he used to take past this house, all those calls he put in to the local estate agent... More than fifteen years ago. Can I remember where he was every night fifteen years ago? Could I even remember where he was on the night of the murders?

Ben might know. He might remember. He said he was away at college when the murders happened, but what about before? What about holidays? Would he have recognized his former school friend hovering around his old house?

"What's wrong, Sarah?" Anna says, and I look at her, blank-faced. How long did I zone out for then? What was she saying?

"Nothing. It's nothing." But even I can hear the lie in my voice. Does she see me jump when I hear a car door slam? Does she wonder why I rush to the living room window to check it's not Patrick?

"Nothing wrong? Really?" Anna says.

"You'd better go. Patrick could be home any minute and he's... It's not a good time."

"I'm worried about you," she says softly. "I see myself when I look at you... I sometimes feel I spent my life learning to swim against the tide. Years and years, building my strength up." She leans in close and her perfume is overpowering. She smells of the sweetpeas she brought around once, strong enough to make my head spin.

"I can see you've done the same. Struggling against the tide all this time. I swam away, but after a while I got tired and stopped swimming," she says. "I stopped swimming and the tide dragged me here." She closes her eyes and takes a deep breath. When she opens them, she stares at me with burning eyes. "Things are escalating, aren't they? What are you worried about, Sarah? I can see it in your face. What's he done?"

I'm awake but not really awake. I lie staring up at the ceiling, listening to Joe get ready for work, Mia for school. My door opens and I close my eyes again, feign sleep.

"Sarah?" Patrick whispers, sighing when I don't answer. The bed creaks as he sits next to me. I feel his hand on the back of my head. "I have to go into the office to speak to David, but I'll come home early."

He puts a glass of water next to the bed. It's the first thing I see when I open my eyes after he's gone. It's to take my pill with. He's done it every morning, put a glass of water in front of me, waiting until I respond to the trigger, like Pavlov's dog, and get up to find my pills. Are the ones I buried in the garden still there? I picture myself digging them up, swallowing mud-caked drops of numbness, and that's the thought that gets me out of bed. I make myself shower and dress and go downstairs. I will not fall into that bloody dark pit again. I won't let myself.

I jump when I go into the kitchen and find Joe there, eating toast. I put a hand on my chest. "God, Joe, I jumped a mile then—I thought you'd gone to work."

He looks at me from under his hair. "I don't start until four today," he says. "It's an evening shift."

I frown and switch the kettle on. "Will you be okay to get a bus or a train home?"

He puts his mug next to mine, spooning coffee into both. "I might stay with a friend."

"One of your old friends from school?"

"What old friends from school? Have you noticed my phone constantly ringing?" He half smiles, but I can see the bitterness. "It's fine, Mum. Don't worry about it. I've never been Mr. Popular, never like Mia."

"So who are you staying with?"

He picks up his mug when I fill it with hot water. "Just…a friend. Someone I met. The one who came out to meet me last week." I think that's all I'm going to get, that he'll take his toast and coffee and retreat to his room, but he puts his mug on the table and turns to me. "Simon. His name's Simon."

I think of seeing Joe that day at the fairground, the boy leaning in to kiss him. I have to turn away for a moment so he won't see the worry on my face. It was me who persuaded Patrick not to push him into going back to school, to let him have this time to recover and work out what he wants to do. I'm trying really hard to let him have his independence, but it's so difficult when the shadows of the attack are still on his face. "Tell me about him."

"He's not from around here. He rescued me," Joe says, and he smiles. "Mia would love that, wouldn't she? I got into a bit of a state on a night out in Cardiff before we moved here and he helped me out. That's how we met." His smile widens. "He's twenty-one and he's just finished university. He's working at the Gap while he waits for a *proper* job. He wants to be a teacher. He doesn't even like clubbing—he was dragged there by coworkers. He doesn't drink either, or smoke, and he's vegetarian."

Joe looks at me and I hold my breath. I have to hide from him sometimes, from all I see in his face, and talking about this boy, what I see in his face is *everything*, all there, open and raw, laid out for this boy called Simon. It terrifies and thrills me at the same time.

"I don't even know why I like him," he says. "He's so… normal. He's quiet. We have nothing in common. But…his smile.

And the pattern of his voice—its rises and falls, the way he... pauses." Joe's voice drops to a whisper.

He's wearing a dark blue long-sleeved top and the sleeves are stretched down, almost covering his hands. I think of his scars underneath, all the things he's never talked to me about etched into his arms. He sees me looking and pulls the sleeves down even farther.

"How..." I stop. Joe is actually talking to me; I don't want to scare him off. "How's it going with the therapist?" He's had two sessions now, making his own way there on the bus. I offered to go with him, but he refused. Patrick doesn't talk about it—won't talk about it.

"It's okay, I guess. She keeps telling me I have to open up and talk about stuff, so I won't always feel the need to..." He fiddles with a cuff. "I told her about Simon and she said to be careful, that I might be too *vulnerable* for a relationship at the moment." He glances up at me. "But we're only friends. That's what he wants."

"Have you mentioned Simon to your father?"

He laughs. "Are you kidding?" The laughter dies. "There's something else I've been talking to the therapist about. You know I said someone was watching the night I was attacked? I thought I saw...I thought it might have been Dad. But she thinks I may have imagined it. Put him there in my mind because of all the issues I have with him."

There's an aching lump in my throat. Oh, Joe. How could we have gotten to the point where my boy could believe his own father would watch him get beaten up and do nothing? But haven't I wondered too? Wasn't I looking for evidence that night in the hospital?

"Do you think she's right?"

"I think she must be. How can I have seen him? It was dark and I was thinking about him. That boy was kicking me and I was thinking about Dad and how ashamed and disgusted he'd be, and suddenly I thought I saw him."

He gets up then, and I think that's it, but he only goes as far as the hall and comes back with his scruffy old backpack. He reaches inside and pulls out a brochure, pushing it toward me. It's a prospectus for a continuing-ed college in Cardiff.

"Here's something else for Dad not to find out about. I know I fucked up my chances of a degree course by leaving school, but I don't want to go back. I can't," he says. "Simon got this for me. There's a part-time course I can do and still work. I could still go to art college." He touches the prospectus. "I never thought it was for me, the happy-ever-after thing. I might look like him, but I sometimes think I'm more like you."

I reach across and put my hand over his. All these secrets... all these lies we're telling each other. The truth burns to come out, but now...I think how much he is offering me and how hurt he would be by the truth. Can I bear to force that pain on him right now?

"Now, though...Do you think I could, Mum?" Joe says, his eyes bright, cheeks flushed. "Do you think I could do this—stop fucking up and get a life?"

Patrick is staring at the pot of daisies Anna brought. I'd forgotten about them and left them on the hall table, still done up in tissue paper with a blue bow.

"Where did these come from?"

"My friend brought them around."

"*Friend?* What friend?"

I don't know how to read the look on his face. "Anna. I told you about her."

"Why daisies? Why these?"

"Patrick, I don't understand—they're just flowers. I thought we could plant them outside. I thought they'd look nice."

He looks like he's going to be sick. "I hate daisies," he says. "Get rid of it."

When I was a kid, I had all these dreams. Stupid fucking dreams about going into space and curing cancer and winning Oscars and all sorts of crap. It settled, eventually, as dreams do, into something so much less bright and fanciful. But even my dull-as-ditchwater dreams got snatched away, ripped to pieces, ground into the dirt.

Dreams do not come fucking true. Ever. They don't. Not even for them, pretending their house is a castle, not the fucking Murder House. Especially not for them, nest of cuckoos with their lies and their secrets.

You're in there, in the house that was once just a house before it became the Murder House. I can see them all through the window, your perfect smiling family. But I know better. I know what's going on in their pretty heads.

How can I still be so invisible?

I step closer to the window, out of the shadows. They're all too absorbed in themselves to see me. I crouch down, dig with my hands in the wet earth under the bay window, dig up the pills I watched her bury. I dig them all up and put them in an empty jar. Now we'll see, won't we? Now we'll see.

CHAPTER 27

I wait for the house to be quiet before I get up. I wait and I plan. I have three passport application forms hidden in my bedside table drawer. All I need is to sell one painting at my exhibition and I'll be able to afford to get the passports and three cheap flights somewhere—anywhere—in Europe. I'll get the brochures out again, not the exotic tropical vacations but the ones that focus on Spain or France. I'm not going to wait anymore for the adventures my mother never had. The moment Mia finishes school for the summer, we'll be on a plane, far enough away that Patrick won't be able to find us.

Anna talks about shelters, but that's not what I want. I'm not going to hide among all those women who've been beaten and battered and tell them I'm scared it was my husband scribbling on a cellar wall, that I'm scared because he nearly slapped his daughter, that he's drinking and he doesn't drink—he doesn't. He doesn't get angry, doesn't lose control.

I'm not going to do that because it's too close. We'll never be free of Patrick and this house if we stay around here. It'll be night and the lights will flicker and the wind will rattle the window and Patrick will be there in my mind, standing outside Mia's room in the middle of the night crying, fixing locks on every door, grinding sleeping pills into my tea. And Joe—what about Joe? He wouldn't come to a shelter with us—he's getting away on his own.

And I'm scared about that too. I'm scared to see Joe ready to go off with all that hope in his face, because what if he doesn't get into that college course? What if this Simon of his rejects him? What if Patrick comes along and grinds salt into that raw hope, drags him back to the Murder House? What if he goes the way his birth mother went? It makes me want to lock him up, hide everything sharp, put bars on his window, and I'm scared that makes me like Patrick or my mother. I think that's what moving here has done to me.

So, no, that's not what we're going to do. We're going to spend the summer on a hot beach where Mia and Joe will lose the dark shadows and get tans. We'll lose the tension we all carry around. I'll get a job and I'll paint. I'll paint a whole damn new life for us, and when we come back, I'll make it a reality.

Two more months, that's all. Two months to find the money for those passports and tickets and then we'll be free.

I wait and I plan, but I don't wait enough, because when I go downstairs, Patrick is in the kitchen. He's sitting at the table and he has my pills in front of him, the lid of the container open.

"What is this?" He says it quietly and all the hairs on my arms stand up. I've been so careful to eat some of the mints each day so Patrick wouldn't get suspicious and check closer, but I can smell them from here. I should have filled it with white stones. I should have been swallowing them. I don't know what to say. I shake my head, but I have no words.

He turns and picks up a glass jar, pushes it next to the plastic box on the table. The jar is full of dirt-clogged white pills, half-dissolved and crumbling. I think I'm going to be sick, throw up all over Patrick, the pills, the table. I don't understand how... Did Patrick see me bury them? Has he dug them up? No, that's... The nausea rises again, higher. Did I do it? I've been thinking about them. As things have gotten worse, haven't I been fantasizing about digging the fucking things up?

No, no—stop. That's not me anymore. I'm in control now, no lost days.

But if not me, if not Patrick, then who?

Someone's been watching. They watched me bury the pills. They've known the whole time they were there and they've waited...

"I found this on the doorstep," Patrick says, nodding at the jar.

"With a note that made no sense." He looks up at me. "It made no sense because how could these be your pills when you've promised so faithfully you've been taking them every day?" He picks up the plastic box and tips out a handful of mints. His voice is shaking. "I don't understand why you've done this."

"I don't need them anymore."

"Don't you? Your paranoia, your obsession with the history of the house...Sarah, you're worse than you were before, not better."

It's not true. It's not just paranoia. "I tried to tell you they were making me feel worse."

"No, you didn't. And if it were true, why didn't you go to the doctor and tell *him* that?"

Because of the cellar. Because of my sketchbooks. Because of the fear on Mia's face, because of Joe in a hospital bed, because Patrick knew John Evans.

"I just...I was becoming too reliant on them. I had to get rid of them right away, while I still had the willpower to do it. It was impulsive, stupid, I know that, but once I'd done it, I couldn't think how to undo it."

He picks up the jar with the mud-caked real pills, holds it up to look at it. From across the kitchen, I'm sure I can see worms and bugs in there and bile surges, stings my throat.

"Someone knew how to undo it. Someone knew what you did." He looks at me. "Who left these, Sarah? Who dug them up and left them for me?"

I don't know, but I think of the watcher I thought was Ian Hooper, that I've been scared recently is Tom Evans, and my stomach lurches at the thought of either of them watching me bury the pills. Better that, though, than the first fleeting thought that came to mind when I saw the jar. (*Mia. Mia did it.*) I don't want it to be my daughter hating me that much.

Picking up the box of mints, Patrick walks over to the garbage can and empties them all in, going back to scoop up the ones on the table, putting them into the bin as well. He fills a glass with water and hands it to me. I watch as he picks up the jar and shakes out a small white pill. It has bits of damp mud clinging to it and he holds it out on his palm.

"Take your medicine, Sarah." His voice is shaking again.

"Patrick." I step away.

He moves closer, still holding out the pill. "Take your fucking pill."

I back up farther, but I hit the wall. I close my mouth and shake my head and I'm back in the old house, the blurry figure coming into my bedroom, the dream of someone pushing pills into my mouth. I think he's going to do it, he's going to cram those mud-covered pills in, feed them to me along with the worms and bugs in the jar.

The front door slams and Patrick freezes, his hand inches from my face. Mia comes in, making for the kettle, stopping when she sees us, me hunched against the wall, Patrick leaning over me.

She stares from me to Patrick and back again. "What's going on?"

Patrick lowers his arm and moves away from me. "Why aren't you in school?" he says to her.

"Study period," she says. Patrick's got his back to her and he's still looking at me, but I see Mia blink, see the lie on her face.

She picks up the jar on the table, dropping it, her nose wrinkling as a centipede wriggles to the top and crawls onto the table. "What's going on?" she says again.

"Nothing for you to worry about, Mia," Patrick says, his voice no longer shaking, looking at the empty bottle, the centipede on the table, the open bin. He turns and smiles at his daughter. Her face is wary. "It's your mother. Your mother has been lying to us all."

"No—Mia, wait. It's not what you think."

I see Mia's face twist. "God—you two. I don't want to be involved in your sick games." She turns and runs, leaves me there with Patrick.

We watch her go, hear her stomp up the stairs. "I'm sorry," he says, after a silence that seems to last years. "I...lost my temper.

I'm sorry. We'll make an appointment with the GP, see if we can't find something that will work for you." He chucks the jar, complete with mud and bugs, into the bin and walks out after Mia.

The centipede is still crawling along the table. I pick it up with a shudder and carry it out into the back garden, setting it free in the grass. I hear a noise and look up. Mia is watching me from the window in Joe's room, a pale ghost half-hidden in the shadow of his curtain. If Mia hadn't come in, would Patrick have fed me that pill? I think of his face. Yes. He would have. If Mia hadn't come back, he would have shoved that pill, covered with mud and bugs and worm shit, into my mouth and he might not have stopped at one.

Why is he so determined to keep me medicated? What is he so scared I'll see if my head is clear?

I get up when I hear the front door again, then the sound of the car starting. By the time I go back through the house, Patrick is gone. I glance at the clock—nearly ten thirty. I don't know what's going on at work, if they've had the disciplinary meeting he told me about, if they've reached a resolution. Every time I ask, he changes the subject. Every day, he puts on his suit, gets into the car, and drives off, but I have no idea anymore if he's going to work.

I scrub away all signs of mud in the kitchen and empty the bin. I have a gnawing ache in the pit of my stomach. It's been there ever since we moved here and it's getting worse. It wakes me at night and it makes me wish, just for a moment, but a dangerous moment, that Mia hadn't interrupted us and that Patrick had made me take that pill. Is that why I buried them within reach, instead of throwing them away to be collected by the garbage men? Is that what I couldn't tell Patrick? I *wanted* the numbness, the disconnection, the fuzzy layer between me and this nagging ache?

"You okay?" Mia's watching me and I realize I'm standing in the middle of the kitchen, a garbage bag in one hand, the other clutching my stomach.

"I'm fine," I say. "Spot of indigestion."

There's so much worry on her face it makes the ache worse. She's abandoned the makeup; she looks pale and tired. "Mum—*stop*. Stop pretending everything's fine."

"I'm not pretending—I don't want you to worry, that's all."

She laughs, a disbelieving sound that's almost a sob. "You don't want me to *worry*? God, Mum, you tried to kill yourself and you don't want me to *worry*? Dad's done everything to try to make you happy, including moving bloody house. And now *he*'s miserable and angry and lashing out."

"It's not—"

"I shouldn't have told you about Caroline. It's made things worse, hasn't it?"

"No—please, Mia, you haven't done anything wrong," I insist.

"Maybe *you're* the one who should go away. Sort yourself out. If you weren't here, Dad would be normal again. He'd have time for me and Joe."

My God, even my own daughter wants me gone. I'd imagined that if I left, Mia would come with me. What would I do if she insisted on staying with Patrick? I couldn't. Couldn't leave her here. "Mia, please..."

"Listen to yourself. Stop pretending everything's going to be okay. Please stop."

CHAPTER 28

I sit in a too-hot bath, but I can't get warm. What am I going to do? Mia's questions echo in my head. I could have told her about my plans—the passports, our summer abroad—but what if she doesn't want to come with me? I can't leave her with Patrick. With Mia, I could fight for custody, but I have a history of anxiety and depression. I'm on record as suicidal. And Joe…I'd lose him. He's not eighteen for another seven months. I can't leave yet. I need money; I need a plan. I need Joe to be out of here, safe.

I don't hear Patrick come up and when the bathroom door opens, I lurch upright too quickly, sending a tidal wave of water over the side, onto the floor, onto his feet. I blink water from my eyes and grope for a towel, vulnerable in my nakedness even after seventeen years together.

He holds out a towel, not moving as I wrap it around myself. My hair is dripping, but he's standing in front of the towel rail so I can't reach for another without him moving. He watches me drip onto the floor, goose bumps rising on my arms.

When he moves I wrap a towel around my hair and follow him into the bedroom. He sits on the bed, taking off his shoes, like nothing happened earlier, but I can see dirt from the muddy jar under his fingernails. I sit on the opposite side and reach for a comb.

"Let me," he says, taking it from me. He used to do that in the early days: I'd wash my hair, he'd comb it and dry it for me. He combs carefully, his hands gentle. He combs out the knots and his breath smells sweet and I wonder if he was drinking downstairs, if he felt the need to drink to settle his nerves before coming up to see me.

He puts down the comb, but he doesn't get up. Instead he leans and kisses my shoulder. I force myself not to tense. His lips move up to my ear.

"Patrick, my head hurts and I'm tired..."

"You're always tired these days," he mutters, and his fingers dig into my biceps. When I wince, he kisses my shoulder again, runs his fingers up and down the red marks he's left on my arms with one hand, unbuttoning his shirt with the other. I close my eyes as he tugs at my towel and slides his hand underneath.

Once. Once upon a time, like in a fairy tale, my mouth would go dry watching Patrick take off his shirt. My heart would pound and I'd rush to help him, impatient to strip him bare. His stomach is still flat, his shoulders wide and strong, but it seems like forever since desire was making my heart pound as he closed the bedroom door.

"Ssh," he says, pushing me backward onto the bed. "Let's take advantage of being alone..."

I close my eyes, but all I can see is him and Caroline.

"No," I say, pushing him away. "I can't." I get up, start pulling on my clothes.

"Where are you going?"

"I need some time alone. I need time to think."

He gets up and stands between me and the door. A trickle of fear threatens to become a flood. What if he doesn't let me leave? I glance at my bedside table. What if he goes looking for other hidden secrets, finds the passport applications?

Does he see the fear in my face? He sees something, because he moves closer to me.

I hear a door open—one of the children's. Music comes on, loud through the wall. Patrick's head turns toward the noise and it breaks whatever spell was building. The tension leaves his body and he sags.

"Okay," he says. "Of course. Fine. Time, yes. Take some time, and then we'll talk. We can sort things out."

I wanted to go to the studio, but I didn't want to see Ben. I've always believed the watcher had to be Hooper or, lately, Tom, someone connected with the house and the murders. But since I saw that painting Ben did, his collections of shells, I've wondered if it could be him. He's walked past the house so many times—he could have been watching as I buried the pills. And it was him who found the baby shoes, wasn't it? Maybe he has some agenda of his own, some weird obsession with Patrick, a long-dead friendship that Patrick has never mentioned.

Instead of going to the studio, I walked into town, constantly looking behind me to check Patrick wasn't following. I went to a pub—a bright, touristy pub near the fairground where I recognized no one and no one recognized me. I sat there for too long, nursing a glass of wine, startling every time the door opened, paranoia and anxiety growing, afraid to go home, but afraid not to because Joe and Mia were back there with Patrick.

An hour. I was only out an hour, but Patrick reaches for me as soon as I step back inside the house. He wraps me in his arms and holds me too tight. I can barely breathe, but he holds me tighter. He's breathing fast and trembling. "I thought you weren't coming back," he says, his eyes red. I try to move, but he won't let me go. This close, I can smell sweat and sour alcohol, and that's not how Patrick smells.

An hour. That's all. What's he going to be like when the three of us get on a plane and leave for a month? What will he be like if he finds us when we return?

He relaxes his hold and I step away. His fear is contagious. This isn't Patrick. This isn't right.

"It's okay," I say, even though it's not. I say it to stop the fear—the fear breaking Patrick into pieces and the fear rising in me. It dampens the anger, douses it, with icy-cold trickles of panic.

"Things are going to get better," he says. "I have a meeting tomorrow at work. Things will be back to normal. The house..."

"This *fucking* house," I say, and he recoils. I take a deep breath and step away. "I can't do this anymore. I can't live here, treading on the bones of that poor dead family. Trying to pretend it's our home, when it's not. It's not, and it can't ever be. All it will ever be is the Murder House, and the only people living here should be the ghosts."

"It's not the house. It's not—"

"If we hadn't come here, Joe would never have been attacked. You would never have lost your temper with Mia."

He closes his eyes. "No. It's pressure of work, not the house. Like my dad... you wouldn't understand."

He opens his eyes and stares at me. "John Evans stole this house. His father bought it while me and my parents lay bloody in the dirt and he gave it to John, like it was a new football. God, I hate them—all of them, with their lying shark smiles, all charm on the surface, rotten inside."

"I thought you were friends. That's what I heard."

"John fucking Evans stole the house and I got it back. *That*'s what matters. Mia and Joe were out of control long before we moved here and things would have been worse if we'd stayed in Cardiff. And you... you, Sarah. You took an overdose and almost died. That wasn't in this house, was it? No, moving to this house is what saved you."

Patrick's face is white. "It was never John Evans's house—he stole it, he ruined it, and I wish he'd—"

"You wish what?"

Patrick shakes his head and pushes past me.

"You wish *what*?" I shout, but he's already gone, slamming the front door behind him.

The next morning I'm standing in the front garden staring down at the border under the window when Ben walks up to the gate. I'm looking for another footprint, a hint of who might have dug up those pills, small or large—wouldn't that give me a clue? But there's nothing. And now here's Ben, passing by again.

"I wanted to check you were okay," Ben says, his hand on the gate. I don't say it to him, but I saw him coming. I was upstairs and he had paused in the exact spot I saw the watcher on the first night.

"Sorry," I say. "There's been stuff going on. I've been distracted."

"I haven't heard you up in the studio."

I didn't know he'd been looking out for me.

"Can I come in?" he asks.

A group of girls in school uniforms walk past and stare at us. One whispers something and they all burst into laughter. What if they tell Mia, if Mia tells Patrick about the man on my doorstep, standing too close?

"I'm gardening," I say, even though I have no gardening tools, even though my feet are bare. "Let's stay out here." All I can think about is that damn painting of him and Patrick, and I don't want to be in the house alone with him.

"What are you going to plant here?" Ben asks, coming to stand next to me.

"I don't know yet."

"It used to be beautiful," he says.

I turn to him. "You saw it?"

He nods. "When we were still friends, I'd come over sometimes. Patrick's parents liked gardening. We weren't allowed in the house very often. Boys can be so messy."

He sounds like he's repeating words he'd heard. I can imagine Patrick's mother saying it, shooing them out when they came in with muddy feet and sticky hands. When I knew Patrick's parents, they didn't have a garden, just that crowded, dark little rented bungalow, a few paving slabs for outdoor space. I don't remember them having a single plant.

I put my foot in the earth, right where I thought I saw that original footprint. There's something hard under my heel. I crouch and dig my hand in, pulling out a plastic figure, a little white Stormtrooper. I wiggle my fingers farther into the dirt and there they are, half the cast of the original *Star Wars* films, plastic corpses emerging from the ground.

I pick them up and clean them off. They're still recognizable, but some of them are warped, half-melted, as if they've been pulled out of a fire. Han Solo is featureless, his head nothing but a melted blob.

They weren't there when I buried the pills. They weren't there when Patrick turned the border over just after we moved in.

"I remember these," Ben says, and I go rigid.

He nods at the tortured figures in my hand. "That was one hell of a punishment."

"Punishment? What do you mean?"

He sighs. "I don't know what Patrick did, but his father threw his *Star Wars* figures in the fire. That's how he got the scars on his arms. He put his hands in to rescue them."

How had he said he'd gotten those scars? A fireworks accident. A rocket gone astray. "Why would his dad do that?"

Ben frowns. "That was what he did. Give Patrick something he really wanted, then take it away. Good thing they never let him have a pet."

That's not what his father was like, no. But most of what I know is from Patrick, and haven't I learned recently that not everything Patrick tells me is truth? I open my hand and let the figures fall back to the ground, scooping earth back over them, burying them once more.

It can't have been Ben who put them there. Can it?

I look at him but can't read the expression on his face. He's staring down at the shallow grave I've made for the *Star Wars* toys.

"Patrick's the friend who needed sanctuary, isn't he?"

Ben hesitates, then nods. "He was off school once, for days. When he came back, it was assumed he'd been ill. He was thin and pale and too quiet. But I saw him when we got changed for PE and he was covered with bruises. I asked him about it—I knew things weren't right at home. But he was hostile. He started distancing himself from all of us. I kept an eye on him, though," he says. "And later, when he came back, I gave him a key to the studio."

"When he came back from where?"

Ben looks at me. "It... I'm sorry. I misspoke."

"I don't know who he is anymore," I say. "Since we moved back here, I've found out all these things."

"Like what?"

Like he was friends with you but I've never heard your name mentioned, I could say but don't. The ease I felt around Ben after our first meeting has all gone. "Like this," I say, pointing down to the half-buried *Star Wars* figures. "Like that he was friends with John Evans. Like that I'm worried he's been sleeping with my best friend."

He blinks, leans down to pull up a dandelion. "Is it the first time?"

"First time what?"

"First time he's been unfaithful."

"Yes. At least, I think so." The doubt grows more doubt, gives birth to a whole litter of doubt that squirms in my belly.

"Are you sure? Can you always account for where he's been?"

Is he still talking about Patrick and another woman? "What do you mean?"

"He was always..."

"Always what?"

"He never had one girlfriend at a time. Never anyone steady. He had a string of girls who'd follow him around."

I can't picture it. I have no doubt girls fancied him at school—I've seen photos: he was as beautiful then as he was when I met him. But I can't imagine him with loads of girlfriends—he's always been so single-minded, so focused on one passion at a time. For all these years, it's been me.

"Patrick? Really?"

"A different girl every other week, it seemed. Never letting anyone get close. I saw it the summer before I left for university. Patrick and John Evans teamed up, worked their way through half the town."

Patrick and John Evans...Tom had been right, then. About them being friends. Which means Patrick is still lying. What else is he lying about?

"He told me he hated him."

"Maybe he did, later. When John got the house. I don't know—I'd left town for college by then. But at the time, before John got together with Marie, they'd hunt together."

Hunt.

"Patrick had a type," he says. "Perhaps that's why I felt the need to give you that key. All his girlfriends looked like you and I remember how he treated them."

Caroline doesn't. You couldn't get any further from me than Caroline. Could Mia have been wrong about what she saw? I haven't been able to imagine it—maybe because it isn't true. What did Caroline say that night in the hospital—*it's not what you think*. I feel a surge of hope. God, I want Mia to have gotten it wrong.

"When Patrick left town for university, and John and Marie moved into this house, I assumed that was the last I'd see of him. But I came back during vacations and I'd see him around sometimes—not regularly, but every couple of months or so. He took up with John and his group again like nothing had happened."

But what about the things Patrick had said about John Evans? It didn't sound like friendship. No mention in his bitter words of evenings spent in the pub, a friendship or acquaintance, or whatever the fuck it was, lasting longer than me and Caroline. *I wish he'd...* What had Patrick been going to say?

I think back to the day the story came out. The house, Patrick's house, now our house, blown up huge on the front page of all the papers, not just the local ones. *Welcome to the Murder House.* Not there yet, the spray-painted graffiti: the walls were bare then.

Oh, God, Patrick, isn't that your old house? I remember saying, and Patrick picking up the paper, staring at the photo.

What did he say? How did he look? Did he go pale? Did his hands shake? I can't remember. He sounded as shocked as I was, I remember that. There was a photo, underneath the house. A photo of the family... *Did you know them?* I asked him, didn't I? Yes, I asked. I close my eyes, make myself go back there, make myself wait for his answer. Patrick, younger, no gray in his hair. Me, longer hair, not as skinny, just a few weeks after Mia's birth. *Did you know them?*

No.

That was his answer. He said *no*, put down the paper, and left the room. I must have thrown out the paper, not wanting to look at the house, at the poor dead faces of that family anymore.

What about before? The few days before the story came out...the day it happened. Was he home every night? Or was he in the pub with John Evans, the last person to see him before he was murdered? I don't know. How am I supposed to remember? It was more than fifteen bloody years ago. Mia was not yet sleeping through the night. I was tired, distracted. Every month or so, that's how often Ben is saying Patrick was coming back here and meeting up with John Evans. Once a month for how many years that I never knew about? What was it Tom said to me, that Patrick knew something about Hooper and the murders? What does he think my husband knows?

All these weeks I've been staring out of the window, looking for the watcher, the monster, the bogeyman, scared that Ian Hooper had come back to town with his bloody knife. What if the bogeyman has been inside the house the whole time?

I hear the wind chimes again, fainter this time.

Please. Does she know you at all? After so long with you, she can worry about such a stupid fucking thing? Of all the things to worry about, you turning serial killer is not one of them. You're good, though. Your mask is almost seamless these days.

I could give her better things to worry about. I could give her things that will keep her awake for years, worms of worry to burrow their way into her brain, eating, eating, eating…

But, really, haven't I already told her enough? Gifts on the doorstep and hints about all the secrets still hidden in the house.

Slide my glass across the bar to be refilled. The barman smiles at me. "I thought it was you," he says.

Thought it was who? The me I am now, or the me I was then?

CHAPTER 29

There's a knock on the door at ten o'clock at night and it sends a jitter of fear through me. I pull the curtain aside and a different kind of fear moves through me as I see not Ian Hooper and his bloody knife, or Tom Evans, but Caroline. I've been expecting her to turn up ever since she came to the hospital. She's left messages and I've deleted them all. The tiny hope that Mia was wrong is still there—but if I speak to her... *It's not what you think*, she said. But what else could it be?

I open the front door and stare at her. She's not wearing any makeup and her face is blotchy and washed-out. I can't remember the last time I saw Caroline without makeup. I used to tease her that it was tattooed on.

"I don't want to talk to you." I go to slam the door, but she grabs it, won't let go.

"I know it's late, but I had to wait for Sean to come home. You wouldn't answer my calls. I had to see you."

"I don't think there's anything left to say."

"Listen to me, Sarah. Do you think it was coincidence that Mia was there when he kissed me?"

Not wrong, then. The kiss was real.

"Do you really think we'd get so carried away we'd do that knowing she was there? He set it up because he knew it would split you and me up, that it would turn you and Mia against me."

I glance behind me, looking for Patrick. He'd said he was going to bed, but what if he'd heard Caroline knocking? I step outside, pulling the door closed behind me.

"Stop it—stop making bloody excuses."

"I won't. Not until you listen and think about it. I don't know what lies he's been feeding you, but do you really think I've been harboring feelings for Patrick? *Patrick?*"

It doesn't make sense. Of course it doesn't. But it happened.

"You know when it was? After you came home from the hospital—I saw the For Sale sign go up on the house and I came around. Did he tell you? Of course he didn't. He wouldn't let me see you—we were arguing and suddenly he grabbed my arm and kissed me. He smiled. I couldn't make sense of it—couldn't work out why he'd done it. I never told you because it wasn't... it wasn't a passionate kiss. There was nothing in it that said he was the slightest bit interested in me. He must have known Mia was there, Sarah. He knew exactly what he was doing." I shake my head, but she presses on. "Think about it. I won't stay now, but read this—Patrick has been lying to you. Read this, even if you don't believe anything else I've said."

She hands me some photocopied sheets of old newspaper reports. "Is this about the house? I know—"

"It's not about the house. It's about Patrick. I told you Sean found something. This is it."

My hands shake as I read the photocopied story, dimly lit by the outside light.

A man and a woman have been questioned in connection with child cruelty charges after a 12-year-old boy was removed from their house and taken to the hospital.

The boy was found with injuries and in a severely malnourished and dehydrated state. He is currently in the care of Social Services.

"What is this?"

"It's Patrick. The twelve-year-old boy was Patrick. He spent months in care—has he ever told you this? He was in the same group home as Eve—that's where they met."

"No, that can't be right."

"It is—I've seen the files. Sean looked them up. He could have been fired for doing it, but I needed to see. You need to know,

Sarah. He was in care with Joe's birth mother and he never told you. He's been lying—why would he do that?" She takes a deep breath. "Didn't you tell me he and Eve were in a casual relationship, then she got pregnant? How casual could it have been if he knew her all those years?"

I feel sick reading the story. That's what Patrick told me, a casual relationship that resulted in a pregnancy. But if they'd met when he was twelve, were they in touch the whole time? And how could he have been in care? What happened? Injured, dehydrated, malnourished— Oh, God, oh, God...The cellar. The writing on the wall. How could he not have told me? How could he keep something so huge a secret?

"I've never liked the way he acts around you," Caroline says. "He shut everyone else out, wouldn't let us near you. He wanted you all to himself, right from the beginning."

"Please stop it."

She opens her mouth, closes it again, then sighs. "I saw it, from the first moment you introduced us...He was controlling. Creepy. I didn't like it."

Everything Patrick had told me about his childhood was a lie. All lies—that bloody perfect life he's been trying to re-create is all a lie.

"I saw his file. I saw what they did to him. He never said a word to the social workers or the doctors. He denied his parents ever touched or neglected him," Caroline says. "His dad went to AA and they let Patrick go back to them. But he was in care, Sarah. Something happened that was so bad, he had to be taken away. And he's never told you about it or about knowing Eve since he was a kid."

"No. It can't be true. It can't."

"How can you still be in denial?"

Denial? It's not denial. Not anymore. I'm shell-shocked. Reeling. I can't...I just can't...

"Sarah, he's been lying to you the whole time. You need to get out. Come to me—bring Mia and Joe. Please."

I stare at her. "I can't just walk out now—he's upstairs. So are Joe and Mia. Do you think he'd let us walk away with you? He'll know—he'll see you." I'm suddenly scared for her as well as us. She has a husband at home—and her boys. They're so much younger than Joe and Mia. I can't bring Patrick roaring after me to her house.

My fear is reflected on her face as she looks up at the house.

"You have to go now," I say. "Before he knows you're here."

CHAPTER 30

I go upstairs on shaking legs, but Patrick's not in bed. His pillow's cold, still plumped up. In the dark, in the silence of the night, my imagination supplies a picture: Patrick spying on me talking to Caroline, or drinking with Ian Hooper, swept in by the storm, Hooper sliding the bloody knife across the table. *Here*, he says. *I've held on to this for you for too long. Have it back.*

I head toward the stairs but stop dead before I take the first step down when Mia's door opens and Patrick comes out. He doesn't see me hovering there: he goes the other way, into the bathroom.

I walk along the landing and push Mia's door open. "Mia, honey?"

She's curled up, facing the wall, barely visible under the quilt, and I think she's asleep. It's okay, she's sleeping, Patrick was just checking on her, like he used to do when the kids were tiny. Maybe she left her light on, maybe he was turning it off...

It's this house, putting bad thoughts into my head. Every time I pass through one of the cold spots, more of them seep in, thoughts of ghosts and cellars and hidden secrets and buried lies. I think she's asleep and then I see her hand clutching the quilt, white-knuckled. She's awake.

"Mia..." I step farther into the room. What can I smell? "Mia, have you been drinking?"

She turns then and my eyes have adjusted to the dark enough to see the fury on her face. Anger and...something else. Fear?

(*I've been bad. I've been very bad.*)

"Me?" she says, in a whisper to match mine. "*Me* drinking?"

I glance at the half-open door. Patrick's still in the bathroom. I push Mia's door closed and go to sit on the edge of the bed.

"I can smell it," I say. "It can't be your father drinking. He said he was going to bed. If he sat in the bedroom drinking alone at half past ten, that would be..."

(*very bad*)

"You don't know *anything*. You're so fucking blind."

"What was he doing in your room?" We're still speaking in whispers, but those words seem too loud and I see Mia flinch.

"It's this house," she says, turning from me to stare up at the ceiling. "Everything was fine until we moved to this *bloody* house."

Was it? I think of my breakdown, my grief after my mother died; Joe's car accident, the older scars on his arms. Mia's only half-right. Everything that's wrong now was wrong before. The house isn't making these things happen: it has been stripping away the lies blinding us all.

"He called me Sarah," Mia says as I get up to leave.

"What?"

"You asked why he was in my room. He's drunk. He staggered when he came in. He was looking out the window at something and he called me Sarah. Don't tell me the house isn't affecting him."

"He must have gotten the wrong room." My words feel clumsy and forced.

Mia thinks so too. I can see it on her face, in that edge of fear.

(*I've been bad*)

"He called me Sarah and he was ranting about secrets and lies and punishments." She sits up, chewing her lip. "You haven't... you haven't lied to him, have you, Mum? Because the state he was in, that would be..."

(*very bad*)

I think of the gallery, of Anna and Ben and Tom Evans, of everything Caroline just told me. Fear rises in my throat, like a physical thing. I'm wrong. Mia is right. It is this house, feeding these evil, creeping thoughts into Patrick's brain, where they sit and fester. The cellar, his parents, John Evans, the murders, Caroline, the watcher, going into Mia's room...

"No—don't worry. No secrets. Nothing for you to worry about. But Caroline has said you can stay with her for a while," I say.

"After what she did?"

I swallow past the lump in my throat. "It wasn't what it seemed—she still loves you. You can stay with her for break and you'll be..."

Safe. I don't need to say it out loud. I see the relief on Mia's face and I feel it myself. I know it's the right decision. It doesn't matter what's gone on with me and Caroline: all that matters is that Mia will be safe with her. I'll have a week and in that week, I'll...Fear grips me, panic of the unknown. In that moment, I feel younger than Mia: I'm the girl who watched her mother fall apart when left alone; I'm the girl who's clung to Patrick and closed her eyes to every hint of something wrong for more than seventeen years in fear he might take Joe away from me.

I step back onto the landing as Patrick comes out of the bathroom. He looks at me and back at Mia's door. "What are you doing?"

"I thought I heard a noise."

His eyes are red, like he's been crying. He looks defeated.

"Are you okay?" I ask, and he straightens up, his face blank, Patrick again.

"I'm tired," he mutters, and walks into the bedroom, leaving me on the landing, poised on a cusp: part of me just wants to run.

Even back then, when the house was just a house, not yet the Murder House, it was a bad *house. You sensed it; I know you did.*

We were there together once. It was locked up and empty—your parents were out. We walked through the house in the dark and when my eyes adjusted, I saw cracks in the walls, felt cold drafts creeping through. It was perfectly tidy, but I saw mold in the corners, rotten window frames. I saw a house your parents had obviously lost, long before the bank took it away from them. It smelled rotten. It smelled dead. If someone had told me then what the house would become, I'd have believed them because I could already see it creeping through.

All those months before you lost the house, you were just the same. The smile never dropped. That time, though, your smile wasn't there.

"Do you want to see the cellar?" you said.

I shook my head, but you took me down there anyway.

CHAPTER 31

"What do you think? Looks good, doesn't it?"

It's not Ben asking; it's Juno, his permanently smiling assistant, already walking away before I can answer. I'm staring at my painting in the window of the gallery. Not the painting of the Murder House—in the end I couldn't exhibit that one. Or the ones still locked in the cellar. Instead there's the painting of Anna's secret beach, with all its glittering colors. Down at the water's edge, someone stands staring out to sea. I think it's me. I think I painted myself onto the canvas and what I can see in that swirl of cobalt blue is yearning: a yearning to sail away, a yearning to drift, or a yearning to drown.

It's Thursday afternoon and the exhibition opens this weekend. I haven't been back to see Ben since he came around, but I brought my paintings down from the studio when I knew he wouldn't be there. I thought this exhibition would be my opportunity. There are half a dozen bottles of Prosecco in the gallery fridge, a box of rented glasses on the counter, and posters are going up all over town with my name on them. I've done all this in secret, encouraged by Anna.

But Patrick's going to find out. He'll see the posters or walk past the gallery and see my work in the window.

I'm finding it hard to breathe.

I can't be in that house when Patrick finds out about this.

What do I think? I think I'm scared.

I walk away from the gallery and take out my phone.

"Caroline? I need your help."

I open the door quietly, but Patrick still hears. He comes out of the kitchen and watches me hang up my coat. It started raining on my way back and I'm leaving a pool of water in the hall. I need to shower and change, but Patrick's blocking my way.

"Where have you been?"

"Sorry I wasn't here when you got home. I went for a walk." The exhibition program burns a hole in my pocket.

"In the rain?"

"It wasn't raining when I went out."

He's turned away from me, but I can tell the rage is there, simmering, bubbling. I can tell in the set of his shoulders, the way he squeezes the kitchen door handle before he opens it.

What would he do if I told him the truth? It's not even about the exhibition—it's the fact that I've lied, gone behind his back.

"I've got dinner in the oven," he says. "Go and change and we can eat."

Mia opens her door as I go upstairs. She looks at my dripping hair. "Where have you been?" she says, an echo of her father, but without the simmering anger under the surface. I hear in Mia's voice the fear I feel.

My hand tightens on the program in my pocket. I want to tell her, but Patrick is just downstairs and he might hear and he might...

"Mum?"

"What?"

"I saw Dad on the beach earlier." She looks down at her feet, then back up at me. "He was...he was in his work suit and it was the middle of the afternoon. He stood right at the water's edge in the rain. He had his shoes on and the sea was going over his feet and up his legs and he looked...People were laughing because he looked mental."

"Mia..."

"Seriously, Mum. It was pissing down with rain and he was there in a suit, getting soaked by the waves and he looked *deranged*."

Has he already been past the gallery? That simmering rage...

"I have your train tickets," I say, over the too-fast beat of my heart. "Pack up your stuff—I've called Caroline and you can go tomorrow as soon as you get home from school. We won't wait until break. You can miss a week—I'll call them, sort it out."

"Have you told Dad?" The fear on her face makes my heart beat even faster and, for a moment, I think I might pass out.

I shake my head. Mia's lip is trembling, but she doesn't say anything else. It's implicit that this will stay secret until she's on that train. Until she's safe.

I press my hands against the sides of my head as I put the shower on. Every morning Patrick gets up, puts on his suit, picks up his briefcase, and drives off God knows where. He hasn't mentioned the suspension in days. I thought...I hadn't thought. I had other things on my mind. But if Mia saw him on the beach, has he been going to work at all? If not, what has he been doing? The water starts running cold and I step out, shivering.

I go down with dry clothes on and my hair wrapped in a towel. Patrick's in the kitchen, stirring something in a saucepan.

"Patrick, Mia said she saw you on the beach," I say.

He doesn't answer.

"Patrick." I say it again, gently, but he turns away, puts the oven mitts on, and bends down to take a roasting pan out of the oven.

"Where have you been going? To work?"

He stands with his back to me for a moment, then spins suddenly. "Here, take this," he says, pushing the pan toward me. He does it so quickly that I grab the pan without thinking and scream as the hot metal sears my bare hands. I drop it, beef and fat spattering across the floor. He grabs my hands and I scream again as he pulls me toward the sink, pushing them under the cold tap. Tears spring to my eyes as the cold water gushes over my red palms, the skin already blistering.

"I'm sorry. God, Sarah, I'm so sorry, I didn't think. It was an accident—I wasn't thinking."

But I'm thinking of his rage, bubbling and boiling over. I'm thinking of the look in his eyes as he pushed that roasting pan toward me.

"Mum?" Joe peeps around my door and I get up, pull it open wider to let him in, trying not to use the tender part of my hand. I'm not sleeping. I've been sitting on the bed, trying to work out what to do next.

"What happened?" he asks, staring at the bandages on my hands.

I put my hands behind my back, like he might forget he's seen them if I do. "I had a silly accident and picked up a roasting pan without oven mitts. I wasn't thinking."

He stares at me. He knows I'm lying. "I have an interview tomorrow for that course. Can I show you my portfolio?"

"Of course." I smooth down the quilt so he can heave it onto the bed.

The first page is another drawing of Mia, bigger than the one I framed. I glance up at him, but he's grown his hair and I can't see his face under the fringe that falls over his eyes.

"I worry about Mia," I say, tracing a finger over her pencil-drawn face.

"I know." Joe turns a page in the portfolio and Patrick's staring up at both of us, a dark, almost faceless figure set at the eye of a swirling maelstrom. I pull my hand away from the page and lean back, as if he could come lurching out of Joe's painting, wrapped up in all that swirling storm.

"She's going to stay with Caroline," I say. "Next week and for the break. Do you want to go as well?"

He shakes his head. "I can...I can stay with Simon. Are you going to Caroline's with her?"

"I don't know." Despite what happened with Patrick and Caroline, it's the first place he'd look for me.

Joe sighs. "Why don't you leave?" he says.

I look at Joe's painting again, searching for the Patrick I fell in love with, the man who danced with me, who had a smile so wide and open I could see all his love. If I can find that Patrick, I can show him to Joe.

"Sometimes"—Joe glances at me—"the way he treats you... Sometimes I've wondered if you like it."

Shame grows sour in my gut. I don't know what to say, so I keep my eyes on the portfolio, now turned to one of his sketches of me. I've always been so scared of living alone—I went from my mother to Caroline to Patrick. The thought of being alone makes fear bloom inside me. But how do I tell that to my son?

I turn the next page. Here Joe has painted the house, the Murder House. He's painted it not as it really is, a pretty Victorian seafront house, but as some Gothic horror house, standing alone on a cliff-top, battered by winds and storms, but it's recognizable. He's painted it like it is in my nightmares. And I recognize myself in the tortured Munch-like figure in the top window, pressing on the glass, shadows creeping up behind her. The tears in my eyes blur the drawing and I reach up to wipe them away. It's the dark twin of the one I painted, with the wrong angles and sense of something off. This is full-on Monster House.

"This is how it looks in my dreams," Joe says. "If I get in," he says, "if I get into college, I'm going to move out. I'll keep my job—Simon's said we can find an apartment together, not as a couple, but share an apartment."

Joe flips over a couple more pages and stops at a pencil drawing of a laughing boy. I recognize him as the brown-eyed boy I saw in Joe's earlier drawings the night he was attacked.

"Is this him?" I ask, and Joe nods.

He's sitting on a chair in the drawing, leaning toward us, bundled in a thick jacket. He looks open and happy, clean-shaven, bright-eyed. This drawing is more intimate than the earlier sketches I saw.

"He kissed me," Joe says. Immediately I want to shake this bright-eyed stranger, make him promise never to hurt my son. He's still so fragile, despite the college application and the therapy sessions.

"I know you're worried," Joe says, rubbing his arm. "I know you're waiting for me to start cutting again. But it's not Simon who made me start. Even if it all goes wrong, it's not Simon who'll make it go bad for me again."

No, it'll be Patrick. It'll be this place. He's been trying to tell me for weeks, but I haven't been listening.

"I have something for you," I say, going over to the wardrobe and reaching back for my treasure box. Right at the bottom, under the postcards from my dad, there is a set of paintbrushes in a roll of fabric.

"My dad gave me these," I say to Joe as I hand them over. "The last time he came home before he stopped coming home. I never...I was angry with him then for leaving, so I never used them. Then they became too precious to use because they were the last thing he bought me."

I watch as Joe unrolls the velvet. They're good sable brushes, too good for the child I was then, still daubing with poster paints. "I want you to have them," I say.

Joe glances at me, then reaches out his hand. "Why does this feel like a goodbye?"

I take his hand, squeeze it lightly, wincing as my burned palm throbs. "You'll definitely get a place," I say. "You're incredibly talented, Joe."

"So are you," he says, zipping up the portfolio. "Don't give up on it, Mum."

"I have an exhibition in town." I blurt it in a rush and the words sit heavy in the air. It's because I've kept it a secret that it feels like I'm doing something wrong. "I'm hoping I'll sell some paintings. Enough to..." I leave the sentence unfinished.

"Does Dad know?" Joe says, and I glance toward the half-open door, back of my neck prickling. All these secrets. "Don't tell him," Joe whispers.

In the cellar, you kept a box. Secret, hidden. Tucked away in the far corner, never coming out of the shadows.

"I kept this here for when..." you said.

"When what?"

"When I was down here. When I'd been bad."

You opened the box and showed me what was inside. Now I remember junk. Tat. Useless things. Now I think, Why not a flashlight? Why not water? Why not food? But that's practical, adult crap. And you were a kid when you hid that box, and it wasn't hunger or thirst or even the dark you were scared of. It was what was in *the dark.*

In the box, you kept a shell. A big one, from some exotic shore a million miles away from that cellar. "I used to think it was full of magic," you said. There was also a key, but you wouldn't tell me what it was for, what it unlocked. And, best of all, there was a necklace with a cross on it to ward off all the evil.

CHAPTER 32

The next morning Patrick unwinds the bandages and lays them on the table. He picks up the first aid cream and gently rubs it into my throbbing palms. I risk a look—they're red and there are a couple of small blisters, but it's nowhere near as bad as I'd thought. When it happened, it felt like I'd burned the flesh down to the bones.

"I'm sorry," he says again, putting soft gauze pads on my palms and opening a fresh bandage. His sleeves are rolled up and I can see his own faint burn scars.

"It's okay," I say. "It was an accident."

He puts a strip of surgical tape on to hold the bandages in place. "Was it?"

I look up at him. He's still holding my hands and I pull them away. "What do you mean?"

"All the way to the drugstore to pick up bandages, I'm telling myself over and over it was an accident, and all the way back I was thinking I was angry with you. For being out again. For lying. Perhaps I didn't plan to burn your hands, but…"

I shake my head. Patrick looks thinner, smaller, older. Eaten up from the inside out by fear growing like a cancer. It's infectious. I feel it blooming in me.

"What if it wasn't an accident?" he whispers. His breath is sour.

Anna comes to the house and I put my bandaged hands over my ears, hunch down at the table, and wait for her to give up. I don't want to see anyone.

I jump, my elbows slipping off the table. Now she's knocking on the front window. "Go away," I mutter, walking into the hall to peer into the living room. I can see her shadow in the clouded glass. She knows I'm in here. She knows I'm always bloody in here.

The shadow retreats and I breathe again. I don't know how I've ended up here, hiding inside from my friend, hiding out there from Patrick. I unwind the bandages from my hands. One of the blisters has burst and I gasp as the cotton tugs at the raw wet flesh. They throb and the pain is fierce, but there's no sign of infection, so I wrap them again, adding a fresh cushion of gauze to protect my palms.

Patrick has gone out, dressed up in his work suit as usual. I wanted to ask him where he was going, but the words wouldn't come. He's left some money on the table, only a few pound coins, but I gather them and run upstairs.

I pull open my top drawer, looking for the envelope I've hidden at the back, slowly filling with any odd bits of money I find. I stuff the coins into it—there's been barely thirty pounds since I bought Mia's train ticket and it makes me laugh, a snort with a hysterical edge. This is my running-away fund? Thirty fucking quid? I can't get money out on my card: we're so far overdrawn that the bank will say no. We're living on Patrick's credit card, which he keeps on him at all times. I've already cut back on the food shopping so I can squirrel away a few more pounds.

A knock on the door makes me jump and I push the envelope back into the drawer. Dammit. Anna's not going to give up. I march to the front door and pull it open, but no one's there. A feather floats up and gets caught in my hair. More swirl around me, and when I look down, I think it's a dead bird on the step, but when I crouch and look closer, it's a box lined with soft gray and white feathers and in it is another shell, the twin of the one I carried around in my coat pocket and then displayed in the cabinet.

Sometimes when I held that shell to my ear, I didn't hear the sea. Instead I heard whispering and strained to pick up the words. Sometimes I could hear the whispers floating on the air, too faint to make out. The children hear them too. Mia wakes up crying and Joe gets jumpier every day.

I think Patrick hears them, but he'd never admit it. He keeps going outside at night, looking for the watcher. After the night he thought he saw the watcher, he stopped accusing me of paranoia. He got someone in to measure up for new curtains, thick, heavy ones that block out every chink of light downstairs and in our room.

"No one can spy on us now," he said, pulling them closed in the living room.

The walls crept closer. I've never been claustrophobic before, but those velvet curtains look stronger than steel bars blocking the window, sealing us in, just the four of us, locked up in the Murder House.

I lift the box up, then Patrick's there, snatching it out of my hand before I can pick up the shell. "Where did you get this?" he says.

"I didn't—it was on the doorstep."

He pushes past me, striding out into the road, looking up and down the street, the box still in his hands. Then he hurls it down onto the rocky beach and all the feathers fly up, a swirling storm around his head. "Leave us alone!" he shouts to the empty street.

Losing it, I think. *He's losing it. Things are escalating, aren't they?* Anna's voice echoes in my head as Patrick shoves past me again, sending me stumbling into the door frame. I watch him snatch up his keys, get into the car, and drive off, swerving across the road and speeding up as he reaches the corner. I hear the wind chimes again, louder, discordant, and press the heels of my hands against my ears.

I lock the door with a painful twist and walk away, ignoring Lyn Barrett's twitching curtains. I'm halfway up the coast path, thinking of nothing but getting away from that bloody house, when the mist starts rolling in. It's nothing new; I've become used to it—the world disappearing. But I'm on the coast path alone, three feet from the cliff edge. The mist is damp and cold and there are footsteps behind me. Is it Patrick? Anna?

I slow and so do the footsteps. I'm poised again, on the cusp Joe paints me on: fight or flight? Always, before, my choice has been run, hide. Block out the world. Pills, wine, hide behind Patrick, hide from the truth, hide from...everything.

But I'm not going to do that anymore.

A second passes and I turn. A man steps out of the fog. "Sarah?"

I should have run. I should have screamed. I should now—run, scream, both. It feels like the world has gone, but it's all still there. I'm only five minutes from the house.

He steps closer and it's Tom Evans. I don't know whether to be relieved or more scared. He looks like a stranger, a man full of demons.

"Don't run," he says, his hand shooting out to grab my sleeve. "I'm not here to...Don't be scared."

We're hidden in the mist, the only people stupid enough to be out. My heart is pounding so hard I believe in this moment that a person could die of fright.

"Let me go," I say.

He drops my arm and moves back, his own hands held up. "I'm sorry, I'm sorry."

I tuck my bandaged hands farther into the sleeves of my coat. "What do you want?"

I can hear Patrick's voice in my head, whispering what he'd said when we watched that row of people staring up at the house: *They're waiting for it to happen again.*

"I saw you come up here. I left you so many messages, but you didn't return my calls."

"You have to stop calling, Tom. I'm sorry I contacted you. I never would have if I'd known you were still so..."

"So what?"

Obsessed. Disturbed. I can't say that to the man standing in front of me trembling, can I? Looking barely older than Joe—Joe with all his pain and scars. "Have you told your doctor you've been calling and visiting me?"

He laughs. "My doctor fucked up."

"I think you need to try to let this go." I wince at my own words. Isn't that what Patrick said to me? *Let it go, Sarah.* If I'd done that, would I be here now? Would everything be such a mess if I'd been able to do as Patrick asked and pretend the murders never happened? That Ian Hooper being released meant nothing to us?

"You were the one who contacted me. You were the one who brought me back here," Tom says, and the additional weight settles on the burden of guilt I already carry for so many things. "And you were right to do that," he says, reaching out and clutching my arm again. "I can help *you* now and you can help me."

"What do you mean?"

"Hooper's out, and he shouldn't be. He should have rotted and died in prison for what he did to my family."

"I know. I'm sorry, but what can I do?"

"Not you—your husband."

I shake my head to rid it of the buzz of his words. I can't hear what he's about to tell me. "Patrick doesn't know anything."

"You're wrong. He was there. He was with Dad the night of the murders. They were in the pub together."

"No—no, that's not true. I'm sorry, Tom, but—"

"He gave evidence in court."

"What?" I'm frozen by his words. He's deranged. Patrick is right: he's delusional. "No, he didn't. I would know." But I stopped looking, didn't I? After I contacted Tom, I stopped my research into the murders. I stopped wanting to know all the horrible details.

"He did. He told the court they were in the pub together until ten, so there was no way..." His voice trails off.

He has to be lying. Patrick would have told me he'd been called to give evidence. But Patrick never told me he and John Evans were friends. Patrick never told me he was visiting this town while I was at home with Joe and Mia.

"There was always doubt," Tom says, looking into the fog, not at me. "I was a kid hiding under the bed while my entire family was murdered."

There's an odd distance to his voice, a lack of emotion that reverberates, sends prickles across my skin.

"I remember...Mum tucked me in, but I had a bad dream and woke up, so I was under the bed playing because I didn't want to go back to sleep. I heard shouting. I heard a man shouting and my mum screaming, and I saw...My door was open and I saw Dad and Mum in their room struggling and Mum was screaming at Dad and she—she fell. Billy rushed out of his room and I closed my eyes then and I put my hands over my ears until the screaming stopped." He takes a deep, shaky breath.

"When I came out, it was quiet and I thought...I thought it was over. But then I heard more voices. I went to the top of the stairs and I saw Hooper with the knife and I saw my dad fall. I told them that the first time." He looks back at me. "But before Mum and Billy stopped screaming, I heard the things Dad said. He was shouting at Mum. He was shouting, *I'm going to kill you. I'm going to kill you all.*"

He gives me a ghost of a smile that chills me inside.

"I spent my whole childhood telling myself I was wrong. I'd been mistaken. Dad wasn't a good man all the time, but he wasn't a monster. I didn't want to be the monster's son. I told my grandfather once and he said the same. He said I was wrong and I should never, ever tell anyone. So I didn't. And then, at the trial, Mr. Walker said he was with Dad and it made me feel better, because I must have gotten it wrong—it wasn't Dad I saw and heard shouting at Mum. I was confused—maybe I fell asleep and was dreaming. It must have been Hooper, because Mr. Walker said Dad was with him."

I breathe in but can't let the breath out. I hold it until my chest hurts.

"But it never went away," Tom says. "Hooper was never convicted of my mum's and brother's murders. Not enough bloody *evidence*. He was there with the knife in his hand...It had to be him."

He looks at me. His hand relaxes on my arm. "I need Mr. Walker—I need Patrick to talk to them again. He knows the truth. He can tell the truth and Hooper will be locked up again. Then this will stop," he says, letting go of my arm. He hits himself hard on the forehead, clenches his hand into a fist, and hits himself again. "I want it to stop—I want to stop hearing my dad say those words." He lets his hand drop and there's a red mark on his forehead.

"It's why I sold Mr. Walker the house—it's why I agreed to see you the first time. He knows the truth about the murders and he knows the truth about the house, what it does to people. You should have listened to me before—you should have gotten out then."

I back away from him, my heart hammering in my chest. Patrick was right about one thing even if he's lied about everything else: Tom is disturbed.

"Sarah?" Tom calls as I turn to run. I stop and glance back at him.

"Did you get the box I left?"

"You left the shell? Just now?"

He looks blank. "Shell? No—the other week. You weren't there so I left it on the doorstep."

"What?" Then I remember the box with my name on it that Patrick took.

"It was photographs. From before. My dad and your husband. The house."

"I haven't... Patrick took the box." I see a shadow cross his face. There are only a few years between him and Joe, but right now he looks decades older.

"When we moved into the house, there was... You should look at the walls," he says.

"The *walls*?" I remember the pictures from those newspaper cuttings, the edge of drawings under Joe's peeling wallpaper.

"Behind the wallpaper. In the room that used to be mine. That's how I know Mr. W—*Patrick* understands about the house. What it does." I don't like the way he says Patrick's name, through gritted teeth, spitting it out.

His gaze skitters away from mine and he stares back down the path toward the house. It drifts into view in a break in the mist, and I see Anna on the doorstep. When I glance back at Tom, I realize he's been watching me watching Anna.

"You should be careful, Sarah."

I turn away, but I don't move. "Leave me alone, Tom."

When I turn back he's gone, swallowed by the mist.

Anna is still standing on the doorstep, hunched over, her hands in her pockets. She looks like she's just gotten up: her hair is all over the place and she's not wearing any makeup. Close up, she smells of stale alcohol and cigarette smoke.

"What are you doing here?"

"I wanted to check you were okay. I saw Patrick leave—he looked angry," she says. I step past her to open the door, fumbling with the keys in my bandaged fingers, trying to hide them with my body.

I haven't invited her, but she follows me inside, still talking. "I saw his face as he left. What do you think is going to happen next? You think he's going to come back and everything will be fine?"

I ignore her and run upstairs, opening the drawer of Patrick's bedside table, searching for Tom's box of photos. There's no box, but my hand closes on one photo, crumpled at the back of the drawer.

I recognize Patrick immediately, even though he looks so much younger. He looks like the Patrick I met. The photo is taken outside the house, and even then, way, way before it became the Murder House, it still looks... dark. The windows are blank black eyes, the red door a bleeding mouth, hiding sharp teeth waiting to gobble up the smiling teenage Patrick.

But it's not the house, or Patrick, that gets my heart racing. It's the grinning man next to Patrick, who's obviously a young John Evans, looking just like a happier, luckier version of Tom. Then my eyes drift to the teenage girl with the wild black hair leaning her head against Patrick's shoulder. It's Anna.

* * *

She's still standing in the hall when I go down.

"You told me you only moved here last year."

"What?"

"Both strangers in town, you said. Always lived in the city, you said."

"Christ, Sarah, what are you talking about?"

My sleeves are pulled down over the bandages, hiding the photo. I'm searching Anna's face, but she gives nothing away, just stares at me in confusion.

"How long have you really been here? How long exactly have you known my husband? How well did you know him when you and he and John Evans were all laughing fucking teenagers together?"

I push my sleeve back and hold out the photo. "Look at this—*look*. It's taken here, right in front of the damn house. Patrick's got his arm around you—were you sleeping with him? Were you his fucking *girlfriend*? Why would you lie?"

She looks shocked, ready to deny it; then something changes in her face and her shoulders sag. She hunches over, her eyes on the floor. "Does it matter?" she says. "I never lived here. I was passing through and we hooked up. He wouldn't even remember me, so does it matter?"

"Does it *matter*? You never told me. You've been lying the whole time." I thrust the photo at her, waving it in her face.

She doesn't answer, doesn't react. Instead she reaches for my bandaged hand, raising her eyebrows when I gasp and snatch it away. "Did Patrick do this?"

"It was an accident. Everything's fine. Stop trying to change the subject."

"What subject? I'm trying to help you, Sarah, and you want to bitch at me about some crap teenage sex a million years ago?" She marches away from me into the kitchen. "So what if I was?" she says. "So what if I was sleeping with Patrick? Or John fucking Evans? So what if I had sex with half the town over one wild weekend by the sea? You didn't know me; you didn't know them. What if I told you we had sex in this house, we had sex on the beach, at the fairground, in the restroom of the pub? Is that what you want to hear? Does that make you feel better?"

"It's not the sex," I say. "It's the lying."

"I'm not the only one lying. You should ask him. Ask him if he remembers."

"Remembers what?"

She's shaking her head, white-faced, her arms wrapped around herself, like she's in pain. "Nothing. Forget it."

"Look, Anna. I think it's best if you stop coming around for tea for a while, okay? I know you're trying to help, but this is my life, not yours, and there are things you don't know."

"You think you can skip off into some bright golden future?" she shouts, stepping closer, yelling right into my face. "I've seen your paintings in the gallery. The exhibition opens tomorrow, doesn't it? What do you think Patrick's going to say about that? Or has he already seen them? Is that what the fucking bandages are about?"

"Doesn't matter now, anyway," I say, to the house, to myself, as well as to her. "I'm leaving. As soon as Mia gets home, we're leaving."

"What about Joe?"

"Joe's with a friend and he's moving out anyway. He's going to get a place at college, an apartment share with a friend."

Anna frowns. "Joe? What are you talking about? He's too young."

"He's almost eighteen. He'd be going away to college soon anyway."

She shakes her head. "You told me he was fifteen."

"Mia's fifteen, not Joe."

She walks over to a framed sketch of Joe and Mia as toddlers. "I thought they were twins," she says, tracing their smiles.

"No, they're not. There's nearly two years between them."

Her hand stills on the drawing. "Two years?"

I nod, even though she has her back to me.

"No," she says. She takes the picture off the wall and stares down at it. "No. What did you do?" she whispers.

"What?"

She whirls around and her face is set in a snarl, her eyes filled with tears. She raises the picture and throws it past me at the wall. I duck and cover my head as the glass shatters and flies everywhere.

"You bitch!" she screams. "You thieving fucking bitch." She rushes toward me and I step back, my shoe crunching on broken glass. She stops a foot from me, trembling, breathing fast, her face still set in that snarl. I think she's going to attack me, but instead she turns and runs out through the door, slamming it behind her.

I crunch over the broken glass and lean to pick up the drawing, brushing shards of glass off it. I'm going over what I said in my mind, looking for the catalyst, for whatever set her off. I blink and then I see. It's not in this picture: it's in the photograph, the one Tom Evans left for me. I see it now. I see it in the spin of her foot, in the wave of her hand, in the edge of her bitter laugh. I finally see it.

I look from one picture to the other.

And there it is.

Eve.

There's writing on the back of the photo from Tom. My hand is trembling so much it takes a moment for the words to sink in. When they do, when I read them and look at the picture again, I have to rush out, to the bathroom, head over the toilet, retching and retching up bile and bitterness.

I've been so stupid. More stupid than I ever thought I could be. So damn *stupid*.

Still time not to do it. I look at the envelope in my hand. I could rip it up, walk away now, go and get shit-faced, keep going until I die. But I've already put the letter in the envelope. You'll know, won't you? You'll know what it means.

This envelope is a bomb. This envelope and what it contains is a grenade, a Molotov cocktail I'm about to push through your door. I know what it'll do and I still have the power to stop it. If I want.

But I don't.

CHAPTER 33

"Joe? Joe—it's Mum. Please call me back as soon as you get this message. Don't come home. Call me first." It's the third I've left and I'm worried. I need to speak to him before— The front door slams and I gasp.

I'm upstairs, throwing clothes into a suitcase. It's not three o'clock yet, too early for Mia, too early for Joe to be back after his college interview. I shove the suitcase under the bed, my heart pounding, tugging the quilt down to cover it just as Patrick walks into the bedroom. The awful truth, all Patrick's lies, Anna's screaming accusations—they hover in me like physical things, wanting to come out in a howl of fury. But I can't speak: he stands between me and the door, and tension fills the space between us. I can see, in the sheen of sweat on his forehead, his trembling hands, his red-rimmed eyes, that any semblance of control has gone. This is the Patrick who threw Joe against a wall. This is the Patrick who went roaring toward Mia.

"We're famous," he says, chucking the local paper and a bunch of flowers onto the bed.

Patrick brought me flowers? I stare at them. I'm reaching for them when I see the card clipped to the bouquet. There's a printout of the photo of the Evans family that was in all the newspapers, the words *Never forgotten* written underneath. I recoil and snatch my hand away.

I go cold, looking at the headline on the newspaper. They've used the same photo, the famous photo from fifteen years ago, fluttering police tape, *Welcome to the Murder House* spray-painted on the front door...and those are the words they've used as the headline. There's a weird buzzing in my ears and the world retreats for a moment. All I can see is the newspaper.

"It's the anniversary of the murders," he says, brushing past me to go to the window. "The *fucking* vultures are back."

I look out, past Patrick, who is white-faced and shaking.

Lyn Barrett is walking up to the gate. She lays a bunch of daffodils and a small stuffed toy on the ground.

"Oh, God," I mutter.

"They do it every year apparently," Patrick says. "Lay flowers and pretend they all knew the murder victims so well. Fucking *vultures*."

I step closer, looking for Ian Hooper, for Tom Evans.

I rub my arms to smooth away the goosebumps.

Run, a voice whispers. *Now, while he's distracted.*

"They lay their flowers and talk about how *awful* it was, such a *tragedy*. But they're all dying for something exciting like that to happen again," Patrick says, not looking away from the window. "Fifteen years to the day...They're just dying to see more blood spilled in the Murder House."

He pulls the curtains closed and turns away. "I've been called into work," he says. "For an urgent meeting. What a treat for a Friday afternoon." He steps closer to me. "Better lock the door, hide the key, keep the murderers out."

I nod. But if we lock the door and hide the keys, we're trapped in here. And I no longer think it's the danger on the outside we need to worry about.

After he's gone, I find myself pulled back to the window. It might be paranoia, but it seems that everyone who passes, the dog-walkers, the joggers, pauses to stare up at the house. I draw the curtains again and reach down to pull out the suitcase.

The newspaper is still on the bed when I put the suitcase next to it. I feel sick as I read all about my husband, his family, and this house. The report gleefully revels in the fact that Patrick has moved back into the family home. I read the last lines and draw in my breath.

Ian Hooper was arrested last week for assault in Liverpool after a fight outside a club. Hooper, who's been living in Liverpool since being released from prison, was charged with assault on a 25-year-old man.

All the things left on the doorstep, the watcher outside the house. If Hooper has truly been in Liverpool all this time, it can't have been him. None of it was him. I *wanted* it to be him, the obvious Big Bad, because otherwise... But it was never him. The Ian Hooper I've been so scared of has never existed. It has to have been Tom, waiting and watching even before I contacted him. Oh, God—I've been so stupid, inviting him into our lives.

I should never have waited this long to leave. Why did I? Was it for my stupid exhibition, which was always a ridiculous dream, wasn't it? Another form of denial. I don't know where I'll go. I won't stay with Caroline, but I can borrow money from her, find a cheap B-and-B and I can— Oh, God, what *can* I do? Doesn't matter. I can figure that out later.

I throw more clothes in, but I need some of Mia's and Joe's things. Mia's only packed for a week. I take my suitcase downstairs and run back up to fill another bag. My heart is racing as I cross the landing to Joe's room. I'm gripped by the conviction that I have to go *now*, that even taking these few minutes to pack is wrong. It's definitely colder in Joe's room than the rest of the house, even when the heat isn't on. I can't blame a faulty radiator.

The wallpaper is peeling again and I pull it off in a big sheet. What did Tom say? Look at the walls. Plaster falls, a shower on the floor. Underneath the wallpaper, beneath the black spots of damp, the whole wall is covered with drawings. Sketched by a child's hand, but not an innocent hand. The drawings are of a family, the stick man and woman with knives in their bellies, being torn apart by sharp-toothed dogs. The stick man strangling a stick child, the stick woman climbing into the stick child's bed, hands outstretched. I put my hands over my mouth and swallow sour vomit.

My legs are shaking as I back out of the room and close the door, wishing there was a fucking lock on it. Joe's been sleeping in there, with those monstrous pictures on the wall. My breath is fast and harsh as I move on to Mia's room. Most of her possessions seem to be scattered across the floor, clean and dirty all mixed up. I crouch to look under her bed for shoes and see something else, tucked right at the back, something shiny. She must have dropped something down the side of the bed. I lie down and wriggle under, stretching my fingers out to reach it.

The chain is dusty, but I recognize it right away. It's my mother's necklace, the gold chain with the sapphire pendant, her "best necklace," she used to call it, always putting it on when we went back to visit. My hands are shaking and I drop it on Mia's rug, where it sinks into the shaggy pile and disappears. I push my hands into the rug until I find it again, the dust all gone, shiny and gold again, so many memories of my mother in every link of the chain.

"What are you doing in my room?"

I hadn't even heard Mia come into the house. She's in the doorway, scowling at me. Guilty, I think, as her attention goes from me to the chain in my hands.

"Did you take this?" I say, standing up.

"Where did you get that? It's mine." She stretches for it, but I hold it out of her reach.

"Yours? You took it, didn't you? You went into my room and took it. Where's the rest? I saw"—my voice is shaking—"I saw my mother's engagement ring in a jewelry shop in town. I thought your dad took it...but you sold it, didn't you? Is that how you paid for the new clothes, how you could afford to go out and get drunk?"

"What the hell are you going on about?" she says. "I didn't take any bloody jewelry. It was a present."

"What?"

She's wary now. It's there in the double blink, the shifting of her feet. "Dad gave it to me. As a present. I haven't worn it—it's gross. I hate gold. I thought I'd lost it."

"It's not his. It was never his. It belonged to my mother. Why did he give it to you?"

"As a reward," she whispers.

"A reward? For what?" I force the words out and she glances behind her as if expecting to see Patrick there.

Mia looks so young and so like me standing in the doorway. There's a moment here, a moment for us to do what we always do, to walk away in opposite directions, ignoring what we don't want to confront. I close my eyes and wait for it to pass.

"He asks me where you've been, who you've been talking to. He told me it was because he was worried about you. After the overdose." She reaches into her pocket and pulls out a crumpled twenty-pound note. "It's what he gives me the money for. I'm sorry. I told him I didn't want the money. He kept insisting he was only doing it because he was worried."

I swallow, thinking of all the places I've been, all the lies I've told.

"It doesn't matter. We're leaving, both of us," I say to her. "I've packed a bag. We're leaving."

"The other day when you were out..." She comes to stand next to me, leaning her head on my shoulder. She traces the bruises on my arm, four perfect circles of purple where Patrick grabbed me. "Oh, Mum, I've really fucked up."

She seems smaller, younger. I kiss her forehead and smooth back her hair. My little girl. How could Patrick have put this on her? This is my fault. Anna was right: I should have gotten out already—I should have found a way earlier.

"He came into my room again," Mia says.

I pause, my hand still on her hair.

"He was drunk," she whispers, and I hold her a little tighter, closing my eyes. "I could smell the whiskey on his breath when he got closer. He was drunk and raving and I was scared, and he kept asking me about you and what you've been doing..."

I hold her so tightly, rocking her back and forth as she cries, whispering soothing words to her, telling her everything will be all right, words meant to be a balm to her raw wounds. I hold her tighter still and try to control my own trembling.

"He was drunk and I tried to tell him nothing was going on, but I saw you, Mum, at the café and then at the gallery with that man. Your paintings in the window. I saw your face. You were suddenly happy while me and Joe were going through so much shit. So I told him. I told Dad you've been painting and I told him about the exhibition and that you've been seeing someone else. I told him everything and he gave me that bloody necklace. I wanted to tell you, but I didn't know how to..."

I go cold. I remember Patrick's face as he thrust that roasting pan at me. Mia told him all this and he didn't say a word, but it's festering inside him, truth and lies. My burned hands are a punishment. He meant it. What's he going to do when he sees the exhibition and recognizes Ben? I can't go with Mia now. I can't run with her—Patrick will come tearing after us if I do. He'll go straight to Caroline's with all his rage and he'll—

"Go," I say to Mia. "You go ahead. Get the train and go to Caroline's and stay there until I come for you."

"You can't stay here, Mum."

"I'll be fine—it's just for a bit, just until you and Joe are away and safe."

Mia's shaking her head, her arms wrapped around her stomach as if she's in pain. "No, no, you have to come too—you can't let him... What will he do? He'll go mental, you know he will. He'll lose it again. He'll—" She stops and takes a shuddering breath. "You don't know, you don't know everything."

"What? What is it?"

"At the old house, when you took the overdose..." I can barely hear her words over the rushing and roaring in my ears.

A car door slams outside.

"After school, Dad picked us up. Dad *never* picks us up—he should have been at work. I told him I was going shopping with you, but he took us home and we found you...It was like he knew. I asked him. After. I asked him and he said I was wrong, he just finished work early and wanted to pick us up."

"I believe you," I say, through numb lips, tasting the bitterness of pills on my tongue.

"I didn't want it to be true—I wouldn't let it be true because I was scared," she says, tears spilling. "I was scared and I took it out on you because I couldn't face thinking that Dad would do that."

"What? Mia..."

"You had Joe. You've always had Joe and your painting, talking about bloody art all the time. I was Dad's girl, so I thought if I didn't let it be true, things would stay the same. But they didn't. We came here and Dad...I didn't have Dad anymore. I don't have anyone."

I can hear a key in the front door.

"He gave you the pills, didn't he?" she whispers, and I close my eyes.

"Go down now," I say. "Run out the back way."

"I can't. He's already in. He'll stop me."

"Okay. I'll go downstairs and meet him," I say. "I'll distract him, take him into the kitchen, and you can sneak out the front."

"What will you do? You won't tell him you're leaving, will you?"

"I'll make something up. I don't know what yet." I put my arms around her, gather her up, like I used to when she was little, hug her as tightly as she hugs me. "I will sort this," I say. "I swear to you I will make this all right. You're my girl. *Mine*. I'll sort it, then I'll come and get you and everything will be okay."

She starts to speak, but I shake my head, pushing her out of the room ahead of me. "Go—wait for me."

CHAPTER 34

My step falters as I get to the bottom of the stairs. I heard Patrick come in, but there are no lights on and the front door is open, swinging back and forth in the wind. I nudge Mia and push her outside. She takes a step away, but I cling to her sleeve. Why is the front door still open? Has someone followed Patrick in? I look down the street, but no one's around. It's so tempting, so tempting, to grab Mia's hand and run away with her.

"Sarah?" I let go of Mia's arm as I hear his voice and I hear her hurrying away as I turn, a fake, bright smile on my face that freezes at the sight of Patrick's face. Something's wrong. Something's very wrong.

"Where are you going?" Patrick's voice drifts from the darkness of the hall and I take a step back. The door's still open. I could still run. Patrick comes forward, out of the shadows.

"Nowhere."

He laughs. I don't like that laugh.

"I was getting worried," Patrick says. "I thought you'd gone."

I step inside to stop him from seeing Mia leaving. "I thought you had a meeting."

"I never made it. Someone put a letter through the door for me and I—I know what the meeting was about anyway. They're firing me."

I see something that looks like blood on his shirt and my mouth goes dry. "Patrick... What have you done?"

He sees me looking and touches the stain. "I've been making too many mistakes, forgetting meetings, not turning up."

Suddenly I remember the suitcase. The packed suitcase sitting in the hall, inches from him. My heart pounds and my stomach turns in lazy waves. I should have run with Mia.

He follows my eyes to the suitcase. "You never intended to give the house a chance, did you?"

"I did. Of course I did. I gave you my mother's money, didn't I? I gave you everything I had."

"And you've never let me forget that, have you?" He opens the suitcase, takes the clothes out by the handful, dumping them on the floor. "The only money you've *ever* contributed to this marriage. Money I had to practically beg you for."

He takes the now-empty suitcase and unlocks the cellar, throwing it down the stairs. "I'm not going to let you. I won't let you leave me like that. I won't let you sneak off."

He grabs my arm, pulls me farther into the house, then leans across me and pushes the door closed. As my pulse rate shoots up, I imagine Patrick's control as a piece of elastic, constantly stretched since we got here and now stretched a little more by Mia telling him about my exhibition and Ben, even more by that bloody suitcase, further again by his job. And the house, constantly nibbling away, eroding the thread that's left.

"We can't stay here anymore." The words come out as a whisper. "I know what you did. I know about Eve..."

"No."

"We have to leave." I try to keep my voice calm, keep my focus on stopping his control from snapping. But when I go to step around him he moves in front of me, blocking my path. "Maybe...maybe you getting fired is a good thing. You can find something else, something less stressful. You can sell the house, give yourself some breathing space. Have a *real* fresh start."

"And you? You and the children? Are you planning on coming with me?"

I hesitate too long.

"No." He says it too loudly and I flinch. "I won't let you leave me. And you'll *never* get the children."

I grit my teeth. "I won't stay here. It's rotten, it's evil, it's bad for me, it's bad for the children, it's bad for *you*. You can see that, can't you? You and Joe and Mia...And now you've lost your job."

"It's not the fucking *house*." His voice rises and I take a step back. "It's you, passing judgment all the time, making me beg for your mother's fucking money when I've paid for everything the entire time we've been together. *You're* the reason I'm stressed. *You're* the reason the kids have gone so far off the rails. *You're* the reason I lost my damn job because I had to spend all my time worrying about you and your state of *fucking mind*."

I try again to push past him, but now his hand is at my neck and he shoves me against the wall, his hand tightening, cutting off my breath. I reach for his arms, dig my nails in, scratch as hard as I can. He swears and lets go of me. I slip and stagger and he grabs for my hair, pulling it until I scream, then hauls me back, raises his fist, and punches me. My face explodes, I swear it does. I fall, both hands clutched to my cheek, afraid to find it shattered. There's blood—my lip, my nose. I can taste it, sour and coppery.

I curl up small. In films, in books, when they fight and get up and run and fight back, how can that be real? I can't move. I can't think. All of me is concentrated here, in this fire on my face.

He gathers me up. He's rocking me like we're dancing and he's crying. I can feel his tears falling on my face and they sting, salt in my wounds.

"I'm sorry, Sarah. I'm so sorry. I never...I won't...I'm so sorry."

He rocks me back and forth and I'm crying too, for the couple we once were, the man who danced with me, who had that smile, all that love, all those plans.

"You're right," he's saying. "It's this house...I thought I could make everything right. When I grew up here, it was so *perfect*. Then I came back and the windows were rotten, it was damp and falling apart. My parents were...There was something wrong with them. There was always something wrong with them. But I thought, when the house was mine, I could make it all better."

He sits me down on the bottom stair and reaches for a tissue from the box on the hall table. He dabs it on my lip, wiping away the blood.

"The house was taken away and I never got the chance. Not then. This, though, now, us, this was my second chance. You were so ill. I was so scared after your overdose. I was so scared I was going to lose you and I thought the house could make everything right."

He leans in. I think he's going to kiss me and I cringe away.

"No, Sarah," he says frantically, pulling me into his arms again, muttering his words into my hair. "No, no—don't back away from me. Don't be scared of me. Please—I never wanted...I thought if I had the house back, I'd have it all. But it's not right. You, the children, the house, none of it is perfect. Not like it should be."

As he says this, he pulls away and I can see the anger simmering again, frustration fueling it. He stares down at the blood-spotted tissue in his hand and his voice drops to a whisper. "When we met, do you remember how we'd plan our lives? All those dreams we had?"

I remember. I remember silly conversations, pie-in-the-sky stuff, the things a new couple says. It wasn't *real*, his talk of the house by the sea, the kids, the dog, his conviction of how perfect it would be. I never thought it was his real bloody life plan.

"Please don't leave me, Sarah."

I back away from the hand he reaches out. *Don't touch me*. The words are in my head, but I can't say them. I'm scared of making that anger burst out again. He touches my face, gently this time, cupping my jaw, his thumb brushing my lip.

"It's the house," he says again. "It's this house. I'll sell it."

"Sell it?" I don't believe him. He's been obsessed with getting this house back his whole adult life.

"You don't believe me, do you? I will, I'll sell it. What's the point in having the house if I'm living here alone? I never meant to live in it alone. It's supposed to be a family house." He rests his forehead against mine. "Please...I'd never have...If we hadn't been here, if I hadn't gotten so caught up in the house and everything, I would never have lost control like that. You've seen it, you said it to me before, it's the house. Give me another chance. We'll sell and we'll move and it'll never happen again."

I don't speak.

"We'll move," he says. "We'll move and it'll be better—it'll be like it was before, you'll see."

I close my eyes as he rocks me and I want to cry. Better like before? When? When I thought we were happy, but he was coming to this town once a month and never told me, drinking in a pub he never mentioned, obsessing about a house I thought was a long-forgotten piece of his past, lying about business meetings when he got home to me and the children?

He's rocking me and it's like we're dancing again, scruffy me in my thrift-store coat and Patrick with the smile that was all for me, and I wonder if there's any of that Patrick left…if that Patrick ever existed at all.

"I'm sorry," he keeps saying. "But I won't—I can't let you leave me."

The cellar door is still open: I can feel the cold draft on my face.

"Where are Mia and Joe?" he asks.

My heart is galloping. "No idea," I say, resisting the urge to look at my watch. Will Mia be on the train by now?

"I wanted Mia to be wrong, but then I got this letter," he says, pulling an envelope out of his pocket.

"What?"

"I went out, driving around, trying to get my head around it, wanting not to believe it. And then I went into town and I saw your paintings in the gallery. I saw your name on the poster and I knew Mia was right and that you've been lying to me for so long. And she was right about the other thing too, wasn't she?"

"What are you talking about?" I can feel the cold spots Mia talks about, but they're not in the house: they're inside me, growing bigger.

He opens the envelope and holds up a photo of me and Ben—and all the cold spots meet. I'm ice inside and, oh, God, oh, God, I have to get out of here. I lurch upright and turn to run, but he's too quick, his hand shooting out to grab my arm, pulling me back and spinning me around to slam against the wall.

"Oh, I don't think so, Sarah," he says, pinning me there. "You're not going anywhere."

"Please, Patrick—that photo, it's not—"

"Not what it looks like? That's what I wanted to believe. It didn't make sense to me... Someone pushed it through the letter box."

Anna, I think. *Eve.*

"I was here, trying to convince myself it was innocent, that someone took the photo for some vindictive reason of their own, but then I remembered what Mia said."

"What did you do?" I whisper, and there's that look again, skittering past me.

"Mia's a good girl," he says. "She told me everything. She told me the truth, but I got angry with her because I didn't want to believe it."

"It's not true," I mutter. Not true. "It's just an exhibition—he's one of the artists from the gallery. I wanted it to be a surprise."

"You think I wouldn't recognize him? You were sketching him, this *artist*. You told me he was made up, a figment of your imagination, but you drew him, his *house*. You've been inside his house. You've been lying to me all this time. *Months*."

"He's a friend, that's all."

He stares down at the photo again and so do I. It's a photograph of us in the café, me leaning toward him. It's like the painting of the couple on the bench—it could be interpreted so many ways. *Friends or lovers?* Anna's voice whispers in my memory.

It was noisy in the café so I leaned toward Ben to hear something he said better, but it looks like we're kissing in the photograph. It looks like we're in love: Ben's hand is touching mine and I remember the feel of it, how intimate it seemed, that brush of skin on skin.

"He was always jealous of me when we were at school. Jealous of me, jealous of this house when he lived in a poky apartment in town. Just friends? Don't lie to me."

"We are just friends," I say again. "I swear to you, Patrick, I have not been unfaithful—"

"Stop." He lifts his hand and touches my face. His hand is cold on my cheek. "I love you. I'll die loving you. You're the same. You can't live a life without me."

His hand squeezes my jaw and I let out a small cry of pain. His shoulders sag, and his hand drops from my face. "Why couldn't I ever be enough for you?"

"You were once," I say, and tears burn in my eyes. "You were all I ever wanted, but you never trusted me. You *lied* to me, Patrick. From the moment we met, you've been lying. You've done this with all your lies—you killed all that love."

"I helped you. I *saved* you."

"Like you couldn't save Eve? That's the story you told me, isn't it?"

He hunches over, like he's in pain. "You know you're killing me?"

I can see it in the agony on his face. But staying with him would kill me. And if the twisted obsession he has that he calls love has to kill one of us, I'd rather it was him. "Let me go," I say.

"You can't leave me. I'll tell Joe the truth about who he is and what you did."

"I don't care anymore."

"You will care. They'll never speak to you again. You'll never get custody, not even of Mia—I'll tell them about the breakdown, the overdoses. You'll be completely alone."

"Better alone than with you."

His hand comes up and slaps me hard. My head bounces back and hits the door. He reaches for me, pulling me to him, hugging me tight and muttering, *I'm sorry, I'm sorry*, holding me so tightly I can't breathe. He follows his words with kisses and my shock turns to panic. I can't get out of his arms and we're alone in the fucking Murder House and he's kissing me and saying sorry.

"Let me go, Patrick," I say. "Please let me go."

He steps back, still so darkly handsome in his suit, his hair getting too long, falling over his eyes. He bends to kiss me, not on the mouth, just below my ear. "Please, Sarah," he whispers in my ear. "Don't make me punish you again."

He starts stroking my arms and I close my eyes and think about the gallery and Ben. He looked so happy as he went through my paintings, talked about us working together. None of it real, the sanctuary he offered me, tainted forever now by his history with Patrick, but those moments... A whole other life there, waiting for me.

Patrick's hand moves up to grab my shoulder, pulling me back toward him when I try to get away, his fingers digging in hard enough to bruise.

"Tell me you love me," he says, like a plea.

"I don't," I say. "I hate you."

I do. Him, this house, this life, the whole thing born from an evil lie. Such a bitter contrast to the other one, the one I could have. I hate him so I tell him. It's all I have, this little ability to hurt.

Before I can think, he's dragging me down the hall, wrenching the cellar door wider. "You think you can do this to me? You think I'll let you?" I cling to the door frame with my raw, blistered skin and he bends my fingers back until I scream, then pushes me in, keeps pushing me so I half fall down the stairs, and he follows me and we're both there, in the cellar, in the dark.

"I'm sorry," he says. But he's not. He's not sorry at all. His voice is ugly with grief and anger and he's not done punishing me yet.

"Please let me go," I say.

He stares at me. "No. Never."

If I'd said yes to that date with Ben, the first time he asked, before I knew who he was, before I knew how much history he had with Patrick, what would we have talked about? What would I have said to him?

I used to be a whole person, not a half, but I got lost somewhere.

I wanted to leave my husband, but I was scared.

This glimpse of a whole new life, you, the gallery, is more precious to me than you could ever imagine.

But maybe I wouldn't have had to say any of that. He's a painter and we could have talked about art, and books, and music. I would have liked him in a muted way.

He has hair the color of wet sand and ocean eyes, that color somewhere between green and blue. He's stocky and broad; everything about him is warm and I would have let him undress me in his cottage by the sea. I would have smiled as he lifted me and carried me through to his bed.

He's not a handsome man, no lean muscle and flat stomach and sharp edges, like Patrick, but I could have lain with my head on my artist's chest and I could have slept and that would have been my sanctuary, not a studio now haunted by memories of a teenage Patrick.

I think of this as Patrick reaches for me, as he stops me from leaving. I think of my artist and his cottage by the sea and what might have been as Patrick pushes me onto the dirty cellar floor, one hand around my throat, choking off my screams as he pulls my jeans down and rips at my panties. His hand digs into my thigh as he forces my legs apart and shoves himself inside me. He rapes me, and I can't breathe and it hurts and—oh, God, stop.

Patrick, *stop*.

But he won't. He doesn't stop and as he cries afterward and says, *sorry sorry sorry*, over and over again, I close my eyes and pretend I'm in a cottage by the sea, my head on my artist's warm chest, sleeping.

Part 4—The Dragon in the Man Suit

Headline from the *Western Mail,* January 2017:

Who Really Killed Marie and Billy Evans?

Ian Hooper, *jailed in 2002 for the notorious Murder House killings, has been released from jail. He was only ever convicted of killing John Evans due to lack of evidence connecting him to the other two murders.*

Hooper was released quietly on Tuesday. As yet, there have been no reports as to his whereabouts, but he has been ordered, as part of his release, not to return to his hometown.

CHAPTER 35

I can't get up off the floor. I'm still in the cellar, still in the dark. A thin line of light shows under the door and I blink and wait for my eyes to adjust. My husband is eight feet away, sitting slumped against the wall with his head in his hands and I can't get up. I don't know how long I've been here—it feels like forever. I'm lying here telling myself to move. I feel numb and I'm clumsy with my bloody, oozing hands as I try to straighten my clothes. He didn't even take off my jeans, just shoved them down around my knees. My lip is stinging. I think I bit it. I don't think Patrick did. I make myself sit up, but I don't think my legs will hold me if I try to stand.

"I'm sorry," he whispers, and his voice is lifeless, all the rage spent. *Things are escalating*, Anna whispers. I know. I know. Anna said something else, when she was still my friend, when she was still who I thought she was. *The only way out is if one of you dies.* I don't want to be the one who dies.

I wipe another trickle of blood off my chin. When he comes over and crouches next to me, I can smell sweat and stale alcohol. I turn my head away, afraid I'm going to be sick. He kisses my cheek and I can't stop a tear falling. I didn't even know I was crying. I don't want to cry.

"I didn't intend to," he says. "I didn't intend to do anything. But your lies, Sarah. I went past the gallery and saw your name plastered all over posters, and Ben was in there and I..."

Oh, God—I think of the blood on Patrick's shirt. "What did you do to him?" I say, despite the pain in my lip—and everywhere else.

"Get up."

He grabs my arm and hauls me upright, his fingers biting into my biceps. I will fall if he lets go of me. He puts his arms around me and rocks back and forth and it's another fucking parody of our dancing days.

"I was going to kill your boyfriend," Patrick says, pushing my hair out of my face, stroking it smooth. "I was going to lock you in the cellar and find him and kill him for touching you."

"Leave him alone," I say. "He hasn't done anything—we haven't done anything."

He leans in closer. I can smell his sour breath, and the stubble on his chin scrapes against my cheek. "I never wanted to hurt you."

I can't stop shaking.

"I wanted…all I wanted was to love you. I wanted it to be so different. I wanted it to be perfect. This house, this town. I wanted to make it right."

I stare at him, looking for the star-gazing and the seashells and the sand in the shoes and the laughter and the warmth. "I know you were taken into care. I know it was never perfect. Are any of the stories you used to tell true?"

He shakes his head.

"And the writing on the walls…it was you, wasn't it?"

There's a long pause. It fills with words written on a dirty cellar wall, a scared child whispering, *I've been bad, I've been very bad*, over and over.

"I had a lot of time down here. I was bad," he says softly. He blinks and looks away from me. "I was sent down here when I was bad."

"Your parents?" He nods, and the air seems to have gotten thicker. "Why? I don't understand."

"They'd lock me in overnight sometimes." He whispers it so quietly I have to strain to hear. "They'd put me down here and they'd take the lightbulb out so I had no light. Then they'd lock the door. Sometimes they let me out after an hour or two—it depended on what they were punishing me for. If I was very bad, they'd leave me here all night. 'Dirty boy,' they'd say. 'Bad, bad boy.' "

The cold, the creeping damp is everywhere around us. It's daytime now and so dark. At night, would any light have come in through the frame of the door? Would he have been able to see his breath fogging in the cold, making shadows in the corners, or would it have been total darkness?

"They wouldn't put me down here right away," he says. "I'd usually done some stupid thing—lost a pair of sneakers, got mud on the carpet, kicked a football through a window. I'd do it, and they'd see, or someone would tell them, and then I'd wait, days and days and days locked in the house with fear and guilt squirming in my belly, growing and growing until that fucking broken window, those lost fucking sneakers would haunt my every waking and sleeping moment. They'd say nothing to me in that time. The house would be silent, and I'd wait..."

I'm trembling, every muscle tense. I'm there with him. I'm him, a little boy pissing himself in terror about what his parents would do over a lost pair of shoes.

"And then eventually," he says, "they'd sit me down and make me punish myself."

I don't understand. I don't understand how the people I met, that vague old couple living in a claustrophobic hothouse, could be so cold to a small child—their *son*.

"I'd been living in fear for however long it was, crying myself to sleep and wetting the bed, storing up more future punishments, and they'd sit me down and say, 'Well, Patrick, what do you think your punishment should be?' And because I'd had all that time to think, all that time for my crime to build in my head to some monstrous thing, I'd always say the most horrible thing I could think of—they should take away my bike for the lost sneakers, they should lock me up in the dark for the mud on the carpet, beat me for the broken window..."

"And they did those things?"

His voice is calm, expressionless. Not his face, though, that's full...

"Oh, yes," he says. "And they'd always make it worse as well.

Two days in the cellar under the stairs, locked in with no light, just a bottle of water and a bucket for a toilet."

"For mud on a carpet?"

I imagine the dark, the damp, the skittering noises that to a child would sound like creeping monsters.

He nods. "That scar on my back? It wasn't a childhood fall—that was the buckle of the belt my father used to beat me for the broken window. The things they could do..." he whispers. "Her with her hands, him with his fists. But outside, to the world, so normal. You'd never know." He looks at me. "Once he put me down here and forgot. Because he was drunk. I was locked in for days and I thought I would die down here. That was when I was taken away."

"Why didn't you ever tell me?"

He moves, putting more distance between us, a sliver of space for the cold to creep in. "I didn't want to be that person, that boy in the cellar. Not to you. The way you looked at me when we first met, I liked the Patrick you saw, with the childhood I invented."

Would I have looked differently at Patrick if I'd known the truth then? Could I have prevented all this? Could I have helped him if I'd known the truth?

He takes a shuddering breath. "When they first moved here, things were different. Dad had just gotten a really good job and they had this house. They had so much *vision*. So many plans. I came along and they included me and I could see it all, even as a little kid. I could see it and I wanted it. It all fell apart so slowly and I could see them battling against it for years—battling against the drinking taking hold, battling against everything going wrong with the house. I saw it beat them down and break them."

"But..."

"But I could still see it—all they had planned. The life they saw. I promised myself I could do better, I *would* do better." He pauses. "I just wanted to make it right... But look at what I've done. I've turned into *him*, my father." He peers down at his hands. "I could see it all start to go wrong and I got so... angry. I punched a hole in my bedroom wall once—the plaster was falling apart and my hand went straight through. I hid...I hid a knife there. I don't know why. I don't know what I intended to do with it. Was I always planning bad things, do you think, Sarah? Always bound to end up like them? Or could I see things spiraling out of control? Did I think it was for self-defense?"

"I know about Eve. I know what you did. You told me she was *dead*. You told me..."

His face twists. "Eve was as bad as them. Rotten inside. She deserved everything."

"And me? You gave me the pills, didn't you?" I feel again the rough fingers pushing across my tongue. It wasn't a dream. It was never a dream.

"I had to get the house back," he says. "You just needed to see reason. I didn't know how many you'd already taken."

"I could have died."

"That was *your* fault. You'd already taken so many."

I'm crying again and I wipe away the tears with the back of my hand. "All for a house? You did it all for a fucking *house*?"

"It's not just a *fucking house*. It was *mine* and John stole it."

"Were you there? The night...the night of the murders?"

He must see it in my face, what I'm thinking, because his mouth twists and I see the anger rising again.

"Don't look at me like that—don't ever look at me like that. You think I did it? You think I killed them? You think I'm capable of that?"

"I've seen what you're capable of."

"No, you've got it so wrong." He shakes his head and there's a silence that lasts an eternity. "I told John what his wife was up to with Hooper. The whole damn town knew, he was being made a laughingstock, but no one had the balls to tell him. I wanted to see his face when he realized the perfect life he'd stolen from me wasn't so perfect after all."

My legs lose their strength and I sink back to the floor.

"He went insane. Berserk. It was so easy to set him off—I told him his wife was having sex with someone else in his own bed, with his children in the house, that they were all laughing behind his back at how stupid he was, how pathetic, half a man. I told him everyone knew. I told him his sons knew and that they *wanted* to run away with Hooper and their mum, that all of them were happy to be leaving John."

He laughs. "And off he went, burning with all that humiliation, shouting for revenge as he stormed up the street, no one to hear his ridiculous vows but me."

"Didn't you try to stop him from coming here?" I ask, through numb lips.

He tilts his head. "Why would I stop him from going home to confront his wife? Wouldn't any man do that if he knew his wife was cheating?" He says it in a mocking tone as he stands over me with Ben's blood on his shirt, the marks of his fist on my face.

"I thought he'd beat Hooper up and I *wanted* that. I *wanted* him to get into trouble. I never thought the stupid bastard would end up dead. I never expected him to kill them." He pauses. "If, indeed, he did. It was Hooper who was arrested, after all."

"But you *knew*. You've always thought it was John. You should have gone to the police." I can barely speak.

"And confess I'd wound him up? Provoked him into storming back there? No. I was being a good friend, telling him the truth. You don't think he deserved to know his wife was sleeping around?"

"But you knew his children were there, his wife..."

"I did him a *favor* in court, keeping his saintly reputation clean, making sure it was only Hooper who was the villain. My hands are clean, Sarah. I did nothing wrong."

"Oh, God." I put my hand over my mouth. Oh, God.

I can see from his face that he believes his own words and I shrink back in horror. He's going to do the same with me, tell himself that I deserved this, that Ben deserved it, like Eve deserved what he did all those years ago. Telling himself he was making things better for Joe. All these imperfect parts of his life rewritten so he can carry on as if nothing has happened.

"But it doesn't matter now. None of that matters. We're going to wipe away the blood, Sarah, that's what we're doing here. We're going to undo it, make it go away."

I scramble backward, toward the door, but he comes over, blocks my path.

"Except...I keep having this dream," he says.

I don't want to hear any more. I'm hovering on the balls of my feet, ready to run when he moves, when the moment breaks, poised on a cusp, the woman in Joe's drawing. I'll snatch up the children and run, let the sea breeze I used to long for carry us far away.

"I dream I'm back in the cellar, but I'm not alone."

I can hear his breathing, harsh and fast.

"My father is here with me and he's whispering things, terrible things. Then I'm a little boy and I'm back in the cellar and my parents are...my parents are torturing me. But then the dream changes and it's me doing it to Mia and Joe and you. Torturing you, hurting you. Killing you."

I don't notice I've been holding my breath until my chest hurts. I let it out with a gasp.

Patrick climbs the stairs and pauses at the top. "I have to think...I have to work out how to make this right."

Before I can run up past him the door closes and I hear the key turn in the lock. He's left me in darkness. I'm alone, but I swear I hear things—skittering, crawling, whispering things. I close my eyes and put my sore hands over my ears, curling up into a ball.

It wasn't a dream. It was never a dream.

CHAPTER 36

My ringing phone pulls me from a broken sleep. I don't know what time it is or how long Patrick has left me here. I open my eyes and see the screen glowing across the cellar by the stairs and the tiny light reveals Patrick, staring down at me. Has he just come in or has he been standing there in the dark watching me sleep?

"You've been very popular. So many missed calls from Mia and Caroline. But I don't know who this is. Will it be him? My old school buddy Ben?" he asks, and I shudder. He glances at the screen, then holds out the phone.

"Answer it. On speaker."

I crawl over on my hands and knees, my heart pounding as I fumble for the accept-call button. I don't recognize the number.

"Mum..."

"Joe?"

There's silence at the other end and, for a moment, I hope he hangs up.

"Are you okay? My phone died so I'm using Simon's." I hear Patrick react to the name, reaching for the phone, but Joe is still talking. "Mia said she's been calling and you haven't answered. She said you were supposed to be meeting her at Caroline's."

My gaze flickers to Patrick to see him staring at me, a tic going in his cheek.

"I'm fine." I close my eyes and clutch the phone harder, wishing I could stop him talking. "I'm fine."

"She got the train back," he says. "She told me about the gallery—the window's been smashed and there was an ambulance outside. She was scared it was you, but your friend was there and—"

"Friend?"

"Anna. She told Mia she's your friend. Mia's with her."

I look at Patrick and gasp. He reacts not to the name but to my gasp. "No, she can't be. She can't—Joe, you have to find Mia. Anna is not who she says she is. Your dad— You have to—" Before I can finish, Patrick takes the phone from me.

"Joe? Where are you, Joe?" He paces back across the cellar, toward the stairs, his voice sickly calm. "Come home, Joe. It's time you knew the truth. It's time I told you the truth about your mother."

I lunge toward him, but he's already ended the call, putting my phone into his pocket. I grab his arm.

"No, you fucking *don't*," he says, pulling my hand away, pressing his thumb into my wounds. I go to scratch his face, but he has my wrist and pushes me back. I stumble and fall.

He pulls a pen out of his pocket and throws it down toward where I lie, sprawled on the dirty cellar floor.

"Write your lines, Sarah, because you've been very fucking bad."

I see he means to lock me in here again and I can't let him find Joe when he's full of so much bitter rage. When he tells him how we've lied all these years, how a stranger, not me, is his mother, Joe will go mad, and then what will Patrick do? I think of him throwing Joe against the wall, almost hitting Mia, everything he's done to me.

No. I won't let Patrick hurt my son.

I struggle to my feet and run up the stairs, reaching for the door as he opens it, but he grabs my hand, squeezing it, crushing it until I cry out. He's bending my fingers back and forcing me away from the door.

"No, you don't," he says. "You're staying right here." He shoves me then, harder than before, and I lose my footing, falling over and over down the steps. My head smashes on the floor and explodes with pain. The world grays and I try, I try to hold on, but I'm drifting and fading and as I fade, I remember, and all I can think is *Don't, Patrick. Don't hurt him. Don't hurt my son.*

SARAH AND PATRICK—2000

James Tucker. That's it, that was his name, the office boy who asked me out. Stood up by James Tucker, I waited outside the pub for twenty humiliating minutes before I realized he wasn't coming. Instead of licking my wounds and going home, I went to a party, downed three tequilas, and was swaying in a corner, my cheeks burning, half-drunk from nervously bolting my drinks, when Patrick came over. Dark hair, dark eyes, broad shoulders, killer cheekbones. I wanted to stick him to a canvas and stare at him forever.

He asked me to dance, then leaned in and suggested we go somewhere and I just said yes. There wasn't a second of hesitation before the yes. He took me to his apartment and laid me on his bed, and it was only when we were halfway through undressing each other that he stopped to ask me my name.

I don't regret it. Not one moment of it. Even when I thought he wasn't going to ask for my number afterward, even when I thought he was never going to call, I didn't regret it. But he did. He asked for my number and he did call.

He took me for a drive down the coast, bought me coffee. We sat in his warm car while a storm raged outside and we talked for hours. I kept staring at him, drinking him in, this beautiful, beautiful man. He kissed me when he dropped me off, but that was it. Then nothing, for days and days, until today. It's been nine days and he's just called to ask me to meet him in the park. Nine days, and winter seems to be fading, daffodil buds already pushing their way up through the ground. Nine days of me missing college and waiting by the phone, filling sketchbooks with drawings of a half-remembered him. The details of that first night are sketchy, but if I close my eyes, I can hear his voice, feel his hands on me; I can remember the smell and warmth of his skin, how he whispered in my ear, then kissed his way down my body.

He's by the lake and I falter. I'm in black leggings and DMs; my perfume is oil paint and turpentine. He's in a suit even at the end of the day. How is this picture ever going to work? I walk forward anyway. I want him to touch me again after those nine endless days.

Then he moves and I sink onto a bench, my breath stolen by shock, like a punch to the gut. Silly me, this isn't a date. This is him here begging my silence.

He's got a stroller.

I was a one-night stand. An aberration. A fling. A mistake.

How brutal, though, to bring his baby here as well. Extra bribery, maybe—please don't tell my wife, please don't hurt my child by telling her.

I won't. I won't tell. I won't tell him he was my first, either. That I'd been waiting, I don't know what for. But then he came along and I forgot I was waiting and he asked and I said yes and he took my hand, like he was sweeping me into a dance, like some old film, and that's what it was like, all of it. I won't tell him that.

He turns and waves, sensing me from fifty yards away, pushing the stroller toward me. He reaches in, lifts out the baby, who's smaller than I thought, a tiny little thing, no more than a couple of months old. Then, without a word, he puts it into my arms. I look down and laugh.

It looks exactly like Patrick, dark eyes and tufty black hair. The baby smiles back at me, a big gummy grin, and I ache, I really do. Nineteen and aching inside for what I could have had with Patrick. Wanting it after one night with him, one long, dancing night. Aching for this baby to be mine.

"This is Joe," Patrick says, sitting next to me. "His mother died."

CHAPTER 37

I move my head and moan as knifelike pain seems to split it open. I reach to touch it and my hand comes away wet. I can't see, but I know it's blood. I've drifted...and as I drifted, I felt again fingers pushing pills into my mouth. I'm shivering one minute, boiling hot the next. The floor is cold and hard, but I stay down anyway because I don't have the strength to stand or even sit. I lie, curled on my side, and my tears soak into the damp floor.

How long did they leave Patrick down here? Patrick, little boy Patrick, locked in the cellar, writing his lines on the wall. *I've been bad, I've been very bad.* Yes, you have, Patrick.

I'm overcome with another fit of shivering. I curl up tighter. My stomach hurts, a bone-deep ache. I don't remember when I last ate, but I'm not hungry: that's not what this gnawing, hollow ache is about. I am thirsty, though. My throat is so dry.

I should have left after Joe was attacked. I should have taken the children and left whether I thought it was Patrick or not. I should have left the second he went for Mia. I should have, and then he would never have...

I wrap my arms around my knees. I can't. I can't. He's right. This is all me. All my fault.

I don't know how long I've been down here, but the house is too quiet. I listen but hear no voices, no footsteps on creaky floorboards. Where's Patrick? Where are Joe and Mia? I wish I had my phone. I wouldn't even call the police first. I'd call the children to tell them how much I love them.

Where is everyone? What did Patrick do to Ben? Did he kill him?

Oh, God, I can't curl up any tighter, but it hurts, it fucking hurts, and even when I wrap my arms around my head, I can't keep Patrick's words out.

I'll tell him, Sarah.

I'll tell him you're not his real mother.

I'll tell him you never wanted him.

I'll tell him what his real mother was like.

I'll tell him you stole him.

And then I'll…

And then I'll…

SARAH AND PATRICK—2000

"She was already taking drugs when we met, but I didn't know. It was a casual thing between us, it didn't last long, but long enough for her to get pregnant. I made sure Social Services knew she was taking drugs. She kept skipping appointments and I was worried about the baby."

Joe's falling asleep in my arms, his eyes drifting closed then snapping open to stare at me before drifting closed again. His eyelashes are long, sweeping down onto perfect rounded pink cheeks.

"He was born healthy, though, and they gave him straight to me. She left the hospital without looking back. It's been a struggle, but better than he would have had with her."

He tucks a loose end of blanket around Joe, his hand brushing my arm.

"Then last month, she took an overdose and died."

"I'm so sorry," I whisper, stroking Joe's cheek with one finger. It's so soft and warm.

Patrick shakes his head. "Joe's better off without her."

I feel sorry for her, the unknown girl who never got to hold her baby.

"I should have told you, that night we met. But it was so beautiful, so perfect, I didn't want anything to spoil it."

It might have scared me off. It might have made me pause long enough to remember I was waiting. He's right, though. It was beautiful and perfect.

"He deserves a better mother," Patrick says.

I hope he doesn't mean me.

CHAPTER 38

I wake with a gasp from a nightmare of blood and pain. What did I hear? It's so dark down here, I've no idea whether it's night or day. My throat hurts. I'm still burning hot and freezing cold. I think I'm bleeding. I can feel a trickling warmth between my legs.

I can hear whispering, a woman's voice, a child's voice crying. I don't know if I'm still in the nightmare, or if Mia's ghosts are here, cold breath on my neck. Patrick's voice echoes in my head, whispering his awful truth as I lie bleeding on the cellar floor. *He deserved a better mother. She was taking so many drugs it was only a matter of time before she overdosed. But I never would have done it if it weren't for you. As soon as I met you, I knew you'd be a better mother for him. I took him for you, Sarah.*

He told me this made me as guilty as him, an abductor: I'd stolen a child. But he'd told me Joe's mother was dead, that Joe was his and his alone. He lied. He's always been lying.

I sit up. Someone's unlocking the door. I scuttle backward, I don't want to see him—I can't, I'm not ready, I'm…

It isn't Patrick who appears in the doorway; it's Anna. She's wearing the same clothes I saw her in yesterday, and she's so still and pale, I wonder if she's been outside the house ever since, watching.

It was her who put the photo through the door. I know why.

"The door was open," she says, in a light tone, like she's just turned up for a cup of tea. "The front one anyway. Hope you don't mind me just walking in. I saw the lock on the cellar door. I knew you'd be down here. This always was the Walker family's favorite go-to punishment place."

"I'm sorry." I don't know what else to say.

She pulls a dirty teddy bear out of her pocket, a tiny thing more gray than blue, worn and fraying. "Do you remember?" she says. "Do you remember when you asked me if I had kids and I said no?" She looks at me, the fake-light tone all gone, and I see she's crying. "I lied."

Would I ever have realized if I hadn't gone looking for that photo? I don't know. I never knew her. I never knew…"He told me you died," I say, and see her look down at her wrists, with their rivers of scars.

"I tried," she says. "I tried really hard for a lot of years. He told me the same lie. He told me my baby died."

"Died?" My voice shakes. "Died? What do you mean, died?"

I see her taking note of my swollen lip and red eyes, the blood matting my hair, the shaking mess of me locked in the cellar. "He got the photo, I take it?"

"And all the other things you left on the doorstep."

She smiles. "Took you a while to work it out, didn't it?"

"Why would I ever have thought it could be you? I thought you were my friend."

Her smile disappears. "Friends? God, you really are fucking stupid, aren't you?"

As soon as I'd figured out who she was, I knew the whole friendship had been false. "I don't understand exactly what you're trying to do, with the letters, the photo. Was it you watching the house? The night we moved in and after?"

She nods. "Before, too. I watched Patrick all suited up and pleased with himself, moving his perfect fucking family into his perfect fucking house." She looks down at the teddy she's clutching. "I was so…not angry, bitter. I was bitter. My life was destroyed. I had nothing left and he just walked away and started a new one, with you, his perfect girlfriend, going on to have the perfect children he always wanted. While I got left with *nothing*." She scrunches up the bear and I think she's going to rip it apart. "That was bad enough. All I wanted to do then was fuck with you. I wanted to make sure your perfect little life was anything but. I know Patrick—I know him far better than you do. I was with him first."

She walks down two steps. "It fascinated me, the act he was putting on, this Patrick he was presenting to the world. When I knew him, he was still working on it. The Patrick I knew was a lot more volatile. It was still easy to push his buttons. His act hasn't gotten that good." She stops and looks down at me. "Did he like the shells I left? I used to collect them. He came to my room in the group home once and I'd done something to piss him off, so he smashed them all, crushed them to dust, and walked out."

She pushes her hands through her hair so it stands on end. All the things Patrick had said about Joe's real mother, the drugs, the neglect: Were any of them true? I can see it now, in the shape of her hands, the way she smiles. Joe. My boy who was never my boy but has always been mine.

"He hates that you paint, doesn't he, Sarah? Hates that you have that talent, that it's something he doesn't share. So I pushed you to Ben, thinking it would be enough to have you showing your paintings in the gallery run by his old school friend, but then I saw you liked him, actually fancied the little creep. I never knew him back then, but Patrick told me he used to watch him, follow him around town. You really have odd fucking taste, Sarah. But it was so hilariously *perfect*—I couldn't have planned it better. I knew it would send Patrick over the edge when he found out."

She laughs. "I saw you pick the shells up and take them into the house. I whispered messages into the shells for Patrick. You took my words into the house." Her smile fades. "I liked seeing Patrick get so mad."

"What exactly were you trying to do?" I ask her again. "Were you trying to get him so angry he killed me?"

"No. No. I wanted... You stole my life. I thought at first you were just a replacement. Then you told me Joe was seventeen and I realized what Patrick had done."

I'm shaking my head but scared to speak. "Anna..."

"Stop calling me that. My real name is Eve."

"Eve. I'm sorry, but Patrick told me Joe's mother was dead or I'd never have—"

"Never have what? Stolen my son?" she says, coming down the rest of the stairs and grabbing my arm.

Her grip loosens and I wish I had the strength to run.

"We were together from the beginning, Patrick and me. We were stuck in the same group home. He always said it was a mistake being there, and then he was released and I was sent to a shitty foster place...I was so damn jealous. He used to come into Cardiff to meet me and tell me all about his perfect home by the sea, this beautiful house and his perfect parents...I grew up yearning for that. He used to say we'd be together forever and tell stories of the life we'd live." She breaks off and laughs again. "That photo you found? I thought I'd surprise him once—come and see this wonderful home of his. He was all smiles and introducing me to John, like he was happy to see me, but underneath he was *furious*. He cut me off for ages, wouldn't speak to me."

I don't know how I didn't see it before, the sense of familiarity I had when I saw her—she looks like Joe. I always thought he was too much like Patrick and that ate him up, screwed him up, but standing here looking at his real mother, all I can see is my boy. He'd see it too, if he were here now: he'd see it right away. His real mother and his fake mother, the liar.

"Then he came strolling back into my life like nothing had happened. I got pregnant and he moved me in here and, hey, the joke was on me, right?" she says. "It was like a prison, some Hammer House of Horror. His parents, those sick fucks. And him—everything he ever told me was a lie, and when I saw it, saw the reality of his life, *he* hated *me* for it. Blamed *me* for tainting it, for ruining his story. He punished me like they used to punish him. He hid me away, never let me out, never let me see any of his friends again. Locked me in the cellar. I'd be down here and I'd hear the baby crying and he wouldn't let me out because I'd been bad. He didn't trust me not to take drugs, or get drunk or fuck around. I was *dirty*. I was *wrong*." She lets go of my arm and paces back and forth.

I try to edge away, toward the stairs.

"I *deserved* to be punished, he said. And they encouraged him. They gave him the key to the cellar, this fucking punishment room," she says. "The Patrick I thought I knew—he was a false god. So he dumped me, destroyed me, went out and found himself a new girlfriend dumb enough to believe his lies. I had to get away, you see that, don't you? I didn't mean to leave my baby. I didn't mean to be gone so long…

"I came back," she says. "But when I came back Patrick told me he was dead. He said I abandoned him and he died because of me. He said all that and I ran and…"

I'm aching, physically hurting, overwhelmed with the horror of what Patrick did to her, to Joe, to me.

"Patrick never let him be mine," I say. "I wanted to adopt him properly because he told me you died, but he wouldn't do it. I've never even seen his birth certificate. I've never…" My voice dies as I take in everything Anna's said. Oh, God—does Joe even have a birth certificate? No—he must have. Patrick must have registered his birth. He wouldn't have…My mind skitters over years of evasiveness and lies and all the terrible things Patrick has done.

"Can't even steal a child properly, can you, Sarah?" Anna mocks.

"I never knew he was stolen. Not then. I would never—"

"Liar."

"What about Mia? What have you done with Mia?"

She smiles. "Worried I'll do what you did? Worried I'm going to steal *your* child, Sarah?"

"Please…"

"She's fine. I told her a few truths, that's all. All the lies she's been told—I told her what you're really like, what you did."

Anna takes a step back. "She didn't want to listen, screamed abuse at me. And Joe…rushing back here to help *you*. After what you did, he still came running back for you."

"What do you mean?"

"He's here."

"What?"

"Joe. He's here. I saw him come in. He left the door open and I waited, then followed. It was so quiet, I didn't..." She blinks and looks up toward the open cellar door.

I struggle to my feet. "We have to help Joe," I say. "Patrick will tell him. He'll tell him—not the truth. More lies. And he'll hurt him. He'll try to punish me by hurting Joe."

She shakes her head. "No, it's good that he knows the truth. He'll find out the truth and I'll get my son back."

"Anna... *Eve*," I say, "that's not how it works. You think Patrick will tell him the truth? He'll tell him the same lies he told me—that you were a drug addict, that you neglected him, abused him, that you abandoned him and left him to die. And what will he do then? Look at me—look at what he did to me."

Anna's still shaking her head.

"You know him, you know what he's capable of. He wants to punish me, and Joe, for leaving him. What do you think is going to happen?"

"No, no, no," she says again. "That's not what's supposed to happen."

"Joe has been self-harming," I say. "Cutting himself. What do you think it's going to do to him when Patrick spews his lies?"

"I'll kill him," Anna says. "I'll kill him if he hurts my son."

Headline from the *Western Mail*, May 2017:

**Two More Bodies Found
in the Murder House**

The bodies of a man and a woman were removed from the house—the police have not yet released their identities.

ANNA

The corridor is longer. In my dream, in the house that's still just a house, the corridor is longer and there's another door. This one is at the end. And instead of running and running and thinking I'll never get to the end, this time I know I will. And I don't want to anymore. There's a door. There's another door and this one is open.

I get to the end. I don't want to look, but I can't help it. It's blue. The room is blue. Blue for boys. There's a cot and the cot is white and the cot is empty.

You left me there, in that house that wasn't yet the Murder House, just a house. You left me there pregnant, living with your parents while you finished university and then started work, coming back at weekends, the odd night in the week.

All the time I was pregnant, I tried really hard—a couple of drinks, a couple of smokes, nothing really. But then you left me there and your parents ignored me and the hours were so long and so empty…

They made me have the baby in the house. Wouldn't take me to the hospital, didn't let the baby out. They told no one he even existed. Our secret, you called it, when you came back.

The house was cold and dark, too many drafts where there shouldn't have been. It sucked the energy and happiness right out of me. I'd go around putting on lights and heat; your parents would go behind me switching them off again. They wouldn't even let me take the baby for a walk. You'd slink off back to work and they'd lock me in the bedroom or the cellar because they knew I'd leave in a second if I could. I'd find one of my old friends and beg for a fucking wheelbarrow full to the brim with drugs, anything, anything at all.

It wasn't only me; it was the baby too. Crying, all the time, all night, all day. Your parents would shut me in your old room with the baby. Lock us up to shut us up, me frantically shushing a screaming baby to stop them from getting angry with us. When they lost the house, their stuff was cleared out bit by bit, until there was nothing left but me, the baby, the locked door. I loved him, I did, our child—but I was so tired. Any sleep I did manage was broken by nightmares or I'd be woken by the rattles and groans and whispers of the house. And the baby got sick and kept crying until I...couldn't. Not anymore.

My turn to leave. Out of the window, climbing down the tree, praying they wouldn't hear me, that they wouldn't lock me up again. I never meant to be gone so long. Thought it was days, not weeks, not months. I disappeared down the rabbit hole.

I called and you told me to meet you at the house, but when I got there it had been sold. Empty, I thought. The front door was open, though. I ran up and you were in your old room, standing next to the cot. It wasn't a big cot: it was one of those basket things on a swing. Don't remember what it was called, crap mother that I was.

You were there, a bunch of daisies wrapped in tissue in one hand, and the cot was quiet and the house was sold and I thought it was okay. I thought I'd stayed away long enough for everything to be okay again. That now your parents had gone, you were there to take me and the baby away and we'd leave the house and you would be the boy I thought you were again and I'd stop the drugs and things would be good, like they were meant to be.

But you were...not angry, I could have handled angry, would have welcomed it, the punch I deserved. You weren't happy, you weren't anything. I stood in the doorway and you faced me, rocking the cot (Moses basket? Is that what it's called?) with one hand, cold and dark as the house.

The cot was empty.

"You left, you didn't tell anybody. My parents didn't know, so they didn't come up. He was sick and you left."

You looked at me and the anger was there then. "He died," you said. "You neglected him and he died. You killed him." You held out the bunch of daisies. "I've brought these to put on his grave."

My skin was crawling and there was a hole inside me, black as night, growing and hurting. The tears, when they came, were so hot they burned my cheeks.

I shook my head, backed away from you. Backed away from that empty cot. No. No no no no.

I couldn't.

I couldn't stand—couldn't...

My legs gave way and I sank to my knees. "Show him to me—let me see him."

"Too late. We buried him. Better run away again," you said, "before I tell the police you're here, before I tell them what you did."

I ran away from the house where I'd murdered my baby, murdered him by not loving him enough. It was me. I made it the Murder House way before Ian Hooper and John Evans did.

Sarah asked me if I had kids and I said no. But I did, once. I had a child I thought had died. I had a son.

I've gotten to the end of the corridor. This is not a dream. This was never a dream. There's a door. There's another door and this one is open. In the room is an empty cot. The cot was empty because the baby died. My baby. Baby powder, soft, warm skin, shock of black hair like silk, big gummy smile.

But.

He didn't.

Didn't die. He didn't die. I didn't run away and leave my baby to die. The cot is empty because Patrick stole my baby and gave him to someone else.

SARAH AND PATRICK—2000

"Are you sure you don't mind?" He already has his jacket on and his hand is on the door. It's not a real question. I can't really say, yes, I mind. And I don't, really. Of course college work isn't as important as his meeting. And he wouldn't have asked me if his babysitter hadn't let him down, leaving without notice like that.

"It's fine," I say. "Like you said, it's just until you can find another babysitter you can trust. I'll catch up with college work." Joe's asleep, heavy in my arms, his long dark lashes fluttering on pink cheeks as he dreams baby dreams.

Patrick leans down to kiss me and I smile, memories of last night still fresh in my head. "Thank you," he whispers.

Joe sleeps for an hour and I just sit staring at him the whole time. Have I ever seen a baby up close like this before? Maybe as a kid, the neighbors' babies. His fingernails are so tiny, little miniature nails on fat starfish hands. Arms and legs with folds at the knee and elbow. And, oh, his skin is so soft. I can't stop touching him—stroking his hair, kissing his cheeks, picking him up every time I pass.

It's been two months and Patrick says he knows me now, and it's true he smiles every time he sees me, this big grin that makes me melt, it really does. He's such a beautiful baby, even more beautiful than Patrick, and I wonder what his mother looked like. I asked, but Patrick doesn't have a photo. That's sad. What's he going to say to Joe when he asks about his mother as he grows up?

My favorite time is when I give Joe his bottle. He holds it with me and guzzles it down, but he stares up at me the whole time, dark eyes fixed on mine, and when I smile, because I can't help but smile, he grins back, milk dribbling out of the corner of his mouth.

I fell in love with Patrick first, but it's a close-run thing.

Patrick is struggling to find a decent babysitter so I've moved in here temporarily. Not that it's a problem: I get to spend all night, every night with Patrick and all day, every day with Joe. Days spent in a dream of bottles and walks through the park, humming lullabies, diaper changes, baby talk, and cuddly toys. I've put away my sketchbooks and painting gear so Joe can't get hold of it. It was Patrick's idea, even though Joe's still too young to crawl around picking up stuff. He's right—it's better to get into good habits early. Shift change is marked by Patrick's return, the kiss on the neck that still makes me shiver, still makes me want to rip off his clothes the moment he comes into the room. There's no space for anything in my life but Patrick and Joe, and I don't want anything in my life but Patrick and Joe. Some days I don't bother getting dressed. What's the point when Patrick's only going to undress me again as soon as gets home and Joe's asleep?

We listen for Joe to go quiet and my mouth dries. Patrick leans across and kisses me; his hand slides under my T-shirt. My pulse races faster and faster as he pushes me down on the sofa and unbuttons his shirt. Sometimes I can't wait. Sometimes I grab his shirt and pull it open, scattering buttons I have to find the next day, crawling on hands and knees, groping under chairs while Joe watches from his baby bouncer.

I don't bother with makeup. Patrick doesn't like it anyway—he always used to wipe away the kohl smudged around my eyes. So I'm not really surprised by Caroline's reaction when she comes around.

"What the fuck?"

"Ssh—Joe's sleeping."

Caroline looks like a caricature of herself, an exaggerated picture of the Caro I know. Her hair is pink, a sharp cerise bob, her eyes lined with black; she has a blue stud in her nose.

I look down and see myself through her eyes: pajama bottoms and T-shirt, bare feet, mousy hair, no makeup, no underwear. I fade into the background while she hurts the eyes. The contrast is jarring.

"You dropped out?" she says, pacing the room.

"No, I'm just taking a break, helping Patrick out."

She stops pacing and turns to face me. "It's been nearly two months since you last came in."

Two months? Has it really? That's nearly a whole term missed.

"It's temporary. I'll be back."

She's staring at me and there are tears in her eyes. "This is all wrong," she says. "It's like Patrick and that baby are brainwashing you or something." She takes my hands, holds them between hers. "Come back to the apartment. You can still visit Patrick and the baby. But come back with me, come back to college."

"Don't be silly. I want *to be here. I need to be here. I feel...This is home, Caroline. I love him. I love them both so much."*

I hear a small cry from Joe's room and glance back. "You'll have to go," I say, pulling my hands away from hers and nudging her toward the door. "I'll call you, I promise."

"Hold on, Sarah. Promise you'll hold on."

"Hold on to what?" I say, laughing.

"Hold on to you,*" she says.*

I smile and give her a hug. "Don't be silly. Of course I'll hold on to me. And I've always got you to remind me anyway, haven't I?"

"Always," she says.

I go back inside and lock the door, leaning against it with a sigh. She just didn't like how different Patrick was from the rest of us, but he was different in a good way. He already had a proper home, a real career, and a child. Of course he was different; different wasn't wrong.

I go to pick up Joe from his cot, cuddling him against my shoulder. He stops crying and lies against me, warm and heavy. I sing to him as we go through to the kitchen to warm a bottle. Anyway, what am I supposed to do? Go back to my student apartment and leave Joe behind? My arms feel empty if I put him down for five minutes. I couldn't possibly leave.

CHAPTER 39

Anna races up the stairs and I stumble after her. I'm almost tempted to stay, to hide down here in the cellar, take my punishment and wait for it all to be over, wait for Patrick to tell me I can come out now. But I've been doing that the whole time, haven't I? Passively waiting for it all to go away. *Good girl*, a voice whispers in my head, and I can taste the bitter pill on my tongue.

I hear voices in the house above me.

No. Wake up, Sarah. It's not Anna's job, it's mine. I have to protect my family.

When I stagger up the stairs, Anna's in the hall, white-faced, her hands over her mouth. I look past her and see Joe. He's in the kitchen, half facing away from us, black hair in his face, looking like Patrick, looking like Anna. He's standing there and he's shaking and he has a knife in his hand, dripping blood onto the floor. There's so much blood. I think Patrick told him and he's done it, found an artery, cut himself too deep. There's so much blood—how is he still standing?

"Joe..."

"He told me. He told me you're not my real mum."

"I wanted—"

I take a step closer, but he holds up the knife with a shaking hand. "Don't. Don't. He told me about my real mother—he told me she was a drug addict. He told me she didn't want me, she never wanted me, that she left me to die."

Anna makes a small noise behind me and I hear her footsteps retreating. Is she running away again?

"Joe, please—we need to get you bandaged up. You might need a hospital."

He looks down at his blood-soaked hands and arms. "It's not mine," he says.

"What?"

He looks away from me, toward the kitchen. "It's his. Dad's. I think I killed him."

SARAH AND PATRICK—2000

"Will you marry me?"

I laugh. I clap my hand over my mouth, but it's too late, the sound is out there: it leaves my mouth and slaps him around the face. His face floods with color and I run over to him, stroke his cheek, as if the sting of my words was real enough to leave marks.

"Oh, God, I'm sorry, that was shock," I say. "I love you so much, you know I do, but marriage? I'm sorry I laughed, but I was shocked. I'm only nineteen—I'm still at college."

"Not really, not anymore. When's the last time you went in? You live here now. You're a full-time mother to Joe. We'll get married, buy a house, and move out to the coast, have more children. I've always wanted to move back by the sea. It'll be perfect."

Yes, but…what about the map? The map of the world I showed him with all the places I want to visit circled or colored in? This was supposed to be temporary, like I told Caroline. I was going back to college, then to paint my way around the world. "I can't. I have to finish college. And travel. I want to travel and—"

"But what about Joe?"

I freeze. I'd forgotten Joe in those few moments, sleeping across the hall in his cot, smelling of milk and baby powder, soft velvet belly full of formula and mashed carrots. Of course I wasn't going to leave him.

"We have our whole lives to travel," Patrick says. "You can go back to college when he's older. We'll do it all, everything you want, but we'll do it together."

Joe starts to cry.

"If you stay, you can be his real mother," Patrick adds. "He'll grow up and call you Mum and he'll be yours forever."

Joe's crying is getting more strident. He's teething again and must be in pain as well as hungry. He has two teeth now and eats solid food. He's started babbling, that baby babbling, not real words, just sounds. But he says ma ma ma over and over, giving me that grin, snuggling into my neck, babbling ma ma ma, and every time he does, I swear it tugs on a string attached to my heart. Patrick leans closer.

"Please, Sarah, think about it. Think about us. *What we have—you, me, and Joe. It's so perfect. It could always be like this."*

Like this? Is this what I want? A stay-at-home mother at nineteen? But I look at Patrick and I'm swept away again, we're dancing again, and I'm thinking of the nights Joe can't sleep, when instead of being angry, Patrick gets up with me to see to him, and how, when I'm humming lullabies, he'll wrap his arms around both of us and we'll dance around the apartment, me humming, Patrick smiling, until Joe stops crying and gives us both that smile. I can't leave him. I can't leave either of them.

Patrick reaches into his pocket and pulls out a velvet box. He fumbles it open and takes out a diamond ring. He holds it out to me and there are tears in his eyes. "Please, Sarah. Marry me. Stay with me. Stay with us."

SARAH, ANNA, PATRICK, AND JOE—NOW

He's not dead. He's lying on the kitchen floor, breathing too fast. There's a rattling sound to it I don't like, but he's not dead. Joe is not a murderer. But my son is standing there with a knife in his hand, covered with his father's blood. If I call an ambulance, Patrick will live, but the police will come and Joe will be locked up. My beautiful, fragile boy will go to jail.

And Anna? Where is Anna? She's disappeared. I'm ice, head to toe. Oh, God, oh, God, what do we do? Anna could be calling the police—they could be racing here right now to take Joe away.

Joe drops the knife and the sudden clatter breaks my paralysis. I make the choice to leave Patrick where he is, the pool of blood around him, and pull Joe away from the kitchen, through to the downstairs bathroom, put his hands under the tap, and start washing the blood off, under water hot enough to scald my tender hands and his, ignoring the pain, adding soap, scrubbing until I can't see a sign of blood. I glance up and recoil from the sight of my bloody face in the mirror. Does Joe even see? He just stands there shaking—I think he's in shock.

"I'm sorry, Joe," I say. "I'm sorry I never told you."

"I thought at first he was telling me I was adopted, but that didn't make sense. Hasn't everyone always told me how much I look like him? Why didn't you tell me?"

"Your father said... he always said it would destroy you. He said you were fragile, and finding out what your real mother was like would break you. I believed him and I went along with it because I wanted you to be mine. I didn't want you to be borrowed. He always said, if you grew up with Eve as a mother, what would you become? And with me as a mother, it would be better and it was, wasn't it?" I'm saying it as a plea. I want him to tell me I did the right thing in believing Patrick's lies for his whole life. "You're painting, you're going to college, you have Simon."

He's staring down at his shaking hands. "All my life I thought I looked like him but got the ability to draw and paint from you. He told me she died, my real mother. That it was because of me, depression after I was born. That she was a junkie, took an overdose and died because of me." He tries to back away from me. "I understand why you don't love me, I understand why no one can ever love me," he says.

"No, don't—don't *ever* say that. I have *always* loved you," I say. "I loved you from the first moment I saw you. You are my son, my baby, my child." I wipe away his tears.

He looks at my bleeding, weeping hands and then at the state of my face. "What did he do to you? Oh, God, what did he do?" He steps away from me, rubbing his arms. "What have I done, Mum? I was so angry—the things he was saying. I didn't think. The knife was on the side and I just grabbed it and..." He goes white, sways. I think he's going to pass out and I put my arms around him.

"What are we going to do?" he says, and the terror in his voice has me gulping back panic of my own. "We have to call an ambulance. I didn't—I never wanted him dead. I just wanted him to stop talking."

"*No*," I say. "Wait." I take a deep breath and step away from him. "He's not dead. You haven't killed him. I want you to go and find Mia for me. You have to explain that everything Anna told her is a lie, but tell her *nothing* about this. Tell her you found me and I'm fine and we talked and that's it. Tell her I'm still in here talking to Patrick but I asked you to leave."

He's shaking his head, but I keep talking. "You have to. I can't stand it if you get into trouble for this, Joe. I need time to make Patrick see..."

Can I? Is he still alive, still conscious enough to listen?

I push Joe toward the front door, not letting him look where Patrick lies. "Go and find Mia."

But when I open the front door, Anna's standing there. She stares at Joe like she's never seen him before and I realize she hasn't. Before, she saw my son; now she's seeing hers, the baby she thought was dead, all grown-up. I ache for her. Whatever she's done to me, I ache for her loss: seventeen years of Joe's life.

"I was going to run again," she says. "But I couldn't. I couldn't leave you again." She's looking at Joe as she says it. "I called you Liam," she whispers.

"He doesn't know," I say to her, reaching for Joe's hand.

"What?" Joe says, looking from me to her.

"He lied," I say. "He lied to all of us. He told you your real mother was dead, but it's not true."

Joe and Anna stare at each other and I can see the resemblance now so clearly. Where has she been? All these years as Joe was growing up, where has she been?

Finally, Anna speaks. "If I'd known…If I'd known, I'd never have run so far. I wanted to die, but I never even wanted that enough to go through with it."

She looks down at her arms and I see Joe rubbing his own. This was why Patrick never wanted Joe told. *He's like her*, Patrick said. *She was always fragile, but it was her family who broke her. Do you want to do that to Joe? She's dead. He never needs to know.*

He said it and, because I wanted Joe to be mine, I went along with it. I believed him; I believed there would never be a birth mother coming looking for her boy because she was dead. I became Joe's mother. I should have questioned it more, but if I'd known Eve was alive, I would never have lied. I wouldn't.

Anna shudders. There are tears in her eyes, but it's not grief on her face, etched into the tense lines and white-lipped mouth. "Is he dead?"

I shake my head. "Anna—Eve, listen." I grab her arm as she tries to push past me. "Joe's going to get into trouble with the police unless we help him."

"We?"

I take a deep breath. "You. His mother. You can help him."

"You're lying. More lies because you want to get away from me. You want to stop me killing that bastard with my bare fucking hands."

"I'm not lying. Look at me—look at what he did to me. We can make this self-defense, but it can't be Joe with the knife in his hand. He'll go to prison—do you want that? Your boy, your son."

She looks down the hallway, then back at me.

"You said it yourself. All your letters, your gifts, they've worked," I say. "Patrick lost control. Things escalated, just like you said. But it's Joe who's going to end up punished for it."

"No, that's not what I meant. It's meant to be him who suffers."

"What do you think he did to me when you gave him that photo? What do you think he did to Mia?" I lean in, looking for a trace of the clear-eyed Anna I thought was my friend. "You know what he did to Ben. You know what he did to *you*. Do you think he'd hesitate for a second to see Joe punished for this?"

She lets go of my arm and her eyelids flutter. I think she's going to faint, and this time, it's my arm holding her up, stopping her from falling. She leans against the wall and sinks down. "What can we do?"

I glance at Joe. "We have to talk to Patrick. If I tell the police what he did to me, to Ben... You can even tell the police the truth about who you are and what he did. Patrick won't want any of this to come out. We can—we can come up with a story." The panic is evident in my voice, the short, sharp breaths I take. I'm saying all this for Joe, but I don't believe my own words. I just have to get Joe away from the house.

"Mum, no," Joe says, watching me. "Whatever you're thinking, please don't. You promised me. You promised me in the hospital you'd never leave."

"It's okay, Joe," Anna says in a flat voice. "We can work this out. Go on now, go wherever Sarah told you to go. Leave it to us."

* * *

I take Joe outside and leave Anna in the house with Patrick.

"I don't understand," Joe says, looking back at the house.

"He lied," I say. "Your father lied. I know I've lied too, but I swear to you, I believed your birth mother was dead. I never would have kept it secret if I'd known she was alive."

"I don't... I can't believe she's my mother."

"Joe, please." I take his hand, grip it tight, ignoring the sting of pain from my palm. "Don't let this break you. I'm your mother. Doesn't matter whose DNA you carry, I am your mother. I know I haven't been the best, but please, please, believe I love you. If you let me, I will sort this out. I will find a way to fix it for you. I will be the mother I should always have been. Find Mia and wait for me. I'll make this right. I promise."

Joe looks at me. "I got that place in college. They told me at the interview. I thought things were going to go right," he says. "I'd get away from here, from *him*. I'd go to college and live with Simon. I'd get to be *happy*."

"You still can. Let me fix this."

He leans down toward me. I see him pause and I know he's waiting for me to turn away, like I always do. I wait and he kisses my cheek. "Come and find us, Mum," he says. "Don't forget your promise."

Patrick is standing when I go back into the Murder House. Not dead. There's still time to think of something to save Joe. He's hunched over, clutching his stomach, face-to-face with Anna.

"You told me he was dead," she is saying.

Patrick's eyes flutter and he sways. "You left him. You walked out."

"But I came back and you told me he died. How could you do that?"

"You were drunk when you came back. Drunk and off your face. You came back after nearly two months and thought you could have him back."

"He was my son."

"No. You didn't deserve him. You didn't deserve any of it." His voice gets louder and he breaks off and gasps.

"That wasn't your fucking decision to make."

"It wasn't really me who decided it, though, was it? You never checked. You never asked where he was buried. You accepted what I told you and you ran away again. You were glad to be rid of the responsibility."

Anna steps away from him. "No, that's not true. I thought he was dead—*you told me he was dead*."

He stares at her, his breath coming fast and shallow. "I saw relief on your face."

He lurches forward and I see he has the knife in his hand, the one Joe dropped. I reach to pull Anna away.

Patrick turns to me, white-faced and bleeding but still with that knife clenched tight in his hand. "Sarah..." he says. Pleads. His eyes flicker from Anna to me. "Whatever she's told you, it's poison. It's lies."

Anna hisses and I hold her arm tighter.

"I asked Joe to do it, you know," he says to me, ignoring Anna. "I told you I'd die if you left me—you've always known that." He breathes in, winces, lets it out with a shudder.

We have to get out of here. We have to stop this.

"I only ever did any of it to make you stay, you know."

I stare at him. "You didn't have to do any of it, though. When we first met, when I was looking after Joe, I *wanted* to stay. You didn't need to do anything to *make* me stay."

He turns away from me. "You say that, but for how long? How long until you got restless or bored, or saw someone else you wanted? I was just making sure that didn't happen."

The romance, the dazzling bright Patrick who'd make me want to dance when there was no music, it faded in those first few years of marriage. I became a housewife, he a career man, and we drifted apart, forgetting to dance. We never traveled; I never went back to college. The map I used to treasure got lost, my paints and canvases grew dusty, and I forgot it all. He was still out there, striving for his ridiculous dream of perfection, this house always in his sights, and I lost track of my own dreams. I became a caricature of the perfect wife Patrick wanted.

I used to wonder what my life would have been like if I hadn't waited so long for James bloody Tucker, if I'd gone home instead to wallow in the humiliation of being stood up. I would have stayed at college, gotten my degree, maybe done the traveling I'd always dreamed of.

Or what if James Tucker had actually turned up? We would have had a drink in the pub, maybe gone for a quiet dinner somewhere. Maybe we'd have fallen in love, gotten married.

But…

Perhaps I'd still have a Mia in some form—maybe younger, a different surname. But I'd never have had a Joe.

And Patrick was right. It could have been so perfect.

"I loved you so bloody much, and I hate you for that. I hate you for not being the man you should have been," I say, and his face twists into anger. Careful. I have to be careful.

"Are you going to tell the police it was you, not Joe? They won't believe you. You never could tell a convincing lie," he says. "What's it going to be, Sarah?"

"They'll believe it if I tell them as well," Anna says. "They'll believe us if you're dead."

"But I'm not dead, am I, Eve?"

Anna's mouth twists into a smile. "Not yet."

The blood underneath him has spread farther and he's white-faced. His eyes close, his white-knuckled grip on the knife relaxes, and I think he's going to fall. For a heart-stopping second, I think this is it, that Joe really has killed him. I could go now, gather up the children and run away, and for a second I'm so tempted. But then I'll always be waiting for that knock at the door, and so will Joe. If I let him live, we'll forever expect to see Patrick raging toward us with a bloody knife in his hand however far we run.

And I can't do it again, can't live through another seventeen years of waiting for the hammer to fall. I just want him to hit us with the damn thing now so I can stand here, arms spread wide, stand in front of Joe and Mia, taking the hammer blow for them, which is all I've ever wanted and so far failed to do.

His eyes snap open, as if he hears my thoughts.

"Sarah..." he whispers.

I can hear cars driving past, which seems so strange, that normal life is carrying on outside this fucking house.

"I want you to stay with me, Sarah."

I shake my head.

"If you stay with me, I'll develop amnesia. I won't remember a thing about who attacked me. It'll be like Ian Hooper and John again—no one has to know the truth. I'll tell them I heard someone come in, but I didn't see who. It won't matter if they find Joe's fingerprints. He's my son: he's meant to be here. No one will believe *her*," he says, glancing at Anna. "And I'll carry on *not remembering*. I'll *not remember* for as long as you're home with me. You know they'll believe me. You know how good I am at keeping a secret. But if you leave again, I'll tell them it was Joe. I'll tell them everything and he'll go to prison." He pauses to get his breath back. "What do you think prison will do to Joe?"

It would kill him. I've already realized that.

"I don't want to be on my own. Stay at home. Stay at home and save Joe."

This was what I wanted. A way out for Joe. But if we do this, Joe will be as much a prisoner as I've been, bound to Patrick forever by this awful lie.

"Don't listen to him, Sarah," Anna says. Does she see indecision in my face?

I stare at Patrick and try to see the man I once loved, who once loved me properly. But I'm not sure he ever existed. Screwed up by his parents, he was frantically manipulating things from the first time we met. But there's worry on his face as he stands there bleeding. This is his final gamble, his very last chance. He's betting everything on this spin.

And he's still holding the knife. There is no happy ending here. There is no *indecision*.

I step forward to whisper my answer to him.

"*Never…*"

I move back. "I will never come back to you. And if you tell the police who stabbed you, I'll tell them why. I'll tell them you raped me." I look at Anna. "I'll tell them about Eve and what you did to her. And I'll tell them about John Evans, what you made him do."

I see the moment he breaks and I can't move fast enough. I'm frozen in place as Patrick disappears, replaced by a monster made of rage. It's all my nightmares come true—the madman with the knife coming toward me. All traces of weakness are gone as he launches himself at me, slamming me to the floor, knocking the breath from my body, one hand at my throat, the knife coming toward my face. I reach for it, black spots floating in front of my eyes as he squeezes my throat harder. I miss the handle and the blade slices deep into my palm. It's slippery with Patrick's blood, my blood, and I can't get a grip. I feel the sting as it cuts my cheek and he pulls it back to stab again.

Anna leaps at him from behind, pulling on his arms, pulling him away from me and I scramble up, lose my balance, fall to my knees, coughing, drawing in whooping, painful breaths through my swollen throat.

I crawl away from them, but Patrick is on Anna and I hear her scream. I turn and she's on the floor, hunched over and Patrick is smiling. Oh, fuck, he's smiling and he's going to kill her. He's going to kill Joe's mother all over again.

"Patrick!" I shout it, scream through the pain, and as he spins to look at me, he slips in his own blood. He throws out his hands to break his fall and drops the knife. Anna lunges to pick it up, staggering upright. She looks at me.

"Run," she says, panting.

I stare at her. I see in her face she's going to finish it. Here I am on the cusp again. I could stop her, or try to. She could kill me as I try. Patrick could kill both of us.

But I will not run away, not again. I take a step forward.

"Mum?"

Oh, God, that's Mia's voice.

"Mia, no!" I shout, running from the room. "Get out, get out."

She can't see this—I can't let Patrick get near her. She's in the hall and I grab her arm, pull her outside, down the path.

"*Run!*" I hear Anna scream again.

We turn to look at the Murder House and, as we do, the door slams shut.

ANNA

It's quiet in the Murder House. As quiet as it was in the dream I used to have, when the house was just a house. You're lying four feet away, silent and still, your eyes open and unseeing.

You got me, with the knife, before you dropped it and I killed you. I haven't looked to see how bad it is, but the pain is bright-white and it feels like the blade is still in my side. I think you did a better job on me than Joe did on you. How long? How long before someone sees Sarah, staggering and bloody, and calls the police, sends them racing here to the Murder House?

There was a moment just now when I thought you'd lost. I had my dead son back and I watched you die, and I thought I'd won and you'd lost. But then I thought of him, this beautiful boy we made, and I looked at myself, at the scars on my wrists that I showed to Sarah, and at the other scars I didn't show, the red and silvery white dots of needle marks on my arms and legs.

Not all of them are old scars.

Sarah, your pathetic, far-from-perfect wife, is weak. But she does love Joe.

She does, at least, love Joe.

This is the story that will be told:

Once upon a time, a queen lived with a king in a castle. Only the king wasn't really a king and the castle wasn't really a castle. The king was really a dragon wearing a man suit who'd put the queen under a spell so she wouldn't realize he was a dragon and the castle was actually a dungeon. She was a woman in the dark and she didn't even know.

A knight came along one day and decided to help save the

queen and her children. The knight pushed and prodded and pushed and prodded at the dragon until the dragon forgot himself and threw off his man suit and showed his true self. The spell was broken and the queen got to live happily ever after in the light with her children.

And the brave knight...the knight slew the dragon.

Do you like that story, Patrick? It's our fairy-tale ending, after all.

How long now? No sirens yet, but it won't be long. As I wait, the blood pumping out of me slows. The pain is fading and I'm growing numb. I don't think that's a good thing. I slump lower and close my eyes.

Do you remember? Do you remember the first time we danced? We were outside, on the beach, looking up at the stars. I was drunk and you whirled me around and around and it felt like we were flying.

I was laughing and giddy and breathless, and we were flying to imaginary music, and I loved you and all I wanted was you, the stars, your arms around me, you and me flying.

It's time for our dance to end.

SARAH

There's a big audience the day they bulldoze the house. The actual event is a bit of an anticlimax—I see it on the faces of the people watching. What are they hoping for? That blood will start streaming down the walls, that ghosts will come screaming out of the rubble? I bet all these people were here that night too, watching the bodies being brought out.

Anna was still alive when the police got here, but she'd lost too much blood and died before she even made it into the ambulance. I told the police the same story I told Joe. I told them Anna knew Patrick would come for me after he beat up Ben, so she rushed over to warn me. I told them he was going to kill me and she saved me. She saved us all. Joe doesn't need to know the bad stuff she did. He only needs to know she died a hero.

I'll never get to tell her I have a job at the gallery. Ben's okay, but Patrick put him in the hospital so I'm helping out. Mia wants to go back to her old school for her GCSE year, and I'd be closer to Joe if we move back to Cardiff. But for this summer, I have sea views from the caravan we're renting, I have a job, and I'm painting again in the studio above the gallery. Patrick's ghost has gone. Ben invited us to stay in his cottage, but he still sees Patrick when he looks at me. There's a shadow that wasn't there before. I don't think he'll stay in touch when we leave.

My exhibition was postponed, but it'll happen before the end of the summer. There's a half-finished seascape on an easel, one I think Anna would approve of, full of all the colors from her secret beach.

"Mum?" Mia walks over and we stand and watch the house together.

There's a collective gasp when it comes down, followed by a sigh I may have imagined. I shiver as a cold breeze creeps around me, one of Mia's cold spots set free.

That's it, it's gone.

Mia stretches out her hand and I take it, holding it tight. I'm not letting go this time.

"They should have done this fifteen years ago after the first murders," the man next to me mutters, coughing as he lights a cigarette.

I look up the cliff path where a figure watches the house fall. I hope Tom will be able finally to move on now that the house is gone.

"Yes," I say. "They should have." They should have done it a long time before that.

Mia and I walk away from the ruins of the Murder House without looking back.

Vanessa Savage is a graphic designer and illustrator. She has twice been awarded a Writers' Bursary by Literature Wales, most recently for *The Woman in the Dark*. She won the Myriad Editions First Drafts competition in 2016 and her work has been highly commended in the Yeovil Literary Prize, shortlisted for the Harry Bowling Prize and the Caledonia Novel Award, and long-listed for the Bath Novel Award.